"Where do we st

Gavin glanced over at
talking about us."

He could tell from her expression that she didn't think that was what they should be talking about.

"We agreed to discuss the dig and not this thing between us," she said.

Gavin wondered if Layla knew that "this thing" actually had a name. It was called *desire*. "I think we should talk about us before discussing the dig."

She gave him an annoyed look. "Why? I told you last night we need to keep sex out of it."

Yes, she had said that, but did she actually think they could when there was so much sexual chemistry between them?

"I want you and you want me."

"And?"

Maybe it was time to explain what he meant. "And…" he said, "we *will* sleep together."

* * *

The Rancher Returns
is part of The Westmoreland Legacy—
Friends and relatives of the legendary
Westmoreland family find love!

THE RANCHER
RETURNS

BY
BRENDA JACKSON

MILLS & BOON®

All rights reserved including the right of reproduction in whole or in part in any form. This edition is published by arrangement with Harlequin Books S.A.

This is a work of fiction. Names, characters, places, locations and incidents are purely fictional and bear no relationship to any real life individuals, living or dead, or to any actual places, business establishments, locations, events or incidents. Any resemblance is entirely coincidental.

This book is sold subject to the condition that it shall not, by way of trade or otherwise, be lent, resold, hired out or otherwise circulated without the prior consent of the publisher in any form of binding or cover other than that in which it is published and without a similar condition including this condition being imposed on the subsequent purchaser.

® and ™ are trademarks owned and used by the trademark owner and/or its licensee. Trademarks marked with ® are registered with the United Kingdom Patent Office and/or the Office for Harmonisation in the Internal Market and in other countries.

First Published in Great Britain 2016
By Mills & Boon, an imprint of HarperCollins*Publishers*
1 London Bridge Street, London, SE1 9GF

© 2016 by Brenda Streater Jackson

ISBN: 978-0-263-91879-3

51-1016

Our policy is to use papers that are natural, renewable and recyclable products and made from wood grown in sustainable forests. The logging and manufacturing processes conform to the legal environmental regulations of the country of origin.

Printed and bound in Spain
by CPI, Barcelona

Brenda Jackson is a *New York Times* bestselling author of more than one hundred romance titles. Brenda lives in Jacksonville, Florida, and divides her time between family, writing and traveling.

Email Brenda at authorbrendajackson@gmail.com or visit her on her website at www.brendajackson.net.

To the love of my life, Gerald Jackson, Sr.
My first. My last. My everything.

To everyone who loves the Westmorelands,
this book is for you!

To the 1971 class of William M. Raines High School,
Jacksonville, Florida. Best wishes on our
45th class reunion. Ichiban!

Plans fail for lack of counsel,
but with many advisers they succeed.
—*Proverbs* 15:22

Prologue

"Hey, Viper, your cell phone was going off upstairs."

Gavin Blake, known to his SEAL teammates as Viper, nodded as he set his coffee mug on a side table in the barracks' common area. Standing, he stretched the kinks out of his body and felt his aches all the way to the bone. Their last covert operation had been risky as hell, but they'd succeeded in destroying yet another ISIS stronghold.

In two days they would officially be off duty and most of his teammates would be heading for home. However he had other plans. Getting laid was at the top of his agenda. It had been too long since he'd shared a woman's bed and he'd already made plans with a beautiful bartender he'd met in Mississippi while helping his teammate Bane out of a fairly dangerous situation several months ago.

Gavin raced up the stairs toward his berthing unit and retrieved his cell phone from the gear in his bunk. He'd missed a call from Sherman Lott, the man who'd lived on the neighboring ranch for years. Panic floated through

Gavin's belly. Had something happened to his grand-mother?

Since his grandmother lived alone when he was away, Gavin had given their closest neighbors his contact information in case of emergencies. Of course the foreman was there, running the ranch in Gavin's absence. Surely if something was going on with his grandmother, Caldwell would have contacted Gavin. But what if this was one of those times when Caldwell had gone to Saint Louis to meet with one of their beef distributors?

Gavin quickly pressed the redial button and Mr. Lott picked up on the second ring. "Hello?"

"Mr. Lott, this is Gavin. Has something happened to Gramma Mel?"

"No, Gavin, your grandmother is fine physically. Not sure what's happening to her mind, though."

Gavin frowned, wondering what the man meant. Although she was nearing her seventy-fifth birthday, Gavin had never known a day in all his thirty-two years when Melody Blake hadn't been sharp as a tack. He'd spoken with his grandmother two weeks ago and she had sounded just fine to him. "What makes you think something is wrong with her mind?"

"She's allowed some fast-talking college professor to convince her that the outlaw Jesse James buried some of his loot on the Silver Spurs, and they plan to start digging up parts of her land next week."

Gavin refrained from correcting the man. The land was *their* property since Gavin legally owned all eight hundred acres jointly with his grandmother. Instead he concentrated on what Lott had said. His grandmother had given someone permission to dig on the Silver Spurs?

"There must be some mistake, Mr. Lott. You know my grandmother as well as I do. There's no way she would allow some man to—"

"It's a woman. A professor by the name of Dr. Harris."

Gavin drew in a deep breath. Who the hell was Dr. Harris and how had she talked his grandmother into agreeing to a dig on Blake land?

Rubbing a hand down his face, Gavin knew he would be flying home and not making that pit stop in Mississippi after all. *Damn!*

"Gavin?"

"Yes, Mr. Lott, I'm here."

"I hated to call you knowing you're probably somewhere doing important work for our country, but I felt you needed to know what's going on."

"And I appreciate you doing so. Don't worry about a thing. I'll be home in a couple of days."

Gavin hung up the phone and cursed in anger. He then placed a call to his ranch foreman, Caldwell Andrews. The phone was answered on the third ring.

"Caldwell? What's going on at the Silver Spurs? Sherman Lott just called and he thinks Gramma Melody has gone loco. He said something about her allowing some professor to dig on the ranch?"

He heard Caldwell curse under his breath before saying, "I wish Lott hadn't called you, Gavin. Your grandmother is fine. She likes the professor. They talked and according to Ms. Mel she read the professor's report and it's legit."

Viper rolled his eyes. "Caldwell, you know as well as I do that there's no buried treasure on the Silver Spurs. If you recall, when I was in my teens, Dad allowed this outfit to come in and dig up parts of the land when they convinced him there was oil somewhere on it. Not a drop of oil was found."

"I remember. But I guess Ms. Mel figured a little digging wouldn't hurt anything since it's a small area, away from the main house and far away from where the cows are kept. It's the south pasture."

"The south pasture?"

"Yes. Nobody ever goes over there."

Nobody but me, Gavin thought. He knew everyone thought of the south pasture as wasted land since it had compacted soil, little or no vegetation and unsuitable irrigation. However, that part of the ranch was where he could escape and find solace whenever he needed to be alone. For some reason, going there always renewed his spirits. It was where he'd gone as a kid whenever he would miss his mother, where he'd gone after getting word about his father being killed in the Middle East. And last year he had camped out there a couple of days after returning from his mission and believing his teammate Coop was dead. It was there in the south pasture where Gavin had dealt with the thought of his good friend dying.

"Like I said, Gavin. Your grandmother has everything under control."

He wasn't so sure of that. "I'll find that out for myself since I'll be home in a few days. Don't mention my visit to Gramma Mel. I want to surprise her." When he hung up the phone, he rubbed a frustrated hand down his face.

"Viper? Hey, man, you okay?"

Viper turned to see four sets of eyes staring at him with concern. His SEAL teammates. They were Brisbane Westmoreland, team name Bane; Thurston McRoy, team name Mac; Laramie Cooper, team name Coop; and David Holloway, team name Flipper. The five of them had survived all phases of SEAL training together and were not only teammates, but like brothers. More than once they'd risked their lives for each other and would continue to have each other's backs, on duty or off.

"Viper?"

He heard the impatience in Mac's voice and spoke up before Mac's edginess got the best of them. "It's my grandmother."

"What about Gramma Mel?" Flipper asked, moving closer. Each of them had at one time or another gone home with Viper and met his grandmother.

"Is she sick?" Bane asked.

Viper shook his head. "No, it's nothing like that. My neighbor called to let me know that Gramma Mel gave some college professor permission to dig on our property. This professor has convinced my grandmother that Jesse James buried some of his stolen loot on the Silver Spurs."

The worried expressions on his friends' faces switched to relief and then amusement. "Is that all?" Coop asked, grinning, resting his broad shoulder against a wall.

"That's enough. Nobody has permission to dig on the Silver Spurs."

"Evidently your grandmother gave it," Bane pointed out.

"Well, that permission is being rescinded, and I'm going to make sure Gramma Mel and this professor know it."

"Did you talk to Caldwell?" Flipper asked.

"Yes, but he'll go along with anything my grandmother says. Now I have to head straight home instead of making that pit stop in Mississippi like I'd planned. Hell, that means I'm giving up a chance to get laid for this foolishness."

Mac grinned. "But what if Jesse James did hide some of his loot on your land? If I recall, he and his gang robbed a number of banks in and around the Missouri area."

Gavin frowned as he zipped up his gear and faced his friends. "There's not any loot on the Silver Spurs and nobody can convince me otherwise."

One

Layla Harris smiled as she accepted the plate of cookies. "Ms. Melody, I wished you wouldn't have gone to the trouble."

She said the words out of politeness, knowing they weren't true. Nobody could bake like Melody Blake and she was glad the older woman not only liked doing so but also enjoyed sharing her baked goods with Layla. Especially when the snack included a delicious tall glass of milk that had been produced right here on this ranch.

"No trouble at all," Melody Blake said, smiling. "Besides, I enjoy your company. It can get lonely in these parts."

Layla knew the Silver Spurs was a good half-hour car ride from town. At least Ms. Melody had neighbors living fairly close who checked in on her regularly. Layla had discovered the land owned by the majority of the people in this area had been in their families for generations and most of it was used for ranching cattle.

There was something special about the eighteen hundred acres encompassing the Silver Spurs and the spacious Blake family ranch home. Layla had felt welcomed the moment she had driven into the yard. The sprawling ranch house was massive and Layla figured it had to be over fifty-five hundred square feet. What she liked most was the wraparound porch with a swing that faced a beautiful pond.

Ms. Melody, a retired librarian, had said she didn't mind living in the huge house alone because she was used to it, and reading and baking kept her busy. The kitchen alone was massive and it was where the older woman spent a lot of her days, creating mouthwatering treats. In addition to the huge main house, there was a spacious guest cottage located within walking distance.

When Ms. Melody had agreed to let Layla conduct her archaeological dig on the property, she'd also kindly invited Layla to stay in the main house, but Layla preferred the guesthouse. She could come and go without disturbing the older woman.

According to Ms. Melody, the Silver Spurs had been a prosperous cattle ranch for years. It had even survived when the majority of the men, including Ms. Melody's husband, left to fight in the Vietnam War. When her husband and son became full-time military men, they'd hired a foreman to keep things running smoothly. Ms. Melody also explained that although her grandson was active in the military as a navy SEAL, whenever he returned home he reclaimed his role as a rancher.

Layla met Caldwell Andrews, the ranch foreman, and found the man pleasant and capable. The same held true for the men who worked for him. They appeared to be hard workers who were dedicated and loyal to the Blake family.

There was so much about Melody Blake that reminded Layla of her own grandmother. Both were independent, in the best of health for women their ages and were active in their churches and communities. Only thing, Gramma Candace wasn't a baker. She preferred spending her time with a knitting needle instead of a baking pan.

"I thought I'd bake chocolate chip cookies this time. They're Gavin's favorite," Ms. Melody said, breaking into Layla's musings.

At the mention of Ms. Melody's grandson, Layla couldn't dismiss the shiver that went through her body. Gavin Blake was a hunk. Although she'd never met him in person, she had seen enough of the man to judge his looks thanks to the numerous framed photographs that hung on several walls in this house. Layla knew it wasn't the man's ego that was responsible, but the grandmother who loved her grandson and was proud of the fact that, like the father and grandfather before him, he was a navy SEAL.

From all the photographs she'd seen, Layla could tell just how well built Gavin Blake was, how drop-dead gorgeous. He was definitely eye candy of the most delectable kind. Any woman would be hard-pressed not to feel some kind of sensual pull whenever she feasted her gaze on his image.

Layla had studied one of the close-up photos, which showed dimples when he smiled, a blunt nose, stubborn jaw and full lips. His angular face made him look so much like the warrior she'd heard him to be. She'd also heard he was quite the ladies' man. That bit of information had been shared by some of the locals she'd met at the café where she occasionally ate lunch. Once they'd heard she was about to dig on Blake property, they didn't hesitate to give her an earful.

According to a very talkative waitress whose eyes lit up whenever she spoke of Gavin, Layla had learned he had been a local football hero who had put Cornerstone, Missouri, on the map after leading his high school team to the state championship. No one had been surprised when he'd gone to the naval academy since he'd come from a military family. His father had been killed in the Gulf War and very little was known about his mother. Rumor had it that she'd been pretty, a few years younger than her husband and the two had married within a week of meeting in New York. Apparently, she'd never adjusted to being a military wife or living out on a ranch and had packed up and left. To this day she had never returned.

"Your grandson and I have something in common," Layla said, returning her thoughts to the conversation, "since chocolate chip cookies are my favorite, as well."

As she bit into a cookie, she thought that chocolate chip being their favorite was *all* she and Gavin had in common. Unlike him, she hadn't spent much time enjoying the opposite sex. She'd spent most of her life in school, getting her advanced degrees and working toward tenure with little time for male companionship. She had doctorates in History and Archaeology, and at twenty-six she was the youngest professor at Flintwood University in Seattle. That position had come with sacrifices such as limiting her social life, especially when it came to dating. The only people bothered by her decisions were her parents. They were hoping a man would come along and put a ring on her finger and a baby in her belly. She was their only child and they didn't hide the fact they wanted grandchildren.

Nor had they ever hidden the fact they weren't happy with her career choice. They were both gifted neurosurgeons and they'd expected her to follow in their footsteps by entering the medical field. They hadn't been pleased when she'd chosen not to do so. The thought of someone digging a hole in the ground instead of saving lives didn't make sense to them. But she'd never felt the calling to be a doctor, and she knew history was important, too. Understanding the past kept people from repeating their mistakes.

"So, Layla, what's the game plan for today?"

Layla smiled. She liked Ms. Melody's attitude. When Layla had shown up on the Blakes' doorstep over a week ago she hadn't known what to expect. She definitely hadn't been prepared for the older woman to believe her story about hidden treasure. She'd faced so much cynicism from colleagues regarding her research she'd come prepared to argue her points. Ms. Melody had listened and asked intelligent questions. Plenty of them. The older woman had also taken two days to review Layla's research, which had resulted in more questions. It was only then that Ms. Melody had agreed, with a request for periodic updates.

Ms. Melody had told Layla that her grandson would most likely not support her decision, but she'd also promised she would deal with him when the time came. Besides, she didn't expect him to return home for a few months, and it was highly likely the treasure would be found by then. Layla hoped that was true. Her creditability with the university was on the line. The possibility of tenure was riding on the success of this dig and publication of her findings and techniques.

She'd participated in several excavations, but this would be the first one she'd spearheaded. Funds from the university hadn't been as much as she'd requested, due to budget cuts, but she was determined to make good use of what she'd been given and show results. The head of her department, Dr. Clayburn, hadn't offered much support. He'd even tried shifting the funds to another project. Lucky for her, he'd been out of the country when the vote had been taken.

She'd worked all her life for this chance to prove she was an archaeologist of note. If her research was correct— and she knew it was—she'd be the first one to find any of Jesse James's treasure, and she'd be the first to use some of the latest technology on a successful dig.

"Since all the permits are in order, I contacted the members of my team," she said, smiling. "They will be arriving in a week." Her excavation team consisted of students from the university, some from her classes and some from Dr. Clayburn's. She had spoken with every one, and they were as anxious as she was to get started.

"You have to be excited about that."

"Yes," she answered, though she knew that's when the pressure would begin. "The equipment will start arriving on Monday." Layla took another bite into her cookie before adding, "Again, I really appreciate you letting us dig on your property, Ms. Melody." It showed Layla that Ms. Melody believed in her work.

"There's no need to thank me. Anyone who took the time to read your research with an open mind would reach the same conclusion. It's historically documented that James and his gang robbed a bank in Tinsel and then headed to east Missouri before a sheriff posse drove them south. I think you're right. Given how fast a horse can travel loaded down with a cache of gold bars, it makes perfect sense that the gang holed up somewhere in this area before taking a chance to continue east. And it makes even more sense that they got rid of some of their loot before heading toward the state line. Like I said, your research was thorough."

An inner glow filled Layla. Although others had read the same documentation they couldn't forget her age or inexperience. Because of that, they assumed Layla was on a wild-goose chase, wasting university funds that were needed to finance more important archaeological projects.

At that moment they heard the sound of a vehicle pulling up in the yard.

Ms. Melody glanced over at the clock on the wall. "It's not even noon yet. I wonder who that could be."

Getting up from the table, Ms. Melody went over to the

window and glanced out. When she turned back around, a huge smile covered her entire face. Layla heard the love in the older woman's voice when she said, "It's Gavin. He's home. The rancher returns."

Gavin grabbed his duffel bag from the truck before closing the door. He tilted his Stetson back on his head and looked at the car parked in front of what his grandmother called the guest cottage and what he called the party house. It was where he and his teammates would hang out whenever they visited.

Gavin hoped that his grandmother hadn't extended an invitation for the woman to stay on their property as well as dig on their land. If that was the case, he intended to send her packing quickly. He didn't want anyone taking advantage of his family.

He thought about what he was missing in Mississippi. He'd looked forward to being in bed with that bartender about now. Calling to cancel had been hard. Promising to head her way as soon as he'd taken care of this unexpected family emergency had satisfied her somewhat.

Walking around his truck, he took a deep breath of the Missouri air. This was home and he'd always enjoyed returning after every covert operation. Silver Spurs meant a lot to him. To his family. It was his legacy. It was land that had been in his family for generations. Land that he loved. He enjoyed being a rancher almost as much as he enjoyed being a SEAL. *Almost.* He would admit that being a SEAL was his passion.

Gavin appreciated having a good man like Caldwell to keep things running in his absence. The older man had done the same thing during Gavin's father's time. And Caldwell's father had been foreman to Gavin's grandfather, so Caldwell and his family also had deep history with the ranch.

While he was home, Gavin intended to return to ranching. He couldn't wait to get back in the saddle and ride Acer as well as help Caldwell and the men with the herd. And he needed to go over the books with Phil Vinson, the ranch's accountant.

However, the first thing on his agenda was a discussion with his grandmother about her giving someone permission to dig on their land. Hopefully he'd have everything settled by next week and he would hightail it to Mississippi. All he needed was one night with a woman and then he'd be good for a while.

He had taken one step onto the porch when the front door swung open and his grandmother walked out. She was smiling, and when she opened her arms, he dropped his duffel bag and walked straight into the hug awaiting him. She was petite, but her grip was almost stronger than that of a man. He loved and admired her so damn much. This was the woman who'd been there for him when his own mother had left. The woman who'd been there for him when he'd laid his father to rest sixteen years ago. She had, and always would be, his rock. That's why he refused to tolerate anyone trying to take advantage of her kindness.

"Welcome home, Gavin," she said, finally releasing him so she could lean back and look at him from head to toe as she always did when he returned from one of his assignments. "I didn't expect you for a few months yet. Did everything go okay?"

He smiled. She always asked him that knowing full well that because of the classified nature of his job, he couldn't tell her anything. "Yes, Gramma Mel, everything went okay. I'm back because I understand you and I need to—"

He glanced over his grandmother's shoulder and he blinked, not sure he was seeing straight. A woman stood in the doorway, but she wasn't just *some* woman. She had to be the most gorgeous woman he'd ever seen. Hell, she looked like everything he'd fantasized a woman to be, even while fully clothed in jeans and a pullover sweater. He didn't want to consider what his reaction would be if she was naked.

His grandmother sensed his attention had shifted. She turned around and smiled at the woman. "Layla, come out here. I want you to meet my grandson."

Layla? Where had she come from? Was she the grand-daughter of one of his grandmother's fellow church members or something? He recalled Mrs. Cotton had a granddaughter who visited on occasion from Florida and her name was Layla…or was it Liza? Hell, he couldn't remember. He wasn't thinking straight. When this Layla began walking toward him, he ceased thinking at all. She was wearing stretch jeans and a long sweater and had an eye-catching figure with curves in all the right places.

Gavin fought for air as she neared. He studied her features, trying to figure out what about them had him spellbound. Was it the caramel-colored skin, dark chocolate eyes, dimpled cheeks, button nose or well-defined kissable lips? Maybe every single thing.

Wow! Was he that hard up for a woman or did this Layla actually look *that* good? When she stopped beside him, a smile on her lips, he knew she actually looked that good. He kept his gaze trained on her face—even when he really wanted his eyes to roam all over her.

Not waiting for his grandmother to make introductions, his mouth eased into a smile. He reached out his hand and said, "Hello, I'm Gavin."

The moment their hands touched, a jolt of desire shot through his body. It's a wonder he hadn't lost his balance. Nothing like this had ever happened to him before and he touched women all the time. From the expression that had flashed in her eyes, he knew she had felt it, as well. Yes, there was definitely strong sexual chemistry between them.

"It's nice meeting you, Gavin," she said softly. He even liked the sound of her voice. "And I'm Layla. Layla Harris."

Harris? His horny senses suddenly screeched to a stop. Did she say Harris? Was Layla related to this Professor Harris? The woman's daughter perhaps? Was she part of the excavation team? She looked young, around twenty or twenty-one. Now he had even more questions and he was determined to get some answers when he had that little talk with his grandmother. "It's nice meeting you, too, Layla."

It was only when she eased her hand from his that he realized he still held it. She turned to his grandmother. "Thanks for the cookies and milk, Ms. Melody. I enjoyed them. I need to run into town to pick up a few items. Anything I can get for you while I'm there?"

"No. I've got everything I need."

Layla nodded. "Okay. I should be back in a couple of hours."

"Take your time."

Giving Gavin one last smile, she quickly walked down the steps toward the parked car. He stood and watched her every move until she was inside the car with the door closed. It was then that he turned his attention back to his grandmother. Not surprisingly, she was staring at him.

"For a minute I thought you'd forgotten I was standing here, Gavin Timothy Blake III," his grandmother said in an amused tone.

So he'd been caught ogling a woman. It hadn't been the first time and he doubted it would be the last. "What can I say, Gramma Mel?" He grinned sheepishly. "She's awfully pretty."

He decided not to mention how he appreciated that

sway to her hips when she walked, or how nice her breasts looked beneath her sweater.

"Yes, she is pretty. Come inside. Just so happens I baked some chocolate chip cookies this morning."

That made Gavin smile even wider as he picked up his duffel bag. His mouth watered just thinking about the cookies. Now if he could only get that image of Layla Harris's backside out of his mind…

"How are the rest of your teammates?" his grandmother asked, leading him through the front door. "You guys were together for over two months on this mission."

He glanced around as he entered. Everything looked the same. However, instead of smelling like vanilla, his grandmother's favorite scent, the house smelled of woman. Namely Layla Harris.

"Everyone is fine, just anxious to get home. Bane and his wife are renewing their vows in a few weeks and I plan to attend the ceremony," he said, placing his duffel bag on the sofa for now. "This was Coop's first covert operation after being rescued and he's good as ever."

The only reason Gavin shared that much info with his grandmother was because when he'd come home last year before the holidays everyone had believed Coop had been killed on assignment. The entire team had taken Coop's death hard. Then right before Christmas, they'd found Coop was alive and being held hostage in the Syrian mountains. Gavin and his team had been sent in to get Coop, as well as other hostages, out alive.

"This was Bane's first time back, too, right?" his grandmother asked.

Did his grandmother not forget anything? Bane, being master sniper, had been recruited to work in DC for six months teaching SEAL recruits. "Yes, we were glad to have him back as well. And before I forget, I plan to head for Mississippi next week. I've got important business to take care of there." His grandmother didn't need to know that the important business was getting laid.

As soon as he entered the kitchen, he went straight to the sink to wash his hands and then quickly headed for the coffeepot. After pouring a cup, he turned and watched Gramma Mel arrange a half-dozen cookies on a plate for him. He smiled. Anyone else would eat just one or two, but his grandmother knew him well. He needed at least a half dozen to get things started. "You need a fresh cup of coffee?" he asked her.

"Thanks. That would be nice, Gavin."

After pouring another cup, he moved away from the counter to sit down and she sat across from him. He placed her coffee in front of her and grabbed for a cookie. She slapped away his hand. "Say grace first."

He chuckled, recalling the protocol she expected of him. After quickly bowing his head in silence, he grabbed a cookie and almost swallowed it whole. He loved his grandmother's chocolate chip cookies.

She shook her head as she took a sip of her coffee. Now was as good a time as any to bring up what had brought him rushing back to the Silver Spurs. "What's this I hear about you giving some professor permission to dig on our land?"

Gramma Mel raised a brow over her cup of coffee. "And you know this how?"

He held his grandmother's gaze. "Sherman Lott called. He thought I had a right to know."

She frowned. "As far as I'm concerned, Sherman needs to mind his own business."

Gavin stared at this grandmother as he bit into another cookie. "The way I figure it, Caldwell is the one who should have called me. He's paid to keep me informed about what's going on around here. But he wouldn't call because he'd think doing so would be disloyal to you. And we both know what you mean to him."

His grandmother didn't say anything. She just stared into her cup of coffee. There really wasn't anything to say. Gavin had known for years that his grandmother and Caldwell had a thing going on. He wasn't stupid. Nor was he insensitive. He wanted the two people who meant the most to him to be happy. He figured that one day they would stop trying to be so damn discreet. In the meantime, what they did was their business. He'd only brought it up now to make a point.

"Caldwell would have told you had he thought it was important," his grandmother finally said.

"Whatever." He took a sip of his coffee. "So what about it? Did you give permission for a dig to take place on our property?"

She leaned back in her chair. "Yes, I gave my permission and I see nothing wrong with it."

Gavin kept his cool. "Well, I do. Honestly, Gramma Mel. You actually bought into this professor's tale about Jesse James's buried treasure?"

"Yes, I read her research and found it thorough and convincing. I have a copy, if you want to read it for yourself."

"I don't need to read anything to know the research is false. There's no buried treasure on our land, and I'm against the idea of anyone digging around for nothing."

His grandmother leaned forward in her chair. "And I happen to disagree. But what you believe is a moot point since I've given Layla permission and from what she told me this morning, her equipment will arrive in a few days—"

"Hold up," he said, giving the time-out sign with his hands. "Why did you give Layla Harris permission? It's her mother who's running things, right?"

His grandmother look confused. "Her mother? I never

met the woman. Layla is in charge or should I say Dr. Layla Harris is in charge."

Surprise made Gavin raise his eyebrows. "Layla is the professor?"

"Yes, and a very competent one."

Gavin shook his head, not believing such a thing was possible. "She's young."

"She's twenty-six. However, I admit she does look younger."

Twenty-six? That was still young and yes, she definitely looked younger. He drew in a deep breath, trying to force back the memories of just how she'd looked… in her jeans and sweater. And then the thought that she'd deliberately oozed her way onto his grandmother's good side made him mad.

"You might have given your permission, but I have not given mine. Something that major means we need to be in full agreement."

"No, it doesn't. If you recall, we agreed that any time you were away on military business, I could make decisions in the best interest of the Silver Spurs."

"I don't consider digging up our land to be in the best interest of anything."

"I disagree. I'm excited about what Layla might find. And I also gave her permission to stay in the guesthouse."

The line of Gavin's jaw tightened. He'd figured as much. Melody Blake was stubborn, but then so was he. He ate the last of his cookies, drained his coffee and stood. "I'm tired and need a full day of sleep. But we will talk about this again, Gramma Mel. In the meantime, I suggest you tell Dr. Layla Harris to hold up on bringing any type of equipment to the Silver Spurs."

And without saying anything else Gavin walked out of the kitchen.

Two

Layla pulled her car off on the shoulder of the road, unable to drive any farther. Once she killed her vehicle's ignition, she forced herself to breathe deeply a few times. Never in all her twenty-six years had any man wreaked havoc on her senses like Gavin Blake. Never had any man left her in such a mind-blowing sensuous state. Who would have thought a man could have her nerves dancing, her mind racing, her stomach swirling and her nipples actually feeling like they'd been stroked? She had been tempted to glide her hands over every inch of his sexy, sculpted body.

She had known he was the epitome of male perfection from all those photographs she'd seen. To be honest, that's where her troubles had started…with those photographs. In one, his lips had curved a little at the corners as he stared at her as if to say he knew exactly what she was thinking. She knew it was her wild imagination, but every time she glanced at that particular photo it was as if he was checking her out with those intense dark eyes of his. As if he knew her fantasies included him. Even in his photo, his muscular power had nearly overtaken her senses.

Pretty much like he'd done today. She hadn't counted on the real thing being even more explosive than his pictures. Before he'd realized she was in his grandmother's doorway, she had stood there spellbound as a rush of emotion made her body ache with desire. Then, when he'd noticed her, those eyes had made her yearn for something she didn't need. Something she had never needed. A man.

Gavin Blake had stood on his grandmother's porch wearing a pair of faded jeans and a T-shirt with his military tag hanging around his neck. Even wearing her sweater, she found the air cool, but the temperature hadn't seemed to faze him. Was he as hot-blooded as he looked?

The one thing she did know was that he was a big guy. Tall. Muscular. Built. She could imagine him as the football hero she'd heard he used to be, tackling players with little or no trouble. And she could definitely imagine him as a SEAL, taking on the bad guys to protect his country.

And she couldn't help but imagine him naked in bed… with her. Unfamiliar sensations raced through her just thinking about it. When he had touched her hand while staring into her eyes, she'd forgotten all about Ms. Melody standing there and had all but purred out loud. Blood had pounded through her entire body. She doubted she would ever use her hand again without remembering the feel of him. If her body reacted from a single touch to her hand, she didn't want to imagine him touching her anywhere else…her breasts, her stomach, between her legs. And when he smiled at her, she'd been a goner. She could still feel the impact in the pit of her stomach.

She had never experienced this kind of need in her life. She didn't even have a battery-operated boyfriend like some of her single female colleagues joked about owning. Sex was something that had never been on her must-do list. She'd put her energy into her academic career. But there was something about Gavin that made her think of heat and desire. Something that made the area at the juncture of her thighs quiver. Made her hormones sizzle.

Drawing in another deep breath, Layla admitted she needed to get a grip. She wasn't in Cornerstone, Missouri, to lust after the man who jointly owned the land she needed as an excavation site. All she wanted to do was stay on schedule and have a successful dig. Besides, Gavin Blake probably looked at other women the same way he'd looked at her. Hadn't that waitress in town enlightened Layla as to just what a ladies' man he was? Now seeing was believing.

Seeing was also a warning to keep her common sense intact and be on guard. An involvement with Gavin Blake was the last thing she needed, even though her body was trying to convince her otherwise.

There was something else she should be concerned about, something she just remembered. Ms. Melody had said that her grandson might be against the idea of a dig on the Silver Spurs. Although Ms. Melody had given the okay, would Gavin's return change anything? The thought of losing the permission she'd gained sent nervous jitters through her.

Maybe she should talk to Gavin Blake herself. She would present her research to him the same way she'd presented it to Ms. Melody. Layla wanted to believe he was reasonable. It wasn't as if she would be digging all over his property. She had narrowed it to one location.

Yes, she would talk to him herself, but only after she talked to Ms. Melody—and after Layla convinced herself she could talk to him without every part of her turning to mush.

* * *

Gavin's eyes flew open and his entire body went on full alert. His ears picked up the sounds around him and it was then he recalled he was back in the United States and not in some godforsaken country where he had to be on guard 24/7.

It was always this way for the first few days after he returned home. He had to regroup and get his mind back in sync with normal life, deprogram from battle mode and ease back into the life of a rancher.

Glancing at the clock on his bedroom wall, he saw it was ten at night. He wasn't surprised that he'd slept nearly nine hours straight. His ears perked up at the sound that had woken him. Was that a harmonica? Granted it was far off, but he could still hear it. His teammates teased him about having sonic ears, because of his ability to hear a sound over a hundred feet away.

He wasn't sure if that was a blessing or a curse when he involuntarily eavesdropped on conversations he wished he hadn't. Like the time Mac was outside the barracks and downstairs in the yard talking to his wife on the phone, telling her in explicit sexual terms what he planned to do to her when he returned home from their mission. Gavin had heard every single word and the details had nearly burned his ears. They had definitely made him horny as hell. For a fleeting moment it had made him wish he had a wife or an exclusive woman he could return home to instead of a little black book filled with names of willing women.

Gavin pushed the whimsical thought from his mind as he lay in bed and listened to the music. It sounded pretty damn good. He sat up and rubbed his hands across his face as if to wipe away the sleep. Pushing the bedcovers aside, he eased out of bed. Not bothering to cover his naked body, he strolled over to the window, pushed aside the curtain and looked out. The October air produced a chill that would send shivers through a normal person's body. But because of his SEAL training, Gavin could withstand temperatures of the highest and lowest extremes.

The way the moonlight crested the rocky bluffs, dissecting the valleys and rolling plains, was simply breathtaking. There was nothing more beautiful than Silver Spurs at night. For as long as he could remember, he'd always been moved by the grandeur of the land he was born on.

The harmonica stopped and he knew the sound had come from the party house where Layla was staying. Since the woman was still in residence, he could only assume his grandmother had not delivered his message. Had she done so he was certain Professor Layla Harris would have left by now.

Maybe he should talk to Layla Harris himself. Make it clear where he stood. He moved back toward the bed. Instead of getting into it, Gavin ignored the voice of reason saying he should wait and talk to Layla in the morning and grabbed his clothes off the chair. After sliding into his jeans he tugged his T-shirt over his head. He put on his socks and boots and headed for the door.

The music from the harmonica started up again.

Layla placed her harmonica aside. Playing it relaxed her and she would always appreciate her grandfather for teaching her. She could vividly recall those summers when she would sit on the front porch of her grandparents' New Orleans home and listen to her grandfather play his harmonica, then beg him to teach her how. When Grampa Chip passed away ten years ago, his request had been that she play the harmonica at his funeral and she had.

Thoughts of losing the grandfather she adored always made her sad and that was the last emotion she wanted to feel right now. Even when she had no idea what would happen with this dig, she wanted happy thoughts. Earlier, Ms. Melody assured Layla that all was well. Her grandson was too exhausted to think straight and he needed a full day of sleep.

Layla hoped that was good news considering she had all that machinery on the way. She figured Ms. Melody knew her grandson better than Layla did. She would wait for Gavin Blake to get his full day of sleep. Hopefully, after another discussion with Ms. Melody, he would see things the way his grandmother did.

Layla glanced around the guest cottage, thinking how much she liked it here. The place was larger than her apartment in Seattle. She definitely didn't have a huge living room with a fireplace or a spacious master bedroom with a large en suite bath with a walk-in shower and Jacuzzi tub. The cottage also had a loft that could be used as additional sleeping space, and an eat-in kitchen. She loved the wood floors throughout and the high ceilings. And because it sat a distance away from the main house, she could play her harmonica without worrying about disturbing anyone. That was something she couldn't do at her own apartment.

She stood to stretch and was about to head toward the bedroom when she heard a knock on the door. Glancing at the clock on the wall she saw it was after ten. Usually Ms. Melody was in bed every night by eight since she was such an early riser. Had something happened? Had the older woman decided not to butt heads with her grandson and didn't want Layla and her team to dig on the Silver Spurs after all?

Layla moved toward the door. It didn't have a peephole so she leaned against the wooden frame and asked, "Who is it?"

"Gavin. Gavin Blake."

Her gaze widened and heat swirled around in her lower belly. She tried forcing the sensations aside. Why would Gavin seek her out at this time of night? Had something happened to Ms. Melody? From their talks, she knew the older woman suffered occasionally with migraines.

She opened the door and the man stood there, almost bigger than life, and looking as yummy as a chocolate sundae. He was dressed as he had been that morning. Jeans. T-shirt. Western boots. But her brain wasn't computing *what* he was wearing as much as *how well* he was wearing it.

Although it was cold, he wasn't even wearing a jacket. He leaned in the doorway looking exactly like any woman's dream. Hot. Sexy. And then some. He was one of those can't-get-to-sleep nighttime fantasies that left you hot and bothered with no relief in sight. It was those thoughts that had her unable to speak, so she just stood there and stared at the penetrating dark gaze holding hers as her heart beat violently in her chest.

She knew SEALs stayed in shape, but the body of the man standing before her was simply ridiculous. She knew of no other man whose body was so well built. So magnificently toned. His jeans appeared plastered to him in the most decadent way. He made her think of wicked temptation and sinful delights.

Doubting she could stand there much longer without going up in flames, even with the blast of cold air, she swallowed deeply and then forced her voice to ask, "Is something wrong with Ms. Melody?"

From the look that quickly flashed across his features, she could tell he was surprised by her question. "What makes you think something is wrong with my grandmother?"

Layla sighed deeply. "What other reason would bring you here?"

That, Gavin thought, was a good question. Why *was* he here? He had heard the harmonica. And had quickly figured out the source was Layla in the party house. So what had driven him out into the night? He definitely could have waited until morning to talk to her about the dig. Had he come here just to stand in the doorway to try and get his fill of looking at her?

"Gavin?"

And why did the sound of his name from her lips send desire throbbing through him? In his horny state, it wouldn't take much to push him over the edge. "Yes?"

"If nothing is wrong with Ms. Melody, why are you here?"

He crossed his arms over his chest. "I heard you playing a harmonica."

Layla's jaw dropped in surprise. She must have been shocked that he heard her. The guest cottage was far away from the main house and on the opposite side of the bedrooms. Gramma Mel had probably told her he would be sleeping hard for a full day.

But he wasn't sleeping. He was here. He rubbed his hand down his face in frustration. He needed to get to Mississippi fast or else…

Or else what? He would begin thinking of Layla Harris in his bed? Too late. His mind had already gone there. More than once. Those thoughts had pretty much settled in the moment he'd laid eyes on her. Having her at the party house wasn't helping matters. Typically, all he had to do was snap his fingers to get any woman he wanted. Why were his fingers itching to be snapped? With Layla Harris, would it be that easy? Why didn't he think so?

"I am so sorry," she said now. "I didn't mean to wake you. I know you need to get all that rest and—"

"You didn't wake me."

"But you said that you heard me playing."

"I did, but that's not what awakened me." Gavin figured there was no reason to tell her how disrupted his sleep patterns tended to be during his first few days back home. Which still left her question unanswered. Why was he here? Why had he sought her out? In the middle of the night? "You play very well," he said.

Gavin thought she was even more beautiful than she had looked this morning. He blamed the easy smile that touched her lips.

"Thanks, but I'm sure you didn't come all this way just to give me that compliment."

No, he hadn't. He'd actually come to give her hell for feeding his grandmother a bunch of crock about buried treasure on their land. So he needed to say what he had come to say. "We should talk. May I come in?"

It was funny he would ask. After all, she was the visitor on his land. This was his house. Ms. Melody had told her that Gavin and some of his SEAL teammates had built it a few years ago as a place to hang out whenever they visited.

Gavin and his friends could get loud and rowdy here at the cottage without disturbing his grandmother. That accounted for why the place was so spacious with the cupboards bare—except for a refrigerator stocked with beer and wine coolers. Not to mention that a deck of cards seemed to be in every room.

"Yes, of course you can come in. You own the place."

"But you're my grandmother's guest."

Had he said that to remind her she wasn't *his* guest? To remind her that her presence on the Silver Spurs was something he didn't support? Layla would find out soon enough.

She moved from the door and he followed, closing it behind him. "Would you like something to drink?" Grinning brightly, she said, "There's plenty of beer and wine coolers in the fridge."

Gavin chuckled. "I'll take a beer."

She nodded. "One beer coming up." She felt his gaze on her backside.

"Here you are. I feel funny doing this," Layla said, coming back into the room carrying a cold bottle of beer.

He lifted a brow. "Doing what?"

"Serving you your own beer."

"No reason that you should. You're my grandmother's guest."

That was the second time he'd said that, Layla thought. Not one to beat around the bush, she crossed the room to hand him the beer, and then wished she hadn't. Their hands had only briefly touched so why was heat filling her? And why was he looking at her as if that same heat filled him?

She quickly took a step back and wiped her hands down the sides of her jeans.

"You think that will get rid of it?"

She met his eyes. She knew what he'd insinuated, but she wanted to be sure. "Get rid of what?"

"Nothing."

He then opened the bottle and took a huge gulp. Afterward, he licked his lips while she watched. Her chest tightened. He lowered the bottle from his mouth and held her gaze. "Want a sip?"

She drew in a deep breath to clamp down on her emotions. Was he offering to share his beer? For them to drink from the same bottle? Doing something like that was way too intimate for her. Evidently not for him. A distinct warmth coiled around her midsection. The way his eyes darkened wasn't helping matters.

She should call his bluff and take a sip. But that might lead to other things. It might give him ideas. The same ideas floating crazily through her head. The last thing she needed was an involvement with a man. Any man. Especially him. Her work was too important to her. The idea of an October fling was not. "No thanks. I had one earlier and one was enough for me."

Instead of saying anything, he nodded and raised the bottle to his lips to drain the rest. She watched his throat work. When had seeing a man drink anything been a turn-on?

When he finished the bottle and lowered it, she asked, "Want another one?"

He smiled at her. "No, one was enough for me."

She couldn't help but smile back at his use of her words. "I don't know, Gavin Blake. You seem like the sort of guy that could handle a couple of those."

"You're right, but that's not why I'm here."

His words were a reminder that he hadn't shown up tonight for chitchat and drinking beer. "Yes, you said you wanted to talk. Is there a problem?" Layla knew there was and figured he was about to spell it out for her.

"Who taught you to play the harmonica?"

She'd expected him to just dive in. His question threw her. "My grandfather," she said, angling her head to look up at him. "He was the best. At least most people thought so."

"And who was your grandfather?"

"Chip Harris."

Surprise made Gavin's jaw drop. "Chip Harris? *The* Chip Harris?"

Layla nodded. "Yes," she said, intentionally keeping her voice light. Very few people knew that. It wasn't something she boasted about, although she was proud of her grandfather's success and accomplishments. He'd been a good man, a great humanitarian and a gifted musician. But most of all he had been a wonderful grandfather. Her grandparents had helped to keep her world sane during the times her parents had made it insane.

Layla saw Gavin's dark, penetrating eyes suddenly go cold. "Is anything wrong?"

"So that's how you did it."

She raised a brow. "That's how I did what?"

"How you were able to talk my grandmother into going along with your crazy scheme of Jesse James's treasure being buried on my property. You probably heard she's a big fan of Chip Harris, and used the fact that you're his granddaughter to get in good with her. Get Gramma Mel to trust you and—"

"You jerk." Anger flared through her. His accusations filled her with rage. "How dare you accuse me of doing something so underhanded, so unethical and low? You might not know me but you know your grandmother. How can you think so little of her to imagine she has such a weak mind she could be taken in by anyone? How can you not trust her judgment?"

Layla drew in a disgusted breath and then added furiously, "For your information, I never once mentioned anything about my relationship to Chip Harris to her. Ms. Melody's decision was based on my research, which she took the time to read. And she asked questions and found some of her own answers. So regardless of what you believe, her decision was based on facts, Gavin Blake. Facts and nothing more."

Gavin was stunned by Layla's rage. When her words sank in, he regretted accusing her of manipulating Gramma Mel. He'd crossed the line and he knew it. He owed her an apology. "I'm sorry. I should not have accused you of that."

"But you did. Save your apology for your grandmother. She's one of the most intelligent women I know. But tonight you made her out to be a woman who can be influenced easily by anything, especially name-dropping. Like I said, you should know your grandmother better than that."

Gavin didn't say anything. Probably because he knew she was right. His grandmother was as sharp as a tack. She'd told Layla so many stories of how he'd tried to pull one over on her…unsuccessfully. Maybe he should do what his grandmother had done and read Layla's report for himself.

"I should not have come here tonight," he finally said.

"No, you should not have, especially if you came to talk that kind of BS. I don't have time for it."

Layla's words seemed to irritate him. "You don't think I have a right to question why you're here?"

She didn't back down. In fact she took a step closer. "You have every right. But you already know why I'm here. If you don't agree with your grandmother or you want to question why I feel a dig on the Silver Spurs is warranted, I can understand that. But what you did, Gavin, is question my integrity. I take that personally."

"You have to admit the idea of buried treasure on my land is pretty far-fetched."

"Maybe to you but not to me. You're a SEAL. I'm sure there are times when you engage in covert operations where the facts lead you to believe your assignment will be successful…although logically it doesn't seem possible."

He frowned. "It's not the same."

"I think it is. I did my research on the life of Jesse James. Five years' worth. I studied his life, specifically that bank robbery in Tinsel. That's what led me here. If you took the time to read my research, you would see it's all there. All I'm asking is for you to give me the same courtesy Ms. Melody did and take the time to read my work."

"I don't have to read a report to know what you're claiming isn't true."

In frustration, Layla blew out a breath and threw up her hands. "Why are you so stubborn?"

Instead of answering he gave her a careless shrug of his broad shoulders. "I'm not being stubborn. Just realistic."

He wasn't even trying to be reasonable. "So what do you want, Gavin? Since you believe that I've hoodwinked your grandmother and I'm a lunatic on the hunt for buried treasure, did you come here tonight to ask me to leave? To tell me to get off your property because you won't allow me and my team to dig?"

When he didn't say anything but continued to stare down at her with those dark, penetrating eyes of his, she knew what she'd just said was true. "Fine. I'll leave in the morning."

She moved with the intention of walking around him to show him the door. He surprised her when he reached out and grabbed her arm. The moment he touched her it seemed every hormone in her body sizzled. She couldn't move away from him. His hand skimmed down her arm in a sensual caress.

"What do you think you're doing?" She heard the tension in her voice and felt her heart rate quicken. Their gazes held and something hot in the depths of his eyes held her hostage. She wanted to break eye contact and couldn't. How could any one man have so much sex appeal? Create such primal attraction?

Layla became angry with herself because of her reaction to him. The man standing in front of her had destroyed her plans. He'd placed her in a difficult position with the administration at the university and with her team. She'd have to cancel excavation and lose her funding. She might never get another chance to prove her theories. Yet at that moment all she could think about was how fully aware of him she was.

"What I'm doing is touching you," he answered moments later, as if he'd needed time to give her question some thought.

Well, she had news for him. He should keep his hands to himself. So why wasn't she telling him that? And why was there a throb inside her? One that had started in her stomach but was now going lower to the juncture of her thighs? And why, when she saw his head lowering, did she just stand there? When his lips touched hers and he wrapped her in his arms, she sank into him. The same way he was sinking into her mouth.

The kiss was making her forget everything, even the fact that he wanted to throw her off his ranch. The only thing she could concentrate on was how his tongue was moving around in her mouth, sending shivers up her spine until she heard herself moan.

But he was moaning as well, and then he deepened the kiss. She recognized this for what it was. Lust. And that usually led to sex. If that was his plan, he could take it elsewhere. She had no intention of getting involved, no matter how fleetingly, with a man who refused to take her work seriously.

She pulled her mouth free and took a step back. "Like I said. I'll be off your property in the morning." She then walked around him to the door.

Before opening it, she glanced back at him. He stood in the same spot, staring at her as if she was a puzzle he was trying to figure out. Seriously? Did he think she was that complicated? As far as she was concerned, he was the problematic one.

He was the man who, with very little effort, it seemed, could tempt her to lower her guard, to surrender to this need he created inside of her. A need she hadn't realized even existed. And it appeared he was dealing with his own need if the huge bulge pressing against the zipper of his jeans was anything to go by. There were just some things an aroused man couldn't hide.

"We need to keep sex out of this, Gavin." She'd had to say it, considering the strong sexual chemistry flowing between them. Chemistry both of them were fully aware of.

He stared at her for a long moment, saying nothing, but she saw the tightening of his jaw. Had her words hit a nerve? Had they made him realize that she wasn't as gullible as he thought?

When he began walking toward her, her heartbeat quickened with every step he took. Never had she felt such a strong primal attraction to any man. Even his walk, his muscled thighs flexing erotically with every step, tripped her pulse. It had her drowning in the sexual vibes pouring off him.

When he came to a stop in front of her, he grabbed her hand to keep her from opening the door. Immediately, like before, they became attuned to each other. Why was there such a strong physical attraction between them? No man had ever made her forget about work. But she struggled to remember that work was the reason she was here. That and nothing else.

"Don't know about you, but I can't keep sex out of it, Layla. I think you know why. Whether we like it or not, there's a strong sensual pull between us. I felt it the moment I set eyes on you this morning, and if you say you didn't feel it as well, then you would be lying. You might pretend otherwise, but you want me as much as I want you."

No matter what he said, she would deny it. She hadn't come to the ranch for this. She had come to Cornerstone, Missouri, to do a job—to prove her theory and move up in her career—*not* to have an affair with a navy SEAL who could overtake her senses. A man who was proving, whether she wanted him to or not, that she had sexual needs she'd ignored for too long. But regardless of that proof, under no circumstances would she sleep with him. Doing so would be a very bad idea. It would be a mistake that could cost her all she'd worked for up to this point. Besides, hadn't he all but told her to get off his land?

Instead of a straight-out denial, she said, "What I want is to be allowed to do my job. I need to do that dig, Gavin."

His gaze hardened. "Why? To prove me wrong?"

"More than proving you wrong, I need to prove to myself and my peers that I am right. There's a difference, but I don't expect you to understand."

Yes, he understood the difference. Hadn't he felt the need to prove that he was his own man? To prove that being a SEAL hadn't been about his grandfather's and father's legacies but about establishing a legacy of his own? The first Gavin Blake had been handpicked to be part of the first special operations unit that became known as the SEALs. And Gavin's father, Gavin Blake Jr, had died a war hero after rescuing his team members and others who'd been held hostage during Desert Storm.

For years, he'd thought being Gavin Blake III was a curse more than a blessing. You couldn't share the name of bigger-than-life SEAL predecessors without some people believing you should be invincible. It had taken years to prove to others, as well as to himself, that he was his own man. Free to make his own mistakes. Now he cherished the memories of the heroes his grandfather and father had been and he was proud to carry their names and to continue the family legacy of being a SEAL. In the end, he'd realized becoming his own man hadn't been about proving anything to others but proving it to himself.

A part of him wanted to believe that Layla's issues were hers alone. They were her business to deal with and not his. But for some reason he couldn't let her go. His curiosity pushed him to say, "Don't leave the Silver Spurs just yet, Layla."

He saw that his words surprised her. Gave her pause. "Why? You ridiculed my years of research, accused me of manipulating your family and told me not to dig on your land. Why should I stay?"

"To convince me that you're right."

He could tell from her expression she thought what he'd said didn't make sense. "I can't do that unless you give me permission to excavate, Gavin. That's the only way I can prove anything."

Gavin was totally captivated by Layla Harris—by her passion for her work, and this passion between them. Why? He wasn't sure. She was beautiful, but he'd been around beautiful women before. She was built—with lush curves, a nice backside and very attractive features—but all those were just physical attributes. Deep down, he believed there was more to Layla Harris than just her beauty, more than her intelligence. There was something inside of her she refused to let surface. And it was something he wanted to uncover.

One thing for certain, he honestly wasn't ready for her to leave the Silver Spurs. But she was right. Why should she stay if he wouldn't allow her to dig on his property? He gritted his teeth at the thought of any woman making him feel so needy that he'd allow her to dig up the south pasture, his special place. But he quickly remembered he'd gone six months without sex, which had a way of crippling a man's senses.

"It's late," he heard himself say. "Let's talk more tomorrow."

"Will talking tomorrow change anything, Gavin?"

All he knew for certain was that he couldn't think straight being this close to her. But the last thing he wanted was to wake up tomorrow and find her gone. "It might," he said. "I'm not making any promises, Layla. All I can say is that right now I'm exhausted and can't think straight." He would let her think his muddled mind was due to exhaustion and not the degree of desire he had for her.

"Will you read my research?"

He wouldn't lie about that. "No. You can go over the important aspects of your work when we meet tomorrow."

She stared at him for a long moment as if weighing his words. Finally, she said, "Alright. I'll stay until we can talk."

Relief poured through his body, quickly followed by frustration and annoyance. No woman could tie him in knots like Layla seemed capable of doing. "I'll see you tomorrow."

When he'd first arrived, her hair had been neatly pulled back. Had he mussed up her hair when he'd kissed her? Maybe that was why the loose curls now teasing her forehead were a total turn-on.

"Good night, Gavin."

That was his cue to go. "Good night." He opened the door and stepped out into the cold Missouri night.

Three

Layla awakened the next morning wondering what she'd gotten herself into. Would remaining an additional day to meet with Gavin really change his mind?

There was always the possibility that it could, which was the reason her bags were not already packed. Besides, she was a fighter, a person who didn't give up easily. It had taken over a year to convince the university to give her funding for the dig, and another six months to get them to ease off some of their restrictions and ridiculous conditions. Even now, she wasn't sure the heads of the department believed in her 100 percent, but at least they were giving her a chance.

Now all of that forward momentum—the work that could change the history books and earn her a tenured position—could end because of Gavin. She drew in a deep breath. What was she going to do? Short of sleeping with him, she would do just about anything to convince him to reconsider.

She shifted in bed to look out the window. She'd thought she had a beautiful view in her high-rise apartment overlooking downtown Seattle—until now. The rolling plains, majestic hills and valleys of the Silver Spurs were awesome. The concrete jungle she saw each morning from her bedroom window couldn't compare.

She loved it here. She wouldn't mind returning to visit. But this time, she wasn't here for a vacation. She had a job to do and she hoped Gavin wouldn't stand in the way of her doing it.

Gavin.

He thought she'd been manipulative enough to use her musician grandfather's name to get in good with his grandmother. Although he had apologized, those accusations still bothered her. Yet in spite of them, she had allowed him to kiss her. And it was a kiss she couldn't stop thinking about. A kiss so deeply entrenched in her mind that she'd thought about it even while she'd slept. She was thinking about it now while wide-awake.

Layla realized that kissing, something she'd never enjoyed doing before, wasn't so bad after all. At least with Gavin it wasn't bad. Evidently other guys had lacked his expertise. Not only did he have a skillful tongue, but he knew how to use it. The feel of being in his strong arms had sent pleasure throughout her entire body.

She drew in a sharp breath as memories flooded her, filling her with a longing for them to kiss again. Yet how could she even contemplate repeating that kiss when she wasn't sure she even liked him? The one thing she did know was that she definitely desired him and he'd been arrogant enough to call her out on that.

In frustration, she rubbed a hand down her face. She needed to rid her mind of thoughts of Gavin. She'd never mixed business with pleasure and she had no intention of doing so now. The most important thing in her life had always been her work, and she deliberately avoided relationships to keep her focus where it should be. She wouldn't let her attraction to Gavin interfere with what she needed to do.

And the first thing she needed to do was get out of bed and start her day. Gavin said they would talk today and she could only hope for the best.

It was early evening when Gavin finally opened his eyes and he immediately thought about the woman staying in the party house. The woman he'd kissed last night.

Layla had mated her tongue to his with an intensity that made every muscle in his body throb. It was as if she had just as much passion bottled up inside as he did. And he'd unleashed it all with that kiss.

He would love to pick up where they'd left off last night. Take the passion to a whole new level. That made him think of other things…like making love to Layla. How it would feel to run his hands through her hair, lock his mouth and his body to hers. Become immersed in all that sexual energy they seemed to generate. He got hard just thinking about the possibilities.

Gavin glanced over at the clock. He had slept the day away, but he had needed the sleep. Images of Layla had sneaked into the deep recesses of his mind, whether he had wanted them to or not. She'd been in his dreams.

He wanted her.

There. He'd confirmed it in his mind without an ounce of regret. He was a man with needs and that kiss last night had totally obliterated any desire for the Mississippi vixen. He'd lost interest in heading south as planned. Nor did he want Layla to leave the ranch. But like she'd reminded him last night, unless he agreed to let her dig on the property, she had no reason to stay.

That meant he had to come up with a plan.

He rubbed sleep from his eyes, remembering that he had detected a few insecurities lurking within Layla last night. Something about her need to prove herself. What was that about? Did he really want to know? Did he even care?

Yes, he cared. He would go so far as to say that he even admired her spunk. Layla was tough and he had a feeling he hadn't even seen half the strength she possessed. She had to be resilient to have become a college professor at such a young age. He could see her holding her own when it mattered. He couldn't help but smile when he recalled her saying that he needed to keep sex out of this situation. Little did she know he had no intention of doing that. Their attraction was too strong and he intended to use it to his advantage.

As he stood to head for the bathroom, he halted upon hearing voices. They were his grandmother's and Layla's. His body immediately reacted to the sound of Layla's voice. They were in the kitchen. And he could tell his grandmother was enjoying the conversation.

He could understand why Gramma Mel was so taken with Layla. Although he never thought about it much, his grandmother probably got lonely around here whenever he was away. Even though she had Caldwell, there hadn't been another woman staying on the Silver Spurs since Gavin's mother had left.

He tried pushing thoughts of Jamie Blake from his mind like he'd always done. Why should he think about the woman who hadn't thought of him? One day she'd packed up and left, drove away leaving only a letter claiming she needed time away and would return. She never did. That's what had bothered Gavin the most, knowing a woman could just walk away from her husband and eight-year-old son without looking back.

Refusing to think about his mother anymore, Gavin

entered his bathroom to shower. He hoped Layla stayed in the kitchen with his grandmother for a while because he definitely needed to talk to her.

Layla's hand tightened on her glass of iced tea the moment Gavin entered the kitchen. She didn't have to glance behind her to know he was there. His presence filled the room and sent all kinds of sensations vibrating through her. She was a little irritated that she was so aware of him. The sexual chemistry she'd hoped was a fluke was back in full force.

"Gavin, I figured the smell of food would wake you sooner or later," Melody Blake said, smiling at her grandson.

When he moved into Layla's line of vision she had no choice but to glance over at him. "Yes, it definitely did," he said, answering his grandmother but staring straight at Layla.

Then he spoke to her. "Layla. How are you today?"

She wanted to tell him she'd been fine until he'd made an appearance. She couldn't stop her gaze from roaming all over him. He stood near the window and the fading afternoon light highlighted his features, his clothing, everything about him. Not for the first time, Layla thought he had to be the sexiest man alive.

When he lifted a brow, she realized she had yet to answer his question. "I'm fine, Gavin. Thanks for asking."

She quickly switched her gaze away from him and back to her plate. Why had she waited so long to answer? Doing so had made it obvious she'd been checking him out. Thoroughly.

"I left your food warming in the oven, Gavin," Ms. Melody said, breaking the tension.

"Thanks, Gramma Mel. All I've been able to think

about these last few days was getting back to your home-cooked meals." Gavin opened the oven to peek inside.

After getting his plate out of the oven, he smiled at Layla and crossed the kitchen to sit in the chair beside her, brushing his thigh against hers. He said grace and then lifted his head and looked over at Layla. He caught her staring at him again. She knew his touch had been no accident. Totally deliberate.

He pasted an innocent smile on his face and asked, "So, Layla, how was your day?"

Layla gritted her teeth. The nerve of him asking how her day had gone when she'd been waiting to meet with him. She hadn't mentioned anything about Gavin's visit last night to Ms. Melody. There was no way Layla could have mentioned it with a straight face, especially when she couldn't help thinking of the kiss they'd shared.

Knowing he was waiting for her response, she said, "My day has been going great."

"Gavin, I'm glad I got to say hello before I leave," his grandmother said, standing to her feet.

Gavin looked at his grandmother. "Where are you going?"

"The civic center. It's bingo night and Viola is picking me up. She should be here any minute."

It suddenly occurred to Layla that she would be left alone with Gavin. That shouldn't be a big deal since they still needed to talk, but it was. Already nerves stirred in the pit of her stomach.

"We'll take care of the kitchen," she heard Gavin say. "Layla and I need to talk anyway."

Ms. Melody looked back and forth at the two of them before directing her gaze to her grandson. "I think that's a good idea." At the sound of the car horn, a smile touched her lips. "That's Viola."

Before Layla and Gavin could tell her goodbye, Melody Blake had grabbed her purse and was out the door.

That's when Gavin turned his attention back to Layla.

When Gavin saw Layla loading her dishes into the sink, he said, "You don't have to help me with the dishes."

She shrugged her shoulders. "I don't mind."

Her back was to him and he couldn't stop his gaze from covering every inch of her backside, wrapped tight in her skirt. And before she'd left the table, more than once he'd checked out her pink blouse, noticing the deep V neck. There was nothing like seeing a little of a woman's cleavage every now and then. Made him wonder what her breasts looked like. How they would feel in his hands. Taste in his mouth.

"Your grandmother forgot to mention she made a dessert," Layla said, breaking into his thoughts and turning around to meet his gaze.

"What is it?"

"Peach cobbler. Do you want some?"

That question was not one she should be asking him. Not when he had an erection nearly hard enough to burst out of his jeans. Yes, he wanted some, but his thoughts weren't on the peach cobbler.

Why did the picture of her standing at his grandmother's sink make a pang of desire shoot through him? The hair she'd worn down and around her shoulders yesterday was now confined in a ponytail. It wouldn't take much to walk across the room and set it free. After doing that, he would proceed to do all kinds of naughty things to her. Gavin shifted in his seat to relieve the pressure against his zipper.

"Yeah, I'd love to have some," he said in a deep, husky voice. And he knew Layla had figured out they weren't talking about peach cobbler.

She didn't say anything, just stared at him. He wished she didn't look so damn sexy while she sized him up, trying to figure him out. There wasn't much to find out on that score. He was a horny bastard and would remain so until he'd taken care of his sexual needs. That meant they needed to talk, and the sooner the better.

"We can talk while eating peach cobbler," he said.

Layla seemed relieved to finally begin their discussion and returned to the table with two plates of peach cobbler. "Where do we start?" she asked, sliding one of the plates in front of him before sitting down.

He picked up his fork and looked over at her. "We can start by talking about us."

Her expression clearly said that wasn't what she thought they should be talking about. "We agreed to discuss the dig and not this thing between us."

Gavin wondered if Layla knew that "this thing" actually had a name. It was called physical desire. "I think we should talk about us before discussing the dig."

She gave him an annoyed look. "Why? I told you last night we needed to keep sex out of it."

Yes, she had said that, but did she actually think they could keep sex out of it when there was so much chemistry between them? So much that even now he would have no problem taking her right here on this damn table? "You're an intelligent woman, Layla. I'm sure you're well aware of how the human body operates. All of us have needs."

"Speak for yourself, Gavin."

He watched her nervously gnaw on her lower lip and heated lust danced up his spine. He was trying like hell to figure her out. Was she denying she had needs, as well? He knew from last night's kiss that that was a lie. Her denial made Gavin wonder about her experience level.

"Are you saying you don't want to have sex with me?"

As if the question shot her to full awareness, she leaned

over the table and glared at him. "I don't want to have sex with you, Gavin. I don't want to have sex with anybody. All I want is to do my job. A job you refuse to let me do."

They weren't getting anywhere. For some reason he didn't want to talk to her about the dig until he found out why she kept certain emotions in check. So he tried another approach.

"Tell me about yourself, Layla."

Layla lifted a brow. That was clearly not what she'd expected. "I graduated from high school at sixteen and immediately went to college. Graduated with my bachelor's degree in history, then went on to get a master's in archaeology. My doctorate is in both history and archaeology."

"And you're just twenty-six?"

"Yes. I went to college year-round. I've worked on dig sites as an undergrad and while working toward my PhD so this won't be my first excavation."

"But it will be the first one you've been in charge of, right?"

"Yes, that's true."

He leaned back in his chair, deciding to keep her talking about the dig for a while, after all. He doubted she realized that whenever she talked about her work she lowered her guard. "So you admit you're inexperienced."

Layla frowned. He could tell she wasn't sure if they were still talking about the dig. "I don't think of myself as inexperienced, Gavin, so you shouldn't think that, either."

"Then tell me what I should think."

After several moments, she said, "You should focus on the fact that my being here is the result of several years of research. I didn't just wake up one morning and decide to do this. I've tracked each and every one of James's bank robberies in this area. Mapped out every possible trail he could have taken, every single place he and the gang could have hidden out. Then I obtained records of this land and the surrounding properties. I had my team digitally re-create how this area would have looked back then.

"The Silver Spurs would have been the ideal place to stop over because of the low-hanging trees. And the lake between here and the Lotts' spread would have allowed the gang time to wash away their scent and stay hidden from the sheriff's posse. I could even see James's gang being smart enough to use a decoy to send the posse racing in another direction. One away from here to give them time to bury their loot and lighten their load."

Gavin was trying not to get caught up in the sound of her voice. He wanted to hear the words she was saying. She was excited about her work and discussing it energized her. He couldn't help noticing the glow in her eyes, the confidence in her voice, the smile on her lips. The same lips he had tasted last night.

She was trying like hell to convince him that she was onto something, that she had researched her findings and believed in everything she was telling him. He knew there had to be a number of doubters...like himself.

When she stopped talking, he shifted his gaze from her lips to her eyes. "I take it you've already surveyed the area, used ground penetrating radar on the location already."

She nodded. If she was surprised by his knowledge of her preliminary assessment, she didn't show it. "I've gone further. I was able to get an infrared spectrum."

He lifted a brow. "How?"

"One of my students is big into digital technology and created it for me. That's the advantage I have over others working on this subject, I'm bringing this excavation into the digital age."

The technological aspect was an area Gavin was somewhat familiar with. The military already used all sorts of futuristic developments. It was important whenever they were sent into enemy territory that they didn't step on booby traps or buried explosives.

She looked at him expectantly, as if he would question what she said. He merely nodded. "I'm familiar with the use of high-tech digital to detect buried items."

She smiled, obviously glad that he was following her. "All the equipment my team and I use is state-of-the-art, some have never before been used in an archaeological context and they were developed exclusively for this dig by students in my department," she said proudly.

Because she was young he couldn't imagine her getting others to rally behind her for the cause. Whether she knew it or not, that spoke volumes about her character as a leader. It would take a strong individual to coax others on board. He knew how that could be.

"It's too late today but tomorrow I want to check out the area you've targeted." What she would discover was that he also had a high-tech camera, one designed by Flipper for marine purposes. However, it had proven effective at detecting objects underground, as well.

"Alright."

He heard the hope in her voice and figured that was because he'd shown interest in the dig site. She probably thought he was almost on board. That wasn't the case. But he wouldn't tell her that yet.

When he didn't say anything else for a while, she lifted a brow and looked over at him. She even had a little smile on her face. That glow brightening her eyes almost undid him. "Any more questions, Gavin?"

There was something else; something he had to know. "Yes, but not about the dig. It's something about you that I want to know."

"What?" she asked, lifting an arched brow.

He held her gaze steadily. "When was the last time you made love with a man?"

Four

Layla gaped, certain Gavin hadn't asked her what she thought he'd asked her. What man would inquire that of a woman…especially one he'd known barely twenty-four hours? However, from the look on his face, he evidently saw nothing wrong with the question. He was sitting there waiting on an answer.

She lifted her chin and crossed her arms over her chest. When she saw his gaze shift from her eyes to her upraised breasts, she dropped her hands. "Do you actually expect me to answer that?" Somehow she managed to get the words past a constricted throat. The way he stared at her was making her head spin.

He shrugged massive broad shoulders. "Don't know why not. We're sexually attracted to each other. Just want to know what I'm dealing with when we decide to go for it and take the edge off."

Go for it? Take the edge off? Layla shook her head, clearly missing something. She knew they were attracted to each other; she got that. What she didn't get was him thinking that attraction meant they would eventually decide to "go for it." She had no intention of going anywhere. She was here to do a job and not indulge his fantasies... or her own, for that matter.

"I think you need to explain what exactly you're getting at. We agreed to keep sex out of this, Gavin."

"I didn't agree to any such thing. You suggested it but I didn't agree to it. Why would I?"

"Why wouldn't you?" she countered, not understanding his way of thinking.

He leaned back in his chair and her gaze watched his every movement. Restrained and controlled. She wondered if his actions were intentional, to put her off-kilter. When he picked up his glass of tea, her gaze automatically shifted to his hands. They were large and callous. They were the same hands that had sent shivers up her spine last night.

Memories of their kiss suddenly bombarded her and then her gaze shifted to his mouth as he took a swallow of iced tea. She was drawn to the way his mouth covered the rim of the glass and the way the liquid flowed down his throat. But what really got to her was the way he licked his lips afterward. When he caught her staring, those penetrating eyes darkened as they held hers.

"Want some?"

She snatched her gaze away. The lump in her throat thickened. She was glad to be sitting down; otherwise it would have been impossible to stand on both feet. The look he was giving her had her weak in the knees.

Somehow she managed to clear the lump in her throat and hold up her glass. "No thanks, I have my own."

His eyes blazed as they continued to hold hers. "I wasn't offering you any of my tea, Layla."

She sucked in a deep breath. He couldn't have set her

straight any plainer than that. There was no need to ask what he was offering. That was the moment she knew Gavin Blake intended to be a problem. One she needed to deal with here and now.

"You never did answer my earlier question. When was the last time you were with a man?"

She set her glass of tea back down on the table. "And you never answered mine about why you wouldn't agree to keep sex out of it." Feeling flustered, she added, "We need to talk."

A smile touched the corners of his lips. "I thought that's what we were doing."

There was no way he could have thought that. What he was doing was deliberately getting her all unglued. If he thought for one minute his arrogant behavior would make her run, then he didn't know her very well. "There seems to be some sort of misunderstanding here."

"Is there?"

"Undoubtedly. I'm here to do a job…that is, if you let me stay to do it. But under no circumstances am I here for your pleasure, Gavin. I don't play those kinds of games. Evidently just because we shared a kiss last night, you've gotten the wrong idea about me. I need to set the record straight now. So hear me and hear me good." She leaned part of the way over the table toward him. Although his face was void of any expression, she was certain she had his undivided attention.

"I am *not* here to engage in an affair with you, if that's why you want to know about my sex life." *Or lack thereof.* But that was something he didn't need to know.

Gavin didn't say anything. He knew she assumed his attention was on her words. In truth his attention was on the mouth delivering those words. Her lips were perfectly shaped with a little cute dip in the center. He liked the play of that mutinous tip whenever she frowned and how those same lips folded pensively when she appeared in deep thought. But more than anything, he couldn't forget how those lips felt beneath his. Their lushness. How delicious they'd tasted. How sweet.

When she got quiet after delivering her spiel, he figured she thought she had set him straight. Far from it and it was time to let her know where he stood. "Are you finished?"

She seemed surprised by his question, but nodded nonetheless and said, "Yes, I'm finished." She then straightened in her chair, her posture a lot more relaxed than it had been moments ago.

"Evidently, there's a lot you don't understand about sex, Layla."

Her body tensed again. And somehow those gorgeous lips looked even more sensual. "What's there to understand?" she asked.

Gavin continued to study her. He saw her nonchalant expression and noted her features had taken on a blasé look. Her apparent indifference to this discussion of sex could mean only one thing. She'd been cheated of something he considered as vital as breathing. Reaching her level of success in such a short period of time meant something had been sacrificed. An active sex life, perhaps?

"I want you and you want me," he said, deciding to point out the obvious.

"And?"

He forced himself not to smile, thinking she was pretending not to have a clue. Then it occurred to him that maybe she wasn't pretending. Maybe it was time to explain to her what it meant whenever a woman became the object of his personal fantasies.

"And…" he said, "we *will* sleep together."

She sat up in her chair, straightening her spine. Her

lips went from sensual to tense but turned him on even more just the same. "No, we will not," she said adamantly.

He smiled. "Yes, we will. It's inevitable."

She frowned. "No, it's not. Just who do you think you are?"

He figured it was time she knew the answer to that. "A man who wants you. A man who intends to have you. A man who will show you, Layla Harris, just what you've been missing."

Layla tried to keep her heart from pounding deep in her chest, while at the same time fighting off the heat stroking through her body. She knew she shouldn't ask but she couldn't hold back.

"And just what do you think I've missed?"

"Hot, raunchy, mind-blowing sex. Evidently over the years you've been too preoccupied with other things to indulge. Don't you know it's not good to deprive your body of meeting certain needs?"

Her frown deepened. "I haven't deprived my body of anything."

"Haven't you? Why do you think you're so attracted to me?"

Layla actually rolled her eyes. Really? Honestly? Had he looked in the mirror lately? When was the last time he'd studied all those photos Ms. Melody had plastered on the walls. Any woman would be attracted to him. Even now he sat there not doing anything and still looked sexy as hell with that well-toned body of his. And here she was sitting across the table from him. Right within kissing distance.

As far as she was concerned, Gavin Blake was eye candy of the richest kind. Passion personified. But she definitely wouldn't tell him that. She would deny everything he'd said with her last breath if she had to.

"I am not all that attracted to you." At least she hadn't completely lied and said she wasn't attracted to him at all.

"You want me to prove otherwise?"

What was it with men always wanting to prove things when it came to sex? "No, thanks. That's not necessary."

"I think that it is."

He'd said the words in a low, vibrating tone with a sexy rumble she wished she could ignore. But there was no way, what with all the shivers oozing down her spine. "Are you trying to scare me off, Gavin?"

He lifted a brow. "Scare you off?"

"Yes. Say all these things so I get angry enough to leave the ranch, sparing you the trouble of making a decision one way or the other about whether I can dig on your land or not."

"Is that what you think?"

To be honest, she didn't know what to think. She needed his land and all he had on his mind was sex. That made her wonder...

"Then are you trying to box me into a corner? Implying that I will have to sleep with you before you'll give me permission to dig?"

Gavin shook his head. "I would never put pressure on you to sleep with me. But be forewarned, Layla. If you hang around here doing that dig, we *will* sleep together. There's no way we won't. Your own body will betray you. When it does, I will be ready for the opportunity."

Seriously? If he thought her body would eventually weaken, he didn't know her. And that was the point, one she couldn't lose sight of. He *didn't* know her. He didn't know about her dedication when it came to her work. Nor did he know of her ability to be single-minded when it came to her career goals. She could put everything out of her mind except what was most important. She was driven to be successful in her field, and she wouldn't let Gavin—or any other man—stand in her way.

He was pretty sure of himself where women were concerned. A man couldn't look like him, be built like him, and not be in demand and get any woman he wanted. All Gavin had to do was snap his fingers and she figured the women came running. Being denied anything from a woman would be foreign to him.

"Think whatever you want, Gavin, but I'm not the kind of woman you're used to. I won't break."

He rubbed his hand over his chin as he studied her. "Would you want to bet on that?"

Layla frowned. She had no intention of betting on anything and she proceeded to tell him that. He only smiled, and it was one of those smiles she was getting to know too well. The one that made her body sizzle when it should make her angry. His smile all but said he had her where he wanted her.

"Would you be willing to bet on it to guarantee your dig on the Silver Spurs?"

That piqued her interest. "Depending on what you have in mind." She hoped she was not setting herself up for something she would regret.

Gavin held back his *gotcha* smile. Little did Layla know but his teammates didn't call him Viper for nothing. To some, a viper might be considered a spiteful or treacherous person, but for him the name meant he knew how to capture his prey using any means necessary. Striking when they least expected it. He wanted her in his bed willingly and he intended to do whatever it took to get her there. It was time to push his agenda.

"I'm willing to make a deal, Layla."

"What sort of a deal?" She held his gaze.

Did she know how beautiful her facial features were?

How striking her bone structure? He could sit for hours and stare, taking her in. But doing so would make him want her even more than he already did. Before he'd met her, he couldn't have imagined that degree of need for any woman. But he could imagine it for her.

He lifted his shoulder in a half shrug as if what he was about to say wasn't of grave importance. As if he really didn't care one way or the other if she took the deal or left it on the table.

"I'm not as convinced about this buried loot as you and my grandmother seem to be," he said. "And I doubt reading any report will make me change my mind. But wanting you in my bed will," he said bluntly, needing her to fully understand what he was saying.

"This is the deal," he continued. "I will let you dig, regardless of what I think. If you find something, great. You will have proven me wrong. I will be happy for you. Be the first to congratulate you on a job well done. However, if you come up with nothing then you admit you want me as much as I want you and we sleep together."

"You are counting on me failing? And plan to take advantage of me if I do?"

The thought was firing her up. He could tell. The flash of fire in her eyes told it all. "You shouldn't worry about failing. Unless you think you will. If there's some doubt in your mind regarding the accuracy of your research, then I understand if—"

"My research is on point. There's no doubt in my mind about anything."

His smile spread across his lips. "In that case, do we have a deal?"

Five

At that moment Layla realized just what was going on. Whether it was his intent or not, Gavin was forcing her to believe in herself, to prove that she was right in her belief that Jesse James had buried treasure on Gavin's land.

"Well?"

The determination was clear in his eyes. He intended to sleep with her. She was just as determined that he wouldn't. She didn't like the deal he'd offered. In all honesty, she should be appalled by it. Instead she saw it as her chance to prove she was above the desire he couldn't stop talking about. She would find Jesse James's loot. She had no doubts. There was no need getting irritated that he was a typical male who thought a good roll between the sheets was the answer to everything. She would never be able to convince him that when it came to sex, she had always been able to take it or leave it, no matter how tempting it was to indulge. He would find that out for himself.

She'd be free to run her dig and make the finding of not only her career but of a lifetime. She wouldn't think about the traitorous voice that said it might be nice to lose this bet and get the consolation prize...

"Fine."

He lifted his brow. "Does that mean you accept the deal?"

"As long as you give me your word you won't try to hinder me and my team in any way."

"I wouldn't do that."

Yeah. Right. There was no reason for her to trust he wouldn't do just about anything to make sure the result worked out in his favor. Another typical male trait. No man liked losing. "Whatever you say."

"You're going to have to trust me."

Layla rolled her eyes. "Sorry to disappoint you, but I don't know you enough to trust you."

"I can remedy that."

"Don't do me any favors." Layla eased out of her chair, feeling like she'd mentally run a marathon. "So will you give me your word as a SEAL that you won't try anything underhanded?"

"You think my word as a SEAL means something?"

"Yes. SEALs are a special team of men who take the job of protecting our country very seriously, and they live by a code of honor and integrity."

Gavin nodded. She was right. "And you know this how?"

"My father's cousin used to be a SEAL. He retired a few years ago, but he told us all about them. At least what he could share. A lot of the stuff he did was classified."

"The majority of our missions are," Gavin said.

"So, will you give me your word?"

"Yes, you have my word."

* * *

As far as Gavin was concerned, getting her into his bed before the dig began would not be interfering with the job she wanted to do.

"Good." She glanced at her watch. "It's getting late. I'm sure you need more sleep. However, if you need help with the dishes, then I—"

"No, I don't need help with the dishes. That's what dishwashers are for."

"Do you still want to see where we plan to dig?"

"Yes. I want to know what you have planned on my property and where."

"No problem."

"Then I'll come by the cottage in the morning," he said, standing, as well. "Come on. I'll walk you back."

She shook her head as she put on her sweater. "That's not necessary."

"It is for me, Layla. I'll walk you back."

She didn't deny him, maybe she didn't want to appear ungrateful. She headed for the door and when she reached out to open it, he moved his hand forward, as well. She didn't seem aware that he'd been standing so close behind her. His fingers closed over her hers and his chest was flush against her back.

"I can open the door, Gavin," she said, glancing over her shoulder, obviously flustered at his nearness. He loomed over her five-foot-three-inch height. He stood so close he could smell her with every breath.

"Your choice." Releasing his hand from hers he eased back. She opened the door and inhaled the cool Missouri air.

"Nice night, isn't it?" he asked her. He walked beside her now.

"Yes, it is a nice night." She glanced over at him again. "Glad to be home?"

A smile touched his lips. "Yes. It's always good to be home. Time to go from SEAL to rancher."

"Is it that easy?"

"I'm used to it now. I have good men working for me who make the transition less difficult."

She nodded. "You love being a SEAL?"

"Yes."

"I understand your father and grandfather were SEALs."

Gavin wondered what else his grandmother had told her about their family. "Yes, they were SEALs. So I guess you can say it's in my blood. What about your folks? Are they college professors like you?"

"No. They're both neurosurgeons. I didn't follow in their footsteps. Medicine didn't interest me."

He hadn't asked her to explain, but the fact that she did led him to believe her choice of a career was a sore spot with someone. "You are your own person, Layla." She was definitely her own woman, he thought further to himself. "Just because following in my father's and grandfather's footsteps worked for me, doesn't mean following family tradition works for everybody."

She didn't say anything for a minute. "My parents wanted me to be a mini-them and go to medical school. But I couldn't. I'm not a healer. I'm a historian."

"Then you did the right thing by following your heart. When did you decide on archaeology?" Gavin wondered if she noted how in sync their steps were.

"In my junior year of high school." She paused as if she was remembering. "My history teacher had gone on an excavation in Egypt the summer before and told us about it. I found it fascinating how her team was able to dig up artifacts, how they found history buried beneath the earth's surface. It made me realize that's what I wanted to do."

"Why Jesse James?"

He heard her chuckle and the sound stimulated him in a way he wished it didn't. "Why *not* Jesse James?" He heard the amusement in her tone. "I used to watch Westerns with my grandfather whenever I visited him in New Orleans. He was a fan of the outlaw Jesse James. He read a lot of books about him. Watched movies and documentaries. I shared his love and interest. That's how my research began. And it's only grown over the years."

He heard the passion for her subject in her voice. It was there whenever she spoke about her work. She believed in it. If there had been any doubt in his mind before, there wasn't now. She would risk sleeping with him to prove her work.

She'd be disappointed not to find what she was searching for. But Gavin looked forward to helping her get over the disappointment. He didn't believe for one minute that James's loot was buried on this land. It wasn't. He recalled years ago when he'd been in high school, his father had given some outfit permission to check out the land because there was a chance of finding oil. They'd come up with nothing then, and he was certain Layla and her team would come up with nothing now.

"I guess this is where we need to say good-night."

They had reached the party house. Her words told him he wouldn't be invited inside. Maybe that was for the best. He doubted he could keep his hands off of her if they were behind closed doors. And regardless of what she thought, she wouldn't resist him. Last night's kiss had proven that. He wasn't worried about the outcome of the deal between them. Like he'd told her, eventually her body would betray her and she would break. What had happened in his grandmother's kitchen when their hands touched at the door was a prime example of the intensity of the desire between them.

"So what time do you want us to meet tomorrow?" she asked, reclaiming his attention.

"I need to ride out with Caldwell and my men at the crack of dawn to check on a few things. I'll be back around ten. Will that time work for you?"

"Yes."

"Good. We can ride in my truck."

"Alright. Good night."

She turned toward the door, intent on opening it quickly and going inside. He was just as determined not to let her get away that easily. Reaching out, he wrapped his arms around her waist and tugged her close to him.

"What do you think you're doing, Gavin?"

"This."

Lowering his head, he claimed her mouth in a long, passionate kiss. She didn't push him away. Instead, she pulled him closer. Emotions he hadn't expected pushed him to let her know with this kiss just how much he wanted her.

The kiss they'd shared last night had been a game changer. This one sealed their fate.

Gavin knew at that moment that kissing her would never be enough. What he really wanted to do was sweep her off her feet, open the damn door and head straight to the bedroom. But he couldn't do that.

He wanted her to admit how much she wanted him, too. He'd give her time; he'd remember their deal. The one he had initiated. The one he intended to end in his favor. There was no way she would leave the Silver Spurs without them making love.

He finally broke off the kiss. As he drew in a deep breath he watched her draw in one, as well. Studying her mouth, he saw her lips were wet and swollen, and he had to fight back the urge to kiss her again.

"Why did you kiss me?" she asked, touching her finger to her lips.

He smiled, tempted to replace her finger with the tip of his tongue. "For the same reason you let me kiss you. I want you and you want me."

From the look he saw in her eyes, he knew she was angry. Why? Because he'd stated facts when she preferred hiding behind denials?

"I'm going inside now."

"I'll see you in the morning around ten."

She nodded, then quickly opened the door and went inside. When the door closed behind her, Gavin shoved his hands into the pockets of his jeans and headed back toward the main house. He knew she was confused. Confusion came with the territory when you tried to deny the truth of your feelings. However, she was smart. He knew she would figure it out. Eventually she would see things the way he did.

He would make sure of it.

Six

Layla, feeling tousled from a restless night, stepped out on the porch with a cup of coffee in her hand. She took a sip. She needed the hot liquid as much as she needed more sleep. Kissing Gavin was hazardous to her health when the aftereffect was a frazzled mind.

What could she have been thinking to agree to the deal he'd put on the table? What woman in her right mind would agree to have sex with a man who counted on her to fail at the most important project of her life? She kept assuring herself that she had nothing to worry about because her research wasn't wrong.

But what if it was?

She shook her head, refusing to second-guess herself or allow something as insignificant as sex to undermine her confidence in years of research. She lifted the cup to her lips again, took another sip and smiled. She couldn't wait to show Gavin just how wrong he was. She would leave the Silver Spurs with Jesse James's loot *and* she'd keep Gavin out of her panties.

She glanced over at the main house and tried to ignore the heat that settled in her stomach. Ms. Melody had called to invite Layla to breakfast, but she'd declined saying she needed to read over a few reports. The last thing Layla wanted was to run into Gavin. She would see him at ten and that suited her just fine. The man had a way of making her distracted.

And then there was that kiss she couldn't stop thinking about. The one that still had her lips tingling this morning. While getting dressed she'd tried to convince herself not to worry about that kiss—not to worry about anything, especially not Gavin Blake. Agreeing to his deal meant nothing more than a reason to work harder to find James's stash. She hadn't lied to Ms. Melody. Layla had used this morning to review several documents. It was important to make sure she hadn't missed anything in her research.

Layla checked her watch. Gavin would be arriving in an hour. That wasn't a lot of time to prepare to see him again. But then she doubted she would ever be prepared for the likes of Gavin Blake.

"So what have you decided about the dig, Gavin?"

Gavin glanced up from his breakfast plate and met his grandmother's eyes. He'd been in bed when she'd returned last night, but there was no getting out of the conversation this morning. One thing was for certain, he would not tell her about the deal he'd struck with Layla.

"Layla is showing me the site this morning. I want to check it out for myself before I make a decision." He then resumed eating, hoping to end the conversation.

"So when are you leaving for Mississippi?"

He looked up at his grandmother again with a raised brow. "Who said anything about me going to Mississippi?"

She lifted her own brow. "Yesterday you mentioned you had important business to take care of there."

Now he recalled mentioning it. "I changed my mind and won't be leaving after all." He resumed eating again, knowing his grandmother was eyeing him suspiciously.

"Why?"

He lifted his head again. "Why, what?"

"Why are you hanging around here?"

He held her inquisitive gaze. "Do you have a problem with me hanging around here, Gramma Mel?"

"Not as long as you don't have some shenanigans brewing in that head of yours, Gavin."

If only you knew, he thought. He pushed his plate away. "Breakfast was good as usual. I'm surprised you didn't invite Layla to join us."

"I did. But she made an excuse for not coming. I wonder why."

He stood. His grandmother was fishing for information and he was determined not to get caught. "I have a call with Phil to go over the books. I'll be in my office for an hour or so."

"Alright. And you may have changed your mind about going to Mississippi, but I'm still scheduled to go to that library conference in Cincinnati. It lasts a week, and I booked it before I knew you were coming home."

Gavin knew his grandmother enjoyed going to those conferences. "You should go," he encouraged.

She looked at him as if he wasn't trustworthy...of all things. "Is anything wrong?" he asked her.

"You tell me, Gavin. You're not fooling me one bit. I know that look. You're up to something and whatever it is, I hope you don't get caught in your own trap."

"What trap?"

"I'll let you figure that one out. But keep something in mind."

He lifted a brow. "What?"

"Layla is not Jamie."

He frowned deeply. "What is that supposed to mean?"

"It means I think something good could develop between the two of you, if you let it. But you won't. You're afraid she will be like Jamie. Whether you choose to believe me or not, your mom loved you and your dad. I would sit and hear her crying for him at night when he was gone."

"Then why did she leave?"

"Loneliness drove her away, Gavin. The Silver Spurs isn't meant for everyone and she was miserable here. Not everyone can handle the isolation."

"But that was no reason for her to desert me and Dad."

Without saying anything else he turned and walked out of the kitchen toward his office.

A lump formed in Layla's throat when she heard the knock at the door. She didn't have to look out of the peephole to see who it was. Gavin had said he would arrive at ten and it was ten on the dot. She glanced down at herself and then wished she hadn't. Why should she care what he thought about how she looked today? And why had she decided to wear her hair down instead of back in a ponytail?

She opened the door and Gavin stood leaning in the doorway. He filled the space, looking like he needed to be some woman's breakfast, lunch and dinner. Why did the man have to be so over-the-top gorgeous? Why did she want to drool, drool, and then drool some more?

And why did she want to snatch him inside and have her way with him?

She had no right to think any of those things, no right to fantasize. She had to stay focused on her work. "Good morning. I'm ready," she said, grabbing her jacket. He moved aside when she stepped out and closed the door behind herself.

"Good morning, Layla. I hope you slept well," Gavin said as they walked off the porch.

He slid his hand to her elbow to help her down the steps and she wished he hadn't. Immediately, a spike of desire shot through her and she was tempted to snatch her arm away.

"Nice day, isn't it?"

"Yes, it's nice." She glanced over at him as he kept his hand on her elbow while he led her to his truck and opened the door.

"And speaking of nice," he said, gripping her elbow a little tighter as he helped her up into the passenger seat. "You look good this morning. Real nice."

"Thank you."

He closed the truck door and as she watched him move around the front of the truck to the driver's side, she couldn't help thinking that he looked pretty good himself. Real nice. A pair of jeans hugged masculine thighs, a pullover sweater and a leather bomber jacket with the crest of a SEAL on the back graced broad shoulders. In her book there was something about a man who wore a leather bomber jacket, whether he was a biker, a model or a navy SEAL.

She kept her gaze trained on him. When he opened the door and slid onto the leather seat, she couldn't help but appreciate how the fit of his jeans tightened on his thighs.

"You went riding around your ranch dressed like that?"

"No. We finished early so I had time to change before joining my grandmother for breakfast. She missed your presence at breakfast by the way."

"I told her about the report I had to review this morning."

He didn't say anything and she wondered if he believed her.

"You okay?"

It was only then that she realized she was still staring. She snatched her gaze away from his thighs, regretting that he'd caught her ogling him. "I'm fine."

A smile curved his lips and her insides felt like they'd turned to mush. "Just checking," he said, snapping his seat belt in place. "I don't want you to start admitting you want me anytime soon."

Layla frowned, remembering what he'd said last night. "Trust me. That won't be happening." She spoke with a degree of confidence she wasn't feeling, especially when he shifted gears, causing those thighs to catch her attention again.

She forced her gaze out the window to view the pastures, valleys and hills they passed. Not for the first time, she thought the Silver Spurs was beautiful. Already they'd passed the new barn and several other smaller buildings. And there were several fenced rolling plains filled with cows. The sun peeked through a bevy of trees that layered the countryside and she knew it would be a beautiful day even with the chill in the air.

"Sleep well?"

She glanced over at him, wondering why he would ask. Did he assume that she hadn't? Well, she intended to crush that assumption right then and there. "Yes, like a baby, straight through the night." Maybe she'd laid it on too thick since most babies didn't sleep straight through the night.

"Glad to hear it. So did I. I slept so well that I almost overslept this morning." He didn't say anything for a minute. "Which way?"

She lifted a brow. "What?"

"Directions. Gramma Mel said the spot is just past the old barn. Which way do I go after that?"

The barn he was talking about was a big empty building painted red. According to Ms. Melody, it hadn't been used in years but the structure looked sound. More than once

Layla had been tempted to take a peek inside but the doors were bolted up. She wondered if Gavin would allow them to keep their excavation equipment stored there. Since he seemed in a pretty good mood this morning, it might be a good time to ask. "And about that old barn?"

"What about it?"

"I'm going to need a place to store my heavy equipment, like the loader backhoe and tractor, for the excavation. May I use the old barn?"

He glanced over at her and she could imagine what he was thinking. Why should he do anything to help her when he was counting on her to fail? He surprised her when he said, "Yes, you can use the old barn."

She smiled. Since he was being so generous she decided to go for the gusto. "There's also a smaller building next to the barn. I understand it used to be the old bunkhouse."

"What about it?"

"May I use that, as well? I'll need somewhere to test soil samples and such."

He looked at her again. "Are you trying to take advantage of my kindness, Layla?"

"Yes, I guess I am, Gavin."

A husky chuckle escaped his lips. "At least you're honest. Yes, you can use that old shack, as well."

"Thank you."

"You're welcome."

She didn't say anything for a minute as they drove. "Make a left turn at the next tree and drive another couple of miles," she said. "You can park in the clearing next to the stumps. I've marked the exact spot where we'll be digging."

"Okay."

The rest of the drive was done in silence. She was glad when he finally brought the truck to a stop a short while later.

* * *

Gavin drew in a deep breath. With his hands still gripping the steering wheel he stared straight ahead at the view out of the windshield. He needed to get his bearings. Everything about Layla was getting to him. The way she looked, her scent, the way she wore her hair. The way that same hair had blown in the wind when his truck whooshed across his property.

"I can tell you miss coming here."

Did she make that assumption because of the way he was still sitting here, trying to keep his mind and body under control? Yet, she was right. He had missed coming here.

"Yes. As a kid I used to come to this area a lot. There's a huge lake not far from here. It separates our land from the Lotts' property and it's on the Lotts' land. But that didn't mean anything to me. Not even the no-swimming-allowed sign Sherman Lott had posted. I used to sneak into the lake and go swimming as a teen every chance I got. On a good day I would swim for hours without getting caught."

"And on a bad day?"

He chuckled. "On a bad day Sherman Lott would call my grandmother and report me for trespassing."

She lifted a brow. "Honestly? He would actually call and tell on you?"

"All the time. He didn't like anyone swimming or fishing in that lake. But I had a lot of years of good fishing there, as well."

He smiled, remembering how defying Mr. Lott had pleased him immensely. "Time to look around. But before we get out there's something we need to do."

She lifted her brow. "What?"

"Kiss. More than anything, I want to kiss you, Layla."

* * *

Layla couldn't believe he'd said that. Kiss? Hadn't they done that enough already? Not that she was counting but he'd kissed her twice. Why was he going for three? Why was she hoping that he would?

"Kiss me?" she asked, softly, hoping he didn't pick up on the yearning in her voice.

"Yes, kiss you. It's either that or talk you into my truck's backseat."

She nibbled on her bottom lip. "And you think doing that will be easy?"

"No, but it will be worth all the effort I plan to put into it. So how about unbuckling that seat belt and leaning a little over here? I promise it will be painless."

Being painless, Layla thought, was the least of her worries. "Haven't you gotten enough? Of kissing me?" she asked, studying the look in his eyes.

"No, I haven't gotten enough, so lean over this way. Let's engage in something pleasurable."

The urgency in his voice was so intense, it sent shivers through her. She knew they shouldn't kiss again. Doing so would lead to assumptions on his part that she'd rather he not have. But she'd had a hard time forgetting how pleasurable their last two kisses had been. Both times his tongue had stroked hers to a feverish pitch, until she had greedily responded.

Frustration spilled from her lungs in a sigh and with very little control left, she unsnapped her seat belt and leaned closer to him. In spite of her misgivings, she was prepared to give him the kiss he wanted because it was a kiss she wanted, as well.

He leaned in to meet her and their lips touched. On her breathless sigh, he slid his tongue inside her mouth and began mating with her tongue. She felt his intensity all the way to her toes.

She wrapped her arms around his neck as he wrapped his arms around her waist. They were sitting in his truck, kissing like oversexed teenagers. Like they had nothing better to do and all day to do it. How crazy was that? But the insanity was lost as she tasted him. He tasted primitive, untamed and wild with lust. How could she detect such a thing in a kiss? Was this a warning that she should back off? That Gavin Blake would be the one man she couldn't ignore?

The latter gave her pause, but not enough to stop her tongue from mingling with his. Not enough to refrain from following his lead when he deepened the kiss. Not enough to stop the moan escaping her throat.

Layla knew then that she was a goner.

Seven

Gavin greedily devoured Layla's mouth. Never before had any woman escalated his arousal to such a state. And never had any woman made him want to kiss her each and every time he saw her.

Every bone and muscle in his body throbbed with a need for her that went beyond desire. Intense heat curled inside of him, threatening his control. And the one thing he was known for was control. So why were his brain cells faltering under the onslaught of such a delicious kiss? Why was his body making urgent demands for him to make love to her right here in his truck? Damn. What could he say?

Nothing. He was totally at a loss for words, which was a good thing since he didn't have time to indulge in any. He preferred using his mouth for this kiss. He intended to get his fill. But a part of him wasn't sure he could ever get his fill of Layla. He saw her and he wanted her. That wasn't good. He had to get control of his body and of the situation. And he needed to do so now.

Gavin reluctantly broke off the kiss. Drawing his mouth away from hers was one of the hardest things he'd had to do. He saw the look of denied need in her eyes before she leaned back, dropped her head against the headrest and closed her eyes. He figured she was as in awe of what just happened as he was.

What they'd shared wasn't just a kiss. It was an acknowledgment of deep sexual desires. He knew what was driving his and he thought he had figured out what was driving hers. She just refused to accept it. She was stubborn. It would take a lot more kisses like this one to bring her around. They'd felt an intense attraction to each other from the first, and from all appearances, things had gotten worse.

He continued to stare at her as heat curled inside of him. He wanted her. Bad. And that pushed him to say, "So tell me again why we can't sleep together."

Layla heard his words but she couldn't respond. Neither could she open her eyes to look at him. There was no point. She knew what she would see in the depths of his dark gaze. A sexual need so hot it was likely to sizzle her insides. It would make her fully aware of her own sexual need. A need he stirred to life inside her whether she wanted him to or not.

"Open your eyes, Layla. I'm not going anywhere."

At least not today. She suddenly remembered Ms. Melody mentioning he had to go to Mississippi on business. "When are you leaving?" she asked, opening her eyes.

Just as she'd expected. The eyes staring at her were dark and seductive.

He lifted a brow. "Leaving for where?"

"Mississippi. Your grandmother mentioned you had important business to take care of there."

"Trying to get rid of me, are you?"

"It wouldn't hurt," she said and saw his eyes get even darker when she moistened her bottom lip with the tip of her tongue. "So when are you leaving?"

He moved his gaze from her mouth to her eyes. "I changed my mind about Mississippi. I'm not leaving here any time soon." She couldn't stop the disappointment that flashed through her.

"But I thought you had important business to take care of."

"My plans have changed. Do you have a problem with that?"

"I just hope you don't plan to get underfoot."

"I'll try not to. Now show me the exact spot where you plan to dig," he said, opening the truck door to get out.

No matter what he said, Layla knew Gavin would try getting underfoot.

When Gavin pulled an odd-looking camera from his backseat, Layla lifted a brow. "What is that?"

He smiled. "A Vericon 12D. It's a high-tech camera that's mainly used underwater. Flipper messed around with it so we could use it on land, as well."

"Flipper?"

"Yes, Flipper. One of my team members. He's into technology and all that high-tech stuff," Gavin said as they walked side by side.

"Surely Flipper isn't his real name."

Gavin chuckled. "His real name is David Holloway. His code name is Flipper."

"Oh," she said, glancing up at him. "Do you have a code name?"

"Yes."

"What is it?"

He saw no reason not to tell her since his grandmother was well aware of it, too. His teammates called Gavin by his code name whenever they came to visit. "Viper."

Layla scrunched up her features. "Viper?"

"Yes, Viper."

"Why?"

"Why what?"

"Why do they call you Viper?"

He stopped walking to answer her, and when he stopped, she did, too. He hadn't noticed before how small she seemed, standing close to him. He figured he'd never noticed because usually when he faced her he was fixated on her mouth.

"The reason I'm called Viper is because when I set my sights on a target, I don't give up until I make a hit. I love taking the enemy down."

She tilted her head to look up at him. "Do you consider me an enemy?"

He didn't hesitate. "No." She wasn't the enemy, but he had every intention of taking her down...right into his bed.

Evidently satisfied with his response, she looked around him, back toward where the truck was parked. Then she turned around. She did it several times and each time he saw her confusion deepen.

"Is something wrong?" he finally asked.

She whipped around to look at him. "Yes, something is wrong."

He glanced around before returning his gaze to her. "What?"

"Someone moved my marker. It's gone."

He lifted a brow. "What do you mean your marker is gone?"

She frowned. "Just what I said. Someone moved my marker. It's not here."

Gavin released a deep sigh. "Why would anyone move your marker? Are you sure you put one down?"

"Of course I'm sure," she answered in an annoyed tone. "Someone moved it."

Gavin raised his gaze upward. "And who would do that?"

"I don't know, but someone did."

He shook his head. "Layla, the Silver Spurs is out in the middle of nowhere. And this particular spot is considered way outside our working area, almost six miles from the main house. No one would deliberately come on this land to remove your marker."

"Well, someone did, Gavin. I marked the digging site," she said with deep irritation in her voice.

Gavin stared down at her. "Are you sure? Maybe your mind is clouded right now. I can understand my kiss leaving you that way."

Her frown deepened. "I'm serious, Gavin."

"So am I, Layla."

Exasperation darkened her expression. "Will you get your mind off sex for a minute?"

A smile touched his lips. "My mind wasn't on sex," he said. "It was on that kiss we shared. But since you've pulled sex into the conversation...it's hard to think of anything other than getting you in my bed when you look so good."

Layla pushed to the back of her mind that she'd deliberately taken more time with her appearance just so he would think she looked good. That was before she'd come out here and discovered her marker *had* been removed.

"You moved it, didn't you?" she asked with an accusing glare.

"Now why would I want to do that?"

When she didn't say anything but continued to stare at him, his amusement was replaced with a deep frown.

"I have no reason to mess with any marker you claim to have put down. This is the first time I've been out this far from the house since returning home."

He rubbed a hand down his face in frustration. "If that marker has in fact been removed, then that means someone trespassed on this land to do it. Although for the life of me I can't imagine who would have cared enough to do such a thing. I just think you're confused as to where you placed the damn marker," he said, glancing around. "The south pasture is rather large. Maybe it's all the way on the other side."

"I am not confused and it's not on the other side. Not only did I map its coordinates, I recall parking near those tree stumps and walking twenty to thirty feet to my right. The marker was a wooden stake with a red flag on it, and I planted it exactly where we would dig."

"If you're sure of that, then you need to consider who knows you're here. And who would want to see you fail."

She lifted her chin. "And why wouldn't your name head the list? The deal we agreed on means I would have to sleep with you if I fail."

Gavin took a step closer to her. "Whether you fail or succeed means nothing to me because I have every intention of sleeping with you regardless of the outcome of this dig."

Layla was taken aback by Gavin's words. Of all the audacity. She placed her hands on her hips. Anger poured through her. "And how do you figure that?"

"Because, like I explained to you earlier, I'm Viper. I set my sights on a target. I don't give up until I make a hit. You are my target, Layla, and I plan to break down your resolve."

She all but stomped her foot in frustration. "And I've told you that won't happen. What part of that don't you understand?"

"This part," he said, brushing his finger across her cheek. She couldn't downplay her sharp intake of breath or the way her body shuddered beneath his touch. "You do something to me and I do something to you," he continued. "We do things to each other. We can only hold out for so long."

She tilted her lips stubbornly. "I will fight you on that with my last breath."

"And I suggest you save that breath for that explosive orgasm you're going to have."

Layla opened her mouth to blast out a resounding retort but then she closed it without responding. What was the use of arguing with him about something she knew for a fact wouldn't be happening, no matter what he thought? So what if his touch warmed her to the core? She would put him out of her mind. She had more important things to be concerned with. Like who'd removed her marker and why. No matter what Gavin might assume, she was not imagining things.

"My marker was removed, Gavin."

He rolled his eyes. "We're back to that again?"

"Yes. The dig is why I'm here. Why I crazily agreed to your deal. If you didn't remove the marker, then who did?"

Gavin drew in a deep breath, trying to hold his aggravation and frustration at bay. He knew for certain she was not incompetent. So someone had removed the marker like she claimed.

"Here, hold this," he said, handing Flipper's camera to her. He then began walking, studying the ground. He slowed when he saw footprints he knew weren't hers or his. He crouched down and pressed his finger to one, touching the indention in the earth. It was cold. The tracks looked fresh, as if they hadn't been made any more than

forty-eight hours ago. Whose prints were they? One of
his men? Possibly, but for some reason he doubted it. All
his men had been working in the north and west pastures
for the past few days. None had any reason to come to
the south pasture.

It appeared more weight had been placed on the left leg
as that impression was deeper. He also noted the sole of
the right shoe appeared more worn than the left.

He stood and backtracked to where Layla said she'd
parked her vehicle when she'd come out here. He walked,
looking down and around the entire time. When he'd gone
about thirty feet he stopped. Crouching down again he
studied the earth and that's when he saw the small plug
where the marker had been. He glanced to the right and
the left, studying the ground. Again he saw footprints.
The same ones.

He stood and slowly walked back to Layla. Without
saying anything, he took the camera out of her hand.
"Thanks."

She raised a brow. "Well?"

She hadn't asked what he'd been doing. She was smart
enough to figure things out. He was using his skill as a
SEAL to determine if there was proof that the marker
had been removed.

He met her inquisitive expression. "I saw footprints.
I also saw where the marker had been. You're right. The
marker was removed."

"Why? By whom?"

"Don't know, Layla." He honestly didn't have a clue.
The Silver Spurs was private property. And although there
were numerous ways to get on the property, he couldn't
imagine anyone having a reason to come to this particular
area. The one thing he didn't see was tire tracks. But the
person could have parked elsewhere and walked.

"I planned on using this camera to scan the area," he

said. "I suggest you make a list of anyone who might have a reason for wanting you not to succeed in your dig. And make sure you take me off the list. I told you my position and I'm sticking to it."

And without saying anything else, he walked off.

Eight

I told you my position and I'm sticking to it.

Later that day, Layla paced the floor. Gavin Blake was bullheaded, stubborn and full of himself. He was crazy if he actually thought he could get her to bend to his will. No way. No how. So why was she pacing the floor, wearing out both herself and her shoes?

She had watched him use that high-tech camera, but she hadn't been impressed with his findings. Gavin agreed there was something buried in the area but he refused to consider it was Jesse James's loot. To his way of thinking, since that area used to be a popular hunting spot, the camera had picked up nothing more than buried bullet shells.

Layla refused to believe her research was wrong. There was buried treasure somewhere in the south pasture, she was sure of it. And as far as who would not want to see her succeed in this project, that could be a number of people, including her parents. But she didn't for one minute think they would go so far as to sabotage the dig site. They were hoping failing at this would make Layla realize she should pursue medical school, after all. Then there was her older colleague Dr. Clayburn and others at the university who felt she'd been too young and inexperienced for such an expensive project. Did the person who removed the marker actually think she wouldn't have kept the coordinates and just re-marked it? That she would give up so easily?

She stopped pacing when she heard a knock on the door. The tightening in her stomach told her who it was. Why was Gavin here? She had spoken to Ms. Melody an hour or so ago when she'd called to invite Layla to dinner. Layla had regretfully declined, knowing she would not have been the best of company this evening. Besides, she needed distance from Gavin. Evidently he hadn't taken the hint.

The knock on the door sounded again. There was no need to pretend she wasn't there when Gavin knew she was. Crossing the room, she opened the door to find Gavin with a tray of food in his hand.

"After you told Gramma Mel you weren't coming to dinner, she strongly suggested I bring you something. I believe she thinks I'm the reason you didn't come to breakfast or dinner."

Layla moved aside to let him in. Tray and all. Especially the tray. Everything was covered but the food smelled good. "I'll let her know that's not the case when I talk to her tomorrow." No need for him to know he *had* been a factor in her decision.

"She might not be here. Not sure when she's leaving, whether it's tomorrow or the day after."

Layla closed the door and followed him to the kitchen. "Leaving? Ms. Melody is going somewhere?"

"Yes, to a library convention in Cincinnati for a week. But I'm sure she won't leave without saying goodbye. And if you expect me to take her place and make sure you don't miss meals…that won't be happening."

She frowned. "I never asked your grandmother to cook for me, Gavin."

He put the tray on the kitchen table and turned to her. "Don't you think I know that?"

"Then why did you insinuate otherwise?"

"Did I?"

She crossed her arms over her chest. "Yes, you did."

"Then I apologize." She couldn't help noticing how his gaze roamed over her. "You changed clothes," he said.

Was that disappointment she heard in his voice? Seeing his gaze had moved to her chest, she dropped her hands to her sides. "I showered."

"I know. You smell good. And you look good in that dress. Nice legs."

She would have appreciated the compliment if she wasn't still so uptight about that marker being moved. "I want to go back out to the dig site tomorrow and look around, Gavin. This time I want to use my own detector."

"If you're still concerned about why the marker was moved, I might have a reason for that."

She came into the kitchen, trying to ignore the way he was checking out her legs and the way her nipples responded to his blatant appraisal. "What reason is that?"

"Clete. He's an older man we hired years ago to keep the grounds clear of trash and debris as well as repair anything that needs fixing. That way Caldwell and the men can concentrate mainly on the cattle. When I mentioned the marker to Gramma Mel, she reminded me that Clete has a tendency to move stuff when he's keeping the land cleared."

"But why would he remove the marker?"

Gavin shrugged. "He probably didn't know what it was and thought it was trash. He and his wife left a few days ago to visit their son who is in the navy and stationed in Hawaii. I'll talk to him when he gets back."

Layla drew in a deep breath, feeling somewhat relieved. The thought of someone tampering with the dig site had definitely bothered her.

"Sit down and eat. I promised Gramma Mel that I would make sure you did."

She raised a suspicious eye. "Why?"

"Why what?"

"Why would you care one way or the other if I eat?"

A slow, sexy smile touched his lips and her womb seemed to contract with the weight of that smile. And his dimples had bone-melting fire spreading through her blood. "The reason I care is because I don't want you to start losing weight."

She crossed her arms over her chest again, and then quickly dropped them by her sides when she saw his gaze shift back to her chest. Could the man think of anything other than sex for a minute? "And what does my weight have to do with you?"

"When I make love to you, I want to feel meat on your bones."

His statement answered her earlier question. No, he obviously couldn't think of anything other than sex. "We won't be making love, Gavin."

"Your food is getting cold."

He was blatantly ignoring what she'd said. "I'll eat after you leave."

He chuckled. "If that was a hint that you want me to go, forget it. I want to make sure you eat."

She frowned. "What do you plan to do? Stay here and watch me."

"Yes, that was my intent."

He was serious. "I don't need a babysitter, Gavin."

"No. What you need is a lover, Layla. And you never

did answer my question from last night. When was the last time you made love with a man?"

"And I don't intend to answer it because it's none of your business."

If he insisted on staying, she would ignore him. She moved to the table where he'd placed her food. Her mouth began watering the moment she uncovered it. Fried chicken, mashed potatoes, broccoli, candied yams and iced tea. And a slice of chocolate cake for dessert.

A smile lit her face. "Your grandmother is something else." Layla walked over to the sink to wash her hands. After grabbing utensils out of a drawer, she returned to the table and found Gavin sitting there. Did he plan to actually watch her eat? Didn't he have anything better to do?

Deciding nothing would stand between her and that food, she sat down, bowed her head and said grace, determined to ignore him. When she slid a forkful of mashed potatoes between her lips, she closed her eyes and groaned. Delicious.

"If you get off eating mashed potatoes, I can only imagine your reaction when we make love."

A part of her wanted to claim she wouldn't enjoy it. She quickly dismissed the idea when she glanced over at him. A woman could climax just from staring at him. Even so, she said, "In your dreams."

"My dreams will one day become your reality, Layla."

She decided not to argue with him anymore. But if he was intent on watching her, she might as well ask him a few questions. Get him talking, so she wouldn't think about how good he looked sitting there. How sexy.

She took a sip of her tea. "You mentioned your teammate named Flipper. Any others you're close to?"

"I'm close to all of them. We're a team."

"How many?"

"Enough."

She rolled her eyes. Had she asked about classified information or something? "I'm sure you're closer to some of the guys more than others."

He leaned back in the chair as if getting comfortable. She couldn't recall the last time she'd shared a private, intimate dinner with a man. And, whether she liked admitting it or not, this *was* intimate. They were alone, sitting at a table with the backdrop of a blazing fire roaring in the fireplace.

"In that case, I would say Flipper, Bane, Coop, Mac and Nick. The six of us went through all phases of training together. A couple of years ago, Nick took a job with Homeland Security. He needed a little more stability in his life when his wife gave birth to triplets."

As if he felt right at home, he stood and went to the refrigerator to get a beer and then returned to his chair. "Bane is a master sniper," he continued, popping the cap. "Coop is the mastermind behind most of our strategic moves. Mac is slightly older than the rest of us and likes to think he can keep us in line most of the time. He's been married for ages, has four kids and likes to impose his words of wisdom on us whether we want to hear them or not. And Flip can hold his breath under water longer than any human I know." He chuckled as he took a swig. "We're convinced Flipper has gills hidden somewhere."

Layla heard the fondness in his voice when he spoke of his teammates. "What's a master sniper?"

He looked at her. She thought he would say she was asking for classified information but then he said, "A master sniper is the best shot on the team. Bane is one badass. He can hit a target with one eye closed. He's covered all our backs more than once." He paused. "Bane and his wife, Crystal, are renewing their vows next month."

"Oh, were he and his wife separated for a while or something?"

"Yes, you could say that."

Layla knew he was being elusive but she was getting used to it. She didn't have to ask if his job was dangerous. Anyone who knew of the navy SEALs was aware of the types of missions they went on. She finished the rest of her meal in silence, with him watching her. She was tempted to ask if he wanted some but knew the trouble she'd gotten into when she'd asked him that question the last time.

She took a sip of her iced tea and looked over at him when she pushed her plate aside. "Satisfied, Gavin?"

He gave her a crooked smile. "Baby, my satisfaction will come when I get inside of you."

The glass nearly slipped from her hand. She recovered long enough to set it down by the plate. The impact of his words had her burning from the inside out. "Why do you say such things?"

"Just keeping it honest."

Gavin liked rattling Layla. Evidently she wasn't used to a man talking to her this way, telling her what he wanted and how he planned to make her feel. While watching her eat, his imagination had run wild. The conversation hadn't distracted him enough to demolish his desire. He doubted that was possible. He wanted her. He'd made that point pretty damn clear and he knew she wanted him as well, so what was the holdup?

"I've finished eating so you can leave now."

He held her gaze, felt the flare of response in their bodies when they looked at each other. Giving in to temptation, he lightly traced his fingertips along her arm. He felt her shiver beneath his touch. He heard her sharp intake of breath. "Why are you fighting this, Layla?"

"And why are you being so persistent?"

He could tell her that one of the reasons was because he hadn't been with a woman in six months, eight days, twelve hours and no telling how many minutes. Being around her was taking its toll. However, telling her such a thing would make him sound like a greedy jerk with only sex on his mind. That was only partly true. The other part was that he found her as fascinating as he found her beautiful.

"Being persistent is part of my nature."

When he saw her lips form a frown, his groin hardened and he couldn't help drawing in a ragged breath. Standing, he said, "I'll leave you alone now and report to Gramma Mel that you ate all your food."

He reached to remove the tray, but she blocked him. "Surely you don't think I'll let you return with dirty dishes."

"We've had a conversation about the purpose of a dishwasher before, Layla."

"That might be your way of doing things but it's not mine. I will wash the dishes and return them to Ms. Melody tomorrow," she said, standing.

Doing so brought her right smack in front of him. Gavin knew that if she inched closer, she would feel his erection. Even so, he intended to kiss her before he left.

"Walk me to the door, Layla."

From the look in her eyes, he knew she was aware of his plan. He watched her nibble her bottom lip. "Relax, baby. I won't bite."

She stopped nibbling her lips long enough to lift her chin and stare into his eyes. "You'll do something even worse, Gavin."

"What is that?"

"You will make me want you."

He eased closer, pressing his body to hers, wanting her to feel his erection. There was no way she could miss it. "Welcome to the club. And you already want me, Layla. Why are you having a hard time accepting that?"

Gavin could tell she was at a loss for words, which suited him just fine. He had other uses for her mouth. He leaned in to capture her lips.

Why was she having such a hard time accepting this? Layla asked herself when Gavin took her mouth. She didn't resist. She couldn't. In fact she felt herself practically melting into his arms. That was why, she reasoned, she wrapped her arms around his neck. Otherwise she would become a puddle on the floor.

He kissed her with an intensity she reciprocated in every part of her body. His mouth locked onto hers, not leaving any part of her mouth untouched. He tapped into areas she hadn't known existed. He was staking his claim on her mouth in a scandalous way. It was as if he was intentionally making her crazy for his kiss.

And then there was the feel of his erection, pressing hard against her middle. What man could get *that* aroused? To know she was the cause sent heated shivers through her body. The hard tips of her breasts pressed through the material of her dress as if eager to make contact with his chest.

Gavin broke off the kiss and when Layla drew in a deep breath, she was swept off her feet into his arms. He sat back down at the table with her firmly planted in his lap. Before she could ask just what he thought he was doing, his mouth was on hers. And just like before, this kiss robbed her of her senses, made her purr deep in her throat. It was a good thing his arm gripped her tightly otherwise she would topple to the floor. His hand was on her thigh, slowly caressing her skin underneath her dress.

Maybe she needed to ask herself why she was letting him do such a thing when she'd never let any man take such liberties before. Hadn't she kicked Sonny Paul in the groin when he thought he could reach into her blouse and touch her breast? Why did she believe this was different? Just because Gavin's mouth was driving her crazy with lust—could she accept this as okay?

And why was she still clutching him around the neck as if her life depended on their mouths being so intimately locked? Red-hot passion was making her dazed.

Somewhere in the haziness of her mind, she noted he had stood, without their mouths disconnecting. He was moving, headed somewhere rather quickly. It was only when he placed her on the bed that she regained her senses. Snatching her mouth from his, she scrambled away from him.

She blinked upon seeing he was about to take off his shirt. "What do you think you're doing?"

He stared down at her, panting like he'd run a marathon. His eyes, she saw, were glazed with heated lust to such a degree it made her heart pound. "About to make love to you, Layla." He then whipped his shirt over his head.

Seeing him bare chested caused goose bumps to ripple all over her skin. She scrambled farther away from him. "No you're not!"

He stared at her. "Can you look at me and say you don't want me to make love to you?"

She nervously licked her bottom lip and looked away. Yes, she could say it but she couldn't look at him while doing so. Mainly because she *did* want him to make love to her. There was no doubt in her mind that the sheets on the bed were calling their names.

"Layla. Look at me."

No, she wouldn't look at him. Nor would she tell him anything. Scrambling off the bed, she stood and began straightening her clothes before quickly walking out of the bedroom. "I'm showing you the door, Gavin," she called over her shoulder.

Once she reached the door, she waited. It took him a few minutes to follow her. He probably needed time to put his shirt back on and get his lusty mind under control.

When she saw him walking toward her he had an unreadable expression on his face. She drew in a deep breath. What thoughts were going through his mind? Did he think she was nothing more than a tease because she'd stoked his fire and then doused it with water? She would admit to having gotten caught up in the moment like he had. However, although he was ready to take things to the next level, she was not.

When he got closer, she saw the way he stared at her and figured he was angry to the point that he would walk out the door without saying anything to her.

She figured wrong. When Gavin stopped before opening the door, he turned dark, livid eyes on her. He then said in a furious voice, "The next time we kiss, Layla, will be when we make love. It's going to be a package deal."

He then opened the door and left.

Nine

Late afternoon the next day, Gavin walked out on the porch with a steaming cup of coffee. He couldn't believe he'd jogged around the ranch house twenty times last night. That would be equivalent to ten miles. When was the last time he'd done that?

On top of his workout last night, he'd gotten up at the crack of dawn to ride the range with Caldwell and his men. Sharing breakfast with them over an open fire had brought back memories. Most of the men who worked for Gavin had worked for his dad and had known Gavin when he'd been a kid. Although they called him boss, he knew they did it out of respect and not because he was involved in the day-to-day operations. Caldwell took care of the place. No matter how long Gavin was away from the ranch, he rested easy at night knowing the Silver Spurs was in good hands. Gavin also knew that whenever he returned Caldwell had no problem relinquishing that leadership role to him.

He took another sip of coffee as he eased down to sit on the steps. The cold weather was settling in. It was hard to believe Thanksgiving was next month. He'd gotten word that morning from his commanding officer that the team would be headed out again in late January. At least his teammates with families would get to spend the holidays with them. Gavin wondered if his grandmother would hang around the ranch this year. Because he was rarely home during the holidays, Gramma Mel usually flew to Saint Louis to spend time with her sister and her family.

"How did things go today with Caldwell and the men?"

Gavin glanced over his shoulder at the sound of his grandmother's voice. "Good, but that's no surprise. They know how to keep things going in my absence. And I covered just about everything with Phil yesterday. We talked again today and the books look good." The only thing he hadn't done that he'd wanted to do today was take another ride out to the dig site.

"When do you expect Mr. Clete back in town?" he asked.

"By the middle of next week," she said, taking a seat in the porch swing.

"Good." Although Gavin felt certain Clete was the one who'd moved the marker, he wanted to be absolutely sure. However, for the life of him, he couldn't imagine anyone else coming onto the property and tampering with Layla's markers. What purpose would it serve?

Flip's camera had picked up something underground, both in her marked spot as well as another spot close by. Like he'd told her, it was probably nothing more than bullet shells or branding irons. One section did have a relatively higher reading than others but he'd figured out a reason for that, as well. Buried Native American artifacts. Gavin's grandfather had claimed this had been Native American land generations ago. If Layla's research was as thorough as she claimed, she would already know that.

"I had a salad earlier, but if you're hungry I can fix dinner."

"No need. I plan to go into town in a few and I'll grab something at the café."

No way he would tell his grandmother that in addition to dinner he intended to make a booty call. Word was out that he was home and a ton of women had left voice mails. On the drive into town, he would decide which woman would be the recipient of his visit. Not having Layla was getting to him. He needed to get laid and then he could be more rational about her, take his time seducing her without losing his cool.

"Looks like you aren't the only one going into town, Gavin. Now, doesn't she look extra pretty?"

He followed his grandmother's gaze. Layla was crossing the yard and walking toward them. He had seen her in dresses before, but this was one with a skirt that was shorter in the front and longer in the back. Instead of boots she wore high heels and she had a knitted shawl around her shoulders.

Her hair was styled the way he liked best, flowing around her shoulders. And he could tell she was wearing makeup—not much…except for the ruby-red lip color. He frowned, refusing to let her get next to him the way she had last night. He'd been stupid enough to think their evening would end differently. Namely, in bed together.

"Good evening, Ms. Melody. Gavin."

He did the gentlemanly thing and stood. He couldn't help noticing she'd given his grandmother a huge smile. But the one she'd given him was forced. Not that it bothered him one iota.

"Layla," he said, letting his gaze roam all over her.

His grandmother moved forward and gave her a hug.

"Now, don't you look pretty. Have big plans for the evening?"

Layla shrugged her shoulders, keeping her focus on Ms. Melody and ignoring Gavin. "Not that big. The equipment arrives tomorrow and my team the day after. Then it's all work and no play. I decided to spend my last day of freedom doing something I enjoy doing but rarely have time for—going to a movie."

"By yourself?" Gramma Mel asked.

Layla chuckled. "Yes, by myself."

"What are you going to see?"

"That new romantic comedy with Julia Roberts."

"Now, isn't that a coincidence. I was going into town to see that one myself," Gavin said.

Both Layla and Gramma Mel turned to stare at Gavin with raised brows. He smiled at both women's expressions. He then directed his next statement to Layla. "Since we're going to see the same movie, is there any reason we can't go together?"

Gavin was certain there was but he knew Layla wouldn't call him out on it in front of his grandmother. When she didn't say anything he leaned closer to ask, "Well, is there?"

As if recovering from her initial shock, she opened her mouth, probably to say something that would blister his ear. Then she quickly closed it, seeming to remember that his grandmother was standing there, listening to their exchange.

"No, there's no reason," she said. "I'm just surprised you would want to see a *chick flick*. I took you for a blood-and-guts sort of guy."

He shook his head. "As a SEAL, I see too much of that in real life. A chick flick should be interesting. Besides, I like Julia Roberts."

"In that case, I see no reason why we can't go together," she said.

Although she'd tried to sound cheerful about it, he knew she wasn't. Was that her teeth he heard grinding? "Great. We can go in my truck. I just need to grab my Stetson and jacket."

"I enjoyed the movie, didn't you?"

Layla had pretty much given him the silent treatment since leaving the Silver Spurs earlier but he didn't seem to mind. In fact he seemed amused by it. "Yes, I enjoyed it."

She probably would have enjoyed it even more had he not been there to cloud her concentration. It had been hard to focus on the huge movie screen with a sexy man sitting beside her.

"When are you going to stop acting childish, Layla?"

She glanced over at him. "Childish? You think *I'm* acting childish when you told me last night that we won't kiss again unless sex is part of the mix?"

"Yes, that's what I said and I meant it."

"Well, sorry if you think I'm acting childish but I'm the one acting more adult than you. All you can think about is—"

"Making love to you."

She swallowed, seeing a picture of that very thing in her mind. "Yes."

"Can't help it. You do things to me, Layla."

When she was honest with herself, she could admit that he did things to her, as well. But she would never admit it to him. He was just like all the other men she'd known, which is why she'd sworn off relationships. All men wanted of a woman was a roll between the sheets. She wanted more from life; she had a career to build. Men and sex only got in the way of her goals.

She glanced over at him. "You were an only child, right?"

"Yes, as far as I know."

When she looked at him in surprise he added, "My mother deserted us when I was eight and never came back. For all I know, she could have married and had more kids by now."

Layla nodded. "She and your dad got a divorce?"

"No, but she might have changed her name and started over. Who knows?"

Layla didn't say anything for a moment. "You've never tried to find her?"

"No."

"Not even when your father was killed in the war?"

His jaw tightened. "Especially not then. If she didn't return to see him while he was living, I sure as hell didn't plan to give her the opportunity to see him dead," he said in a biting tone. "Dad always believed she would come back to us. Even said he understood her need to get away. After all, he'd talked her into coming to Cornerstone."

"Where was she from?"

"New York. Manhattan. They met while he was on military business at the United Nations. They'd only known each other a week when they married. They met one night at a restaurant, a month after her only family, an aunt, died."

"So when they met, she had no living family?"

"No."

He didn't say anything else for a long moment, and then he added, "According to Dad she lasted out here longer than he expected her to. She tried being a good wife, and I remember her being a good mom. Dad placed a lot of blame on himself since he had to carry out a lot of missions, leaving her here with Gramma Mel and Grampa

Gavin. And when I came along a year later, he thought she'd adjusted."

"But she hadn't?"

"Evidently not. One day she up and left. She told my grandparents she needed to get away for a while and asked them to watch me. She said she'd be back before Dad returned from his overseas tour. Then she got in her car—the one Dad bought for her—and drove off."

"And she never came back?"

He shook his head. "No, she never came back. Months later, when Dad returned home and found her gone, he was heartbroken. She left him a note saying she would come back. But she never did."

"And after all this time, you've never tried finding her?"

"No. She decided she didn't want me or Dad in her life."

Gavin inwardly admitted that more than once he had thought about locating his mother, if for no other reason than to ask her why she never came back. One of his former SEAL teammates, Nick Stover, worked for Homeland Security. All Gavin had to do was give Nick her name and there was no doubt in his mind that Nick would tell Gavin her whereabouts. A part of him knew the main reason he hadn't done so was his fear of what he would find out. What if his mother had never wanted him or loved his dad? At times it was easier to do what his father had done and believe the best…even if it was a fairy tale.

He drew in a deep breath. Why had he shared any of that with Layla when he'd never shared it with a woman before? For some reason, when she'd asked if he was an only child, the floodgates had opened. Emotions he usually kept locked inside had come pouring out.

"Any other family besides Ms. Melody? What about aunts, uncles or cousins?"

He figured she was asking for conversational purposes only, so he obliged her. "My grandmother has a younger sister living in Saint Louis. Her only grandson, Benjamin, and I are close. We're more like brothers than cousins. He spent a lot of his summers here. Ben's a year older and in the Marines. Right now he's stationed in Afghanistan, and we're hoping he'll be home for the holidays."

He glanced over at her. "What about you? Any cousins?"

She shook her head. "No. My grandparents didn't have any siblings and they had one child. I never knew my mother's parents. They died in a boating accident when she was in her teens."

He said nothing as he drove. They were ten minutes from his home and although there had been sexual chemistry between them as usual, they'd managed to keep it under control. That was a surprise since his plans for this evening had originally been to end up in some woman's bed. A part of him couldn't believe he'd given up the chance for sex just to spend time in Layla's company. And he had to grudgingly admit that although she'd tried to ignore him for most of the evening, he had enjoyed being with her.

Moments later, he pulled into the yard in front of the ranch house. His grandmother would be leaving tomorrow and he would have the house all to himself. Bringing the car to a stop, he cut the ignition and turned to Layla. "I'll see you inside."

"That's not necessary," she said, already opening her door to get out. "Thanks for driving me into town and joining me at the movies."

Although she'd said he didn't have to see her in, he

walked beside her anyway. "You're welcome, although I know you really didn't prefer my company."

When she didn't deny what he'd said, he chuckled. "No wonder you don't have a boyfriend."

She glanced over at him. "What makes you think I don't have a boyfriend?"

"I asked Gramma Mel if any man had visited you here and she said no."

Layla frowned. "That doesn't mean anything."

He chuckled again. "Yes, it does. If you had a boyfriend he would have come here, if for nothing else but to check on you. To see how you were doing. To feel out the competition. To stake his claim."

Even in the moonlight, he saw her roll her eyes. "Not all men are territorial, Gavin."

"Any man connected to you would be."

They had made it to the porch. When he offered her hand to assist her up the steps, she said, "No need." And then she walked up to the door without his help. He knew why. All it would have taken was one touch and they would have lit up like the Fourth of July and they both knew it.

"Thanks for seeing me home. At least my temporary home."

"No problem. What time does the equipment arrive tomorrow?"

"Sometime before noon. Thanks again for allowing me to store the equipment in that old barn."

He nodded. "When will your team get here?"

"Some will start arriving the day after tomorrow and will be staying at a hotel in town. We're hoping to finish the dig in a couple of weeks and then we'll be on our way."

A couple of weeks. He had every intention of making love to her before she left. In the meantime, he planned to stick to his resolve about not kissing her until she was ready to give in to their desire—even if it killed him.

"Good night, Layla."

When she just stared at him, he smiled. Evidently she'd expected him to kiss her good-night. "I'll stand here until you go inside."

She nodded. "Good night." And then she quickly opened the door and went in.

He didn't move until he heard the lock click in place. Then he tilted his Stetson back from his face as he moved down the steps. Not kissing her had been hard but he meant what he'd told her yesterday. The next time they kissed would be when they made love. Just thinking about how intense that kiss would be sent heat through his body, especially to his lower extremities.

If he hadn't needed to meet with Caldwell and his men first thing in the morning, he would have taken another ten-mile run around the ranch.

Ten

Three days later, while out riding Acer, Gavin came upon Layla and her excavation team in the south pasture. Most of them had arrived a couple of days ago but he hadn't been around to meet them. He and his men had driven the cows to the north pasture where they would be kept during the winter months.

Over the next few weeks, the cows would be fed to maintain their good heath during the cold spell. Unlike the south pasture, there was plenty of grazing land in the north and a small pond to help irrigate the area. The pregnant cows had to be separated and tagged and the process had taken a lot longer than expected.

Just as well, he thought, as he brought Acer to a slow trot and then a complete stop at the top of the hill. He'd needed distance from Layla. With his grandmother in Cincinnati and him being out on the range for the past three days he'd assured their paths didn't cross.

But now he was back and as he looked down at the activity going on below, he couldn't stop his gaze from seeking her out. At first he didn't see her, but when the crowd dispersed somewhat, there she was, looking as beautiful as he knew she would be.

He rubbed his hand down his face. Nothing about this seduction was working out like he'd figured it would. It seemed he would be the one to break before Layla. He just didn't get it. They wanted each other. That was definite. So how could she keep fighting the attraction? Desire had to be eating away at her as much as it was at him.

He hadn't seen her since that night they'd gone to a movie. Seeing her now made him realize that after all those hot and steamy kisses, and copping one good feel of her thighs, she had gotten into his system. That was crazy. Women didn't get into his system—ever. So how had she managed it?

He fixed his gaze on her as if three days could have changed her. They hadn't. Even from where he sat unobserved on Acer's back, he could still see her flawless skin. She looked just as young as the members of her team. Her students. Wearing her hair in a ponytail, jeans, a pullover sweater and boots should have made her fit in. Yet there was something about Layla that stood out. Something that made his stomach churn and his groin ache every time he saw her.

He never did make it into town just for that booty call. The only woman he wanted was Layla.

Bottom line—she had stirred something deep inside of him that wouldn't go away. At least not until he was inside of her, all the way to the hilt. It was only when his body connected with hers that he would be able to rid his mind of the belief that she was the only woman for him.

Watching her team work, he remembered something else. Namely that phone conversation he'd had with Clete yesterday. The old man recalled seeing the marker. He'd known why it was there, since he'd heard talk in town about someone digging on the property. But according to Clete, he hadn't moved it. That made Gavin wonder who had. Both he and Clete agreed the wind could not have blown it away nor could it have gotten washed away by the rain. Which meant someone had come on Gavin's property and pulled it out. Why?

Gavin hadn't been receptive to the idea of Layla digging on the Silver Spurs. But if someone was intentionally setting her up to fail, they would have to deal with him. Flip's camera had picked up something buried here. That made Gavin wonder if someone intended to unearth whatever was buried before Layla did so they could get the credit? His jaw tightened at the thought. Not on his property. And not on his watch. And not with his woman.

His woman...

How in the hell could he consider her his woman when he hadn't bedded her yet? Besides, Gavin Blake never claimed any woman. But as he fixed his gaze on Layla, he knew that she was his. Bedded or not.

Layla had been reading what looked like a report when suddenly, as if she felt him watching her, she tilted her head up and stared straight at him.

A lump formed in Layla's throat. Beneath the brightness of the noon sun sat a gorgeous man on a beautiful horse. She'd seen the horse before. One day after arriving on the Silver Spurs, she'd noticed when one of the men had taken it out of the stall to groom it. She had been admiring the animal when the man, Curtis, told her the horse's name was Acer and that he belonged to the boss. This was the first time she'd seen Gavin on the horse and the sight took her breath away.

It had been three long days since he'd taken her to the movies and later walked her to the guest cottage, leaving her there and blatantly ignoring her since. Honestly, what had she expected? For him to have kissed her good-night regardless of what he'd said the night before? What he'd done was to toss the ball in her court. He probably figured she didn't have the guts to play it.

But it wasn't that she didn't have the guts. She didn't have the time or the inclination... Oh, who was she fooling? Definitely not herself. If anything, not seeing him these past few days had made her realize that out of sight, out of mind didn't work when it came to Gavin.

"Who in the blazes is that?"

Layla didn't have to move her gaze from Gavin to know one of her students, Tammy Clemons, stood beside her looking at Gavin, as well. "That's Gavin Blake. He and his grandmother own the Silver Spurs. They were kind enough to let us dig here."

"Um, maybe I should thank him. Properly."

A sudden stab of jealousy ran through Layla, and as much as she tried pushing it back, she couldn't. *Properly?* She didn't have to wonder just what Tammy meant by that. It was rumored around campus that Tammy often bragged about sleeping with her professors to get better grades.

Layla knew not to believe everything she heard, but Tammy's behavior made Layla think there was some truth in that claim. Especially since Tammy was here on this dig. Some said her latest conquest was Dr. Clayburn. That wouldn't surprise Layla since the married man and father of two was known to have roving eyes. More than once she'd heard about his late night meetings with female students. Those meetings were something Layla was certain the college president had heard about but had chosen to ignore.

Tammy's grades should have made her ineligible for this team, but Dr. Clayburn had personally added her name above other more well-deserving students. When

Layla had brought it to Dr. Clayburn's attention, he'd gotten upset that she'd questioned him. He'd reminded her that he had the power to withdraw the school's funding for the excavation.

"That guy is what you would call a real cowboy. And I didn't have to travel to Texas to get one."

Layla saw the twenty-one-year-old lick her lips with her gaze trained on Gavin. It shouldn't matter to Layla. But it did. Why? She didn't want to be Gavin's bed partner so why should it bother her if someone else did?

"Need I remind you, Tammy, that you're here to work on this project?"

Tammy frowned. "No, Dr. Harris, you don't need to remind me of anything. Just like I'm sure I don't need to remind you that although we're dedicated to this dig during the day, the nighttime hours are ours to enjoy. And I intend to enjoy him."

The young woman stated the words so matter-of-factly that Layla had to take pause. Was Tammy the type of woman Gavin wanted? The kind who could handle both work and play without breaking a sweat? A woman who enjoyed the challenge of both?

Layla was about to reply when a huge smile covered Tammy's face. "He's seen me checking him out and is coming down for me."

The thought that Gavin might be showing some interest in Tammy made Layla's chest ache.

She turned her attention back to Gavin. He was sprinting down the hill on the huge horse and she recalled something he'd once said. When he saw a target he wanted he went after it. Was he now galloping down the hill because he wanted Tammy? The young woman evidently thought so.

He looked good on the horse, wearing a Stetson on his head. Tammy was right. He was the epitome of what a cowboy should be. Tough. Rugged. Fearless. But then she could probably use those same adjectives to describe him as a navy SEAL. Gavin slowed his horse to a trot when it hit level ground and then he headed in their direction.

"Didn't I tell you he was coming to check me out?" Tammy said, with a ton of confidence in her voice.

The young woman didn't lack any faith in herself as a woman who could draw a man's interest. Gavin reached them and brought the horse to a stop. A lump formed in Layla's throat when she saw his attention hadn't even flickered to Tammy. He was staring straight at Layla.

"Gavin."

"Layla."

"And I'm Tammy," the younger woman quickly said, not waiting for an introduction. She flashed Gavin a huge, flirty smile.

Gavin switched his gaze from Layla to Tammy. "Hello, Tammy."

"You look good on your horse. I would love for you to give me a ride."

Gavin released a smooth chuckle. "Sorry. Acer is temperamental. I'm the only one he lets on his back."

"Um, I'm sure there are other ways we can ride," Tammy purred suggestively. "Without your horse."

Layla cleared her throat. Did the young woman have no shame? Tammy had pretty much offered herself to Gavin. Talk about being over-the-top brazen. The smile, she noticed, didn't leave Gavin's features when he said, "Thanks. But no thanks." He then turned his full attention back to Layla. "Have dinner with me tonight."

Layla swallowed. "Dinner?"

"Yes. I figured we could grab a meal in town."

Before Layla could say whether she would go or not, Tammy spoke up in an irritated tone. "Dr. Harris is in charge of this project, and I'm sure she has a lot to do tonight since we start digging in a few days. There are preliminary reports she has to complete and soil samples that need to be reviewed. But I'll be glad to go out with you tonight."

An annoyed frown replaced the smile on Gavin's lips when he turned to Tammy. "Are you her spokesperson?"

It was obvious Tammy had been caught off guard by Gavin's question. "No."

"I didn't think so. As far as taking her place, I didn't ask you to, did I?"

He couldn't have been I'm-not-interested-in-you plainer than that, Layla thought. Rage appeared in Tammy's face, making it quite obvious she wasn't used to men rejecting her and she didn't appreciate Gavin doing so. Instead of answering his question, she turned and angrily strutted off.

Layla watched her go and then turned her attention back to Gavin. "You might have hurt her feelings."

He shrugged massive shoulders. "She'll get over it. Besides, someone needs to teach her some manners." He leaned back. "So what about it? Will you have dinner with me tonight? We can even take in another movie if you like?"

Layla nibbled at her bottom lip. Tammy had been right about her having a lot of work to do to prepare for the start of the dig. But then hadn't Tammy also reminded her that although they were dedicated to this dig during the day, the nighttime hours were theirs to enjoy? Besides, after witnessing Tammy come on to Gavin the way she had, Layla had realized something. He could have taken Tammy up on her bold offer but he hadn't. He had even made it crystal clear that Layla was the woman he wanted.

Though she had convinced herself that she could do without him even if she wanted him, she now knew she couldn't. And why should she? She'd spent her whole life proving she could accomplish what she set her mind to. Now, she was setting her mind to finishing this dig and having Gavin, too.

She had set her target and she was going after what she wanted. In other words, she was about to become Viper Jr.

She met Gavin's gaze. "Dinner and a movie sound nice. Yes, I'd love to go out with you tonight."

Eleven

The moment Layla walked up the porch steps her nerves tightened. Was she doing the right thing? Was following her desires rather than common sense the best move for her tonight?

Her gaze swept over at the man at her side. Gavin had been quiet since parking his truck. Now he was walking her to the door and she knew it would be her decision how tonight would end. He wouldn't even kiss her good-night unless he knew for certain more came with that kiss. Was she ready to give him more?

They had been careful not to touch all night. Holding hands would have led to heaven knows what. The sexual chemistry between them was that explosive. She had been aware of everything about him all evening. His breathing pattern, the sexual vibes that poured off him and the heavy-lidded eyes that stared at her.

Even now, there was this sensuous pull of desire between them. She was aware of it and she knew he had to be aware of it, as well. That consciousness was a slow roll of longing in her stomach and a throbbing intensity at the base of her throat. Never had she felt such primal awareness of a man before.

When they reached the door she turned to him. Although his Stetson shaded his eyes, she felt his stare. She inhaled his masculine scent. The man was a living, breathing sample of testosterone at its best.

Drawing in a deep breath, Layla tightened her hands on the shoulder straps of her purse. "Dinner was wonderful. So was the movie. It's been a long time since I've seen a musical." His taste in movies surprised her. Last time it had been a chick flick and tonight a musical.

"Glad you enjoyed both."

She smiled up at him. "I did. Thanks for asking me to go. To be with you."

He nodded. "I can't think of any other woman I'd rather have been with tonight, Layla."

His words sent profound happiness spiraling through her. He could have spent the evening with Tammy, who was almost six years younger, and to Layla's way of thinking, a lot prettier. But she was the one he'd asked out. "Thank you for saying that."

"It's the truth."

When she didn't respond, she heard Gavin draw in a deep breath before saying, "I know you have a lot of work to do so I'll let you get to it."

He was giving her an out. He wouldn't pressure her. He'd stated days ago where he stood. If things between them escalated it would be up to her.

Swallowing deeply, she asked, "Would you like to come in for a drink, Gavin?"

He held her gaze for a long moment before smiling. "Yes, that would be nice, Layla."

As she opened the door to let him in, Layla knew it would be a whole lot better than just nice.

Gavin followed Layla inside. Removing his Stetson, he placed it on the rack by the door. She walked ahead, toward the living room and his groin tightened with each sinfully erotic sway of her hips.

"Beer or wine cooler?" she asked over her shoulder.

"Beer." He closed the front door. He actually needed something a lot stronger. A straight shot of bourbon might do the trick, to stop his testosterone from overloading. But then he figured there wasn't a drink on earth that could deaden his desire for Layla. It went too deep. He could actually feel a throb in his veins. Drawing in a deep breath he inhaled her scent.

"Here you are," she said, reentering the living room.

He recalled the last time she'd offered him a beer and what had occurred when their hands touched. What he'd felt. Would she avoid touching him this time? There was only one way to find out.

When she handed him the bottle, he deliberately held her gaze. Intentionally, he rubbed his finger against her hand. Hearing her sharp intake of breath, he'd gotten the reaction he'd hoped for. Unlike the last time she didn't wipe her hands on her jeans.

Still holding her gaze, he opened the bottle and took a huge gulp. He then lowered the bottle, licked his lips and asked the same question he had asked that night. "Want a sip?"

He'd given her an opening. Instead of retreating like she had before, she covered the distance separating them. "Yes, I want a sip." But instead of taking it, she said, "I'd rather sip it from your lips."

He lifted the bottle to his mouth. Then she took the bottle from him and placed it on a nearby table before leaning up on tiptoes to place her mouth over his. With a boldness he hadn't expected from her, she wrapped her arms around his neck and began sipping the beer from his lips.

Gavin felt light-headed and hot at the same time. Never had a woman stirred such passion within him. Never had any woman made his erection throb to this point. Layla was full of surprises and she was driving him insane with need.

As their mouths mated, he wrapped his arms around her. He wasn't surprised by how fluidly her body aligned with his. Sensations swamped his body. He knew from the way she was tasting him that tonight would not end with this kiss. The mating of their mouths was just the beginning. Tonight they were on the same page.

He swept her into his arms. Breaking off the kiss, he whispered against her lips, "I'm taking you to bed, Layla. If you have a problem with it, you need to say so now."

A seductive smile touched her lips. "I don't have a problem with that, Gavin."

Sexual excitement rushed through his veins as he moved quickly toward the bedroom.

Twelve

When Gavin placed Layla on the bed she looked up at him and saw eyes filled with intense desire gazing down at her. She'd meant what she said about going to bed with him. But he might not feel the same way after she said what she had to say.

"We need to talk first, Gavin."

He pulled her sweater over her head. "Okay, I'm listening."

Was he really? Or was he concentrating on undressing her? "A while back you asked me when I last did this. Do you remember that conversation?"

Her sweater was off and his swift hands went to the front clasp of her bra. Within seconds he had her breasts tumbling free. She watched his eyes get smoky as he stared at her nipples, which hardened as he watched. When he brushed against one with a feathery stroke of his fingertips, she drew in a sharp breath.

"Yes, I remember that conversation," he said in a husky

voice, stroking her other breast as if fascinated with its size and shape. "What about it?"

Layla had to think a minute to remember the conversation. His hands were driving her insane. And when he began stroking her nipples in earnest, it created a throbbing ache in her center. She couldn't help but moan.

"Layla?"

"Um?"

"What about the conversation?"

What conversation? Her brain was turning to mush and she fought hard to recall what he was talking about. Then she remembered. "Are you ready for an answer to the question you asked?"

"Doesn't matter now."

And before she could draw in another breath, he lowered his head and eased a rigid nipple between his lips. He sucked hard, feasting in earnest. Greedily. Ravenously. At the same time, he eased the hem of her skirt toward her waist.

And then he pushed aside her panties to ease fingers inside of her. The moment she felt the intimate invasion, she shuddered in pleasure. How could his mere touch do that? Make her come so unglued? Make her feel like a woman?

And when those same fingers stroked her down there, with the same rhythm his tongue was using to suck on her nipples, she moaned aloud.

"That's it. Get all wet for me, baby. Your scent has been driving me mad for days now. I can't wait to taste you."

She wasn't sure what he meant. All she knew was Gavin Blake had fingers that should be considered illegal and a mouth that should be banned. Using both, and at the same time, should be forbidden.

Sensation gathered force in her stomach and when he sucked harder on her breasts, while at the same time inserting his fingers deeper inside of her, she could not bear the pleasure any longer. Her body began to shake with the need for release. A climax ripped through her body. On instinct, she threw her head back and screamed his name.

"Now for my taste."

Before she realized what Gavin was doing, he had pulled off her skirt and tossed it aside along with her panties. Before she could ask what he thought he was doing, he lifted her hips to his mouth and firmly settled his head between her legs.

Layla tried pushing him away—until the moment she felt his tongue ease between her womanly lips. He kissed her down there the same way he'd kissed her on the mouth. Deeply. Thoroughly.

She stopped pushing him away. Instead she grabbed his shoulders and held on. Held him. She needed him to stay right there and continue what he was so expertly doing. When she felt his tongue delve deeper inside, flicking back and forth, her body shattered into what felt like a million pieces.

"Gavin!"

He didn't let up. He continued using his mouth to drive her over the edge yet again. Never had she experienced anything so powerful. So utterly amazing. For a minute she thought she had passed out. Maybe she had. She was completely drained. Limp. Too weak to move. So she lay there, nearly convinced she had died and gone to heaven. Surely there was nothing on earth that could make her feel this good. This satisfied.

She didn't move. She couldn't find the strength to open her eyes. Not even when she heard him remove his clothes before he pulled her boots and socks from her feet. Not even when his hands stroked her thighs and eased them apart.

And not even when she heard the sound of a condom packet being ripped open.

Moments later she heard Gavin's deep voice directly above her. "Open your eyes, baby. Look at me."

Although her eyelids felt heavy, she somehow found the strength to force them open. Gavin's naked body was braced above hers and desire-filled eyes stared down at her. Was it her imagination or were his eyes getting even darker as she stared into them?

"I'm looking," she said softly. Not only was she looking but she was being held in some sort of hypnotic trance.

"I wanted you this way from the first moment I set eyes on you."

That was nice. And she was about to say something, she wasn't sure what, when she felt the hot tip of his erection press against the core of her womanhood.

Her gaze widened and she knew she needed to tell him. Now. "Gavin?"

He leaned in and kissed the words off her lips. Using that scandalizing tongue of his, he began driving her crazy. Instinctively her legs opened wider and she felt him pressing down gently, as he tried entering her body.

He broke off the kiss and stared down at her. She knew from his expression exactly when he realized the *something* she'd tried to tell him about. The *something* he'd said no longer mattered.

"You're a virgin," he whispered in shock.

"Yes." Would he change his mind? Would it matter? She swallowed and said quietly, "I'll understand if you no longer want me."

Something flickered in his dark gaze. "Why wouldn't I still want you? Because you're a twenty-six-year-old virgin?"

When she nodded, he smiled and said, "Doesn't bother me if it doesn't bother you."

That was the moment she knew she had fallen in love with Gavin. She had tried denying it, had even called herself several kinds of a fool for letting it happen. She'd never loved a man before, but she knew what her feelings were. For all the heartbreak it would cause when she left the ranch in a week or so, it didn't make much sense for her to love a man now. But her heart had declared Gavin was it and there was nothing she could do about it.

Making love with him seemed right in a way it had never been with any other man...which was the real reason why she had remained untouched all these years. Sex had never interested her. She had never been turned on by the mere thought of it. Things were different with Gavin. Even before she'd met him face-to-face, his pictures had done something to her. They had pretty much warned her of her fate but she'd refused to accept it until she'd welcomed him inside tonight.

"Layla?"

She held his gaze. "Doesn't bother me, either." *Please don't ask me why I chose you. At least not now.*

He didn't ask her anything. Instead he kissed her before using his knee to widen her legs. And then she felt him, easing inside of her, inch by inch. He was big and she sucked in as he filled her deeply, her body stretching for his invasion. Her muscles clamped down—not to stop his journey but to make it even more sensuous for the two of them. He continued to ease deeper until there was no place left for him to go. He was fully embedded in her in a fit so snug and tight she couldn't tell where her body ended and his began.

When her muscles tightened even more, she actually felt his erection throb inside of her. "If you keep that up do you know what's going to happen?" He leaned in close to ask her.

"No."

"It's going to make me want to do this."

Then he began thrusting, gently, in a sensuous rhythm

that drove her to lift her hips with his every downward stroke. When her inner muscles clenched him harder, he thrusted harder, with a steady fluid beat.

Too steady. Each stroke inside her body pushed her to a place she'd never been. He'd made her come using his mouth. But this was different. It was more intense. Insanely gratifying. And when he went faster, harder, deeper, she screamed his name as sensations washed over her. She clawed at his back, bucked upward to tighten her legs around him and lock their bodies together.

An intense explosion swept her away in an earth-shattering release. Although this might be the first time she'd made love with a man, she knew that this wouldn't be her last with Gavin.

That had been totally unreal, Gavin thought, a short while later as he lay flat on his back staring up at the ceiling. When had making love to a woman ever left him so physically sated and mentally drained? Hell, he was used to making out with women, sometimes all night long. And as a SEAL he was physically fit for all the rigors of combat. Yet, the woman sleeping beside him had practically drained him, made him weak as water with their first sexual encounter. How was that possible?

And she'd been a virgin. Gavin didn't have to wonder how that was possible, given her status in life. To accomplish what she'd accomplished at her age meant she'd made sacrifices. He'd suspected her experience with men had been limited, he just hadn't figured it to be nonexistent. Not that it bothered him. Normally, he preferred not to be any woman's first, but he was glad he'd been Layla's. The thought that no other man had been inside her body before him felt good, made him want to beat on his damn chest like a caveman. He'd branded Layla as his.

His?

Where in the hell had that thought come from? This was the second time he'd thought of her as being his woman. His. He needed to remind himself once again that he wasn't into possessiveness. He'd even participated in a ménage à trois a time or two during his college years. So the idea of laying claim to any woman didn't sit well with him. Sex was sex, no matter how good it was. No need to act crazy.

So why was he?

As he tilted his head to stare down at the woman sleeping peacefully beside him, he had to admit the sex had been better than good. Off the charts. He had studied her face when she'd come. Her expression had been utterly and incredibly spellbinding. Beautiful. Touching. She was such a passionate being it was hard to believe she'd held out for this long. Her presence on the Silver Spurs was the best luck he'd had in years. With sex that good she could dig up the entire damn ranch looking for whatever treasure she wanted. His treasure was right here with him in this bed.

Gavin frowned. He was thinking like a love-struck puppy, and he refused to go there. Isn't that what had happened to his father? He'd quickly fallen in love with a woman only to die of a broken heart in the end? Okay, it had been an enemy's bullet that had taken him out, but Gavin of all people knew of his father's heartache.

Layla shifted her weight. Her leg, which rested between his, touched his groin. Immediately, he got hard. His erection had no problem coming to life. He glanced over at the clock. It was almost two in the morning. He should leave but the thought of waking up beside her in the morning had an appeal he couldn't dismiss.

And then there was the temptation to wake her now and make love to her all over again. Move between her legs and slide inside of her. Go deep until he couldn't go anymore. Then he would thrust hard like he'd done before. Even harder since she was no longer a virgin. He even thought about how it would feel not to wear a condom. To blast off inside of her. Fill her with the very essence of him.

Now that was taking his imagination a little too far. He was a man who played it safe so he would never be sorry. Babies of any kind were not in his immediate future. So why did the thought of a daughter who would be a mini-Layla appeal to him? Make his erection even harder?

Gavin closed his eyes. He had to stop thinking with the wrong head. Doing so could get him in serious trouble. He couldn't let sexual feelings take control of his common sense no matter how wrapped up he wanted to get with the woman beside him. No matter how much inhaling her arousing scent was getting to him.

Shifting his body, he pulled Layla closer and let sleep overtake him.

Thirteen

The strong aroma of coffee woke Layla. She blinked, and then sluggishly realized where she was and what she'd done last night and with whom. If there had been any doubt in her mind about what had happened, all she had to do was tilt her head to gaze across the room to where a half-naked man lounged in the doorway holding a steaming cup of coffee.

Gavin.

She blinked. Okay, since he was wearing jeans, he wasn't half-naked but half-dressed. Still, that was all he was wearing. And those jeans were riding low on his hips, making it pretty obvious just what a well-built body he had. His pose was picture perfect. He was the epitome of a sexy cowboy. A wealthy rancher. A scrumptious navy SEAL. How could one man exemplify all three and do it so well?

Her gaze roamed over him, from the top of his head all the way down to his bare feet. She'd paused when she'd seen that his zipper was undone. He'd either dressed quickly and hadn't bothered to zip up, or he had plans that included her so he'd figured why bother.

Those tantalizing thoughts made her recall last night. Her first time. And she knew without a doubt it had been worth the wait. She couldn't help it. Her gaze traveled the full length of him all over again. This time when her gaze settled on his midsection, she saw something she hadn't seen before. A huge erection. She drew in a deep breath and swore that it got bigger as she stared at it.

"Want some?"

She snatched her gaze from his groin up to his face. The smile that touched his lips was priceless and way too sexy for words. "What are you offering?" she asked.

"Whatever you want."

Reluctantly, she broke eye contact with him to glance outside the bedroom window. It was still dark but she knew it would be daybreak soon. Her team would be arriving from town within an hour or so. Her gaze returned to his. "I should take the coffee, get up, shower and get dressed."

"But…"

How had he known there was a *but* in there? "But I much prefer taking the man holding the coffee."

His smile widened. "And the man holding the coffee doesn't have a problem with you taking him."

Layla was only beginning to fully understand what heated lust was all about. "Did I tell you that last night I thought of myself as Viper Jr?"

He lifted a brow. "Viper Jr?"

"Yes. I set my sights on my target and went after what I wanted, and you, Gavin Blake, were my target."

A wry grin split his lips. "Was I?"

She nodded. "I wanted you."

"And I wanted you."

Layla then saw a somewhat serious look appear in

his eyes as he said, "How do you feel? I wanted you so much…because of that you're probably sore. You sure you're up to another ride this soon?"

Ride? She inwardly chuckled. Yes, he'd definitely ridden her last night. And yes, she was sore from it. However, as far as she was concerned, he could ride the soreness away.

"I'm sure."

"In that case." Placing the coffee cup on a nearby table, he crossed the room to the bed. "But first I want to see something." Before she could blink, he threw the bedcovers aside to expose her naked body.

Surprised, she scrambled to get back under the covers but he tossed them aside again. "No. Don't cover yourself. I just had to make sure I hadn't imagined anything. That you were as beautiful and delectable as I remembered. My mind didn't play tricks on me last night."

His words touched her. Made her feel wonderful. Made her feel like a real woman who had sexual feminine powers over a man. And when she watched him lick his lips with the tip of his tongue, she couldn't help remembering just where that tongue had been and what it had done.

Recalling that part of their lovemaking sparked an ache between her legs. As if he knew what sensations were enthralling her and where, he slowly eased his jeans down his strong, muscular thighs. Just as she'd thought. The jeans were the only thing he'd been wearing. He hadn't bothered to put back on his briefs.

"Now for this."

His words grabbed her attention and she watched him slide a condom over his erection. And boy was it large. How had it gotten inside of her last night? But he'd managed it and she knew he would again. This was the first time she'd seen a man prepare himself for sex. From the way he was doing it, it was obvious he was used to doing it.

"Ready?"

"Yes." She drew in a deep breath. The ache between her legs had made her nipples harden like tight buds.

"We're going to try something different this morning. It will be easier on you and help with your soreness."

In a way, she felt embarrassed engaging in such a conversation with him...about her body. But she pushed her discomfort aside. After last night—and all he'd done to her and how he'd done it—there was no room left for shame. "What?"

He smiled as he moved back toward the bed. "I want you to ride me."

She swallowed. "Ride you?"

"Yes. Do you know how to ride?"

She nodded. "Yes. My parents own several horses." And she'd ridden them often enough.

"Good. So show me what you know," he said, lying back on the bed beside her, then lifting her over him. Just like that. As if she was weightless.

"I'll do my best," she said, sliding into position. The long, hard length of his erection was like a rod, standing straight up, ready for her to mount. So she did. Widening her legs, she took him into her body. The hot texture of his male organ seemed to blaze her insides as she took him fully inside of her.

She watched his face, the same way she'd known he'd watched hers last night. Their gazes held. No words were spoken. This was all about feeling. And she felt him in each and every part of her body. Her muscles clenched around him. Holding tight. And then as if of one accord they shivered with a need they both felt.

"Okay Viper Jr. Ride me, baby. Hard."

Gavin's words incited her to move up and down. She

felt him grip the sides of her hips—to hold on to her, to guide her. Then, as if something elemental had taken control, she threw her head back and rode him hard.

What was happening to her? It was as if she'd lost control of her mind and her body. Having sex with Gavin this way, with her on top, riding him, sent an exhilarated feeling through her, one she couldn't explain.

When he leaned up and whispered naughty words in her ear, sinfully erotic words, she went mad with lust. She heard the bedsprings as she continued to ride. Each time her body came down against him, his came up to meet her.

Suddenly her quivering became uncontrollable and she felt her body explode into a thousand pieces. It was then that Gavin caught the back of her head with his hands and brought her mouth down to his, kissing her with a hunger that made her climax all over again.

Once again he came with her. She felt it. As their tongues continued to mingle, she knew that she loved him with a passion she would never rid herself of, no matter the distance between them. While she was here on the Silver Spurs, she intended to make memories that would last her long after she returned to Seattle.

"Well, how did your dinner date with the handsome rancher go? Did the two of you do the nasty, Dr. Harris?"

Layla didn't immediately look up from studying the soil samples. Tammy was the last person she wanted to talk to, but to ignore her student would be rude. Yet no student had the right to inquire how their professor spent their evening. Layla had always maintained a distance between herself and her students. Because of her age, she took pains to ensure they never lost sight of the fact that she was their professor. As far as she was concerned, Tammy's question was out of line and lacked respect.

Layla raised her head from the microscope and met

Tammy's gaze. "I don't think that should be your concern, Tammy. Did you finish your report?" Layla knew she hadn't. Several students had brought it to her attention that Tammy was slacking. It seemed whenever there was hard work to do, Tammy had a tendency to disappear.

Tammy scrunched up her features. "No. And why do I have to be the one to do that report? Donnell has a lot of free time."

"Only because Donnell has finished all his assignments. You haven't."

A smile touched Tammy's lips. "Doesn't matter. I'll still ace this class."

Layla frowned. "Not if you don't do your share of the work. And if you're not going to be a team player, I will have to replace you. There are several students who would love to be here."

"Doesn't matter. They don't have the connections I have," Tammy bragged. "I'm on this team, Dr. Harris, whether you want me here or not. I thought you understood that."

Layla refused to get into a confrontation with a student. It was clear Tammy thought that being Dr. Clayburn's occasional bed partner meant she could do whatever she wanted. Wrong. Not on Layla's team. "The only thing I understand is that I expect you to carry your load. If you can't, then you're out of here."

Tammy tossed her hair as a smirk touched her lips. "Wrong. You'll be out of here before I will. I'll make sure Mark… I mean Dr. Clayburn knows I'm being harassed." She then turned and sulked as she walked out the door.

In frustration Layla rubbed her hand down her face. Tammy might be right. Layla wasn't one of Dr. Clayburn's favorite people and it was obvious the man was quite taken with Tammy. And Tammy knew it.

"She'll eventually hang herself and Dr. Clayburn. Don't waste your time worrying about her, Dr. Harris."

Layla turned to find another one of her students, Donnell McGuire, standing in the doorway. Had he overheard her conversation with Tammy? Did he and the other students suspect something was going on between Tammy and Dr. Clayburn? The one thing Layla wouldn't do was discuss one student with another, no matter how much she wanted to sound off to someone about Tammy's atrocious attitude.

Before she could say anything, Donnell added, "And don't worry about that report Tammy hasn't done. I'll take care of it. I do have some free time."

His words told Layla he *had* overheard her conversation with Tammy. "That assignment was given to Tammy, Donnell, and I expect her to do it. Besides, I have something else for you to do. I just got a call that the last of our supplies arrived at the post office in town. I need you to go pick them up. If everything looks good, we'll start digging by the end of the week."

A huge smile touched Donnell's face. "Alright! I can't wait." The young man rushed off to tell the others.

Layla chuckled at his enthusiasm. She would give anything for more students like Donnell who took being a team player seriously. He was a hard worker. Most of the students on this team were. Although being an archaeologist was Donnell's first love, she knew he was also good with a camera and had won a number of photo contests. At twenty-two he would be graduating in the spring with a major in archaeology and a minor in photography.

She refused to let Tammy put a damper on her day, especially when it had started off with the promise of being wonderful. She'd had such a wonderful night with Gavin. Then this morning, before the crack of dawn, she'd proven just what a great horsewoman she could be. Memories of what they'd shared still sent shivers down her spine. She couldn't help but blush. Being intimate with a man had never been anything she'd thought about until now…

She glanced at her watch. She had a full day planned here on-site and then Gavin had invited her to dinner again. This time he would be the one cooking. He claimed he wasn't bad in the kitchen. Tonight she intended to see if that was true.

Gavin had always prided himself on being a man in control. As a SEAL, he couldn't be any other way. The success of any mission called for it. There was no time to let your guard down. Weakness of any kind wasn't acceptable. Then why did he lose control every time he entered Layla's body? Why did overpowering weakness overtake him whenever they made love?

He had prepared dinner for her tonight at the party house. He'd fed her well. Surprised the hell out of her with his culinary skills. At the moment, he contemplated impressing her with another skill. One of seduction. When he'd arrived at the party house with his arms filled with groceries, Layla had opened the door wearing an outfit that only made him think of filling her.

She'd tempted him the entire time he was in the kitchen. There was no doubt in his mind that she'd known exactly what she was doing as she'd sat at the breakfast bar watching him. She had known each and every time she crossed and uncrossed her legs that she was showing him a portion of her thigh and exactly what that did to him. How he had managed to finish cooking and then sit across from her and eat was a testament to his control.

Now it was payback time.

"So how was your day, Gavin?"

He'd cleared off the table and was loading up the dishwasher as he fought to retain control. "It was the usual day in the life of a rancher. The cows are finally settled in for the winter, which is good since forecasters predict a cold wave coming through first of next week."

"I heard. I'm hoping bad weather won't delay the completion of the dig. Our goal is to start later this week."

He closed the dishwasher door, then turned around and watched her gaze shift from his face to his midsection. She saw the evidence of his desire for her. That couldn't be helped when she was sitting there looking as sexy as any woman had a right to look. "Did I tell you how much I like your outfit?"

She chuckled and the sound made his erection thicken even more. "Yes, you told me. I figured you would like it since I understand men like to see skin."

She understood right. Men liked touching and tasting skin as well, which was something he'd shown her last night. Her short dress showed a lot of her thighs since the hem barely covered them. And the top had a neckline that showed a lot of cleavage, reminding him of how much he enjoyed her breasts. He wanted her bad. He wanted her right here. Right now.

He slowly crossed the room toward her. Any other woman would have run after seeing the predatory look in his eyes. But Layla stood her ground. That was fine with him. When he reached her, he removed her dress with a flick of his wrist and a little muscle power, leaving her totally naked. Like he'd suspected, she hadn't had a stitch of clothing on underneath that dress. He knew he had surprised the hell out of her with how quickly he'd undressed her.

He smiled at her shocked look. "A SEAL pays attention to detail. While sitting across from you at dinner I studied the design of your dress and figured out the best way to take it off without ripping it to shreds. I like the dress too much to tear it."

He stepped back. "Now to remove my clothes."

Gavin undressed quickly. And then he picked her up and spread her across the same table he'd cleared just moments ago. "Open your legs for me, Layla."

He intended to bury himself inside of her as deeply as he could go. He was certain the hot and hungry look in his eyes said as much. But he knew all this was still new to her and he wanted her to be comfortable with everything they did together.

She lay there, on his table, with her legs spread. For a minute he just stood and looked at her. Remembering her taste, he couldn't help but lick his lips. Tasting her would have to come later. Right now he needed to *come*. Quickly putting on a condom, he settled his body between her thighs. She held his gaze when he entered her, filling her completely. Being inside her, feeling her muscles clench around him, felt so damn good. Her muscles were trying to pull everything out of him and the sensation was driving him insane.

Gavin held tight to her hips as he moved in and out. She wrapped her legs around his waist, locking him inside of her. He wanted her to feel every stroke, the same way he was feeling it. On and on, each thrust was hard and precise. Back and forth, he rocked inside of her. Steady, with meaningful precision. He thrust hard, creating pleasure that spread like molten heat throughout both of their bodies. The sound of Layla's moans only increased his desire to please her. When he felt her body explode, his explosion soon followed.

That's when he realized why things were so different with her. Why with her he so easily lost control.

As much as a part of him wished it wasn't true, he knew he had fallen head over heels in love with Layla Harris.

Fourteen

"So what are you going to do about Tammy?"

Layla lifted her head off Gavin's chest. It was two days after the night he'd prepared dinner for her. She had arrived at the guest cottage to find him sitting on the steps waiting for her. Her heart had pounded the minute she'd seen him sitting there. He'd stood when she got out of the car and her gaze had taken him in. With the Stetson on his head, his Western shirt, a pair of well-worn and scuffed boots, he looked like a quintessential cowboy. She wondered how he would look dressed as a SEAL. Too bad she would probably never see him that way. Gavin as a rancher would be the memory of him she would keep in her heart forever.

He had taken her hand into his and once they were locked inside the house, he had swept her into his arms and headed for the bedroom where they'd made love a number of times. Then he'd told her some troubling news. It seemed earlier that day he'd overheard one of his men bragging about sleeping with Tammy. The man had said she'd told him she was into group sex, so if he had any friends who were interested, she was available.

Gavin hadn't liked what he'd overheard and felt he needed to bring it to Layla's attention. She was glad he had. Unfortunately, she was battling her own issues with Tammy. The young woman's promiscuity wasn't Layla's number one concern. Tammy's entitled attitude was impairing the success of the dig. The report Layla had assigned to Tammy had yet to be done, and Tammy's slacking off on her duties had increased to the point where the other students were complaining. Low morale was the last thing Layla needed to deal with.

Layla had confided in Gavin, telling him of her own issues with Tammy including Tammy's ongoing affair with the head of Layla's department and how Tammy was blatantly using that affair to do whatever she wanted...as well as avoiding the things she didn't want to do.

Finally answering Gavin's question, Layla said, "There's only one thing I can do about Tammy and that is to release her from the team and brace myself for the backlash from Dr. Clayburn. She isn't a team player, she lacks respect for everyone and she isn't pulling her own weight. I refuse to give her more chances than I would give anyone else, no matter who she's sleeping with."

Gavin nodded. He thought Layla was making the right decision by releasing Tammy from her team. He'd known Tammy had been trouble from day one. "So you'll start digging on Friday?"

"Yes. We got delayed when one of the supply shipments was late. We haven't had any other problems, but I wanted to ask, did you ever talk to that guy to see if he was the one who moved my marker?"

"Yes, and Clete said he didn't move anything. So what happened to your marker is still a mystery."

"It doesn't matter since we're moving ahead. I'm excited."

He pulled her tighter into his arms. "So am I. I can't wait to see what you find."

She pulled back and stared up at him. "And now you think I will find something?"

"Yes. I told you I'd gotten a good reading from Flip's camera. I'm sure you'll find something, I'm just not certain it's the loot you're looking for."

She smiled up at him. "Well, I am certain, Mr. Blake." She then pulled his mouth down to hers.

Hours later, the ringing of his cell phone woke Gavin. He looked down at the woman plastered to his side. The phone had awakened her, as well. He glanced at the clock and saw it was three in the morning. Who would be calling him at this hour?

He reached for the phone on the nightstand before it could ring again. "Hello."

He heard the words his foreman said and was out of bed in a flash. "We're on our way."

Layla sat up. "What's wrong, Gavin?"

He glanced over at her as he reached for his clothes. "That was Caldwell. The old barn is going up in flames."

It didn't take long for them to both make their way to the south pasture.

"Arson?" Gavin asked, staring down Cornerstone's fire marshal. He knew Josh Timbales well since the man had been good friends with Gavin's dad.

"Yes, Gavin. Arson. And the person didn't even try covering their tracks. You could smell kerosene a mile away."

"But who would do such a thing?" Layla asked, staring at the building that was now burned to the ground as well as the charred remains of the equipment that had been stored inside.

"I don't know," Josh said to Layla. "My investigative team has been called in as well as the sheriff. Hopefully they will come up with some answers."

In the meantime… Layla turned to stare at her students who were huddled together a few feet away. They'd gotten word about the fire and had rushed from town. She could see the disappointed looks on their faces. They'd worked hard and now this. "I need to talk to my team," Layla said, and walked off.

Gavin watched her go. He could feel her anger and disappointment. He turned a livid gaze to Josh. "No matter what it takes, I intend to find the person responsible for this."

Layla approached the group. Before she could say anything, one of her students, Wendy Miller, spoke up. "Is it true what the firemen are saying? Did someone deliberately set fire to the barn?"

Layla drew in a deep breath. "Yes, the fire marshal has ruled it as arson. The sheriff is on his way."

"Looks like you have an enemy, Dr. Harris," Tammy said with a smirk. "Well, with no equipment for the dig, that means we're free to leave and return home, right? I didn't like this place anyway."

Layla had had enough. "Yes, you can leave, Tammy. I was going to release you from the team in the morning anyway. Have a safe trip back to Seattle."

Fury shone on Tammy's face. "You're dropping me from the team? You can't do that."

"I just did."

Tammy lifted her chin. "It really doesn't matter because there won't be a dig team. Once Dr. Clayburn calculates the cost of all the equipment that was destroyed in the fire, he will call off the dig."

"The college probably insured the equipment. It won't take long to get more in here," Donnell said angrily. He stared at Tammy suspiciously. "And just where were you tonight, Tammy? I was in the hotel's lobby and saw when you came in rather late. It wouldn't surprise me if you torched this place."

From the looks on the faces of her other students, Layla could see they were thinking the same thing. Evidently Tammy saw it, as well. She backed up, away from the others. "I was with someone, so I have a concrete alibi. But I plan on giving Dr. Clayburn a call to tell him everything."

"And how do you have his phone number?" another student asked, making it pretty obvious all of them had an idea.

"That's none of your business," Tammy snapped. And then she angrily walked off.

Layla turned back to her students. "I will call Dr. Clayburn in the morning myself. Regardless of what Tammy says, I doubt he will shut down the project."

Although Layla said the words, she truly wasn't so sure of that.

The next day, an angry Layla slammed down the phone. She could not believe the conversation she'd just had with Dr. Clayburn. She could not believe the audacity of the man.

"What's wrong, Layla?"

She turned and saw Gavin. She hadn't heard him enter the cottage. She saw the care and concern in his expression and she loved him even more than she already had. He had been so understanding and supportive. Incredibly, he'd been more concerned about the loss of her equipment than he had for the loss of his barn.

Last night they had both talked to the sheriff, whom she'd discovered was a high school friend of Gavin's. Sheriff Roy Wade was just as determined as Gavin to find the person responsible for the fire. And after checking for footprints, Gavin mentioned the ones around the burned barn were the same ones he'd seen when her marker had gone missing. It was obvious someone was trying to sabotage the dig. But who, and why?

She drew in a deep breath. "That was Dr. Clayburn."

"And?"

She blew out a frustrated and angry sigh. "Tammy got to him first. She probably called him last night like she threatened to do. He really didn't want to hear anything I had to say."

Gavin crossed his arms over his chest with a furious look on his face. "You mean to tell me he's taking a student's word over yours?"

Layla frowned. "Remember Tammy isn't just another student. She's also the man's side piece. I didn't want to believe it before, but I definitely believe it now. The influence she has over him! If I didn't know better I'd think there's more to it, that she's blackmailing him with something."

Gavin dropped his arms and came to stand in front of her. "Why? What did he say?"

"He wanted to let me know my students were notified this morning by email that the dig has been canceled and they are to return to campus." She paused. "He also wanted me to know that I've been terminated from my position at the university."

"He fired you?"

"Yes. He claims I botched things up. As far as he is concerned, the fire was my responsibility. I should have been more attentive to my work rather than indulging in an 'illicit affair with one of the cowboys.'" There was no doubt in Layla's mind Tammy had fed the man that BS and he'd believed it without question.

"Can't you go to the president of the university with your side of the story?"

"Yes, but Dr. Clayburn and President Connors are good friends. If I was terminated that means Dr. Connors approved the termination because he believed whatever Dr. Clayburn told him about me."

"Let them believe whatever they want. You came here to do a dig and that's what you'll do."

Layla dropped into a nearby wingback chair. "Gavin, didn't you hear what I said?"

He squatted down in front of her. "What I hear is the sound of you giving up. Letting them defeat you."

She touched his cheek. "What am I supposed to do? I don't have a job. Nor do I have a team. Did you not hear me say that Dr. Clayburn sent everyone an email telling them to return to Seattle?"

"You'll get another job. You're too smart and intelligent not to. As far as I'm concerned, losing you is the university's loss. Besides, I want to see what their reaction will be when you find James's loot. You don't have to be affiliated with any university to dig or publish your findings, right?"

Layla shook her head. "No, I can conduct an independent excavation, but I no longer have funding, or a team."

Gavin pulled her out of the chair. "I'll replace your equipment. And you might not have a team, but I do. They will come to help out if I call them."

Layla stared at him, not believing what he was saying, what he was offering. "B-but I can't let you do that. Like you, they just got back from their last operation. They need to spend time with their families and—"

Gavin lowered his mouth and kissed the words off her lips. He then deepened the kiss. By the time he released her mouth, she was panting. "Trust me on this, will you?" he said. "I don't want to brag or anything, but we will do it in half the time your team would have."

"But it will take time to get more equipment."

"We will get the equipment we need without any delays."

Layla knew he had money and influence. She just hadn't realized how much. Then she thought of something crucial. "What about the person sabotaging the dig? Things could get dangerous."

A sinister grin touched Gavin's lips. "If he or she is crazy enough to try something with a team of SEALs around, then let them go for it. We will be ready."

He quickly kissed her again, silencing any more questions. When he released her lips, he said, "Trust me. We've got this. We'll have your back."

There was a knock at the door. Gavin lifted a brow. "Gramma Mel isn't due back until tonight, so it might be Roy. Maybe he's found something."

Gavin crossed the room with her following beside him. Opening the door they found three of her students standing there. "Donnell? Wendy? Marsha? What are you doing here?" Layla asked them. "Why aren't you on your way back to Seattle? Didn't you get Dr. Clayburn's email?"

"Yes, we got it," Donnell said, frowning. "But we didn't want to leave until we talked to you. Until you say there won't be a dig, we are staying put."

"You could get into trouble if you defy Dr. Clayburn," she warned them.

The three students looked at each other and shared what looked like conspiratorial smiles before Donnell said, "We aren't worried about that. They'll be faced with their own troubles soon. So, are you still planning to dig?"

Layla wondered what they meant by "troubles," but before she could ask, Gavin said, "Yes, the dig is still on."

She could tell from the look of respect in his eyes that he admired the stance these three students had taken. Like his team had his back, these members of her team had hers.

Donnell, Marsha and Wendy let out loud cheers and gave each other high fives. Then Donnell said, "When we find James's loot, the university's going to regret letting you go."

Fifteen

"So…you're the fast-talking college professor, huh?"

Layla swallowed as she watched the four men standing in front of her. Gavin had introduced them as Flipper, Bane, Coop and Mac. It was Flipper who'd asked the question, the depths of his blue eyes dancing with amusement.

All four were big men. Muscular. Well built. Extremely handsome. Two wore wedding rings and two did not. Gavin had told her that Brisbane Westmoreland and Thurston McRoy were happily married and that Flipper and Coop were happily single.

"I don't know. Am I?" she asked, switching her gaze from them to Gavin, who stood by her side with his arms around her waist. It was as if he was intentionally making a statement regarding the nature of their relationship. If that was the case, then she wished someone would tell her where they stood. All she knew for certain was that they enjoyed spending time together and they shared a bed every night. She definitely didn't have any complaints about that.

Gavin muttered the words, "Smart-ass," to Flipper, then leaned down and placed a kiss on Layla's lips. He then turned to his friends. "She's more than a professor."

He knew his friends were checking out Layla and with good reason. The four men knew about his don't-get-attached policy when it came to women. But it was obvious that with this particular woman, he'd gotten attached. They would be shocked to discover just how attached he was.

Like he'd known they would, his friends had answered his summons for help. No questions asked. But now that they were here and had been briefed on the situation, they were also eyewitnesses to his possessiveness of Layla. They would have questions about that later. Fair enough. He would address them then. He would admit he'd fallen in love. Bane and Mac would understand. Flipper and Coop would suggest Gavin have his head examined.

"Did you get the equipment I asked you to bring?" he asked them.

"Yes. Two of my brothers will be towing the backhoe loader and tractor in this evening," Flipper said.

"And I've got the rest of the stuff in my truck," Mac added.

"Good," Gavin said. Flip had four brothers. All SEALs. And Flip's dad had retired as a SEAL commanding officer. Gavin had thought he'd had it bad living in his father's and grandfather's shadows—until he'd met Flipper. His friend had five legacies to compete with since all the male Holloways before Flip had stellar reputations as SEALs.

"So where are we staying, Viper? The party house?" Coop asked.

Gavin shook his head. "No. Layla's at the party house."

Flipper chuckled. "So? It's big enough. You don't mind if we crash, do you?" he asked Layla.

Before she could answer, Gavin said, "But I mind."

All four men laughed. Gavin scowled.

"Easy, Viper, let's not get territorial," Flipper said, grinning.

But he did feel territorial, Gavin thought. He figured it was all a part of being in love. He still wasn't sure what to do with his feelings. He didn't want to get caught up in a woman like his dad had done. He didn't want to ask her to give up her career to wait out here on the ranch through all his missions. He didn't want a repeat of what had happened with his mom.

Pushing all that aside, he said, "Gramma Mel got back from her trip a few days ago and she prepared rooms for you guys at the main house."

"Yes!" Bane said, pumping his fist in the air. "We'll get to eat her mouthwatering biscuits for breakfast."

Gavin shook his head. He had to admit he'd missed these guys.

"So, are you going to tell Layla how you feel about her, Viper?"

Instead of answering Bane's question Gavin stared into his beer bottle and shook his head. "Won't do any good. She doesn't feel the same way."

"How do you know?" Mac asked, taking a sip of his own beer. "Women like to hear stuff like that. And often."

Coop and Flipper, Gavin noticed, were keeping their mouths shut. His admission that he'd fallen in love had shocked them into silence. The five of them were sprawled in the living room of the party house. Layla was at the main house assisting Gramma Mel with dinner. Gavin figured his grandmother would go all out and prepare a feast. She'd been happy to see his friends and they'd been happy to see her. Of course Bane would be getting those biscuits for breakfast in the morning. Mac had put in his order for an apple pie and both Coop and Flipper requested peach cobbler.

"So who do you think is trying to sabotage the dig?" Flipper asked, obviously trying to change the subject to one he and Coop could take part in. Gavin was glad to leave the topic of his love life behind.

"Don't have a clue but I intend to find out," Gavin said. "I thought it was someone connected to the university, but now I'm not sure."

"Sounds like someone doesn't want anyone digging in the south pasture, Viper," Coop said, standing, stretching out his limbs. "You all know I'm a suspicious bastard by nature. I can smell a cover-up a mile away."

Mac leaned forward in his chair. "You think someone is covering up something?"

"Possibly," Coop said. He glanced over at Gavin. "Other than Caldwell, how well do you know the men who work for you?"

Gavin shrugged. "Most have worked here for years, some even during my dad's time. There are two new guys we brought on last year." He recalled both were single, and he specifically remembered that one of them had shared Tammy's bed.

"What if someone knows for certain the loot is buried around here, heard about the dig and doesn't want anyone else to find it before they do?" Flipper suggested.

Gavin nodded. That possibility had crossed his mind, as well. He knew these four men. In addition to helping with the dig, they intended to solve the mystery of who'd removed the marker and burned down the barn. So far, the sheriff hadn't found anything other than those footprints.

Gavin had mentioned the prints to his friends. "Um, that gives us something to go on," Mac said pensively.

"We start digging in the morning," Gavin said, leaning back in his chair. "Whoever doesn't want us to will either try to stop us or will hope whatever they don't want us to find is kept hidden."

Later that night, after making love to Layla, Gavin pulled her tighter into his arms as he tried to bring his breathing under control. She had ridden him again. She was getting too good at it. He was convinced the woman was trying to kill him.

"I like your friends, Gavin."

He decided not to tell her that they liked her, as well. They had joked with her at dinner and Bane had even told her about his wife, Crystal, who, like Layla, had gotten her PhD at an early age.

"I'm glad you like them."

Dinner had been a grand affair. Not only had his grandmother cooked enough food for his friends and Layla's students, she'd invited Caldwell and his men to stop by for a plate. Several of their neighbors who'd heard about the fire stopped by to make sure all was well. Gramma Mel had sent them home with boxed dinners.

"Are you worried about the dig tomorrow?" he asked Layla.

She snuggled closer to him. "Sort of. I want to make sure my students stay safe."

"They will. I'm glad Gramma Mel insisted everyone stay at the main house. She has plenty of room and loves all the company."

"I'm glad she made the offer. Without the university footing the bill, my students couldn't afford to stay at the hotel any longer. But there's plenty of room here," she said, smiling.

"No way anyone is staying at the party house but us. This is our special place. I like coming here every night." No matter how late he worked out on the ranch, he liked coming back here to Layla. Before he parked his truck he would hear her playing her harmonica and the sound would lure him to her. He didn't want to think about how involved they were getting.

Layla lifted her head and looked up at him. "Has your grandmother asked you anything about us?"

He smiled. "She didn't have to. I think it's pretty obvious we have something going on. She's fine with it. We're adults."

What Gavin decided not to say was that his grandmother hadn't needed to ask anything because he'd told her his true feelings for Layla—and about his doubts that it would go anywhere long-term. Needless to say Gramma Mel hadn't been surprised.

"Besides, she has her hands full with Caldwell now that she's back. They've been apart for a week."

Layla lifted an arched brow. "Caldwell?"

Gavin smiled. "Yes, Caldwell. Don't tell me you haven't picked up on what's between them."

Layla shook her head. "No, I hadn't. But you have?"

"Yes, for years. He's a widower and she's a widow. Never understood why they preferred being so discreet. I guess they like their privacy.

"Since the dig starts early in the morning I guess we need to get to sleep," Gavin said, but he wasn't very convincing, even to his own ears.

"Um, I have other ideas," she said, moving on top of him again. "I like riding you."

Gavin grinned. He definitely liked Layla riding him. More than ever, he was convinced the woman was trying to kill him. But he would enjoy every minute until the end.

* * *

Hours later, the ringing of his cell phone woke Gavin. He immediately grabbed it when he recognized the ring tone. "Coop?"

"Yeah, Viper, it's me. We couldn't sleep so we thought we'd set a trap."

Gavin sat up in bed as knots tightened in his stomach. Layla had awakened as well and quickly sat up beside him. Drawing in a deep breath, he asked, "And?"

"And I think you need to get here. I've already called the sheriff. We're here at the shack and we got our man."

Sixteen

Gavin made it to the shack in record time, but he wasn't surprised to see several vehicles already there, including the sheriff's. Roy must have been in the area.

With Layla walking quickly by his side, he moved toward the shack but stopped when the door opened and his grandmother stepped out. Her crestfallen features and the tears in her eyes made him pause. *What the hell…?*

He looked past her to Caldwell, who had his grandmother's hand tucked securely in his. The older man shook his head sadly. Gavin felt Layla move closer to his side and he placed his hand in hers.

"I'm taking your grandmother to my place," Caldwell said. "That's where she'll be. You need to go on in now. He's already confessed."

Gavin frowned. *He who? And why was his grandmother crying?* Tightening his grip on Layla's hand, he entered the shack.

Everyone looked up when he and Layla walked in. Roy

and Gavin's four SEAL friends. Was he imagining things or were the five looking at him strangely? A funny feeling settled in his gut. Stepping into the room, he glanced around. "Okay, guys. What's going on? Where is he?"

The group shifted and he saw the man seated in a chair with his hands handcuffed behind his back. Gavin shook his head as if to clear his brain. "Mr. Lott?" he said in shock.

Sherman Lott couldn't even look at him. Gavin shook his head again and looked over at his friends. "There must be some mistake. Mr. Lott has been our neighbor for years. He was a friend of Dad's. He—"

"I was never a friend of your father's!" Lott all but screamed. "Gavin Jr. always got anything he wanted. He was the town's hero in high school. I could never compete. Then he became a SEAL and was a war hero, and I couldn't compete there, either. He got all the girls. After my leg got banged up that time when a horse threw me, the women around here wouldn't give me the time of day."

Gavin stared at the man who was now glaring back at him with cold and hate-filled eyes. Gavin let go of Layla's hand. Evidently he had misunderstood this man's relationship with his father all these years. "Okay, so there was a rivalry between you and Dad, and he wasn't your friend. What does that have to do with you sabotaging a dig on my property?"

Instead of answering, Lott shifted his gaze from Gavin to Layla. "I removed that marker so you'd forget where you were supposed to dig, but that didn't stop you. I burned that damn barn down and that didn't stop you, either. You were determined to dig anyway."

"Why didn't you want her to dig, Mr. Lott?" Gavin asked.

The man didn't answer. He looked away as if ignoring the question.

Gavin looked over at his friends. "Would any of you care to explain just what the hell is going on? Why didn't Lott want Layla's team to dig up buried treasure?"

Roy cleared his throat and said in a somber voice, "It wasn't the buried treasure he was concerned with anyone finding, Gavin."

Gavin frowned. Now he was even more confused. "Then what was it?"

The room quieted and he felt Layla pressing her body closer to his. Then she again placed her hand in his. When no one answered, Lott hollered out, "Your mother! I didn't want you to find your mother's body."

Layla felt weak in the knees and wondered how Gavin could still be standing. His friends evidently wondered the same thing as Bane and Coop crossed the room to flank Gavin's other side. Suddenly, she realized they hadn't done so to keep Gavin steady on his feet. They'd moved to intercede if Gavin took a mind to kill Sherman Lott.

"You refused an attorney, Mr. Lott," Roy said angrily. "Like I told you before, any confession you make will hold up in court."

Layla saw Flipper hold up his phone, letting everyone know he was recording everything. Gavin moved forward, and she, Bane and Coop fell in step. It was apparent the shock of what Lott had said had worn off.

"What do you mean 'my mother's body'?" Gavin asked, standing less than five feet from Lott.

Layla thought she actually saw regret fill Mr. Lott's eyes when he said, "I didn't mean to kill her. Honest. It was an accident."

Gavin drew in a breath so deep, it seemed the room rattled from the effect. She felt it. She thought everybody in the room felt it. "You killed my mother?" he asked in an incredulous voice. "But how? She left here."

The man shook his head. "No, she didn't. She never left. I came across her one day with a flat tire. Said she'd planned on going away for a while but changed her mind and turned around before even making it to town. She missed you and your dad too much to go anywhere. She was on her way back home. Had made it to the main road to the Silver Spurs when her tire went flat. I offered to help. She was pretty. She smelled good. I thought she was too good for your dad. He didn't deserve her. What man would leave a young wife who looked like her all alone to go play soldier?"

The man paused. "I told her as much. I must have made her nervous by what I said. By the way I was looking at her and all. And then I don't know what happened but I tried to touch her. She slapped me and I got mad. I slapped her back. I admit to hitting her several more times. She managed to get away and she ran from me. That made me angry. I ran after her and she fell and hit her head."

"And you didn't go get help?" Gavin asked in a voice that was as hard as steel.

"No!" Lott snapped. "Too late. Blood was everywhere. I knew she was dead. Besides, had she lived she would have told everyone what I tried to do. So I dug a hole and buried her."

Layla could almost see steam coming out of Gavin's ears. He was breathing deeply. The hand holding hers tightened in fury.

"What about the car?" Roy asked. Maybe the sheriff figured the best thing to do was keep the conversation going. Otherwise the deathly silence might put crazy ideas into Gavin's head. Like crossing the room and breaking Sherman Lott's neck with his bare hands.

"I drove the car into my lake," Lott said.

"You bastard!" Gavin roared. He would have moved closer but Bane and Coop blocked him. "You buried my mother in a hole not knowing if she was alive or dead? And then you drove her car into the lake?"

Lott had the nerve to glare at Gavin. "Why do you think I wouldn't let anyone swim or fish in my lake? Why I kept it off-limits to you or anyone? Especially to you. I knew how well you could swim and figured one day you might dive too far down and see the car."

Layla saw fierce rage on Gavin's face and she felt it in his entire body. The thought of him being *that* enraged scared her. She glanced over at Bane and Coop. They looked just as enraged as Gavin.

Coop then said in a menacingly calm voice, speaking directly to Gavin but not taking his eyes off Lott. "Now you know why he tried keeping anyone from digging in the south pasture, Viper. Let Roy take him in."

"No!" Gavin roared. "That bastard killed my mother."

"We know," Bane said in a chilling tone, giving Lott one hell of a lethal stare. "We all heard. And although we want to get a damn machete and chop his ass into little pieces, we won't. Let the law take care of him, Viper. In the end he's going to get exactly what he deserves."

The room got quiet and all eyes shifted to Gavin. Even Lott looked petrified upon seeing the deadly glint in Gavin's eyes. There was no doubt in Layla's mind that everyone in that room remembered that, when he needed to be, Gavin Blake could become a killing machine.

Then suddenly Gavin pulled his hand free of hers, shoved both of his hands into the pockets of his jeans and began slowly backing up, not taking his eyes off Lott. It was as if he was trying to pull himself together. As if he knew that staying in that room with Lott one more second meant he would lose control and do the man bodily harm. Gavin kept backing up until his back touched the door. He turned to open it and then stopped. He paused before turning back around.

Layla held her breath, not knowing what Gavin intended to do next. From the tension in the room, she knew his SEAL friends were poised, anticipating his next move. Then his gaze shifted from Lott to her. She saw both pain and anger in his features and her heart hurt for him. The man she loved. She wanted to think he needed her, but would he shut her out of the emotions he was feeling?

The room was deathly still as he continued to stare at her. Then he moved forward…toward her. When he stood right in front of her, he took her hand in his again. Then, without saying a single word, he led her out the door.

Seventeen

Gavin wanted to pull his truck to the side of the road and catch his breath. But he couldn't. Something propelled him to keep driving until he reached the party house. He needed Layla as much as he needed to breathe. She wasn't saying anything. Just sitting in the bench seat beside him and staring straight ahead. It was as if she knew he needed complete silence. His mind was in a state of shock and he was fighting to keep control. Fearful that at any moment he might lose it.

Every time he thought about what Lott had confessed to doing, his mind would spin. Become filled with deadly thoughts and tempt him to turn the truck around and go back to the shack and beat the hell out of the man. How could anyone do what Lott had done and live with himself all these years? And to think no one had suspected a thing until Layla had shown up wanting to dig on their property.

Gavin released a deep breath when he turned into the

driveway. Moments later he brought the truck to a stop beside Layla's rental car. Then he was out of the vehicle and moving to the passenger side of the truck. He was there when she opened the door.

Sweeping her into his arms, he headed for the porch, taking the steps two at a time. Grateful that in their rush to leave they'd left the door unlocked, he pushed it open and went inside. Barely taking time to close it behind him, he put Layla on her feet and began ripping off his clothes. She followed his lead and quickly removed hers.

He needed to be inside her. Now.

Taking hold of her waist, he lifted her up and released a throaty growl while pressing her body against the door, spreading her legs wide in the process. Then he was at her entrance, filled with an adrenaline high so potent he could feel blood rushing through his veins, especially the thick ones at the head of his shaft. Desire, as intense as it could get, became a throbbing need pulsating within him.

He thrust hard into her. Over and over again. Needing the release that only her body could give him. Leaning in, he captured her lips with his as sensations, too overpowering to be controlled, rammed through him. When she wrapped her legs around him, she propelled him to make his strokes harder and longer.

Their kiss was so sexually charged he wasn't sure how much longer he could last. He was being robbed of any logical thought except becoming a part of this woman's body. This woman, who had come to mean so much to him. This woman, who made him feel things he'd never felt before with anyone else.

And when she tore her mouth away from his just seconds before her body detonated, her spiraling climax triggered his own and he stroked her with hard and steady thrusts. He hollered her name, drowning in emotions so powerful they seemed to rock his world. A world that a short while ago had been torn apart. He couldn't stop his heart from racing at the magnitude of what he felt. At the magnitude of all he desired.

He knew then that if he'd had any doubt before re-garding what Layla had come to mean to him, there was none now.

"Sorry. I should not have taken you that way. But I needed you so damn much, Layla."

They lay together in bed. After making love against the door, Gavin had picked her up and carried her into the bedroom. Then they'd slid beneath the covers and he had held her. She had held him. Layla knew that sleep wasn't an option.

She snuggled closer, needing his heat. Needing a re-minder of how much she had been desired. "No apology needed. I liked it."

"I was rough."

"You were good as usual." He had needed her, just like he'd said. Layla had felt that need with every stroke.

"I lost control," he admitted in a low voice. "That's never happened to me before. Hell, Layla, I didn't even take time to put on a condom."

She'd noticed. Had exhilarated in the feeling of being skin to skin with him. Had loved the moment he had blasted off inside of her. The feel of his hot release had felt so right. How could she tell him that? But she knew she had to.

She lifted her face from his chest, met the dark eyes staring down at her. "I liked the feel of you inside me with-out a condom, Gavin. And don't worry about me getting pregnant. Although I was never sexually active, I decided to get the birth control implant anyway. Better to be safe than sorry. I didn't have to think about it, not like the pill where you have to remember to take one every day." She paused. "And I'm healthy so you don't have to worry about me giving you anything."

He shifted their positions in bed, slipping his arms around her and holding her close. "I'm healthy, too, and you don't have to worry about me giving you anything, either."

He then cupped her chin. "Although I didn't like being rough with you, I enjoyed making love to you without a condom, too."

And then he didn't say anything and she didn't, either. She figured he needed the silence. But when it stretched for what she thought was too long, she moved to lie on top of him and stared into the face she loved so much.

"Talk to me, Gavin. Tell me what you're feeling."

A part of her wondered what right she had to stick her nose into his business, to assume he wanted to tell her anything. But another part of her knew she couldn't let him withdraw. Just like he'd needed her physically, she wanted him to need her emotionally, as well.

She knew his eyes well. Just as well as she knew the shape of his mouth and the fullness of those lips that had kissed her earlier. He would try to fight her on this but she wouldn't let him. He'd been by himself this way for so long she figured it was hard for him to allow another person into his space. Especially a woman. But she had news for him. She wasn't just any woman. She was the woman who loved him.

And for some reason, although he'd never given her reason to say the words, a part of her believed he knew how she felt. A part of her wanted to believe that he knew she wouldn't share her body with just anyone. This wasn't just an excavation fling for her. It was more. But maybe he didn't know. Men had a tendency to be dense when it came to the I-love-you stuff.

"For a minute I felt like a loose cannon, Layla," he

said, interrupting her thoughts. "So out of control. I could have snapped and killed Lott with my bare hands. It would have given me pleasure to hear the sound of his neck breaking."

His words, spoken with deep emotion, invaded her mind. She had felt his anger and she'd seen how he'd managed to hold it in check after hearing everything the man had said. Of course the sheriff had been there to stop Gavin from taking matters into his own hands. And his SEAL teammates had been there, too, although she wasn't sure if they would have stopped him or helped him.

"But now you know the truth, Gavin. Your mother never left you and your dad, after all. She's been here all this time. Here on the Silver Spurs."

She watched his eyes flash with confusion. She explained further. "You remember when you told me how the south pasture was your favorite area and your father's, as well. How the two of you would often camp out there. How you loved the feel of sleeping under the stars?"

"Yes."

"I want to think that although the two of you didn't know it, the reason that area meant so much was because your mom was there. She was *there*, Gavin, and when you were there, without knowing it, you were close to her."

She saw the moment when her words sank in. Something broke within him. His eyes might not have been expressive to others but they were expressive to her. Without saying anything, he cupped the back of her neck and brought her mouth down to his. Their tongues tangled in a mating so intense that when he finally released her mouth, she felt light-headed and breathless.

Layla was glad she had given him something to think about. But she knew he must still feel guilty over what he'd believed all these years—that his mother had deserted him and his father. His next words proved her right.

"But I didn't know, Layla. I thought she had gone. I thought she was living another life somewhere without us. I thought—"

She placed a finger to his lips. "What you thought was understandable. You were only a child when she disappeared. But your dad knew his wife. He knew their love. He always believed she would come back. And she did. In fact, she never left. She's been here for the two of you the entire time. And I know she was proud of your dad and was just as proud of you. The man you've become."

He pulled her close, buried his face in her neck. And she held him. Held him tight and near her heart. A part of her wanted to tell him now how much she loved him, but she knew it wasn't the time. That admission would come later. For now this was what he needed. To know she was here and that he wasn't alone.

Bane's ringtone woke Gavin and he glanced out the window as he sat up. It was daybreak. "Yes, Bane?" He nodded. "We're on our way."

When he clicked off the phone, he said, "Let's get dressed. Both your team and mine are ready. Now they have two treasures to find."

A short while later, Gavin pulled his truck to a stop in front of what Layla knew should have been the excavation site. Instead it resembled a crime scene with yellow tape marking the area. Upon hearing the sound of the truck, everyone turned their way. A blanket of snow covered the hillside and forecasters predicted even heavier snow by the weekend. They would need to work quickly.

Layla saw her students standing in a huddle. They'd probably heard what was going on and were trying to figure out how they'd slept through it all. She also saw Ms. Melody standing close to Caldwell, the man's arms wrapped protectively around her. Nothing discreet there.

If anyone hadn't realized they were a couple before, they sure knew it now.

Roy was talking on the phone and Gavin's teammates stood next to the digging equipment. She wondered if they'd gotten any sleep, although they looked wide-awake and ready for any action that might come their way.

She'd been so busy observing everyone that she'd failed to notice that Gavin had gotten out of the truck until he was opening the passenger door. He leaned over her to un-snap her seat belt and then effortlessly lifted her out of her seat. "Thanks," she said, when he'd placed her on her feet.

"Don't mention it."

Taking her hand, he walked to where the others were standing. His grandmother left her place by Caldwell's side and walked over to Gavin. He released his hold on Layla's hand and pulled Ms. Melody into a big hug. Giving the two some privacy, Layla joined her students. She figured they would have a lot of questions.

After talking to her team, she returned to Gavin and his teammates. Coop explained how they'd fingered Sherman Lott as the bad guy. "After you told us about the footprint and how it was apparent more pressure was being placed on one foot than the other, we knew we were looking for someone with a leg injury or some kind of impairment and who was wearing worn shoes. When we saw Lott's shoes and saw him rubbing his leg more than once, I got suspicious. I offered him my chair so he wouldn't have to stand. I told him that I noticed his leg seemed to be bothering him. That's when he said it occasionally did and was the result of a horse riding accident years ago."

Coop then nodded for Bane to continue.

"Last night after everyone had gone to bed," Bane said, taking up the tale. "Mac and I decided to go to Lott's ranch and snoop around, to see if we could find the kerosene can. Imagine our surprise when we got there and saw him loading up a kerosene can onto his truck, with plans to head back over to your place to burn down the shack. We called Coop and told him to contact you and to call the sheriff. Lott was caught red-handed about to pour kerosene around the shack to torch it."

Roy approached with an angry look on his face. "What's wrong, Roy?" Gavin asked.

"One of the disadvantages of a small town is not having manpower when you need it," Roy said, drawing in a deep breath. "I talked to the sheriff in Palmdale and he said it would be four to five days before their dive team could get here."

Gavin nodded as if he wasn't concerned with that news. "Is there any reason we can't start digging?" he asked.

Roy frowned. "Yes, there's a reason. This is a crime scene."

Gavin shook his head. "Technically it's not. Although I believe everything Lott said, until I find my mother's body there's no proof a crime has been committed. Besides, I'd rather be the one to find her, Roy. And those students over there are entitled to their treasure hunt."

Roy didn't say anything for a minute and then nodded. "Okay, but I will stay here to help and step in if any evidence is found."

"Absolutely," Gavin assured him.

Roy drew in a deep breath and ordered one of his deputies to remove the yellow crime scene tape.

Less than an hour later, the remains of Jamie Blake were found. And within twenty feet of where she'd been buried, a strongbox filled with gold pieces—Jesse James's loot—was also recovered.

Deciding not to wait on the dive team from Palmdale, Flipper had jumped into Lott's lake without any diving gear. When he hadn't resurfaced in five minutes, Roy became worried. Gavin and his other teammates had not. They explained that although the water was icy cold and Flipper had been under longer than normal, Flipper was far from ordinary. They were proven right when a short while later Flipper resurfaced with the license plate he had removed from the car. The license plate was identified as that registered to Gavin and Jamie Blake.

The charges against Sherman Lott were changed from suspicion of murder to murder.

Eighteen

Layla stood at the window. It was snowing and what had begun that morning as small flakes was now huge and covering the earth in a white blanket. Four days had passed since the dig, and activities on the Silver Spurs were returning to normal. Once Gavin's mother's remains had been unearthed, the town's coroner had been called and the yellow tape had been reerected. But not before Jesse James's strongbox filled with gold bars had been uncovered.

The Silver Spurs became the focus of two big news stories—a decades-old murder and the first recorded discovery of Jesse James's loot in the state of Missouri. No-trespassing signs had been posted when the media had converged on the ranch.

Gavin had given his one and only statement regarding the recovery of his mother's remains. "I am glad the truth about my mother's disappearance was discovered and I hope Sherman Lott rots in hell."

A news conference had been held regarding the discovery of Jesse James's loot, which was making international news. Dr. Clayburn arrived in town and tried to claim the university was associated with the dig. Layla refuted his statement since she had documentation in the form of an email from both Dr. Clayburn and the president of the university advising of her termination prior to the dig. The following day, the two men were in even more hot water when photographs surfaced of the two of them involved in illicit affairs with female students. Not surprisingly, Tammy was in many of the photographs, arriving and leaving various hotels with both men.

Layla didn't have to guess where the photographs had come from. Apparently Donnell and some of the other students had exposed the sordid activities. Within twenty-four hours of the photographs being splashed across the front page of the *Seattle Times* and making the national news, the two men, along with a few other faculty members, had turned in their resignations.

Donnell, Wendy and Marsha had joined Layla at the news conference and were acknowledged for their participation on the dig. The Missouri Archaeological Society had authenticated the loot as that stolen by Jesse James from the Tinsel Bank.

Already offers of employment from numerous universities had arrived for Layla, in addition to offers of book deals and television interviews. Yesterday she'd received a call from her grandmother and one from her parents. She had been surprised when her parents told her how proud they were of her. They'd even said she'd done the right thing by following her own dream and not theirs. They invited her to spend the holidays with them in DC.

She drew in a deep breath and moved away from the window to sit on the bed she'd just left a few moments earlier. She had awakened to find Gavin gone. He must have left to check on the ranch with his men. Even with the no-trespassing signs clearly posted, a couple of reporters and their camera crews had encroached on the property only to have Gavin's men run them off again.

The coroner had released his mother's remains and yesterday morning a private memorial service had been held. Jamie Blake had been reburied beside her husband in the family cemetery. Layla had stood beside Gavin along with his grandmother, Caldwell and Gavin's team-mates. Even his commanding officer had flown in to attend the service.

After dinner, Gavin's teammates left to return to their various homes, but not before each one had given her a huge hug and told her how glad they'd been to meet her. She had gotten to know the four well and could see why they and Gavin shared such close relationships. Bane, Coop, Flipper and Mac were swell guys who were fiercely loyal to each other. She couldn't thank them enough for their part in recovering Jesse James's loot.

Now that the dig was over, Layla could feel Gavin withdrawing from her. She had tried ignoring it but she knew something was bothering him. She thought it was related to his mother but, to be totally honest, she wasn't sure.

There was no reason for her to remain on the ranch any longer and she had mentioned that she would be leaving in a couple of days to return to Seattle. She had hoped he would ask her to stay but he hadn't. Instead he'd merely nodded and hadn't said anything else about it. Was that his way of letting her know she had outstayed her welcome?

The thought that he wanted her to leave his ranch had tears welling up in her eyes. She'd known when she fell in love with him that there was a big chance he wouldn't love her back. So why was the thought that he didn't break-ing her heart?

The time they had spent together on the Silver Spurs had been special but now she had to move on.

Gavin placed his coffee cup on the table, stared at his grandmother and then asked, "What did you just say?"

Melody Blake smiled brightly. "You heard me right, Gavin. Caldwell asked me to marry him. This was his third time asking and I finally said yes. We don't want to make a big fuss about it and Reverend Pollock agreed to perform the ceremony next weekend. I'll be moving into Caldwell's place afterward."

Gavin didn't say anything for a long moment. He was happy for his grandmother and Caldwell. It was about time. "Congratulations. I'm happy for you, Gramma Mel. Caldwell is a good man and I believe the two of you will be happy together."

"Thank you. What about you? What are your plans regarding Layla?"

He lifted his coffee cup and took a sip before saying, "What makes you think I have any?"

His grandmother frowned. "Don't try pretending with me, Gavin Timothy Blake III. You love Layla. You've admitted as much. I would think you'd want to take the next step."

Yes, he had admitted it to her and he didn't regret doing so. "Sometimes taking the next step isn't always possible."

"Why not? I'd think you'd want something permanent between the two of you."

He shook his head. "Layla and I are very different. Dad took Mom out of a big city and brought her here and she was miserable. Layla is from Seattle. She'd be just as unhappy and miserable here as Mom was."

"Have you talked to Layla about it? Have you asked her how she feels?"

"No."

"Then maybe you should. You're basing your opinions on assumptions. I know for a fact Layla loves the Silver Spurs. She said as much."

"But that doesn't mean she loves me. If she doesn't love me, then there's nothing to hold her here. She's gotten a lot of job offers from a number of big universities, including Harvard. All we have in Cornerstone is a small college. Why would she settle for that?"

"Well, I think you'll be making a big mistake if you don't talk to her about it, tell her how you feel. Let her decide what she wants to do. You might discover that she loves you as much as you love her."

An hour or so later, Gavin entered the party house. He removed his hat and shook off the snow from his jacket before hanging both items on the rack.

The first thing he noticed as he headed for the kitchen was that the curtains were still closed. Everything was just as he'd left it at daybreak, which meant Layla hadn't gotten up yet. Placing the box containing the breakfast his grandmother had prepared on the table, he moved down the hallway to the bedroom. Opening the door, he stuck his head inside and saw Layla curled up in bed still sleeping.

The bad weather had pretty much dictated that everyone stay inside. He knew his men had a card game going and he could certainly join them. But he much preferred staying here and joining Layla, right in that bed. What if Gramma Mel was right? What if Layla wanted to stay on the Silver Spurs with him? Would it be fair to ask her to stay when a call from his commanding officer meant he would drop everything for a covert operation? Would she want that?

He sat in a chair and removed his shoes and socks before standing to take off the rest of his clothes. No matter the temperature, he preferred sleeping in the nude, something he couldn't do while away on missions.

Crossing the room, Gavin slid into bed with Layla and pulled her into his arms, to warm his body as well as his heart.

Layla thought she was dreaming when she felt a hot and husky whisper against her ear. It took a moment to open her eyes and gaze into a pair of sexy dark ones staring back at her. Gavin's body was pressed close to hers. It was warm, even hot in certain places, and she knew without a doubt that he was naked.

"We need to talk, Layla."

She heard the seriousness in his voice. Why did they need to talk? He was ready for her to leave. She got that. But why was he rushing her away? Did he already have another woman lined up to share his bed? The thought made her mad and she buried her face in the pillow, but not before saying, "I don't want to talk. I have nothing to say to you."

He pulled the pillow away from her, frowning. "What the hell did I do?"

"Just being a typical man. You share a bed with a woman, and then you tire of her and want her gone so you can replace her with another."

He stared at her. "You think I would do that?"

"Why wouldn't you? You're a man, aren't you? You're not tied to any woman, especially not to me. It's not like I didn't notice that reporter flirting with you."

He frowned. "What reporter?"

Layla rolled her eyes. "The one that kept putting that microphone all in your face and kept touching your shoulders every chance she got, even when she didn't have to." Layla hated that she'd said something about that. Now she sounded like a jealous hag. Just because they'd slept together a few times didn't mean she had dibs on him.

Before she could catch her next breath, he had flipped her on her back. He loomed over her and held her hands in a tight grip above her head.

"Why would I want another woman, Layla?"

That was really a silly question. "Why wouldn't you want another one?"

He stared down at her with an intensity that made a rush of desire claw through her insides. "Because you are all the woman I need. Hell, I can barely keep up with you, Layla."

Lord knows that's the truth, Gavin thought, as he felt familiar need hammer through him. Only Layla could do this to him. Make him feel so consumed with desire for her, he would go up in flames. More than once his teammates had told him to take a cold shower when just looking at Layla heated an entire room.

Gavin just stared down at her. She was wearing a nightgown, but barely. It was made of flimsy material and part of it was bunched up around her waist, leaving her bare below. Her hair was loose and tousled around her shoulders. Because of the way he was holding her hands, her breasts jutted up, firm and hard. He could see the impression of rigid nipples through the thin material of her gown.

Just that quickly, her breathing changed. He heard it and then he felt the sinfully erotic movement of her hips against him. After all the times they'd made love right here in this bed, not to mention the times they hadn't made it to the bed, didn't she know how much he wanted her? Her and no other woman? She actually thought she had a reason to be jealous of some damn reporter who couldn't keep her hands to herself?

He knew from the eyes staring back at him that his grandmother was right. Layla had no idea how he felt about her. The woman hadn't a clue. He had told her they needed to talk, and then she'd gone on the offensive. Why? Had his grandmother been right on both accounts, that Layla cared for him as much as he cared for her?

There was only one way to find out.

"Let's backtrack for a minute, Layla. Earlier I asked you why I would want another woman, and you asked why I wouldn't want one. I don't think I made myself clear enough. The main reason I don't want another woman is because I love you. I've fallen in love with you, Layla, and when a man falls in love with one woman she takes away his desire for other women. She becomes the one and only woman he wants in his life, his bed, his home, his mind and his heart. You are that woman for me."

She stared at him for a long time without saying anything. And then he saw it, the tears forming in her eyes. "But if you love me, why were you sending me away?"

He frowned. "I wasn't sending you away. The other night you told me you were going. What was I supposed to do, tell you that you couldn't go?"

She frowned back at him. "You could have told me you loved me."

"Why would I tell you that when I didn't know how you felt? Hell, I still don't know. With your credentials, you can teach anywhere. I know about all those job offers that have come in. Why would you want to stay here? My mother hated it here."

"I love you, too, Gavin, and I love it here. I fell in love with the Silver Spurs the minute I drove onto the land. There are times when I will leave to do speaking engagements and interviews. Maybe even teach a class or two for a semester. However, I will come back. You leave, don't you? To go on your covert operations. Yet you come back.

You return and step into your role of a rancher. Why can't I return and step into a similar role."

"As a rancher's wife?"

She lifted her brow. "Wife?"

He smiled down at her. "Yes, wife. You don't think you'll hang around as my live-in lover, do you? I want to marry you. I want you to one day have my children. I want you to live here on this ranch with me."

"And be here whenever the rancher returns?"

He chuckled. "That would be nice."

A smile touched her lips. "That can be arranged." She didn't say anything for a minute. "About all those offers. I don't want to decide on anything just yet. After dealing with the likes of Clayburn and Connors, I just want to chill for a minute. Possibly write a book. I'd love to take my time and do it here."

He nodded. He needed to let her know something.

Layla waited for him to speak.

"Gramma Mel told me this morning that she and Caldwell are getting married. She's moving to his place. That means you'll be here by yourself whenever I'm away. I'm supposed to report back for duty at the end of January."

"I'll be okay. I will have enough to keep me busy."

Layla wouldn't tell him yet that she wanted lots of children. She'd always wished for siblings and would make sure she had more than one child. And she didn't want to wait a long time before she began having them.

Before Gavin, she'd never thought beyond her career goals. But now she'd achieved those. With him by her side, she could have everything—success and a family and the man she loved.

"So, will you marry me?"

That question, as far as she was concerned, was a no-brainer. "Yes, Gavin, I will marry you."

He released her hands as he lowered his mouth to hers. She wrapped her arms around his muscled back.

She loved her SEAL, her rancher. For them, the best was yet to come.

Epilogue

Layla couldn't help but dab at her eyes. The vow renewal ceremony for Bane and his wife, Crystal, was simply beautiful. The words they spoke to each other in the presence of family and friends were filled with so much love that Layla couldn't help but shed tears.

Gavin had told her how Bane and Crystal had eloped as teens, and then had been separated for five years when her family had sent her away. But what Layla found so precious was how their love had survived. They had reunited a year ago and since no family members had been present for their first wedding, they'd decided to renew their vows in front of everyone.

What was doubly special was that Crystal and Bane had announced to everyone earlier that day that they were expecting a baby. Everyone could tell from the smiles on the couple's faces that a baby was something they both wanted. Gavin and the guys couldn't wait to tease Bane about impending fatherhood. Mac, who had a number of kids of his own, said he would give Bane pointers on changing diapers.

Today was officially the couple's sixth wedding anniversary and Crystal's twenty-fourth birthday. Layla thought it refreshing to find someone even younger than her with a PhD; they had a lot in common. Crystal was beautiful and Layla thought she was just the woman for Bane.

It was a lovely November day in the city of Denver. And since one of Bane's brother's had married an event planner, the home belonging to Bane's older brother Dillon, where the ceremony took place, had been decorated beautifully in colors of blue and gold. Layla had already talked to Alpha Westmoreland about planning Layla's dream wedding, which would take place in June.

"You okay, baby?" Gavin whispered before boldly using his tongue to lick away one of her tears.

"Behave, Gavin," she whispered back in a warning tone, knowing when it came to her he wouldn't behave.

She glanced around to see if anyone had noticed what he'd done. Bane certainly had a big family. There were Westmorelands everywhere. Gavin had warned her but she hadn't believed him. No wonder the locals referred to this section of Denver as Westmorcland Country. There were also some Westmorelands who lived in Atlanta, Montana and Texas. She'd even discovered Bane's cousin was married to a king in a country in the Middle East. All the Westmorelands she'd met were friendly and made her feel so welcome.

Another couple she'd met and liked right away was Bane's cousin Bailey and her husband, Walker Rafferty. They lived in Alaska. Layla hadn't wanted to keep staring at Walker but she remembered when he'd been a movie star years ago. He'd been a heartthrob then and he was definitely one today. She recalled seeing his picture on the cover of a recent issue of *Simply Irresistible* magazine. When she'd mentioned it to Bailey, the woman had chuckled and looked up at her husband adoringly before saying, "There's a story behind that. One day I will have to tell you about it."

It was good seeing Gavin's teammates again. Layla was glad to meet Mac's wife, Teri. The mother of four was simply gorgeous. Everyone planned to visit the Silver Spurs in June for Gavin and Layla's wedding. They'd agreed to spend Thanksgiving at the ranch and Christmas with her family. Ms. Melody and Caldwell had married and seemed to be very happy together.

Layla looked down at her engagement ring. It was beautiful. They had talked about Gavin giving Layla his mother's wedding set. Jamie had still been wearing the rings when her body had been unearthed. But Gavin had said he wanted Layla to have her own special rings and he would keep the rings his father had given his mother to pass on to their first son… Gavin Blake IV. She smiled at the audacity of Gavin thinking he would one day have a son to carry on the Blake name.

When the minister told Bane he could kiss his wife, everyone cheered. Bane pulled Crystal into his arms and gave her one hell of a kiss. What the couple shared was definitely special. Just as special as what Layla and Gavin shared.

Bane then leaned over and whispered something in Crystal's ear, which made her blush. Layla leaned over to Gavin. "I guess you heard that." He had told her about what his teammates dubbed as his sonic ears.

Gavin smiled. "Yes, I heard. Every single naughty word."

"The ceremony was beautiful," Layla said, fighting back more tears.

Gavin took her hand, brought it to his lips and kissed

her knuckles. "And so are you. I can't wait until the day you will officially have my name."

Layla couldn't wait, either. He'd been trying to talk her into eloping in January and having a huge wedding reception in June. He wanted them to be married before he left for this next covert operation. She was giving his suggestion some serious thought.

"And I can't wait until later, when I get you back to our hotel room," he added, whispering close to her ear.

Layla smiled as they linked hands and walked out of the church. She knew her life with her SEAL/rancher would never be boring.

* * * * *

Trent's arms were around her, his lips descending, before she could guess his intention.

Fire flashed along her nerve endings at the first touch of his hot mouth against her skin. She gasped as his lips trailed down her throat. In the space of one heartbeat, she transitioned from wary to wonderful. His teeth grazed the sensitive joining of neck and shoulder and her toes curled. He knew her weaknesses. Every single one. Obviously he intended to capitalize on her bad judgment.

So what?

It had always been like this between them. Hot. Delicious. Inescapable. She groaned, surrendering to pleasure. Why not? They were both consenting adults. She was no longer married to his brother. She'd discovered the folly in trying to create a traditional family. Failing at that, what more did she have to lose by giving in to this rush of desire? And if she convinced Trent to help her in the process, what was the harm in that?

She wanted him, needed this. Why deny it? Later she could chastise herself for this rash act.

* * *

The Black Sheep's Secret Child
is part of Mills & Boon's No.1 bestselling series,
Billionaires and Babies: Powerful men…
wrapped around their babies' little fingers.

THE BLACK SHEEP'S SECRET CHILD

BY
CAT SCHIELD

All rights reserved including the right of reproduction in whole or in part in any form. This edition is published by arrangement with Harlequin Books S.A.

This is a work of fiction. Names, characters, places, locations and incidents are purely fictional and bear no relationship to any real life individuals, living or dead, or to any actual places, business establishments, locations, events or incidents. Any resemblance is entirely coincidental.

This book is sold subject to the condition that it shall not, by way of trade or otherwise, be lent, resold, hired out or otherwise circulated without the prior consent of the publisher in any form of binding or cover other than that in which it is published and without a similar condition including this condition being imposed on the subsequent purchaser.

® and ™ are trademarks owned and used by the trademark owner and/or its licensee. Trademarks marked with ® are registered with the United Kingdom Patent Office and/or the Office for Harmonisation in the Internal Market and in other countries.

First Published in Great Britain 2016
By Mills & Boon, an imprint of HarperCollins*Publishers*
1 London Bridge Street, London, SE1 9GF

© 2016 by Catherine Schield

ISBN: 978-0-263-91879-3

51-1016

Our policy is to use papers that are natural, renewable and recyclable products and made from wood grown in sustainable forests. The logging and manufacturing processes conform to the legal environmental regulations of the country of origin.

Printed and bound in Spain
by CPI, Barcelona

Cat Schield has been reading and writing romance since high school. Although she graduated from college with a BA in business, her idea of a perfect career was writing books for Mills & Boon. And now, after winning the Romance Writers of America 2010 Golden Heart® Award for Best Contemporary Series Romance, that dream has come true. Cat lives in Minnesota with her daughter, Emily, and their Burmese cat. When she's not writing sexy, romantic stories for Mills & Boon Desire, she can be found sailing with friends on the St. Croix River, or in more exotic locales, like the Caribbean and Europe. She loves to hear from readers. Find her at www.catschield.com. Follow her on Twitter, @catschield.

For my Desirable sisters, Jules, Sarah and Andrea.
You inspire me every day with your fabulousness.

One

Savannah Caldwell bypassed the line of partygoers held in a queue by velvet ropes and headed for the burly linebacker with the crooked nose guarding the nightclub's front entrance. Club T's was only open Friday through Monday. Without a table reservation, the average wait for general admission on a Monday night was one to three hours. Savannah had no intention of standing around that long to get in to see her brother-in-law.

A driving beat poured from the club's mirror-lined doorway. At one o'clock in the morning, Club T's was in full swing, and Savannah was actively second guessing her impulse to hunt down Trent to discuss business at this unorthodox hour. But she'd been turned away from his office earlier when she'd tried to make an appointment with his assistant, and so coming here seemed the only way she could get him to acknowledge her.

A wave of melancholy caught her off guard. She'd been fixated on Trent since age eleven when she'd left Tennessee and moved to LA to live with her aunt Stacy, the Caldwell family's live-in housekeeper. At first Savannah had just wanted him to like her. As she entered high school, she'd developed a full-blown crush on him. But it wasn't until she'd moved to New York City at eighteen and began modeling that Trent finally noticed her as a woman.

When she'd married Trent's brother, Rafe, sixteen months ago, Trent had severed all contact with her. The loss had been devastating. To cope she'd buried her sadness. But suppressing her emotions had turned her into a poorly crafted replica of who she used to be. She spoke less. Dressed and acted like a matron twice her age. She'd lost all touch with the optimistic young woman who dreamed of a loving family, and a husband who adored her.

Savannah stepped up to the blond bouncer with the well-defined cheekbones. In four-inch heels, she stood six feet tall, yet the top of her head came no higher than the second button of his snug black polo with Club T's logo. Where ten minutes ago she'd been truly determined, she was suddenly awash in hesitation. Even if Savannah was comfortable with confrontation, she was no match for this man. He was accustomed to subduing intoxicated, belligerent troublemakers twice her size.

WWCD. What would Courtney do?

She drew in a breath to counteract her rising anxiety and ran through the centering exercises her acting coach had drilled into her. Playing the part of wealthy mean girl Courtney Day on a soap opera for three years had enabled Savannah to summon the demanding character at will, even two years after she'd stopped acting.

In the early days of working on the show, Savannah had struggled in a role as foreign to her as Courtney. While she'd certainly encountered enough rich, entitled and manipulative women during her years of living in the Caldwell household to draw from to create Courtney, Savannah hated the sort of conflict the socialite thrived on. Savannah would rather retreat than stick up for herself and had a hard time acting as if everyone should rush to do her bidding.

She'd landed the role because of how she'd looked in Courtney's designer clothes, with her hair and makeup done by professionals, not because she could act. Within the first two days, it was obvious she was going to be fired unless she learned to embrace Courtney's mean-girl persona. A fellow actor recommended her acting coach. Bert Shaw was tough and smart. He convinced her to live the persona 24/7 until she was more familiar with Courtney than Savannah. It had taken two weeks, but once she surrendered to Courtney's strengths, her flaws were easier to accept.

With a slow blink, Savannah wrapped herself in her alter ego once more. "I need to speak with Trent," she told the gatekeeper.

To her shock, the man nodded. The smile he gave her was surprisingly gentle for one of his imposing bulk. "Of course, Mrs. Caldwell. He said to let you right in."

Savannah wasn't sure whether to be delighted or worried that Trent had at long last made himself available after ignoring her phone calls for the last seven days. What sort of game was he playing? Knowing Trent the way she did, it could be any number of things.

"He'll be in the VIP section upstairs." The bouncer unhooked the rope from the stanchion and gestured her toward the entrance.

Courtney treated most people as if they existed only to serve her. Savannah should have sailed through without giving the bouncer another glance, but she sent him a grateful smile as she went by.

Once upon a time she might have enjoyed being here, but not tonight. Club T's catered to twentysomethings who favored short dresses that bared long tanned legs and impressive amounts of cleavage. As she eased through the press of bodies, she was feeing positively archaic.

She'd had fun taking in the LA and New York City nightlife at Trent's side. But that was before she'd entered a loveless marriage, given birth to her son and become a widow all in the space of a year and a half. Not what she'd hoped for herself.

When she thought about the girl who'd dreamed of living happily ever after, she missed her a lot. Naive and very foolish she might have been, but she'd also been brimming with optimism. Undaunted by a lonely childhood where she'd been more burden than someone's pride and joy, she'd craved a traditional family lifestyle, with a husband and children, a cozy house with a dog, and a white picket fence. Instead, she'd fallen for Trent Caldwell and picked the one man who would never make her dreams come true...

Handsome and confident, with an irresistible charm, Trent could also be difficult and moody when things didn't go his way. His family brought out the worst in him, something Savannah had often witnessed during the years she'd lived with them.

When Trent's father, Siggy, went after his younger son for his wild nature and reckless behavior, the whole house had resonated with his denigrating monologues. Siggy saw himself as the head of a dynasty and viewed Trent as the bad seed. During the seven years Savannah had lived with her aunt, it became clear that while eldest son, Rafe, could do no wrong, younger son, Trent, did nothing right.

In the aftermath of those arguments, Savannah had always gone to Trent. In him she saw reflected the loneliness and isolation that defined her situation. Believing they were kindred spirits fanned her girlish crush on him. She supposed that Trent acted the way he did because it was expected of him rather than because it was his nature. Just as she was confident that if he'd been raised by a father who'd been supportive and kind, rather than a tyrant, he would have ended up totally different.

She paused at the edge of the dance floor and searched for the stairs that would take her into the VIP section. Since Savannah had never visited Las Vegas before, she had no idea where she was going. The photographs she'd seen of Club T's didn't do the enormity of the place justice. The club occupied forty thousand square feet in Cobalt, one of the premier hotels on the Strip. In addition to the enormous dance floor inside, the club boasted a sprawling outdoor patio and pool area.

The club was owned by three men—the T's that made up the club's name. Trent Caldwell, Savannah's brother-in-law, who managed the day-to-day business, had a 50 percent stake. The other half was split between Kyle Tailor, former Cubs pitcher and part owner of the LA Dodgers as well as the boyfriend of Trent's sister, Melody, and Nate Tucker, Grammy-winning singer/songwriter, Free Fall's lead singer, producer and owner of Ugly Trout Records.

Before Savannah could start moving again, a medium-size man with brown hair snagged her arm. "Hey, there, beautiful. If you're looking for someone, here I am. Let me buy you a drink."

"No, thank you."

"Come on. One drink."

"I'm meeting someone."

"I'm sure he won't mind."

She'd had too many encounters with men like this. She didn't need a basket filled with cookies or a red cape to attract the wolves. Something beyond being blonde and pretty made her prey. And all too often she had a tendency to trust when she should question instead.

"I mind."

The bodies around them shifted, allowing Savannah to slip away without further confrontation. She angled away from the bar and the dance floor. Sheer luck allowed her to blunder in the right direction. Another mammoth guarded the VIP entrance, but he let her in without challenge. Noting the earpiece he wore, Savannah assumed he'd been warned to expect her.

She wound her way past plush, curved couches loaded with celebrities from the music industry and Hollywood. Her brother-in-law was easy to locate. She just needed to look for the most beautiful women.

Trent was completely in his element. Like an emperor accustomed to being adored, he sat on a curved couch, arms spread wide to allow the brunettes flanking him to snuggle close. Each girl had a drink in one hand and rested the other hand possessively on Trent. If they hoped to pin down this elusive bachelor, Savannah wished them luck. From the look on his face, he wasn't into either of them. Not that that would stop him from showing them a good time. And from their blatant pawing, it appeared that's what they were looking for.

Savannah stepped up to Trent's table and spoke his name. The DJ picked that second to talk over the loud music and drowned out her voice. Nevertheless, whether he heard his name or just noticed her awkwardly standing there, Trent turned his attention to her.

As his eyes met hers, longing slammed into her, as inescapable as it was four years ago when he'd kissed her for the first time. Strong emotions bumped up her heart rate and released butterflies in her stomach. Squaring her shoulders, she ignored her body's disloyalty. She couldn't let Trent get to her. She'd come to Las Vegas with a business proposition and that's what she needed to focus on.

"Savannah, what a surprise." A welcoming smile curved

his lips, but to someone who'd seen Trent unguarded and truly happy, it looked fake. "Come join us."

She shook her head. "I'm not here to party."

He mimed that he couldn't hear her and waved her closer. Savannah held her ground, not relishing the idea of becoming one of his groupies. If she'd felt out of place downstairs, that was nothing compared to the humiliation of standing on display for Trent's fashion-forward friends. Pity, boredom and mockery made up their expressions as they judged her.

In the year and a half since she and Rafe had become a couple, she'd adapted to his preferred style. Her husband had dictated that she wear her hair sleek and fill her closet with elegant clothes worthy of a CEO's wife. Tonight, she'd been thinking along the lines of business rather than clubbing when she'd left the suite wearing a sheath of red satin and sheer checkerboard squares over a nude lining. It covered her from collarbone to knee and made her stand out from the crowd in the worst way possible.

"I need to speak to you." As much as she hated raising her voice, the loud dance music required her to shout to be heard.

"Just one drink." He signaled the waitress. "One drink and we can talk right here."

She was not going to go sit beside Trent and pretend that the way he'd treated her this last year and a half hadn't bothered her. Because it had. She'd been angry with Trent for refusing to even consider making a commitment to her and tormented by guilt for marrying his brother for all the wrong reasons.

Savannah crossed her arms over her chest. She might have to beg for Trent's help, but she wouldn't let him see her humiliation at needing to do so.

"I'd prefer our conversation to be a private one."

She'd never negotiated with Trent and won. The man

never seemed to care whether or not he got what he wanted. He was always ready to walk away from the bargaining table, which gave him an advantage.

They stared at each other—each determined to have their way—until the music and the lights faded to insignificance in the background. Trent's gaze toured her body with lazy intensity as he waited for her to surrender to his will. It bothered Savannah how much she wanted to give in to him.

His power over her hadn't faded one bit. Her thoughts were jumbled as she was overwhelmed by the urge to taste his sexy mouth and feel his hands roaming all over her. Their lovemaking had always been hot and satisfying. He'd spent an exceptional amount of time getting to know her body's every sensitive spot. An ache blossomed inside her. It had been nineteen long months since she'd last been with him, and her every nerve was on fire with anticipation.

Coming here tonight had been a bad idea. She should have held out for a civilized meeting in his office. Instead, she was filled with a recklessness inspired by the dance music's heavy beat and her own dangerous desire.

She had to go.

As a child Savannah had coped with her father's temper and her grandmother's frequent illnesses by hiding somewhere she felt safe. By the time she'd become a teenager, the habit of fleeing difficult situations was fully ingrained in her psyche. Retreat and regroup. Now that she was a mother, she'd grown better at standing her ground, but when overly stressed she fell back on what was familiar. Which explained why she turned away from Trent and headed for the exit.

The club seemed busier than it had five minutes earlier. Savannah wormed through the press of undulating bodies, familiar tightness building in her chest. The ever-changing lights and the hammering beat of the music combined to batter her senses. Her legs shook as she wound her way past the dance floor, and she wrenched her ankle during an awkward sidestep. Her head began to spin. Pressure built until she wanted to scream. She had to get out of the club. But which direction was the exit?

"There you are." The man she'd escaped earlier sneaked his arm around her waist and breathed alcohol at her. Her brief encounter with Trent had stripped away her Courtney armor. Locked in her panic attack, she was vulnerable to the man's boldness. "Thought you could get away from me, didn't you?" His lips met her cheek in an untidy kiss.

"Let me go," she said, but her voice lacked energy and the man was too drunk to hear her even if she'd shouted.

"Let's dance."

"No." She tried to squirm away but found nowhere to escape as the crowd pressed in on them.

All at once a large hand landed on the man's shoulder and tightened. With a yelp, the guy set her free.

"Hey, man. What are you doing?"

The drunk might have been a wolf, but Trent was a ferocious lion. "Leave this club before I have you thrown out."

If she hadn't been so rattled, Savannah might have enjoyed the way her assailant scrambled away from Trent.

Despite the heat being generated by a thousand dancers, Savannah's skin prickled with goose bumps. The urge to turn tail and run seized her, but before the impulse worked its way into her muscles, Trent slipped his arm around her waist.

Through modeling Savannah had gained an understanding of her physical appeal. Training to become Courtney Day had shown her how to act more confident. By the time Trent had come to New York to visit his sister, Melody, at Juilliard, Savannah was no longer an insecure girl, but a confident, sensual woman he desired. And more importantly, one he could have.

Falling back into old patterns with Trent was easy and comfortable, and she didn't resist as he drew her away from the crowd. He led her to a nondescript door, used a key card to activate the electronic lock and maneuver her through.

As the door clicked shut behind them, leaving them alone in a brightly lit hallway, Trent brushed her ear with his lips. "I see you still need someone to watch over you."

Being in his debt before she'd asked for his help wasn't a successful approach. "You didn't give me the chance to handle him."

"Would you like me to fetch him back?"

Savannah fought to control a shiver, knowing that to give in was to let him know how much she appreciated being rescued. "No."

Trent smirked at her. "You said you wanted a private conversation. How private do you need it to be?"

"Somewhere we can talk uninterrupted." She glanced up and down the twenty-foot hallway, seeing no one but hearing voices and laughter from around a corner.

"My office is quiet," he said, fingers sliding along her spine in a tantalizing caress. "Unless you're afraid to be alone with me?"

She twitched as his touch sent a lance of pleasure through her. "Why would I be?"

"You're quivering." He nuzzled her hair, voice deep and intimate. "Makes me think of the last time we were alone together."

"That was almost two years ago." But already the increased agitation in her hormones signaled that the chemistry between them remained as combustible as ever. *Damn.* She hadn't counted on lust being a factor in her negotiations with Trent.

"In the past, we've had a hard time keeping our hands off each other."

"That explains why you stayed away from me. Why did you stop taking Rafe's phone calls? It really hurt him."

His blue eyes narrowed. "Ask me if I'm worried how Rafe felt. He was my older brother, yet he never once stood up for me against Siggy. Not when we were kids or when Siggy refused to bring me into the family business. Rafe was the golden child and he liked it that way. So, what? I'm supposed to forgive and forget because he has a change of heart on his deathbed?"

There it was. That chip on his shoulder. The one he'd developed in response to every slight his father had delivered. Trent had been the second son. The spare heir. The boy with eclectic musical interests and strong opinions.

She couldn't disagree with his perception of his relationship with his brother and father. She'd heard the arguments. They didn't appreciate just how brilliant he was. The only opinions Siggy Caldwell entertained were his own. Rafe had learned about the business at his father's knee, never challenging Siggy's decisions.

"Still want to talk?" Trent asked. Had he noticed something in her manner that led him to believe she regretted coming here tonight?

"Yes."

"Good. I'm dying to hear what brought you to Las Vegas."

"I need your help."

"You must be pretty desperate if you came to me." Trent scrutinized her expression for a beat before taking her by the arm and leading her down the hall. "Let's go to my office. You can tell me all about it."

As soon as Trent escorted Savannah into his office and closed the door behind them, he knew this was a bad idea. He blamed curiosity. She'd been trying to get a hold of him for a week.

Yet, he could've picked up the phone at any time and discovered what was on her mind. But he'd resisted. What had changed?

Long-buried emotions, aroused by the familiar scent of her perfume, provided the answer. His fingers itched to slide over her smooth skin. From his first sight of her in the club tonight, he'd been fighting the longing to back her against a wall and ease his mouth over her quaking body.

He released her arm and turned his back to her. Picturing her naked and moaning his brother's name reminded him why he'd been keeping his distance.

He slipped behind a wet bar that ran perpendicular to the wall of floor-to-ceiling monitors tuned to various key areas in the club. Fixing her a drink gave him something useful to do until the urge to crush her mouth beneath his abated. Trent gave himself a hard mental shake. Obviously he hadn't thought through this scenario when he'd suggested they use his office for their private conversation. Being alone with Savannah shouldn't trigger his libido. He thought he'd gotten over her the instant she'd said "I do" to his brother. Damn if he'd been wrong.

Disgusted, Trent pulled a bottle from the fridge and surveyed the label. "Champagne?" When she shook her head, he arched an eyebrow. "Aren't we celebrating?"

Her frown asked, *Celebrating what?* "You know I don't drink."

"Oh," he drawled. "I thought perhaps after being married to my brother, you might have started."

Savannah made a face at him but didn't rise to the bait. "I'll take some sparkling water if you have it."

Amused, Trent dropped ice into a glass and poured her a drink. Fixing a lime to the rim, he pushed the glass across the bar toward her. As much as he could use a scotch to settle his nerves, he refrained. Dealing with Savannah was complicated enough without a fuzzy head.

A familiar mixture of fondness and rage filled him as he watched her sip the drink.

From the moment the naive eleven-year-old with the big blue eyes had moved into the servants' quarters of his family's Beverly Hills home, he'd been drawn to her. Unlike his twelve-year-old sister, she'd exhibited none of the gawkiness of preteen girls. And her lack of street smarts had driven Trent crazy.

As a kid he'd slipped into rebellious and resentful mode pretty early. Being a troublemaker came easy. He wasn't anyone's hero. But he'd come to Savannah's rescue more times than he could count. She'd been a magnet for anyone eager to take advantage of a young girl from some backwoods town in Tennessee. To look at her you'd think she would turn to smoke if you touched her, but in fact there was supple muscle beneath her soft skin, something he'd discovered firsthand when he'd taught her a couple self-defense moves.

In some ways, she was still the same ragamuffin who'd needed protection from the mean girls in school and the boys who thought to take advantage of her naïveté. But being on her own in New York had given her a new set of skills. For one, she'd learned how to go after something she wanted. And for a while it was pretty apparent that what she'd wanted was him.

Which was why it had come as such a surprise that she'd chosen to marry his brother. Despite the years she'd spent in LA and New York, she remained a small-town girl at heart. She had no lofty dreams of fame and fortune. She'd never known stability growing up, so as an adult, Savannah craved marriage and children, a secure, safe life.

Her vision of a traditional family situation was completely foreign to Trent. His father was an ambitious tyrant who'd married late. His misogynistic behavior had driven his wife away not long after Melody was born. The prenup their mother had signed granted her nothing if she fought for custody of her children. Trent had never been surprised that she'd chosen the money.

Was it any wonder he had so little interest in marriage and family? But knowing how important it was to Savannah should've warned him to keep his distance. He might have, but she was irresistible to him.

No matter how many times he'd cautioned himself to stay away, he couldn't stop coming to her rescue. Only once had he abandoned her to trouble—the day she'd declared her intention to marry Rafe.

"Widowhood becomes you," he said. If he'd hoped to shock her, he failed.

Reproachful blue eyes fixed on him. "That's a terrible thing to say."

"Perhaps, but it doesn't stop it from being true."

Young Savannah had possessed a guilelessness that left her open for the world to read. And take advantage of. He'd expected her to be eaten alive in the cutthroat world of modeling and acting in New York City, but she'd figured out a way to survive. When he'd visited Melody during her junior year at Juilliard, he'd been checking in on Savannah, as well. At first he'd been surprised. The naive girl wasn't gone, but she'd become a little wiser. She'd also gained an air of mystery. He'd been intrigued.

He still was.

"Perhaps you should tell me why you're here, dear sister-in-law."

Her lips formed a moue of distaste at the specific emphasis he put on the last three words. Trent took no pleasure in highlighting the chasm between them, but it needed to be done.

"I have a proposition for you."

Trent had been dodging her for a week, assuming something of this sort. For sixteen months he'd been waiting for her to admit that marrying his brother had been a mistake. It irritated him that she hadn't. And now she wanted something from him.

"I'm not interested."

"You haven't even heard me out."

"We have nothing to talk about."

Her facial muscles tightened, lending her expression a determined look he'd never seen before. She'd always seemed untouched by demons that drove most people, unfazed by success or obstacles. What had changed? Marriage to his brother? Motherhood?

These were questions best left alone. Trent didn't need to venture down the rabbit hole of turbulent emotions conjured whenever he spent time with Savannah. Better to speed her on her way back to LA and be done with temptation.

"Maybe we don't have anything to talk about, but *I* have a great deal to say."

"Why don't you make an appointment with my office for some time next week." He knew he was taunting her but couldn't help himself. She'd become another in a long list of people who brought out his bad side.

"I've already been here five days and you've been avoiding me. I'm closing on the sale of my house tomorrow afternoon, so Dylan and I are leaving in the morning. I had hoped to have everything settled before we returned to LA."

Against his better judgment—because he was playing directly into her hands—Trent asked, "What exactly did you intend to have settled?"

"When Rafe died, he left his shares of West Coast Records to Dylan. That means until Dylan's eighteenth birthday, I'm in charge of the business." She shook her head. "I need help."

Now Trent was starting to see where she was going.

"You've got Gerry." Gerry Brueger had been Siggy's second in command for twenty years. Passed over for president when Siggy stepped down and installed Rafe as the head of the company, Gerry would jump at the chance to take over.

"It's not that simple. I need a CEO I can trust. Someone who gets the business and can turn things around."

"So hire someone."

"That's what I'm trying to do." She cocked her head and scowled at him.

"Me?" This was not at all what he'd expected. Trent shook his head. "Not interested."

"It's your family's company."

"It's my *father's* company." And his brother's. They'd never wanted him to be a part of it. "Besides, my father isn't going to welcome my interference." He noticed that her gaze shifted away. "Have you talked to Siggy about this?"

"It's my decision." But she sounded less confident than she'd been moments earlier.

"So you haven't mentioned any of this to Siggy?"

"He sold a majority of his shares in the business to Rafe. Dylan inherited them. Siggy isn't in control of the company anymore."

Her naïveté was showing. She might think she was in charge, but she was in for a huge battle if she thought she could bring Trent into the record company. He almost felt sorry for her.

"Sell the company back to Siggy and wash your hands of it."

"It's not that cut-and-dried." She set her untouched glass of water on a nearby table and squared her shoulders. "He won't buy back Rafe's shares, but I know he's planning to control things behind the scenes. Siggy intends for Dylan to run the company someday." Savannah paused and compressed her lips into a thin line. With a sigh, she continued, "In the meantime, I can't run it and I don't trust your father to be able to turn things around."

"Turn things around?" Trent had heard rumblings that West Coast Records was having financial problems. No surprise there—Siggy Caldwell's approach to the music industry was uninspired and his eldest son had been a chip off the old block. "What's going on?"

"I'm not exactly sure, because I've been getting the runaround from Gerry, but I think they're behind on paying royalties to their artists."

"When did this start?"

"I don't know. Shortly after we were married, Rafe confided to me that the company was struggling financially before your father retired." That had occurred three years earlier. "And after the cancer started eating away at Rafe, he wasn't making the best decisions. I'm sure things got much worse then."

Trent ignored the compulsion that demanded he step in and fix everything. "While this is all fascinating, what does any of it have to do with me?"

"The company needs you." Her big blue eyes went soft and concerned in the way that always kicked him hard in the solar plexus.

Trent's first impulse was to laugh. He never got the chance. Questions crowded in. He didn't give a damn about the company. But did *she* need him? Trent crossed his arms over his chest and regarded her through half-closed eyes. She was beautiful. Poised. But not happy. He should've felt triumphant. Instead there was a dull ache in his gut.

"You know, better than most, that isn't going to sway me. Try again."

She gazed at the blank walls that made up his office. If she was looking for some clue about how to appeal to him, she wouldn't find it there. He was a man who didn't give a damn about anything. Or that's the face he showed the world. It made it much harder for someone to hurt him if he showed no vulnerability.

"Prove to your father you're a better businessman than he is."

He should be gloating. Trent—not his father or brother—would be the one to save the struggling West Coast Records, but his only emotion was bitterness.

"He would never believe that." The great Siggy Caldwell never owned up to his mistakes. He sure as hell wouldn't admit that his pitiful excuse for a second son was a better anything. "If that's the best you have, I'm afraid I'm going to have to disappoint you."

She let the silence fill the space between them for a beat before speaking. "I need your help."

He resisted the urge to sweep her into his arms and pledge his support. She was staring at him in desperate hope, as if he was her knight in shining armor. That was the farthest thing from reality. Sure, maybe he'd helped her out a time or two in the past, but she wasn't his responsibility anymore. The time for rescuing her had ended sixteen months earlier when she'd promised to love, honor and cherish his brother.

"And just like that, you expect me to drop everything and rush to your aid?" It cost him, but he gave his words a sardonic twist and hardened his heart. "It's not going to happen."

Two

Despite all the times he'd rescued her in the past, Savannah knew she shouldn't have counted on Trent helping her. She'd committed the ultimate sin. She'd married his brother.

And now she was stuck in an untenable position. Her one-year-old son had inherited stock she couldn't sell to a third party without her father-in-law's permission. This meant as an asset it held no value for her. And because of the way the record label was hemorrhaging money, the stock would be worthless in no time.

Begging to be rescued was too humiliating and probably wouldn't work anyway. Negotiating was a much more palatable option. Once again, she channeled Courtney Day. Relaxing her shoulders, she spoke in her alter ego's confident tone.

"What can I say or do to change your mind?"

"I don't know." Something flickered in Trent's eyes. "What are you offering?"

"I have nothing to bargain with."

Cards on the table, she maintained her poker face while his gaze raked over her. Heat rose to her skin. It wasn't humiliation she felt, but desire. If confronted, he would deny that he wanted her, but the flare of his nostrils and the way his pupils dilated hinted that the chemistry between them hadn't faded.

"You have something."

Savannah shook her head, unsure if what she was picking up off him was real or wishful thinking. "Rafe burned through all our cash chasing alternative medical treatments that didn't work," she said. "After he died, I had to sell the house to pay off his debts."

And she'd come up short by a million. She'd counted on selling Rafe's shares back to Siggy for enough money to clear the debt and maybe have a little bit to start over somewhere new.

But Siggy didn't want his shares back. He wanted Rafe's son.

"The only thing of value left is Dylan's shares in the company," she continued. "But I can't touch that."

"I don't want money," Trent said.

No, of course not. He could buy West Coast Records three times over. "What do you want?"

That she was putting herself in his hands occurred to her the instant the words were past her lips. But what else could she do? Siggy was willing to clear her debt but insisted she and Dylan move in with him. Her father-in-law's opinion of her was low. He hadn't approved of his son marrying her and he'd let her know that on several occasions. The thought of living in that toxic environment made her panic.

"Why did you marry my brother?"

The question came out of nowhere, and for several seconds Savannah didn't know what to say. Discussing her marriage with Trent was fraught with too many complications. Trent would never understand or approve of what she'd done, because he couldn't understand how her circumstances had left her feeling vulnerable and alone.

"You knew what I wanted. What was the most important thing to me."

Something Trent was never going to give her—a family. They stared at each other while her unspoken answer hung between them. Speaking of her longing would open up old wounds and she couldn't bear that.

I can't give you what you want.

Her heart had shattered when he'd uttered those words two years earlier.

At last she sighed. "I wanted to be married. To have children."

"I don't understand why you chose Rafe. Was it because you were pregnant?"

Savannah noticed he didn't ask her if she'd loved his brother. Why bother when the math was obvious? Dylan had been born six months after Savannah and Rafe had promised to love, honor and cherish each other until death.

"That played into it." She'd been devastated that the man she loved couldn't give her what she wanted and terrified of raising a child on her own.

Why had she chosen Rafe? Because he'd wanted her.

"Rafe was excited about being a father. Family was important to him."

More important than she'd initially understood. And he'd been very persuasive. At the time she'd believed she could trust him. She wouldn't have married him if he'd been like Trent. But he'd never once made her doubt his desire to be a father, and he'd been over-the-moon excited that she was carrying a boy.

"Rafe and Siggy were exactly alike," Trent scoffed. "People mean no more to them than as a means to an end."

It was humiliating to know just how right Trent was about that. She'd thought Rafe was her friend. Growing up he'd been the nice one, always upbeat and well mannered. He'd never hurt Savannah's feelings when she'd tried to cheer him out of a bad mood. He'd been the one to lift her spirits.

From when they were kids, he'd known how she felt about his brother. A couple times he'd come upon her crying in the midst of teenage angst over Trent. And he'd made her feel less unwanted.

Rafe had been the one who'd encouraged her to take the modeling job in New York. And after she quit the soap opera and returned to LA, he'd been the one who'd helped her find a rental.

She'd never questioned why Rafe was so accepting about the circumstances surrounding her pregnancy. Nor had her suspicions been aroused by the fact that he'd been the one who'd handed her a box of condoms and sent her to Las Vegas to visit Trent and get him out of her system once and for all.

It wasn't until after Dylan was born, when Rafe collapsed and she discovered the illness he'd been hiding, that she'd learned how he'd tricked her. That he'd sabotaged the box of condoms. Gambled that she would get pregnant.

He'd bought into his father's notions of a dynasty. Wanted a son, but his cancer treatments had left him impotent and sterile. So he'd taken a chance and tricked her into getting pregnant by his brother.

At first she'd been shocked and appalled at being manipulated by someone she trusted. But in the end she couldn't hate a man who'd made such poor decisions with a death sentence hanging over his head.

"That last time we were together," Trent began, his voice pitched low. "Were you and Rafe already involved?"

Savannah came out of her musing to find Trent standing

within arm's reach. Closer than she'd expected. He stood
with his head cocked, his manner watchful, as if waiting for a sign from her. Suddenly she was having trouble
catching her breath.

He hadn't touched her. He showed no inclination that
he wanted to. So why was she suddenly craving his kiss?

"Does it matter?" She should back away. Put the width
of the room between them. A table. A chair. Better yet, a
door. Several corridors. A couple dozen floors.

"Not to me." His tone was light but his gaze was intense. "But my brother might have appreciated knowing
you were cheating on him with me."

"I wasn't cheating on him. With you or anyone else."

In her rush to vindicate herself in his eyes, she neglected
to remember that little matter of math. Would Trent realize that nine months after they had been together in Las
Vegas, she'd given birth to Dylan? The thought terrified
her. What if he wouldn't help her after discovering she'd
kept the truth about his son from him? It was a practical
concern, but not her bigger fear.

It hadn't taken a lot for Rafe to convince her that once
Trent learned the truth that he would still reject her and
his son.

Which is why she hadn't told him about Dylan when
she'd discovered she was pregnant. Was it cowardly of
her to hide the truth because she was assuming the worst
outcome? Of course, but nothing Trent had ever said to
her gave her reason to hope that he'd miraculously alter
his way of thinking because he was going to be a father.

"I don't want to talk about my marriage."

"Then we've run out of things to say to each other."
Trent gestured toward his office door.

"That isn't necessarily true," she countered, snatching
at something to keep the conversation rolling. If she kept
him talking, he wouldn't be able to throw her out of his

office and maybe she could get the topic back around to the record label.

"What else did you have in mind?"

"You could ask me about Murphy."

He'd gotten her the French bulldog as a Christmas present three years ago. At the time she'd thought he'd bought the cream-colored snore monster because he was starting to get ideas of taking their relationship to the next level. She'd been in heaven.

Having Trent all to herself for those two weeks had been magical. They'd snuggled on the couch and opened presents at midnight on Christmas Eve. The week leading up to New Year's, they'd walked the puppy, browsed through Chinatown and the East Village, taken in a couple Broadway shows. They'd rung in the New Year with a bottle of champagne and the most perfect lovemaking of Savannah's life.

Then, six weeks later, he'd canceled on her last minute, and she'd spent Valentine's Day crying into Murphy's soft puppy coat. She'd realized that the long-distance thing wasn't working for her and she'd decided to quit the soap opera and move back to LA.

"How is he?"

"Wonderful. He's devoted to Dylan. Follows him everywhere. Curls up with him at nap time."

"How did Rafe enjoy sharing his bed with the dog?"

Questions like these were a minefield. How did she answer? She couldn't reveal that she'd entered into a loveless marriage and had never shared a bed with her husband.

"He didn't." Which was at least true.

"I'm not surprised. Rafe was never an animal person."

Unlike Trent, who'd fostered several rescues over the years. He liked helping out—something he'd deny—but the temporary nature of providing a home for dogs who after a couple months moved on to permanent situations demonstrated his unwillingness to commit and his distaste for being tied down.

She'd been so hurt by his refusal to move their relationship forward, even though she'd known that's how he was when she'd gotten involved with him. She kept hoping that he'd change. That she'd be the one he'd fall in love with and would be unable to live without.

Instead, in her sorrow and loss, she'd let his brother manipulate her. In her heart she'd known Trent was a better man than his brother, and a small part of her had expected him to save her one more time.

Only he hadn't. And she couldn't blame him for leaving her to rot.

"I'm sorry," she murmured.

"For what?"

"It was wrong of me to get involved with Rafe."

"I've been waiting a year and a half for you to admit that."

Trent's arms were around her, his lips descending, before she could guess his intention. Fire flashed along her nerve endings at the first touch of his hot mouth against her skin. She gasped as his lips trailed down her throat. In the space of one heartbeat, she transitioned from wary to wondrous. His teeth grazed the sensitive joining of neck and shoulder and her toes curled. He knew her weaknesses. Every single one. Obviously he intended to capitalize on her bad judgment.

So what?

It had always been like this between them. Hot. Delicious. Inescapable. She groaned, surrendering to pleasure. Why not? They were both consenting adults. She was no longer married to his brother. This had nowhere to go. She'd discovered the folly in trying to create a traditional family. Failing at that, what more did she have to lose by giving in to this rush of desire? And if she convinced Trent to help her in the process, what was the harm in that?

All these thoughts flashed through her head in the instant before Trent's hand slid over her butt and pulled her pelvis into snug contact with his arousal. She fisted her hands in his hair and tugged to bring his mouth to hers. She wanted him, needed this—why deny it? Later she could chastise herself for this rash act.

Trent captured her mouth in a hot, sizzling kiss. The ache between her thighs pulsed with more urgency as his tongue plunged past her teeth. She met the thrust with ardent fervor. A growl vibrated in her throat. That they could be discovered at any second should have bothered her. On the other hand, maybe Trent had entertained enough women in here to make his staff wary of interrupting their boss.

That thought too should have disturbed her. But Savannah was beyond logic and reason.

She drew him toward the couch and pushed him onto it. He bounced a little as the cushions gave beneath him. With a sassy grin, she hiked up her skirt and climbed onto his lap. Settling her hot center against his erection caused them both to shudder. She wasn't sure when the Courtney Day persona had fallen away. What she was doing now was pure Savannah.

Breath ragged, palms gliding up her thigh, he regarded her. His guards were up. He'd tightened his lips into an unyielding line and a sharp line appeared between his strong, dark brows. Questions gathered in his eyes. Savannah rocked her hips in a sultry move that caused him to exhale sharply in a low curse.

He started to speak. She shushed him and captured his face between her hands to keep him still while she flicked her tongue against his lower lip and then pulled it between her teeth and sucked gently. Strong fingers dug into her thighs hard enough to leave bruises. She smiled as she kept up the tantalizing seduction of his mouth.

Earlier when he'd pulled her against him, she'd felt the familiar square of tin that held breath mints and a little something extra in his suit coat pocket. Now she reached for the box and slipped it free. Trent heard the familiar rattle and leaned away from her kiss.

Savannah sat up straight and held the tin between them. "I see you haven't changed your habits."

"I like being prepared."

She popped the lid and slipped a mint into her mouth. Sharp and cool, the peppermint flavor exploded on her tongue, making it tingle. "Want one?"

Eyes locked on hers, he opened his mouth and let her feed him one. While the mint dissolved, they regarded each other in silence. His gaze held challenge, but curiosity, as well. He wanted to know if she intended to get to what else the tin held. Savannah savored his anticipation. He liked being in charge. It's why he hadn't stuck around to be a part of his family's business, but had struck out on his own.

No one was going to boss around Trent Caldwell.

But Savannah had found him to be a wonderful partner in bed. For as often as he'd swept her into his passion and demanded her surrender, there had always been opportunities when he let her take the lead. Because of this, her confidence had flourished, not only with regard to her sexuality, but also in her worth as an individual.

The heavy pulse of desire between her thighs hadn't diminished one bit during this exchange. In fact, as she grew more committed to this next step, her hunger for him had only increased.

Savannah plucked out the square foil package and held it up. "Only one? You used to carry at least two." She might have sounded confident, but she wasn't. Courtney

Day might not have thought twice about a quickie with her sexy ex, but Savannah was rapidly losing her nerve.

"What makes you think I haven't used one already today?"

Trent had a healthy sexual appetite, and she wouldn't be surprised if he'd already had sex with three other women. She shouldn't care. But it hurt all the same. Several deep breaths later she'd pushed down panic and dismay. This couldn't become about what she'd had and lost. She needed a brief interlude to escape her troubles and there was no better man to rock her world than Trent.

But why was he baiting her? She could see from his flat stare that he expected her to back off.

"For a second I forgot who I was dealing with." She closed the tin with a metallic snap and tossed it aside.

Aware that he was scrutinizing her every move, she placed the wrapped condom between her teeth and set her hands to loosening his belt. Up until now she'd been doing a good job of appearing confident. But beneath Trent's unreadable gaze, she felt a tiny fizz of nervous energy dance along her spine, making her fingers clumsy. Trent made no attempt to help her. In fact he didn't move at all, except for the unsteady rise and fall of his chest.

At long last Savannah slid down his zipper and freed him. His erection sprang into her hands, eager for her attention. Overwhelmed by joy at what they were about to do, she paused for a moment, fingers coasting along his hot silken length. With a half smile she tore open the wrapper and unrolled the condom, sheathing him. His head had fallen back against the couch while his breath hissed out between clenched teeth. He squeezed his eyes shut and held perfectly still, every muscle in his body tense beneath her.

In her stylish but conservatively cut dress, Savannah might not have appeared as if she'd planned for a hot night at the club, but she'd chosen a red lace bra and thong set to wear underneath. Had she thought in her wildest dreams she would be in this position? Perhaps her subconscious had wanted this all along.

Before she could change her mind about what she was about to do, Savannah cupped Trent's erection in her palm, slid aside her thong and brought his tip into contact with her wet heat.

For the first time in several seconds Trent shifted. He cupped her butt in both hands and moved her forward and down until he was sheathed inside her. They groaned simultaneously as she came to rest, fully seated on his lap once again. Savannah put her hands on his shoulders, needing him for balance as her head began to spin.

This wasn't just sex. It had never been just sex between them. But there were no words of love or affectionate looks exchanged. This was a crazy, impulsive interlude that she desperately needed. Her goal was oblivion, and being with Trent always enabled her to forget her problems. Even when what was troubling her was Trent himself.

They rocked together in a familiar rhythm, maintaining a steady, relaxed pace.

"Take your hair down," Trent demanded, his voice an unsteady rasp.

Happy to oblige, she reached up and pulled out half a dozen pins and demolished the smooth, controlled hairstyle with a languid shake of her head. Long blond waves tumbled around her shoulders and tickled her cheeks. Trent had always loved her hair. He sank his fingers into the thick silky mass and brought her lips back to his.

Trent wasn't sure how he'd come to be on his couch buried deep inside Savannah, her tongue dancing with his in a passionate kiss, her manner every bit as wild as he remembered. Another woman might have pleaded with him for help or screamed abuse when he refused to fall in

with her plans. He'd had only the briefest suspicion that
Savannah intended to seduce him into helping her before
he rejected the idea. Her hunger for him was as all-consuming as his for her.

- That didn't make this a reunion between lovers. Not in
the traditional sense. Sixteen months of bitter silence lay
between them. Part of him didn't want to open the door to
her. The part of him that did was in charge at the moment.
Maybe what they were doing was saying goodbye. But as
her teeth nipped at his lower lip, driving him closer to orgasm, he knew this brief taste of her had only revived his
unquenchable desire.

Trent fought to make the moment last. But he was only
able to hold on until he could determine that she hovered
on the brink of a climax.

Her soft keening and the accelerated rhythm of her hips
pushed him over the edge and they came together. Heart
thundering, Trent sat perfectly still, his body drained, his
heart twisted wreckage. *Damn her.* She'd made him do
what he promised he wouldn't. He'd let her back in. His
first instinct as he labored to breathe was to kiss her long
and deep and never let her go. His second instinct was
to remove her from his lap and kick her out of his office.

He did neither.

Instead, he sank his fingers into his hair, let his head
fall back and stared at the ceiling. It was the pose of a man
wondering what the hell he'd done.

Displaying no regret, Savannah pushed off the couch
and got to her feet. Hips swaying in unconscious allure,
she crossed to the bar and found a towel, bringing it back
to him. By the time Trent had cleaned up and disposed of
the condom, she was putting the last hairpin into her im-
promptu updo. The only signs of how she'd spent the last
ten minutes were her flushed cheeks and smeared lipstick.

He glanced up and down the length of her as she stepped

back into her tall heels, and all he saw was a tranquil, confident woman. Gone was the femme fatale. Trent couldn't decide if he was glad or sorry.

"This doesn't change anything." His tone was brusque, his words more clipped than he'd intended. "I'm not going back to LA to bail out West Coast Records."

She looked at him askance, her eyebrows lifted in disbelief. "That's not what this was about."

"No?" But he knew she wasn't lying. Savannah frequently ended up in trouble because she wasn't calculating. The fact that he'd just accused her of unscrupulous behavior demonstrated that their unexpected sexual encounter had thrown him off his game. He hated that. It was time to take the situation back in his hands. "Where are you staying?"

His question surprised her. Something flickered in her eyes. "I'm not taking you to my hotel suite, if that's what you're thinking."

It wasn't what he'd been thinking, but now that she'd mentioned it, that sounded like a great idea. He'd like to strip that conservative dress off her and make love to her properly. But it was too late for that. Two years, one marriage and his brother's son too late.

"Where are you staying?" he repeated, letting her see that his patience was waning.

"Upstairs."

Cobalt had been Trent's first choice of location when he and his business partners decided to open Club T's. The hotel's owner, JT Stone, was a brilliant businessman with a great reputation and solid ethics. The rent was high for this exclusive real estate, but the hotel drew a chic crowd with deep pockets who liked to party and could easily afford Club T's high-end table service.

"I'll walk you back to your suite."

"There's no need."

Savannah wouldn't meet his eyes, and it was the first indication Trent had that the encounter had ruffled her composure.

"It's two in the morning." And Trent had no intention of returning to the club tonight. He'd lost his taste for partying the instant Savannah had appeared at his table. All he wanted was to head home, pour himself a liberal amount of scotch and brood. "And you've already had one run-in with a man you couldn't handle."

She gave an offhand shrug. "I think I handled you just fine."

He fought back an admiring smile. "I meant the guy in the bar."

"Oh, him." She shook her head. "I was on the verge of crushing his toe with my heel."

Unsure if she was kidding, Trent caught her by the elbow and turned her in the direction of the office door. He led the way through the back halls of the club and hotel to a service elevator. Once inside he turned an expectant expression on her. Rather than tell him her floor, she reached to push the button herself.

"It's no good, you know," Trent said as the car began to move upward. "If you try to bring me in at West Coast Records, Siggy will fight you with everything he has."

"But you're exactly what the company needs. You're brilliant. Your father and Rafe never understood that."

Trent stared at her in bemusement. She'd always been on his side. How had two people who only had each other's best interest at heart failed so miserably at being together?

Because he didn't want what she did. Family for him meant nothing but heartache.

"You're wasting your time and mine. Let the company fold. You and Dylan will be fine without it. I'll make sure of that."

Three

Savannah turned Trent's words over and over in her mind as he escorted her to the suite. His offer made no sense.

At her door, she stopped and faced him. "You'll make sure how? I don't intend to take your money."

All she'd ever needed was for him to love her. She'd wanted to be his wife and raise his children. To make a secure life for her family and feel safe in turn. Being shipped between her father and grandmother for eight of her first eleven years had never allowed her any sense of belonging. That wasn't to say she didn't have good memories of the small town in Tennessee where her grandmother lived.

"You said you sold your house to pay Rafe's debts. Where are you going to go and what do you intend to live on?"

"I'd hoped to return to Tennessee." California was expensive and she wanted to start a new life far from the Caldwell family.

She never should have settled in LA after leaving New

York. Originally she'd intended to move to Las Vegas to be close to Trent. He'd not been thrilled at having this plan sprung on him. It had been the first time she'd asserted herself and made her longing for marriage and a family clear to him. The fact that she'd pushed had caused their breakup. With her future up in the air, she'd gone to LA and reached out to Rafe.

He hadn't hit her with *I told you so* or made her feel worse about herself. He'd been supportive and friendly. A hundred times since then she'd wondered how her life would've turned out if she'd done any one of a dozen things differently.

"What's in Tennessee?" Trent asked.

Not a single thing, but at least it was somewhat familiar. "It's home."

He didn't look convinced. "And with no money, what are you planning on doing there?"

She'd considered returning to acting, but that would require relocating to New York or staying in LA. But with the terrifying load of debt hanging over her head, she was slowly coming around to the idea.

It meant giving up her dream of raising Dylan where neighbors knew each other and pitched in to help. At least for the time being.

"I had thought to move to Gatlinburg. The population is small, but it's a big tourist destination and I'm sure I can find something I can do."

"You didn't deserve to be put in this position by my family. You want to move to Tennessee, I'll help you with some cash to get you started."

She was okay with the idea of moving away, but Trent's offer of help made her feel as if he wanted her gone. Ridiculous. One brief sexual encounter with him and she was on her way to becoming emotionally attached again. *Damn*.

This was not why she'd come here. She needed him to save the record label so Dylan would have something to inherit.

"The only help I need is for you to take over West Coast Records." Despair swept over her, but she couldn't let Trent see her distress. "Beyond that, there's nothing I need from you." She used her key card and let herself into the suite. "Good night, Trent. It was nice to see you again."

With a cheeky Courtney Day smile, she waved at him and slipped through the open doorway. She thought she'd gotten the final word in, but Trent had one last parting shot before the door closed.

"Take the night and think about my offer."

Savannah opened her mouth to tell him he was wasting his breath, but he'd already turned and walked away. She resisted the urge to call after him. She was tired of arguing.

With her plan to escape her current predicament amounting to a major failure, Savannah sought solace in the one spot of light. Her son, Dylan. She entered her bedroom, found him sleeping peacefully in his crib and turned off the baby monitor so as not to wake Lori, the babysitter Savannah had used on and off in the months since Rafe's death. Dylan was a sunny, healthy baby who'd begun sleeping through the night by the time he was six months old.

Having never known her mother, Savannah hadn't known what to expect when her son came along. Although she'd long craved a family of her own, reality was never the same as daydreams. In Dylan's case it was so much better.

Savannah left her sleeping son and crossed to the bathroom. She stripped off her dress and examined her bare thighs. Sure enough, a bruise was forming where Trent's fingers had bitten down. She brushed her fingertips across the spot. Letting her body dictate the encounter with Trent hadn't been the best idea, but she didn't regret what had happened. Yet she knew her impulsiveness would have emotional consequences.

Maybe she should take Trent's help to get out from under Rafe's load of debt. Let Siggy destroy the company. What did she care as long as she and Dylan were free? Besides, even if she could convince Trent to take on the leadership of the record label, she might be inviting more trouble from her father-in-law. He was leveraging her situation to keep Dylan close. What if he came after her with some ridiculous legal ploy that she couldn't afford to fight?

Savannah changed into pajamas but doubted her ability to sleep, so she turned on the television and sat on the couch in the living room to watch a show about tiny-house hunting. Her mood lightened somewhat as she considered the idea of finding a four-hundred-square-foot house where she and Dylan could live a simple life.

The sort of life she might have had with her mother if she hadn't been killed while deployed in the Middle East when Savannah had been three. She'd give anything to recall even the blurriest image of her mother, Libby. Instead, all she had were the stark memories of being passed back and forth between her father and maternal grandmother like an endless tennis volley.

Her parents had indulged in a brief fling that resulted in Savannah being conceived. And despite her resolve never to follow in her mother's footsteps, she'd done exactly that. From what she'd gathered from her grandmother, Libby hadn't planned to tell Chet Holt he was a father. Nor had Savannah's dad been thrilled to be saddled with the responsibility of a daughter he'd never expected.

When her father's bad decisions landed him in prison for burglary, and with her grandmother's health making it too hard for her to care for Savannah, she'd been shipped off to LA to live with her aunt, who worked as a housekeeper for the Caldwells.

Savannah closed her eyes and recalled the discomfort of her first few months in LA. The Caldwells' house was not a happy place. Siggy's second marriage was on the rocks, and Melody fought with her stepmother nonstop. At sixteen, Trent was raising hell at school and driving his father crazy at home. Only Rafe seemed above the fray. He'd been breezing through his senior year of high school and was on track to finish in the top 10 percent of his class.

With those unhappy days filling her thoughts, it was no wonder that when she fell asleep in front of the TV she had a nightmare about her and Dylan living in the Caldwell home with Siggy. She woke to the sounds of her son stirring in his bedroom and stumbled in a fog of lingering dismay to get him changed before Lori woke. Savannah loved these quiet early hours with Dylan.

Snuggling him enabled her to escape her worries for a little while. His smiles lit up a room. He was such a happy, inquisitive child and since he'd begun to walk two weeks ago, she had to keep a close eye on him at all times.

Both Savannah and Dylan were still in their pajamas when the babysitter emerged from her room. Savannah had given him breakfast and was on the couch reading to him from his favorite picture book.

"What time is it?" Savannah asked Lori, standing with Dylan in her arms.

"It's a little after eight."

"Why don't you order us some breakfast," Savannah said. "I'd like an egg-white omelet and toast."

The closing on her house was at two thirty that afternoon. Their flight back to LA was at eleven. Savannah handed over her son and headed to the bedroom to get ready. She didn't linger over her morning routine and had her bag packed in short order. By the time she emerged, a waiter was pushing a room service cart toward the large window that overlooked the Strip. Savannah signed for the breakfast, and the man headed for the door. When he opened it to leave, Trent was standing in the hall outside her suite.

"Good morning," he said, not waiting for an invitation to enter the room.

Trent's abrupt appearance threw her for a loop. She'd considered he might call. But never in her wildest dreams did she think he might actually show up in person this morning. Dressed in an impeccable navy superfine wool suit with a crisp white shirt and cobalt tie, Trent looked ready to do business.

Savannah shot a quick glance toward her son. He sat on the floor surrounded by books and toys, happily gnawing on a plastic key ring. Lori had seated herself at the dining room table and was removing the metal domes from the plates of food. She seemed uninterested in Savannah's visitor.

In the dark hours of late-night Vegas, reconnecting with her ex-lover had been relatively uncomplicated. In the cold light of day, with her son—Trent's son—less than ten feet away, she was feeling overwhelmed by her past mistakes and future missteps.

"What are you doing here?"

"You aren't really planning on moving to Tennessee, are you?"

After her troubled sleep and her dream about living in Siggy's house, Savannah was feeling less confident than she had been the night before. Despite what she'd told Trent, the truth was she had no place to go once she signed the papers on her house. She'd been so convinced she could get Trent to help her she hadn't focused at all on what would happen if she failed.

"I…" Her chest grew exceedingly tight. She couldn't get any words out.

"Are you okay?"

"Fine." The word had very little conviction behind it. Where was Courtney now? Savannah had lost her connection to her confident alter ego.

"Where are you planning to go, then?"

Misery engulfed her. "I don't have a plan." He'd never know what it cost her to admit that. Too many times he'd viewed her as helpless. "My only option was for you to help me with the company."

"But that doesn't help you with your immediate problem of where to go once you close on your house."

She knew he was right.

"I called Melody last night," Trent continued. "She's in Australia at the moment, and with the time difference it was afternoon. She told me Siggy wants you to move in with him. You're not planning on doing that, are you?"

Not if she could help it. Even as a temporary measure, becoming beholden to her father-in-law was a bad idea. Savannah exhaled in frustration but didn't respond to Trent's question. She couldn't blame Melody for telling Trent what was going on. Melody was just as upset as Savannah about the situation. Trent's sister had worked hard and suffered much to get out from beneath her father's weighty expectations.

"It's a bad idea."

"It's not what I want to do." She crossed her arms over her chest and stared past his shoulder. "I'd prefer to move to Tennessee and buy a small house there."

But was it really the place for her and Dylan? Savannah had latched on to Gatlinburg because her grandmother's house had been in a town twenty miles away, and she'd built it up in her mind as a great place to raise Dylan.

As if aware of her thoughts, Dylan gave a happy gurgle and stood. Trent's attention swiveled toward the toddler as Dylan began his ungainly waddle toward them.

"He's walking already?" Trent regarded the boy impassively. "I didn't think he was quite a year."

Savannah's pride shone through as she answered, "He's a little ahead of the curve." Seeing his mother's smile, Dylan came at her in a rush. With her heart thumping painfully hard, Savannah scooped him off the floor and settled him on her hip. He wrapped his hand around her three-tiered strand of pearls that complemented today's collared black sweater dress with three-quarter-length cuffed sleeves.

"Dylan, right?" Trent was inspecting the boy through narrowed eyes.

"Yes."

Father and son stared at each other while Savannah waited for what would happen next. She'd been dreading this encounter since the day her son had been born. Part of her hoped to see recognition in Trent's eyes. She wanted him to claim Dylan. Then she could stop feeling guilty for denying her son his father.

"You can't do this to him."

Savannah wasn't sure what she'd expected Trent to say, but that wasn't it. "Can't do what to him?"

"Let my father get his hands on him."

"You make it sound so ominous." She'd become an expert at appearing more confident than she was. "What can Siggy do?"

"He could ruin his childhood the way he did Rafe's and mine."

From the expression on Savannah's face, she'd already considered this, and Trent's irritation grew. How could she even consider putting her son into such a toxic environment even for a few weeks? And then he realized her finances had to be in rough shape. What hadn't she told him?

"All right," he said, "let's stop dancing around."

Her eyes went round with apprehension. "What are you talking about?"

"I want to know exactly what's going on with you."

Savannah turned away and carried her son back to his toys. She then took her time pouring a cup of coffee and offering it to him. Trent shook his head.

"Dylan and I are returning to LA on an eleven o'clock flight. I have a closing on my house this afternoon. There's nothing else to tell."

Trent glanced around at the young woman working her way through a thick Belgian waffle and understood that Savannah would prefer not to air her business in front of the young woman.

"I was planning on heading to LA on business tomorrow. There's no reason why I couldn't go a day earlier. Perhaps you and I could celebrate after you close on your house and then tomorrow morning you could give me a tour of the company."

Savannah grimaced. "I'm not sure closing on my house is a reason to celebrate."

"Then just consider it an opportunity for the two of us to get reacquainted."

"Do you really want a tour of the company?" She sounded uncertain.

He hoped she was worried about how his father would react to her bringing Trent into West Coast Records. Her notion that he could do something to help her save the company was crazy.

"Absolutely. Why don't you give Gerry a call and tell him you're bringing by your financial adviser to look over the books."

Savannah gave him the first genuine smile he'd seen. "He's not going to be happy about that."

"Do you really care?"

"Siggy isn't going to be happy about that, either." It

didn't appear as if that bothered her, but Trent suspected it did a little. His father was bound to make her life miserable if he discovered she'd teamed up with Trent. "Are you going to help me with the company?"

"No." His intention was simply to let his father think that's what he intended to do. Perhaps then Siggy would buy back his company from Savannah, allowing her and Dylan to head off to her new life in Tennessee.

She looked confused by his answer. "Then why do you want to see the books?"

"Something has to be going on," he said. Overnight his curiosity had been aroused by what she had told him. While he'd heard West Coast Records was struggling, things didn't sound as if they were bad enough for them to stop paying their artists. "It doesn't surprise me that profits are down, but something more serious must be happening if things are in the state you say they are."

"What if Gerry refuses to give me the information?"

"Then we'll have our answer as to who is at the center of what's going on there, won't we?"

"You think Gerry has something to do with this?"

"With Siggy retired and Rafe sick, he was in the perfect position to mismanage the company." And Trent had never been particularly impressed with the man's business savvy. "So let's go see what's going on, shall we? I've chartered a plane. I'll pick you up downstairs at ten thirty."

"We're already scheduled on a flight to LA."

"It will be easier if I'm not chasing all over LAX looking for you." He softened his tone. "And it will be more comfortable for you."

Trent felt a tug on his pant leg and looked down. His nephew was standing, looking up at him. The boy's blue eyes, so reminiscent of Rafe's, were fixed on Trent's face. Something in his chest tightened. All at once he couldn't breathe.

This was Rafe's son. Savannah's son. Like a man drowning, Trent saw his past with Savannah flash before his eyes. The joy on that Christmas morning when she'd woken up to Murphy's sweet puppy face and adorable snuffles. What had he been thinking? He'd bought her a dog. She'd been feeling gloomy about spending the holidays alone. So he bought her something to take care of and flown to New York to give it to her. Making a woman happy had never been as easy as it had been with her.

And then because she'd misinterpreted his gift, he'd felt compelled to distance himself for months after.

When the toddler continued to stare at Trent, he bent down and picked the boy up. He didn't have much experience with children, but something about his nephew made it a simple thing to settle the child against his chest as if he'd done it a hundred times before. The amount of curiosity in the infant's eyes intrigued Trent. What could possibly be going on in that developing brain of his?

Dylan latched on to Trent's tie the same way he'd grabbed Savannah's pearls, and Trent heard her soft cry of dismay.

"He's going to ruin your tie," she said, stepping toward them with her hands outstretched as if to take her son.

"It's just a tie." Trent pivoted away from her advance. He couldn't explain his sudden reluctance to give the child up. "It looks like your breakfast is getting cold. Why don't you sit down and eat? Dylan and I will be just fine."

The distress in Savannah's eyes made no sense. It wasn't as if he was going to spirit the infant out of the suite. He had no interest in his nephew outside of satisfying a brief bit of curiosity about him.

Rafe had died within months of his son being born. Having a father like Siggy, Trent had little positive experience when it came to father-son bonding. Would Dylan suffer never knowing his dad? On the other hand, once

Savannah settled in Tennessee, she might marry again and Dylan would be raised by a stepfather. Either way, at least he would grow up dearly loved by his mother. That much was clear.

Trent picked up one of the picture books from the floor near Dylan's toys and sat down on the couch with the boy.

"That's his favorite," Savannah said, sitting with an untouched plate of eggs before her. "He'd love it if you read it to him."

Left on his own with the boy, Trent opened the book and began reading while Dylan patted the pages with his fat little hands and wiggled. Trent found himself smiling. For the last year he'd avoided thinking about his nephew. Although he'd never intended to saddle himself with a wife and children, the fact that Savannah had given his brother a son ate at him.

Rafe had gotten everything. Their father's love and approval. The family business. And Savannah. The first two Trent had come to terms with. The last one had blasted a hole in his heart big enough to drive a semi through. But it was his own fault. He could've had her. Dylan could have been his son. Except the conventional family Savannah craved wasn't what he wanted.

The idea that anyone would rely on him was a suffocating weight. Sure, he'd helped her out several times in the past, but those had been random acts when it had been convenient for him. He had to do things on his terms, not on anyone else's. Even now, stepping up to help her with the label, he wasn't doing it for her. He was doing it to piss off his old man.

Trent wanted to see if Siggy hated him enough to bankrupt the record label before he would let his son be in charge. To Trent's recollection, his father had never shown him anything but disdain. Rafe had been the favorite son. Siggy's firstborn. He'd taken after his father in appearance and mind-set: a businessman mired in ego and lacking vision.

Like his sister, Melody, Trent had inherited his mother's voice and musical talent. Not that he had any interest in pursuing a career in the business. He left the songwriting, piano playing and singing to his younger sister. Trent could not be more proud of Melody.

She'd struggled to find her wings in a household that didn't appreciate what she could do. Forced to attend Juilliard as a classic violinist when what she really wanted to do was compose pop songs for others to perform, Melody had dropped out of school midway through her junior year of college.

The gap in their ages had kept Trent from knowing Melody as well as he could. But when he'd gone to visit her in New York City and she'd come clean about her passion for writing music, he'd been behind her 100 percent about quitting school. She needed money to rent studio time to make a demo of her music and he'd happily provided it. He'd also put her in contact with the people in the music industry who could help her get started.

This bit of assistance and support had only added to the acrimony between Trent and his father. It was shortly after this that Siggy stopped speaking with Trent. The owner of West Coast Records had a vision in his head regarding his daughter, and it had nothing to do with her lowering herself to being someone else's songwriter.

Trent hadn't understood his father's perspective. Melody was immensely talented. She could have become an incredible star if she'd been interested in the spotlight. But she preferred being behind the scenes and having her music developed by others. At least that's the way it'd been until his friend and partner in Club T's, Nate Tucker, had convinced her to bring her violin on tour with Free Fall. Seeing a star in the making, Tucker had pushed her to sing one of her songs during his set. It had gone so well that she was now opening for him.

And as far as Siggy was concerned, this was Trent's fault, too.

"How are things going?"

Trent looked up from the book and spied Savannah standing before him. Although her makeup was flawless, he thought she looked pale. Was that brought on by stress or lack of sleep? He'd had a hard time settling down after walking her to her suite. Although he was no stranger to spontaneous encounters, usually the moments lingered in his mind for a short time and then faded away.

With Savannah everything was different.

He couldn't just revel in a quickie with his brother's widow, chuckle at the irony and move on. There was too much history between them. Too much he couldn't stop himself from needing.

"Great," he said. "You're right about him liking this book."

"He enjoys being read to." She smiled fondly at her son. "I guess what kid doesn't."

"I don't remember anyone reading to me, do you?"

Savannah shook her head. "My grandmother used to tell me stories about when she was a little girl. She grew up on a farm in Kansas and talked about milking the cows and barn cats having kittens. She described what it had been like to be in the cellar while a tornado took out the chicken coop but missed the barn and house."

Her distant gaze and fond smile clashed with Trent's attitude about his own upbringing. His childhood memories mainly consisted of watching TV and playing video games. His mother had never read to him. She'd been busy maintaining her appearance and chasing her own happiness. Personal trainers, self-help quacks and an assortment of assistants had kept Trent's mother lean of body and calm of spirit. Or at least they had tried to. Living with someone as critical as Siggy Caldwell was debilitating for anyone without sufficient self-esteem.

These days Naomi was a very different person. She laughed all the time and allowed herself to age gracefully. After leaving Siggy, she'd moved to New York and gotten some off-Broadway work. It was there she'd met and married her second husband, investment banker Larry Fry.

"I'm going to get Dylan ready to leave."

"I have to check out a couple things at the club before I go."

Trent gave up the boy, surprised at his reluctance to do so. Despite the fact that Dylan was a baby, he'd enjoyed the child's company more than he'd expected. But there was a huge difference between playing the part of fun uncle who spent ten minutes reading a book and a lifetime of caretaking as a father.

Savannah settled her son on her hip and spoke in a light voice. "Dylan, can you wave goodbye to your uncle Trent?"

The nearly one-year-old child did as he was bidden and followed it up by blowing a kiss. Trent was impressed by the boy's tricks and wondered if this was average for kids his age.

He didn't want to like his nephew any more than he wanted to get embroiled in Savannah's problems. But something was going on with West Coast Records, and his curiosity wouldn't let him turn it aside.

Besides, there might be an opportunity here and he'd be a fool to pass that up.

Four

While Trent negotiated the LA traffic, Savannah sat like a stone beside him. As of twenty minutes ago, she was officially homeless. Sunshine poured through the car window, but Savannah enjoyed neither the soothing brightness nor the warmth.

"Are you okay?" Trent had been casting glances her way since he'd picked her up from the closing.

"Dylan and I have nowhere to go." Her vision blurred as her eyes filled with unshed tears. She blinked them away. What was wrong with her that she stumbled from one desperate situation to another? "I'm a complete failure as a mother."

"Don't say things like that."

"I haven't done a good job providing for him or protecting him."

"This isn't a problem you created."

While she appreciated Trent's attempt to make her feel better, she couldn't ignore the string of bad decisions that had led her to this place. On the other hand, one of her choices, foolish or not, had given her the light of her life, her son.

"Maybe not a problem I created, but when I discovered how bad things were financially, I should have gone back to work and found us a place to live." She dug her fingernails into her hands to keep a grip on her anxiety. "Instead I stuck my head in the sand."

"Stop being so hard on yourself."

"Tell me you would've acted the same and I won't say another word."

"We don't come at problems the same way."

"Ha." To her surprise, arguing with Trent was making her feel better. She might be down, but she certainly didn't have to be out. "What do you think we're going to find at the label?"

Trent's expression darkened. "This is probably the wrong thing to say to you right now, but you probably should brace yourself for some unpleasantness."

"Too late," she said. "I called Gerry this morning before leaving the hotel, and he was not pleased by my request. So I'm completely convinced we will have a fight on our hands."

"Did you tell him I was coming?"

Savannah smiled. "And lose the element of surprise?"

Ten minutes later, Trent entered West Coast Records' parking lot and pulled into a visitor's spot. She put her hand on his arm as he made to open his door.

"Thank you," she said, seeing Siggy's car parked in Rafe's spot. "I know coming here isn't easy for you."

"It doesn't bother me."

From his expression, she couldn't tell whether or not that was true. She indicated her father-in-law's car. "Have you spoken to Siggy since Rafe's funeral?"

"No. We have nothing to say to each other."

To Savannah's relief, there'd been no father-son blowup at Rafe's funeral. The two Caldwell men had stood apart from each other the entire day and never indulged the ongoing animosity between them. She might not have loved Rafe, but Savannah had wanted his family and friends to mourn him uninterrupted by squabbling.

As much as Savannah longed to take strength from Trent's solid presence at her side, she kept her chin up and a respectable distance between them as they entered the building and strode across the bright, open lobby. West Coast Records had been located here since the '50s. Siggy had bought the company in 1976.

It had done well for a lot of years, but with the shift into digital, the label had been too slow to evolve and hadn't developed a solid plan of action to make money in the age when people didn't have to download an entire album but could pick and choose which songs they wanted.

From what Savannah had come to understand from her own research and what Trent had explained during the flight, West Coast Records had signed a bunch of artists and flooded the marketplace with mediocre music. They were trying to re-create the huge revenues they used to enjoy instead of spending the time it took to develop real talent and accepting that they were going to make smaller amounts than they used to.

Savannah led the way past the unoccupied reception desk toward Rafe's office. She hadn't been here more than a half-dozen times, but she knew the way well enough. As they moved through the halls, she noticed an abundance of empty desks. The whole building had a stillness to it that made her uncomfortable. At four in the afternoon, it was possible that the staff had gone for the day, but the lack of personal items at the desks made the office feel like a ghost town.

"Where is everyone?" she asked Trent, slowing down to peer around her. "It looks deserted."

"Maybe they've laid off some people."

The anxiety that had plagued her for months increased. What if she'd brought Trent in too late? If the company failed, the stock would be worthless. Right now she was using a small income she received from the company to pay the minimum on the debt until she could figure something out. If the label failed, that would dry up. Then, her only recourse would be to declare bankruptcy to get out from beneath Rafe's massive debt.

On the way to Rafe's office, they passed Gerry's.

"Any idea where Gerry is hiding?" Trent asked, arching one eyebrow. His reaction to being here was the polar opposite of hers. The worse things appeared, the more relaxed he became.

"I haven't been here since I found out Rafe was sick. Maybe Gerry took over Rafe's office."

When they entered the president's office, they found not only Gerry, but also Siggy. The old man was seated behind the desk as if he was still in charge. At the sight of him in her dead husband's executive chair, Savannah's anxiety became annoyance.

"What are you doing here?" Sigmund Caldwell demanded, getting to his feet in an explosive movement. Palms planted on the desk, he scowled at his younger son.

"Hello, Siggy." Trent took a step past Savannah, positioning himself like a protective guard dog. "I'm surprised to find you in the office." Thanks to the amusement in his tone, he didn't sound surprised.

"Trent is here because I asked him to come." Savannah held her expression neutral as her father-in-law's sharp gaze shifted to her. "I need to know what's going on with the company's financials."

"You don't need to know anything," Siggy said.

"That isn't true. With Rafe's death Dylan inherits his shares, and I'm his mother. It falls to me to make sure his inheritance survives." Savannah knew immediately she'd gone too far.

"Nothing falls to you. You are just a grasping woman who took advantage of my son's illness. If you think I'm going to let you make decisions about this company, you are sadly mistaken."

"Fine. Then buy the shares back." She was shaking, but the confrontation with her father-in-law was not as bad as it would have been without Trent at her side. She could never have done this without him.

Siggy looked her over, his disdain apparent. "I have a better idea. Why don't I pay you to go away? You leave the boy with me, and I set you up somewhere far away."

It was the deal he'd made with his first wife, Naomi Caldwell. "I have no intention of giving you my son."

The way Siggy smiled broadcast his skepticism. And given his ability to manipulate both his former wives, that didn't really surprise her.

"As you said, this company will belong to my grandson one day. The shares are his. I will manage it until he is ready to take over."

"But you are no longer the managing partner, nor are you the majority shareholder," Trent pointed out in a reasonable voice.

The instant he spoke, his father's attention swung back to him once more. "You do not belong here. If you don't leave now, I'll have security throw you out."

"Security? Word on the street is you can't afford security anymore."

Siggy's face grew ruddy. "Get out," he spat.

"Not without the financials," Trent retorted. He was as calm as his father was upset. "As guardian of the majority shareholder, Savannah needs to see what's going on."

Observing the exchange between father and son, Savannah almost felt sorry for her father-in-law. If Siggy hadn't been such a domineering bastard, perhaps they could've work through their differences amicably. But Siggy wanted to maintain control of his company, and to do so he needed control over her son.

With the four of them staring each other down, Savannah wasn't sure what would happen next. Without access to the computers, she had no idea how they could force Gerry or Siggy to open up the books.

But apparently, Trent knew exactly what he was doing. "Things will not go well for you if we get lawyers involved," he said ominously.

As a privately held company, West Coast Records was not required to file any public documents regarding its finances. The board membership was composed of six of Siggy's cronies but Savannah doubted they would be interested in being on the receiving end of any legal action she might take against them on behalf of her son.

"Gerry, give them access." Siggy slid from behind the desk, stalked up to his son and glared at him. "You might have won this round but I'll burn West Coast Records to the ground before I'll let you anywhere near this company."

Bold words, Savannah thought. But as she watched her father-in-law exit the room, she wasn't completely sure if it was bravado or a touch of madness that drove him where Trent was concerned.

Gerry did something with the computer and then left the room, as well.

As Trent slid behind the desk and began tapping away, Savannah sank into a guest chair opposite him.

"How do you do it?" She sat with her hands clasped tight in her lap and exhaled to calm herself. "How do you face him down so calmly? Doesn't he get to you?"

"Years of practice have taught me to cope." But stress

lines had appeared beside his compressed lips and his eyes were guarded.

Long minutes ticked by while Trent looked through the computer records. Savannah had a hard time containing her restless energy. Any second she expected Siggy to reappear and begin to berate her once more. If before this she'd been determined to keep Dylan out of his clutches, now she was even more convinced she couldn't let her son be anywhere near him.

She paced around the room, paying special attention to the photos and awards that lined the walls. From the look of things, the label hadn't had any great success since the early '90s. And she had a hard time finding Rafe's stamp on anything. This made her sad. In many ways her husband had been trapped by his position as eldest son.

Could he have done as Trent had and made his own way? Savannah wasn't sure Rafe had it in him to break free of his father's hold. Rafe was firstborn. His father's pride and joy. The weight of expectation had turned him into a mini Siggy.

"Finding anything?" She came to stand behind Trent and peer over his shoulder at the monitor.

Despite the seriousness of her situation, the stressful confrontation with Siggy and her fears for her son, she couldn't stop herself from snatching a lungful of Trent's familiar cologne. Her head spun as her senses came alive. His long fingers darted across the keyboard and she couldn't help herself from remembering how they'd felt biting down on her skin as she came the previous night.

His thick, wavy hair enticed a woman's fingers to roam. Not a speck of lint dotted the shoulders of his dark blue suit, but that didn't stop Savannah's craving to sweep her fingers across the material. Last night's reckless encounter had stirred up a beehive of longing. She hungered to touch him again and was willing to make up lame excuses to do so. Before she succumbed to temptation, she put her hands behind her back.

"What are you doing? That doesn't look like financial records."

At her question, Trent didn't glance up. "A friend of mine lent me a program." He removed a flash drive from the computer's USB port and slipped it into his pocket.

"What sort of program?" Savannah stepped back as he got to his feet.

"I'll tell you in the car."

"Is all this really necessary?" She wasn't sure what to make of Trent's cloak-and-dagger routine. Was he behaving this way for her benefit? Acting as if the trip to West Coast Records' offices was more productive than it had been?

Trent spread his fingers across the small of her back and nudged her toward the hallway. "Let's go."

Obviously he wasn't going to say another word while they were still in the building. As badly as she wanted to know what was going on, Savannah was enjoying the warmth of his palm far too much to be hurried.

As on the way in, they encountered no one, but the boardroom door was closed as they passed. Once in the parking lot, Savannah couldn't restrain her curiosity one second longer. "What's going on? Were you able to determine anything from the financials?"

"They gave us only the most rudimentary access."

"What does that mean?"

"That means they were ready for us. We got a year-to-date profit and loss statement and balance sheet. It shows that the company is profitable."

"How profitable?"

"Enough that they should be paying their artists. But you say they aren't."

"That's the impression that I was given. Maybe they are paying some but not all."

"Money is going out," Trent said, opening the passenger door so she could slide in. "I just can't determine if it's actually going to the artists." Without saying another word, he shut the car door, leaving her to mull over his last statement.

She waited until he'd slid behind the wheel and started the engine before repeating her earlier question. "What was with the USB drive?"

"I figured we wouldn't get much. So I came prepared. A friend of mine in Vegas runs a security company. And he wouldn't want it spread around, but he's a gifted hacker. I called him this morning, explained the problem, and he gave me a worm to implant in their system."

"A worm?" Savannah had watched enough TV to know what he was talking about. But she had never considered that real people used them. "Are you telling me you planted some sort of spy software in the company's computer system?"

"As good a hacker as he is, he could've cracked their system from the outside, but why bother when it's so much easier to do it from the inside?"

Savannah was starting to feel hopeful. "So what does this get us?"

"Full access to their system."

Leave it to Trent to come to her rescue once again. Savannah would never have conceived of something so clever and potentially illegal.

"So you'll be able to see what's actually going on?"

"That's the idea."

"Is it illegal?"

"I'd say it's a gray area. Dylan is the majority shareholder in the company. They are denying you access to the books." Trent backed the car out of the parking spot. "But it doesn't matter. Logan assures me his software's untraceable. They'll never know what hit them."

* * *

Adrenaline buzzed through Trent's veins as he negotiated the LA traffic on the way to the hotel Savannah had chosen until she found a more permanent place to settle. The fight with his father had gone as expected. Trent glanced at Savannah. She hadn't reacted well to Siggy's vicious attack. It had taken a great deal of willpower to keep from acknowledging her distress and comforting her back at the label. He didn't want either her or his father to get the idea something was going on between them.

In the old days when he and his father had fought, she had often come to him with comforting words. Initially he'd rebuffed her attempts to make him feel better, not understanding what she needed was reassurance that he was all right.

He glanced at her now. She stared out the passenger window. Her face was impassive, but her hands, clasped around the purse in her lap, were rigid with tension. He recognized that she was stressed. He gathered breath, refrained from speaking. What was he going to say? That everything was going to be fine? He didn't know that. And what was he doing getting more deeply involved in her problem with his father when he'd determined a decade earlier that he was done with the family drama?

"Dealing with Siggy isn't going to be fun or easy," he said, stating the obvious. "Are you sure you don't want me to help you get back on your feet somewhere besides here?"

When he made the offer the night before, he hadn't done so as an ex-lover or a brother-in-law. They'd been friends long before either of those things, and whether he'd always been able to admit it or not, she'd been there for him during some very dark days.

"I told you last night that I'm not going to take your money."

"You could think of it as a loan."

Her features relaxed into a wry expression. "I've considered that," she explained in an overly patient tone. "My answer is still no."

When had she become stubborn? Trent caught himself frowning. She wasn't the same woman he'd broken up with two years earlier. And he wasn't sure what to make of the change.

"Why are you so opposed to letting me help you?"

"I wouldn't be in the car with you if I was opposed to letting you help me."

"Then why won't you take money from me? It's not as if I'd notice it was gone."

She cocked her head and stared straight forward. "I can't explain it. Getting you to help me sort out what's wrong at West Coast Records isn't personal. I could hire a lawyer to do that."

"I thought you were broke?"

"I might be able to afford a really bad attorney," she retorted with a trace of a smile. And then she sighed. "To be honest, I wasn't thinking straight before last night."

"Last night? What changed last night?"

"Have you forgotten already?" Her voice packed just the right amount of sultry amusement to stir his lust.

He tightened his grip on the steering wheel to keep his hands from wandering across the space between them and slipping beneath the hem of her dress to find her bare knee. It drove him crazy that ever since she'd been married his brother she'd started dressing to repress her sensuality. A beautiful woman shouldn't hide the way Savannah did.

"Hardly." But after glancing in her direction, he wasn't sure if they were referring to the same thing after all. "You are talking about what happened in my office, aren't you?"

"You sound worried that I'm not."

"I don't sound worried." What was going on that he wanted last night's encounter to have changed her somehow?

It had been an interlude between ex-lovers. Nothing more. It certainly hadn't changed anything going on with him. So why did he expect her to be any different? Trent ground his teeth together, disliking his uncertainty. To his relief, Savannah chose to elaborate without his prompting.

"Being around you reminded me of the girl I used to be. You taught me how to take care of myself. I'd forgotten how to do that in the last year and a half."

As long as he could remember, he'd lectured her on the need to question people's motives before agreeing to something. She'd lost much of her naïveté while living in New York, but obviously she sometimes forgot to be wary of people eager to take advantage of her.

"Why didn't you take care of yourself while married to my brother?"

"In a lot of ways, your brother was like your father. He wanted a particular kind of wife. One who did as he asked and never argued. I didn't realize our marriage wasn't going to be a partnership until too late."

For the first time, it occurred to Trent that she hadn't been happy. Again came that urge to comfort her. Again he resisted. She wasn't his to worry about. Helping her sort through what was going on with the label was about getting back at his father. She'd hit the nail on the head last night when she'd encouraged him to demonstrate to Siggy that he was a better businessman.

"I'm sorry things didn't work out the way you'd hoped."

"I'm not sure I had an idea what I was hoping for."

Again her remark prompted questions, but Trent refrained from diving in. Last night she'd said she didn't want to talk about her marriage. He sure as hell didn't want to hear about it today.

He parked the car in the hotel parking lot and they went in the front entrance together. She'd chosen a budget chain, with none of the bells and whistles she might have enjoyed if his brother hadn't left her in debt. Whatever else had changed with her, she remained fiscally responsible.

Trent had booked himself into the Wilshire for the night. Although he could very easily have dropped Savannah off and headed to his hotel, he felt as if he owed her some idea of what he had planned.

Her standard hotel room was empty when they arrived. A crib had been set up by the window, but Dylan wasn't in it and the babysitter was nowhere to be seen.

"Shouldn't they be here?" For some reason the sight of the empty hotel room alarmed him. Maybe it was the way Savannah had tensed.

"I told Lori not to go anywhere until I got back." Savannah fumbled in her purse for her phone and scrolled through her contacts. "She didn't send me a text and she's not answering her phone. Where could they be?" The pitch of her voice registered anxiety.

"How long have you known this girl?"

"I first hired her to babysit Dylan right after Rafe's death. I knew there would be a lot to do and that it would disrupt Dylan's routines too much if I brought him everywhere I needed to go."

"And you checked her out?"

Savannah shot him a dark look. "I hired her through a reputable agency that had her thoroughly vetted."

"And she hasn't done anything like this before?"

"If by *like this* you mean taken Dylan somewhere without telling me, not to my knowledge."

Trent could tell his interrogation of Savannah wasn't helping the situation, and she was looking more upset by the minute.

"What is it you aren't telling me?" Trent demanded.

"Nothing really."

"I don't believe you."

"It's just that your father…"

Savannah had been dialing as she'd begun her explanation. Now she spoke to the person who'd answered. "Aunt Stacy," Savannah said into the phone. "I was wondering if Lori is still there with Dylan?" She paused and her entire body slumped with relief. "No, that's fine. I wasn't expecting him to be gone. Lori didn't say anything about heading over there." A pause. "Oh, he did? No, he didn't say anything to me about it."

Fury rose in Trent while he waited for her to finish chatting with her aunt. The part of him that wasn't plotting his father's downfall admired Savannah's ability to remain calm and think under pressure.

"No need to mention I called," Savannah was saying, her voice showing no stress at all. "I'll be by in a bit."

When she disconnected the call, she sank onto the bed and put her face in her hands. Her body shook as she gasped in a ragged breath. Trent put his hand on her shoulder. She jerked away as if burned. Her blue eyes were hot as she gazed up into his face. But as quickly as her temper flared, she calmed down.

"Sorry. That wasn't directed at you." She waved her hand in a random gesture. "Lori took Dylan over to Siggy's."

"Without saying anything to you or asking if it was okay?"

"He told her he'd cleared it with me." She rose, her movements stiff and slow as if every muscle in her body ached. "I guess I messed with him so he messed with me."

"I should have anticipated something like this."

"Neither of us had any way of knowing." Her neutral tone was at odds with the fear and anger she'd demonstrated moments earlier. "I'm sorry to ask for another favor, but do you mind driving me over there? It looks as if Lori helped herself to my car."

"Whatever you need."

Five minutes later, they were back in the LA traffic. Savannah's fierce demeanor invited no conversation. Trent kept his focus on the road. The drive to his father's house took over an hour. It was a tense sixty minutes. He couldn't imagine what she was going through, the panic she must have felt coming back to the hotel and finding her son gone, the roller coaster of emotions when she figured out the nanny had taken Dylan to his grandfather.

Trent wanted to be there when she faced down Siggy, but when they pulled up to the enormous Beverly Hills mansion, she shook her head when he shut off the car.

"I need to do this on my own."

"Are you sure that's your best option? My father will try to bully you."

"He's gone too far this time."

"Call me when you're on your way back to the hotel." Everything in him was clamoring to accompany her into the mansion and act as her champion. "I need to know you're okay."

"I'm going to be just fine."

"Regardless. Call me."

With a nod, Savannah got out of the car and Trent stared at the mansion's front door long after she was lost from view.

Five

Savannah's heels clicked against the travertine tile of the wide entryway as she let herself into Siggy's mansion. The earlier heat of anger had been replaced by icy determination. Ever since she'd come to live in this house at age eleven, she'd been intimidated by the man who lived here. She'd seen how he criticized his sons, dominated his staff and intimidated his business associates.

But today he'd stopped being someone to fear. Today, he'd interfered with her son, and she would do whatever it took to make sure that never happened again.

Set on a half-acre lot, the modern house had a wide-open floor plan that was perfect for entertaining. As a child, Savannah had witnessed hundreds of parties, and when she was old enough, she'd served at many.

The backyard had enough space for a large pool with a broad black-and-white marble surround, a pool house and a separate outdoor dining area for twelve beside an expansive fire feature.

Although the house was fifteen thousand square feet, there were only six bedrooms, and the way the public spaces opened onto each other, it was easy for her to find Siggy and Dylan in the main living room.

Lori was the first one to catch sight of her. Siggy was on the phone near the middle set of French doors that opened onto the backyard, his back to her. Dylan toddled along the espresso-toned hardwood floors that flowed into the dining room. Savannah made straight for him and snatched him into her arms. Pausing for a brief second to hug him and breathe in his familiar scent, she then turned to her babysitter.

"Give me my car keys and get out of here before I have you arrested."

The girl backed away from Savannah's advance, obviously terrified. "I didn't do anything wrong," she protested. "He asked me to come by with the baby. He said it was okay. He told me you knew."

"I don't care what he said. I hired you. You only answer to me." Savannah felt no remorse at scaring the girl after what she'd done. She put her hand out and stared daggers at Lori until she put the car keys in Savannah's palm.

"How am I supposed to get home?"

"I couldn't care less."

Savannah turned her back on the girl and headed for the foyer. While a part of her wanted to confront Siggy, she knew she would lose the battle. However, before she could reach the foyer, a tall broad-shouldered man in a black suit stepped in her path.

"I can't let you leave."

A little dazed by what he'd just said, Savannah was momentarily stumped for a response. Was she to be a prisoner? Savannah considered the surge of independence with which she'd turned down Trent's offer of support. Never in a million years had she thought Siggy would prevent her from leaving.

First she scowled at the man blocking her way, but seeing he had no intention of moving, she glanced over her shoulder at her father-in-law. He was still on the phone and didn't acknowledge the standoff happening twenty feet away. The righteous fury that had carried her this far had started to subside, but mounting panic gave her an adrenaline boost. She'd prepared herself to reclaim her son and fire Lori. She hadn't planned on having to save herself, as well.

"Step aside," she told the man and silently cursed when she heard the slight tremor in her voice. The entranceway he blocked was ten feet wide, leaving plenty of room to go around him, but with Dylan in her arms and four-inch heels on her feet, she doubted she could move fast enough on the marble floor to make a break for it.

"I can't let you go until he says it's okay."

Unwilling to argue with the man further, Savannah turned her back on Siggy. Frustration and helplessness washed over her. She hated feeling this way. It was how she'd felt from the moment she'd slid Rafe's ring onto her finger. Why had she let him talk her into marrying him? She should have toughened up and trusted she could handle being a single mom.

Siggy concluded his call and headed in her direction. Savannah barely let him take three steps before venting her outrage.

"How dare you try to keep us here." She didn't care if this was the wrong tack to take with her father-in-law. "Call off your gorilla. Dylan and I are leaving now."

"We need to talk."

"There is nothing to talk about. Dylan and I are leaving."

"To go where?" He might have sounded reasonable, but

his eyes flashed with disdain. "You have no money and you are deep in debt."

"Thanks to your son."

"He was sick."

"Yes, and he made a lot of bad choices. It left me with a huge financial burden and barely anything for Dylan and me to live on. You know he would hate that."

"I know that he would like for me to take care of his son."

His son. But not her. Instinctively, Savannah tightened her hold on Dylan and shifted so that her body was between her son and the two men who flanked her. Would they try to take him by force? Savannah pushed down dismay. She would not leave here without her Dylan, but couldn't bear the thought of staying. They would be prisoners.

"Then please buy back the stock Rafe left Dylan. Give us the chance for a fresh start."

"A fresh start? What sort of fresh start are you looking for?"

"I thought I would find a small house for just the two of us, and go back to work."

"You mean acting." He said it with a great deal of derision. "That wouldn't be necessary if you moved in here."

Around and around the argument went. She and Siggy had been wearing out this topic since shortly after Rafe's death nine months ago.

"I want Dylan to live in a neighborhood filled with children who come over after school to play."

She had this idyllic image in her head of small-town living, where her house was the most popular one on the block with the kids. Siggy's Hollywood home was a showplace and not one bit kid friendly.

"He's not old enough to go to school."

And by the time he was, she'd be well and firmly trapped. "Do you plan on keeping me here by force?"

"Of course not. You're free to go whenever you wish."

"Thank you." She turned to go, but her way was still blocked. "I wish to go now."

From behind her came Siggy's smooth voice. "Dylan stays."

Savannah fought down panic. "We're both leaving."

For a span of several heartbeats, no one moved. Then the front door opened and Trent stepped inside.

Trent left the front door open as he crossed the expansive foyer. The man barring Savannah's path had two inches and thirty pounds on Trent, but he didn't see this as a problem.

He looked into Savannah's eyes and hoped she'd follow his lead. "We have a plane to catch. And you know how the traffic is."

"Yes, of course." Her gaze searched his.

"She's not going anywhere." Siggy actually appeared to think he could get away with compelling Savannah to stay by bullying her.

"That's not true," Savannah stated, her relief obvious. She took the hand Trent held out to her and came to stand beside him. "Dylan and I were trying to leave, but your father was threatening me."

"Is that true?"

Siggy didn't answer Trent's question but instead asked one of his own. "So you're cheating on your husband with him?"

"Rafe is dead. She can't cheat on his memory."

"And it's no business of yours who I'm with." Savannah shook her head. "Trent is family and he's helping me. Something you should be doing."

"Neither one of you is going to get anywhere near the company again."

"Dylan owns a majority share. That means I'm in control until he turns twenty-one. You have nothing to say about it."

"It's my company. I built it. I have everything to say about it."

"Not unless you buy the shares back."

"I don't have to buy the shares back," Siggy said, his eyes burning with malice. "All I need is control of my grandson."

Beside him, Savannah stiffened. Trent stepped forward. "Do not threaten her."

Siggy sneered. "Or what?"

Trent wasn't a reckless teenager anymore, but his father continued to treat him with contempt. Since striking out to make it on his own, Trent was less and less bothered by his father's low opinion. He'd come to accept that no matter how successful he was, nothing diminished Siggy's disapproval.

"Try me and see." Trent gave his father a cold smile, set his hand on Savannah's back and guided her toward the front door.

She was trembling as they crossed from the cold foyer into the bright afternoon sunshine, but as they headed across the driveway to her car, she released a shaky smile.

"I've never been so happy to see anybody in my entire life."

"That's probably not something you would've said yesterday."

She opened her car's back door and settled Dylan into his seat. "You might be surprised."

Trent waited for her to say more, but she simply buckled her son in and closed the door. At last she faced him, and her gorgeous smile hit him like a two-by-four. Unfortunately it was gone as fast as it had arrived.

"I don't have to tell you how frightening that was. He wants to take Dylan away from me."

"You need to contact a lawyer and get ahead of this."

"You're right." Her shoulders slumped. "But right now I need to get out of here."

While Trent followed her back to her hotel, a plan began to form in his mind. He parked next to her in the hotel's large lot and intercepted her as she was getting out of her car.

"You can't stay here."

She didn't look happy as she gazed toward the hotel's shabby facade. "But it's only temporary."

The longer he was with Savannah, the more he felt driven to fix things for her. It was an old pattern. One he thought he'd abandoned when she'd married Rafe. "I don't mean the hotel. I mean LA."

"I don't want to, but with everything that's going on with the company, I can't leave until things are settled." She wasn't acknowledging how dire her situation was. Alone in LA, she would be at Siggy's mercy.

"You and Dylan are coming back to Las Vegas with me."

Trent didn't second-guess his decision to get further entangled with Savannah and her son. A week ago, he'd been avoiding her, refusing to get involved in her troubles. But what was going on between her and his father kept him from being neutral. She might have been foolish to marry his brother, but she didn't deserve to lose her son because Siggy had lost his.

"I can't."

"What's stopping you?" The question came out with a sardonic spin. "You have no ties to LA. In Vegas you have me."

She opened her mouth and looked ready to refuse. He could almost see the wheels turning. Was she trading one bad situation for another? He could have reassured her, but no matter what else had happened between them, he'd always been honest with her.

"I don't like the idea of you and Dylan alone here." Trent couldn't imagine returning to Las Vegas and leaving her to fend for herself. "And I don't trust Siggy."

She gripped her keys tight and looked a little like a defendant awaiting a verdict. "How long will it take to sort out what's going on with the company?"

"I don't know. It will depend on what Logan finds in the company's files."

"I suppose I could find an inexpensive rental in Vegas."

"I think you and Dylan would be better off staying with me."

"Absolutely not."

"I live in a gated community, on an estate with two acres of land and a guesthouse. My housekeeper loves children and is completely trustworthy. Rhoda can watch Dylan whenever you need her to."

Although he thought he'd made a terrific pitch, Savannah looked unconvinced. "I don't understand."

"What's there to understand?"

"We haven't spoken since I married Rafe. Just yesterday I had to hunt you down in the club because you wouldn't answer any of my calls. Now you're bending over backward to help me out. I don't get it."

He didn't want to dig too deep into his motivations. "Don't look a gift horse in the mouth."

"You'll have to do better than that."

"What do you want me to tell you?"

She cocked her head and regarded him through narrowed eyes. "What changed? Why are you suddenly my knight in shining armor again?"

"I'm not." But he could see where she might be misinterpreting his helpfulness. "My motives are purely selfish."

"How, exactly?"

"Didn't you see the look on my father's face?" The memory of it made Trent grin. "He is beyond frustrated that I'm helping you."

"So this is about you and your father?"

"Yes." And in the spirit of honesty, Trent continued, "I also feel responsible for you getting involved with my brother and in this mess."

"Why do you think that?"

"You obviously were in a vulnerable place after we broke up, and Rafe took advantage of that."

She stared at him for a long moment before nodding. "I'd better go get Murphy and our things."

"Does that mean you're coming with me to Las Vegas?"

"It makes sense for the time being." She didn't appear happy or relieved.

"Why don't you stay here with Dylan and I'll take care of collecting your stuff?"

She shook her head. "Is it weird that I'm uncomfortable waiting in this parking lot alone?"

Trent realized then what a good job she'd been doing hiding her anxiety. "Not weird at all. Grab Dylan and we'll do this together."

Ten minutes after she'd checked out and left the babysitter's suitcase with the concierge, they were headed back to the Van Nuys airport. Both she and Trent had been driving rental cars. They dropped them off at the agency before heading to the chartered plane.

All through the day, from the plane ride to their confrontation with Siggy and now a second flight, Dylan had proven to be a sunny, spirited child. Trent sat across from the boy and regarded him in bemusement. "He takes after you."

"He definitely has my nose."

"Yes, but that's not what I was referring to. I meant his temperament."

"What about his temperament?"

"Dylan is a happy baby. Rafe was a fussy child. At least that's what my mother says. And he turned into a difficult adult."

"Your brother had his moments." Savannah kept her attention fixed on Dylan. "I don't know how I got so lucky with Dylan. He's been easy since the day he was born." She laughed. "Makes me want to have several more."

Whenever she'd made statements like this, Trent visualized her surrounded by little girls with heart-wrenching blue eyes and blond ringlets. For some reason, he'd never pictured her with boys. Yet here sat a handsome lad with dark brown hair and curious blue eyes, and Trent wondered how many more sons were in her future.

"You're an excellent mother. Of course, that's no surprise to anyone."

"It was a surprise to me," she said. "As much as I've always wanted a family, I really wasn't sure if I was capable of taking care of one."

Her confession surprised him. "But you've always seemed so determined…"

How had she been so eager to do something when she wasn't sure if she could? Trent had always been confident in everything he did. He couldn't imagine taking on something he knew he couldn't handle. With her inability to stick up for herself, she'd always struck him as insecure and unwilling to take chances. Maybe she was braver than he'd ever realized.

"Just because I'm scared of something doesn't mean I won't do it. If that had been the case, I never would've gone to New York City. Never modeled. And I sure wouldn't have acted on a soap opera." She gave him a melancholy smile. "I didn't believe I could do any of it. Especially after I saw how beautiful the other girls were and heard the stories of how hard the modeling business was."

"When you left LA, I never imagined you doubted yourself. Why would you? You were beautiful."

"I was short."

"You're five-eight."

"Most models are five-ten and taller. I didn't book a lot of jobs because of that. And it kept me off the runway. Which made me feel inadequate. It's why I traded modeling for acting."

"How did I not know you felt this way?"

"I saw the girls you dated. Not only were they beautiful, but they were also over-the-top confident. They had to be to keep up with you."

But none of those girls had stuck. None of them lingered in his thoughts like Savannah had. Like she still did.

"What do you mean, keep up with me?"

"You know, your party lifestyle. The clubs, the celebrities you hang with. All that can be pretty intimidating for a girl with small-town roots, raised in the servants' quarters."

"I never saw you like that."

"I saw me like that." She tickled her son and made him giggle.

Trent let her words sink in. Why, in all the years they'd known each other, had she never spoken of this? She made it sound as if she didn't think she was good enough for him. That wasn't true. The trouble in their relationship had been that they wanted different things.

Besides, she'd considered herself good enough for his brother. Or was it that Rafe had never made her feel less than utterly desirable and truly wanted? A vise clamped down on Trent's chest.

"Well, you shouldn't."

He checked his watch and then turned his attention to

the darkening sky outside the aircraft. They would be on the ground in twenty minutes. Trent could feel Savannah watching him, sensed her desire for him to elaborate, but he had no more to say.

An hour later, he was carrying his sleeping nephew through his house. Before taking her out to the guest-house, Trent gave Savannah a tour of the wide-open first-floor living area.

Despite her years in his father's mansion and her year and a half living in her own enormous house, for some reason she was goggling at Trent's nine-thousand-square-foot spread.

"You live here?"

He wasn't sure what to make of the laughter in her voice. "Obviously."

"It's a little over-the-top, don't you think?"

"I bought it for the outdoor space," he explained, feeling slightly peevish at her criticism.

While the traditional French country style wasn't his cup of tea, the amenities more than made up for the elaborate plasterwork on the fireplaces and overabundance of pillars and crown molding. Floor-to-ceiling windows and French doors filled the house with light. The place had come furnished with faux antiques that complemented the builder's vision of a French château.

"I can't wait to see it."

Trent guided her through a set of French doors that let out onto a wide, covered terrace. In addition to the guest-house, his backyard hosted a large pool with a swim-up bar and a pool house, an outdoor movie screen and a putting green. Savannah put on the brakes as soon as she stepped outside.

"Is that a slide?" She pointed out the towering water slide that spiraled from the second-floor terrace to the pool. "I'm not sure this is going to work out for Dylan and me."

"Why not?"

"It's a big boy playground." And from the way she was looking at him, he was the big boy.

"What does that have to do with anything?"

"Don't you think having your sister-in-law and her infant son living in your guesthouse will cramp your style?"

"I'm not planning on throwing any wild parties while you're here, if that's what you're insinuating."

She sighed and gave him her full attention. "We'll stay just a couple days. Long enough for me to get my feet back under me and to find a place we can rent for a little while."

"Stay as long as you want," Trent said and meant every word. "Now that that's settled, are you ready to see the guesthouse?"

Six

Shaded by the palm trees that dotted the landscape, Savannah sat beside Trent's pool with her feet dangling in the lukewarm water. No breeze stirred the air and sweat trickled down her skin. She was ready for the break in the heat the forecasters promised for later in the week. Apparently in the weeks leading up to Halloween, the highs in Las Vegas dropped from upper nineties to low eighties.

Beside her on the terra-cotta tile sat a plate with half a tuna sandwich and a glass of iced tea. Nearby, Dylan slept peacefully in a portable crib and Murphy snored happily on a shaded lounge chair. They'd been living in Trent's guesthouse for four days. With his backyard as gorgeously landscaped as any five-star resort, Savannah felt as if she was on vacation, not in the midst of a personal crisis.

She felt safe for the first time since she'd found out that Rafe was sick. Already her guards were coming down. Which troubled her because she hadn't only been motivated by fear of what Siggy might try next when she let

Trent talk her into returning to Las Vegas. She'd also been swept up in a giddy euphoria that he'd cared enough to worry about her. In short, Savannah's reasons for coming to Las Vegas were more about what might happen with Trent than what had happened with Siggy.

Today she would stop procrastinating and corner Trent about what was going on with the label. She knew he and his friend had been digging into the company's files, and she needed to know what they'd found. But given the way he'd avoided answering her inquiries so far, she worried that what they'd found was really bad.

Just then, Trent came out onto the patio from the main house. Over the past few days, Savannah had noticed more and more that if she thought hard enough about Trent, he either appeared or called. In the old days she might have thought this meant they were in sync. These days she chalked it up to her infringement on his bachelor lifestyle.

"You look happy," he said, keeping his voice low as he approached. Today he wore a pair of khaki pants and a white polo that brought out his tan. His blue eyes flicked toward Dylan's crib. "I think Vegas agrees with you."

"I think what agrees with me is feeling safe for the first time since Rafe died and I found out how bad our financial situation really was."

"It's going to be okay."

She studied his features and felt reassured by his sincerity. "Can you tell me what you found out about the business?"

"It's as you expected. The financials are not in good shape. They haven't been paying their artists everything they're owed. One or two probably won't sign another contract."

"What can we do?"

"West Coast Records has several strong artists. But there are too many who've done nothing. It's not their fault. They weren't well managed. A few of them could be kept on, provided their next albums are better produced."

"But who's going to do that? I don't know anything about the music side of things. I might be able to run the business side with help, but when it comes right down to it, the label needs someone like you who can do both."

"I know what you're thinking, but it's not going to happen. My father will never allow me to take over the company."

"Not even if you can save it from going under?"

"From the correspondence between him, Gerry and Rafe, Siggy doesn't believe the company is in trouble."

"How is that possible? Surely even if Rafe kept how bad it was from him, Gerry would have told Siggy the truth."

"And been the one to shatter the old man's vision of his perfect firstborn son?"

Savannah heard the bitterness in Trent's voice. No matter what he said to the contrary, it still stung that his father showed him so little respect.

"Besides," Trent continued, "Gerry has had his own agenda these past couple of years."

Not liking the sound of that, Savannah asked, "What sort of agenda?"

"Some of the company's troubles stem from Gerry's embezzling."

"Embezzling?" Savannah shook her head, unable to believe what she was hearing.

"Apparently he's been stealing money from the company for years. He's been in the perfect position to steal and hide it. I'm sure as years went on and he wasn't caught he grew bolder. And when he was passed over for CEO in favor of Rafe, he probably figured he'd get whatever he could and get out."

"What do we do? Do we call the police?"

"Unfortunately Gerry is a lot cleverer than my father

ever gave him credit for. Not only did he steal money, he made it look as if Rafe took it. Only by digging into Gerry's finances was Logan able to find out that Gerry's spending outpaced his salary and bonuses."

Savannah's hopes plummeted. Nothing they'd found helped her situation. The company was likely on the verge of bankruptcy and so was she.

"Come on," Trent said, stripping off his shirt as he headed toward the pool house. "Let's go for a swim."

When she'd packed for Vegas the first time, she hadn't planned to be vacationing. "I don't have a suit."

The most she'd done in the last few days was to wade in the shallow end of the pool so that she could let Dylan frolic in the water. Given how hot the last few days had been, this hadn't been satisfying, but she'd been reluctant to venture off the property and go shopping for herself.

"I keep all sorts of suits in the pool house," Trent replied, disappearing into the building. Less than a minute later, he was back wearing swim trunks, his glorious chest and abs bare to the sun. "Try one of these."

It did not surprise Savannah one bit that the bikinis Trent held up were on the tiny side. "I don't suppose you have a one-piece in there somewhere."

He shook his head. "The last thing you need is a one-piece. You have a gorgeous body. You should show it off."

She'd had a gorgeous body. Now she carried a little extra weight on her hips and knew Trent liked his girls lean and fit. Almost as soon as the thought arrived, she dismissed it. What did it matter how Trent liked his women? She wasn't one of them. With a heartfelt sigh, Savannah got to her feet and took the bikinis Trent held out.

"I know he's sleeping, but could you keep an eye on Dylan while I change?"

After what had happened in LA, she was having a hard time letting Dylan out of her sight. If Trent had noticed her paranoia, he hadn't said anything. Savannah knew she would have to eventually leave her son in someone else's care, but for right now she was more comfortable keeping him close by.

Trent was peering at a sleeping Dylan when Savannah returned. In this unguarded moment Trent's expression captivated her. With his features softened in wonder, he looked younger and happier. Even though he didn't realize Dylan was his son, he was growing attached to the boy. This made Savannah's stomach tighten in an uncomfortable knot. Part of her wanted to tell Trent that he was Dylan's father. But would he believe her? Or would he see this as a ploy to manipulate him?

Better that the secret remain hidden. Trent liked his bachelor lifestyle and his freedom. No reason to disrupt either. She appreciated his help with the company and wouldn't burden him with the one thing he never wanted— a family.

"What?"

"Hmm?"

She came out of her thoughts and found him staring at her.

"You are looking at me funny. I'm not a complete idiot when it comes to kids, you know."

"You're not?" She retreated into friendly banter. "And where did you get all your experience?"

"For a couple months last year, I dated a woman who had two."

"Two what?"

"Two children. Agnes and Theo. They were four and eight. Great kids."

This news caused Savannah's confidence to implode. After everything he'd said about not wanting a family, he'd dated a woman with children. It felt like betrayal, which was ridiculous. He could date anyone he pleased. It was no business of hers. After all, she'd married his brother.

"That's nice." The urge to run over, pick up her son and hug him close was almost painful in its intensity. Savannah recognized her need for comfort.

"She was great. The kids were great."

"Sounds great."

"Aren't you going to ask me what happened?"

Savannah shook her head. "Are we going to swim or talk?"

Without waiting for his answer, she dived into the pool. The tepid water felt refreshing after the afternoon heat, and Savannah swam beneath the surface until her lungs burned. She rose, snatched a quick breath and dived again. Not until her fingers touched the pool's far wall did she come up again. Sucking in huge gulps of air, she turned and pushed off to stroke back the way she'd come.

Damn Trent for making her feel jealous. She had no right to the emotion where he was concerned. Most of the women she pictured him with were young party girls. She'd never imagined him dating someone with baggage. In the back of her mind a distressed voice called, *Why not me?*

At some point during her frantic swim, Trent had entered the pool. He stood near the center, his expression unreadable as she approached. Savannah stopped several feet away and gazed toward the portable crib. Through the mesh sides, she could see Dylan sleeping peacefully.

"She didn't mean anything to me."

Savannah couldn't believe Trent was continuing the conversation. "Really, it's none of my business."

"It was six months after you and I broke up. I wanted to see what dating a woman with kids was like." Obviously, Trent was not going to let it go.

"And what was it like?"

"Not bad. Different. We didn't really date. More like hung out. Right off the bat she told me she wasn't interested in someone like me."

"A party boy?"

"She wanted someone she could build a future with."

Savannah knew what that was like. "But she dated you anyway."

"She'd been divorced about a year and was looking to getting her feet wet in the dating pool." Trent ran his fingers through his hair, making it stand up in all directions. "I met her at the club. We went out once and both of us knew right away it wasn't going to work out."

"But you kept seeing her."

"There was no pressure."

Savannah had tried to keep things free and easy while they'd dated, but she hadn't always been successful. In her heart, she'd longed for a future with him. A life filled with children and happiness.

"Why are you telling me all this?"

"I don't know."

"That's not like you. You always have a reason for what you do."

"I usually have a reason for what I do. Except when it comes to you."

"Trent—"

Before she could finish whatever it was that she'd been about to say, his arms went around her and his lips found hers. Held tight against his strong body, Savannah gave herself to the powerful emotions surging through her. With her fingers buried in his hair, she hung on for dear life as he devoured her mouth. The water gave her buoyancy and she floated in a bubble of joy.

She wanted him. She wanted this.

The privacy offered by the lush landscaping around the pool eased Savannah's doubts as Trent released the clasp holding her bikini top in place. She gasped as his lips drifted down her neck and settled over the wildly beating pulse in her throat. She wrapped her legs around his hips, feeling his erection hard against her stomach. His right hand came between them and settled over her breast while his other hand cupped her butt, lifting her partially out of the water.

She reveled in the sweep of his tongue over her nipple. It tightened into an aching peak as he laved it once more before pulling the hard bud into his mouth and sucking. She closed her eyes and let the delicious sensations wash over her. After the first time they'd made love, the passion she and Trent shared left Savannah convinced that they belonged together. But no matter how overpowering and all-consuming the connection was between them, Trent wasn't about to settle down and give her the life she craved.

Over the heartbeat thundering in her ears, she heard the soft sounds Dylan made as he stirred to wakefulness. Her hands had worked their way down Trent's torso to the waistband of his swim shorts. Desire clouded her mind, but Savannah's maternal instincts were stronger. With a shudder she broke off their kiss and pushed against Trent's shoulders.

"Dylan," she gasped, shuddering as Trent's fingertips grazed the edge of her bathing suit bottoms, tantalizing inches from where she ached. "He's waking up. I need to get to him."

Without a hint of reluctance or disappointment, Trent set her free. As she swam to the pool's edge, she wasn't sure whether to feel relief or regret that he was being so understanding. With conflicting emotions churning in her gut, Savannah quickly toweled off and went to check on her son.

Dylan was rubbing his eyes, but when she spoke his name, he looked up at her with a wide grin. Savannah's heart melted. How lucky she was to have such a wonderful baby boy. Hearing Trent emerge from the pool, she glanced over her shoulder at him. If she couldn't have the love of her life, at least she had his son.

"I'd better get back to the guesthouse so I can change him."

"Savannah, about what just happened…"

"There's no need to say anything." Her heart contracted at his need to make excuses. "It's always been like this between us."

"And that's it?"

"What more is there? Nothing else about our situation has changed. We're the same people who broke up two years ago because I wanted a family and you didn't."

"I guess we are." His neutral expression told her nothing. "It's just always been easy to forget our differences when I'm kissing you."

He was certainly right about that. And the more time she spent around him, the more likely they would be to indulge in their passion for each other. But there was no future in that. She needed to start thinking about where she was going and what she was going to do.

"Do you have some time this afternoon to start coming up with a plan for straightening out the company?"

"I have a couple of meetings at the club that should take me into early evening. How about we do a late dinner here?"

"Seven?"

"Sounds about right."

Savannah wrapped herself in a dry towel and then picked up Dylan. She offered Trent a bright smile that hid her heavy heart. "I'll see you then."

As soon as Savannah disappeared in the direction of the guesthouse, Trent dived back into the pool. To burn off some of his sexual frustration, he swam hard for several laps before levering himself out and flopping onto a nearby lounge chair. For the last four days he'd been tormented by Savannah's proximity. Night was the worst. Knowing she slept mere steps from his big empty bed had summoned every memory of their time together. To keep himself from acting on his fantasies about her, he'd taken to spending long hours at the club and not returning home until the sky lightened toward dawn.

All of which had simply stoked his hunger, making him unable to keep his hands off her moments earlier. And now he'd agreed to a late dinner under the guise of talking business.

With a growl, Trent got to his feet and headed inside. She would expect him to have answers, and if he couldn't provide any she might get frustrated enough to head back to LA and take Siggy on by herself. He needed to sort through their options. Just as important, he needed to chat with one of his partners in the club, Nate Tucker.

Trent showered and dressed in gray slacks and a bright blue shirt. His impulses pointed him toward the back of the house, where he might run into Savannah again. Cursing his weakness, Trent headed for his garage.

The gated community where he lived was a twenty-minute drive from the Cobalt. Negotiating the heavy Las Vegas traffic gave him plenty of time to ponder what had led up to that fantastic kiss in the pool. What had possessed him to tell Savannah about Karen? He wasn't the type to dredge up past romances. And to belabor the fact that he'd dated a woman with children could only hurt Savannah.

Had he hoped to reiterate that he wasn't a guy who wanted to be tied down with kids? An observer of the conversation might have wondered if Trent was trying to give the impression that he'd at least experimented with being a family guy.

When Trent got to Cobalt, instead of heading to his office at the club, he headed for the hotel's executive offices. JT Stone, owner of the hotel, was a brilliant businessman and would have solid advice about how to deal with the failing record label. The two men had bonded over similar experiences growing up with difficult fathers and running family businesses. In JT's case, he'd fought to regain control of the company that had been in the family for years and won. But in the end, he'd sold the family's overleveraged hotel chain to his cousin in order to own Cobalt free and clear. That JT's father had ended up in prison for fraud had been icing on the cake.

Trent approached JT's executive assistant. "Is he around?"

Nina nodded. "He has a meeting in half an hour, but he's free until then."

"Thanks." Trent stepped into the doorway that led to JT's office and knocked on the frame. "Nina said you have a couple minutes."

"Sure, come on in." JT stood and came around his desk to shake Trent's hand. "What's up?"

"I have a little business dilemma I'd like to talk to you about."

JT's expression lit with interest. He'd dealt with more than his share of business dilemmas in the last two years. Gesturing toward the comfortable sitting area near the large windows that overlooked Cobalt's extensive grounds, JT grabbed a couple bottles of water and joined Trent.

"What's going on?"

"You know how things are with me and the family company."

"Sure."

"My sister-in-law came to me a few days ago wanting my help. When my brother died, he left his controlling interest in the business to his son. That puts Savannah in a position of overseeing the majority shares."

"Let me guess—she asked you to step in as CEO."

"Not exactly. Both of us know there's no way my father would go for that. But she needs my help sorting out the company's various problems."

"Such as?"

"For one thing, they're not paying their artists all the royalties owed to them."

"Because they don't have the money?"

"The company has been doing poorly for years, but things got worse once my brother got sick." Trent cracked the seal on the bottle of water and drank. "Then there's the problem of embezzlement. West Coast Records' general manager has been stealing for quite a few years."

JT arched an eyebrow. "And you know this how?"

Trent gave a little shrug. "I might have had Logan digging around in their computers."

JT and Logan were related through marriage. Their wives were two of the three Fontaine sisters, who ran resort and hotel properties on the Strip. Trent had often wondered what it was like for JT to be married to his competition. His wife, Violet, managed two of the three Fontaine properties.

"Did Logan find anything else troubling?"

"I haven't spoken with him in a couple days, but it's possible." Trent rubbed his eyes, noting a mild twinge in his temple as he considered what else might be going wrong. "In the meantime, Savannah is deep in debt thanks to her husband's reckless spending, and the only asset she has is her major stake in a failing company."

"She should try to dump the company now before the word gets out."

"Unfortunately the way the corporation was set up, she has to get approval from the board in order to sell. And since my father controls the board, he's making things difficult for her."

"Why?"

"He wants control of his grandson and Savannah out of the picture."

JT nodded his understanding. "She's not willing to let that happen."

"Siggy isn't going to let Dylan go without a fight. He already made an attempt to kidnap his grandson."

"You're kidding, right?"

"I wish I was." Trent went on to share the details of their visit to the company and how they'd come back to find Savannah's hotel room empty. "She and Dylan are staying with me at the house. The whole thing really spooked her. She hasn't left the property since she arrived."

"But he can't actually force her to give up her son."

"No," Trent agreed, his mind running through all the things Siggy could do. "But he knows how to play dirty, and I wouldn't put it past him to take her to court over some sort of manufactured evidence that makes her appear as if she's a bad mother."

"But she could fight him."

"She doesn't have the resources for a prolonged battle."

JT was assessing him through narrowed eyes. Trent could read his thoughts easily enough. The owner of Cobalt was wondering why Trent wasn't doing everything in his power to help his sister-in-law fight.

"I've offered financial help," he explained, preempting the man's question. "She's being stubborn about taking money from me. I don't think she'd be living in my guesthouse if Siggy hadn't spooked her by having the nanny bring him Dylan without Savannah's permission."

"You guys go back a ways, don't you?"

"We dated." As much as Trent liked JT, he wasn't about to open up about his complicated relationship with his brother's widow.

But that didn't stop JT from asking. "And yet she married your brother?"

"Yeah." Trent would've liked to leave it at that, but JT was staring at him and didn't appear as if he was going to take Trent's brief response as a hint to drop it. "She wanted family. Kids. You know."

"Seems pretty cold of her to take up with your brother after you two stopped seeing each other."

Trent would never describe Savannah as cold. "I don't know that she chose my brother to spite me. She'd always liked Rafe. And she got pregnant."

None of this showed Savannah in a flattering light, which didn't strike Trent as being fair. And yet, wasn't this exactly what he'd been thinking about her for the last year and a half? What was with his sudden urge to defend her?

"She's been through a lot," he concluded.

"She's pretty lucky to have you." JT's demeanor went from curious to brisk and businesslike. "So it sounds like the problem you're facing is this. Her son owns a majority share of a company that's going under and she has no way of selling the shares and raising the money she needs to pay off her husband's debts."

"You summed it up perfectly."

"But if I know you," JT said with a smile, "you've plotted half a dozen ways to get her out of her predicament."

"Actually, I've only come up with three. And I wanted to run them by you to see which you think might work out the best."

"Fire away."

Seven

Courtney Day's unflappable smile concealed Savannah's disappointment as she carried a glass of wine across Trent's enormous living room to Scarlett Fontaine. All afternoon Savannah had been alternately nervous and giddy about the upcoming alone time with Trent. Instead of an intimate dinner between just the two of them, Trent had shown up a half hour late with Logan Wolfe and his wife in tow. To hide her disappointment, Savannah had donned her alter ego and was playing the perfect hostess, the way she'd done a hundred times as Rafe's wife.

"It's really nice to meet you," Savannah said, in awe of Scarlett's beauty. She'd seen her dozens of times on TV, but the real woman was so much more charismatic. "I'm a huge fan."

"Ditto." Scarlett gave a little laugh at Savannah's expression. "What? You don't think I know who you are? I'll have you know *Loving New York* has been a total obsession of mine for years. I thought you were great on it."

"Thanks. It was an interesting three years."

"Do you miss it?"

"Sometimes. I thought about getting back into acting, but I'm not sure LA or New York is where I want to be." Savannah recognized she might not have a choice.

"I totally understand where you're coming from. I'm lucky I've been able to coordinate my filming schedule so I only have to be in LA once a week. It's been a bit of a challenge balancing the management of Fontaine Richesse with my acting career. Fortunately I have an amazing husband who supports me one hundred percent." Scarlett shot a heated glance toward the two men standing out on the terrace.

"Fontaine Richesse? You mean the hotel on the Strip?" Savannah's admiration for the woman went up several degrees. "You manage that and have an acting career?"

Scarlett's husky laugh echoed around the two-story living space. "I have excellent people in place to help me with the hotel, and my sister Violet is always on call if something comes up when I'm not around."

"Still." Savannah was feeling woefully inadequate. What had she done in the last year and a half? "I'm feeling overwhelmed and I'm not even working at the moment."

"But you have a baby to take care of, and you just lost your husband. Plus from what Logan tells me, the company your son inherited is having all sorts of problems."

Savannah wasn't surprised Scarlett knew some of her background. After all, Logan was helping Trent. Obviously the couple would have talked on their way here, and Logan would've explained what the meeting was about.

"It's a bit of a mess," Savannah agreed. "I don't know what I'd do if Trent hadn't agreed to help me."

"How long have you two known each other?"

"My aunt is his father's housekeeper. I moved in with her when I was eleven."

"So you grew up with him?"

"Sort of. It's weird living in someone else's house and being separated by the whole employer/employee thing. I probably shouldn't have gotten to know Trent and his siblings as well as I did."

"Had you always been in love with his brother?"

"No." It was an awkward situation to try to explain. "Actually, Trent and I dated for a few years while I was living in New York." Perhaps *dated* was not quite the right term for what they had done. She knew he'd seen other women when they were apart. But every time they got together, he'd made her feel like she was his only one.

Scarlett's eyes widened a little at Savannah's confession. "That explains a lot. You sure know how to make things complicated."

"I don't try to complicate things," Savannah said, "but they often seem to end up that way. I'm not very good at getting what I want."

"Maybe you just don't believe that you deserve to get it."

"You might be right." She'd never really believed that Trent would give up his bachelor ways for her. And that had kept her from fully committing to their relationship, as well. "I've always shied away from disappointment. It's kept me from going after what's really important."

"It's not too late."

"No, I suppose it's not." But she was lying.

Savannah glanced in Trent's direction once again. She'd really blown it with him when she'd agreed to marry his brother. If she'd chosen any other man, Trent might have been willing to give their relationship another chance. But Trent's resentment of his brother ran deep and her desperate decision had built an insurmountable wall between them. There was no going back from that.

Trent might be willing to help her, but that was because he had his own agenda when it came to West Coast

Records. The chemistry between them might be as hot as ever, but in her heart she knew what had happened in his office last week and had almost happened today was more about looking backward than moving forward.

"I was planning on moving to Tennessee once I found someone to run West Coast Records," Savannah said. "But lately I'm not sure I belong there or that I belong anywhere." Her gaze drifted toward Trent.

"You should give Las Vegas a try. If you're still interested in acting, it's a short plane ride to LA."

"When I left New York, I intended to continue acting, but then Rafe and I got involved and he didn't want his wife to work."

"Do you have an agent?"

Savannah shook her head. "I had one in New York, but we parted ways when I moved to LA. I wasn't sure if I wanted to work in film or TV and figured I would do something about representation once I got to there. Only… things happened and I never did."

"I'll put you in touch with a couple agents I know. Either one would be great to represent you."

"Thank you."

To her surprise, she felt a flutter of excitement in her chest. She'd connected working as an actress with living in LA. Savannah had opened her eyes to other possibilities. If she worked in film, she might go on location anywhere in the world. Lots of actresses balanced children and careers. No reason why she couldn't.

"I'll bet Trent would like it if you stuck around Las Vegas."

"Once we get things sorted out with the company, I'm not sure he'll notice if I stick around or not." But was she being honest with herself or was this another attempt to protect herself from getting hurt again?

"You don't believe that." Scarlett regarded her somberly.

"When my sisters got involved with JT and Ashton, I knew before anyone else that they belonged together. I get the same vibe when I look at you and Trent."

Savannah shook her head. "You've seen us together for less than a minute. How could you possibly tell anything about our relationship?"

"I've known Trent for two years, and Logan and I have been to his club a lot. I've never seen him look at any woman the way he looks at you."

Afraid of how much she wanted to believe Scarlett, Savannah gave a little laugh but decided not to argue. It didn't really matter how Trent looked at her. Two years ago, he hadn't wanted a future with her. In the meantime, she'd married his brother and given birth to Dylan. Trent might desire her—and that's probably what Scarlett was picking up on—but he most certainly was not going to give up his lifestyle and ask her to marry him.

And since that's what she wanted, wasn't she a fool to let herself get caught up in him once more? She needed to move out. That meant she had to stop burying her head in the sand, get a job and a place for her and Dylan to live.

"I'm really glad I met you," Savannah said. "I need to get back to work, and I'm thinking the sooner the better."

"I'm heading to LA in a couple of days. If you'd like to come along, I'd be happy to introduce you to some friends who could get you started on the right path."

Maybe by the time she got herself reestablished in LA the situation with Siggy would be less stressful. And if not, a new source of income meant she could afford to fight him and keep her son safe.

Savannah smiled at Scarlett in appreciation. "That would be terrific."

Trent glanced over his shoulder and saw the two women engrossed in their conversation. "You were right," he told

Logan, delighting at the rare smile curving Savannah's beautiful lips. "Savannah looks a lot more relaxed."

"My wife is like that. She has a knack for making people feel better. And if Savannah wants to go back to acting, Scarlett can help her out. She has some great contacts in Hollywood."

That made Trent frown. He hadn't considered that Savannah might return to LA so soon. It had only been a week since Siggy had pulled his stunt, and there was no reason to think he wouldn't try something equally despicable if Savannah and Dylan returned to LA.

His concern grew over dinner as Scarlett and Savannah chatted about the industry. It was apparent that his sister-in-law intended to return to work.

The two couples lingered over the meal and then moved outside for dessert. Trent hadn't done a lot of this sort of entertaining. A low-key evening with another couple was a nice change from the sort of parties he usually threw here. Between the game room in the upstairs loft that overlooked the living room and the big backyard with the pool, slide and outdoor movie screen, he usually hosted groups that liked to dance, drink and get a little crazy.

Savannah had taken a couple minutes as everyone moved outside to go check on her son. She came back with the baby monitor and explained she'd sent Rhoda home. The conversation between the women changed then to talk of babies and future plans for children.

Scarlett patted her husband's knee and shot him a sly smile. "We've decided to put off having children for at least another year. He's not happy about it, but I don't think my husband has any idea how demanding I'm going to get when I'm pregnant."

"It can't possibly be any worse than you are right now." Logan's words didn't match the tenderness in his eyes as he gazed at his gorgeous wife.

"Then you're in for a rude awakening. Violet was the sweetest thing until she got pregnant with Rowan. Poor JT was beside himself." Scarlett rolled her eyes in dramatic fashion.

"Beside himself with joy, maybe." Trent recalled JT being nothing but thrilled in the months leading up to becoming a father. He laughed at the sharp look Scarlett shot at him. "And Logan will be no different."

"You're not helping," Scarlett said, turning to Savannah. "I suppose you're going to side with them, too."

"I used to want a big family," Savannah said, not letting her gaze stray anywhere near Trent. "But now that I have Dylan, I'm content."

Trent felt an awkward *whump* in his chest. If he hadn't known better, he would've thought it was his heart breaking. Savannah was trying hard to spin her situation into something positive, but Trent had known her a long time and didn't believe for one minute that she would give up on her dreams unless they'd been crushed by disappointment.

"Melody and I are your family, too," he reminded her.

"I haven't forgotten. Which is why I've decided not to move to Tennessee."

"That's great."

"I'm glad you're okay with it," Savannah said, giving him a weak smile. "And if I can swing a few acting jobs in LA, I can afford a little house for Dylan and me here."

She made it sound as if she was intended to move out as soon as possible. "No need to rush. You can stay here as long as you want."

"I appreciate your generosity, but I think I've relied on you far too much already."

How did he explain to her that he liked it when she relied on him? When he came to her rescue she always gazed at him as if he was larger than life. In her eyes he was a hero, not the troublemaker everyone had to watch out for.

Trent kept an eye on the clock as the evening wound down. He'd hoped for some alone time with Savannah before she turned in, but the hour grew later and later. At long last, Scarlett patted her husband on the knee.

"I think you mentioned needing to get some more work done this evening," Scarlett said, standing up. "A security expert's job is never done."

"I think everyone here can sympathize," Trent said, trying to keep his relief from showing as everyone made their way to the foyer. "All of us have been known to work some pretty unorthodox hours."

"Thanks for the invite," Logan said. "Next time, let's do it at our house."

The two men shook hands while the women hugged. Minutes later, Trent and Savannah stood alone in his empty house. He wasted no time pulling her into his arms and kissing her. From her passionate response, she'd been feeling the same sensual pull. Her fingers tugged his shirt free from his pants and dived beneath the hem.

He groaned at the pleasure of her palms skating along his bare back. Lifting her into his arms, he made for the guesthouse, instinctively knowing she would want to be nearby if Dylan needed her. His frantic heartbeat made it hard for him to take things slow, but as he lowered her feet to the floor beside her bed, he sucked in a calming breath, pushed her out to arm's length and closed his eyes.

"Tonight we're going to take our time," he said, opening his eyes and peering at her.

She was flushed, her expression slightly dazed. She backed away and put her hands to her cheeks for a moment. Trent thought for sure she'd come to her senses. To his relief, instead of ordering him to leave her room, she stripped her asymmetrical tank over her head and cast it aside. Standing before him in a nude bra and khaki leggings, she threw her hands wide as if in surrender.

"I don't know if I can."

Trent loosened the buttons on his shirt and sent it sailing to join her top on the floor. "We have the rest of the evening to get it right."

Her pale eyebrows rose. "That's a relief, because I'm pretty sure we're seriously out of practice." She stuck her thumb inside the elastic waistband of her leggings and stretched them away from her body. "Would you like me to take these off, or do you want to do the honors?"

Trent's mouth went dry. He stepped into her space and bracketed her waist just above the material. Her smooth skin was warm beneath his palms. Moving with slow deliberation, he dipped his fingertips below her waistband. His hands rode her curves downward, taking her leggings with them. She was trembling as he helped her step out of the snug pants.

While she unhooked her bra and slipped it free, he dropped a kiss on her stomach. Eager to revisit every inch of her, he trailed his fingertips from her instep to her knee. Her breath grew shallow, uneven. She set her hands on his shoulders and leaned on him for support as her legs shook. Still kneeling, he hooked his fingers into her cream lace panties and eased them down her thighs.

"I don't know how much more of this I can take," she gasped as his mouth grazed down from her belly button.

"Let's see about that, shall we?"

Getting to his feet, Trent eased her back onto the bed and quickly divested himself of his clothes. She lifted onto her elbows to watch him, and he was aware of every greedy flicker in her blue gaze.

She propped one foot on the bed and waggled her knee in an enticing manner. "Come get me."

He hesitated only long enough to fish several condoms out of his pants pocket. She raised her eyebrow as he dropped them onto the nightstand.

"It's been too long," he said, setting his knee on the bed.

Her hands slid up his ribs and across his back as he covered her with his body. "Too long since what?"

"Since I've had you all to myself."

He kissed her then, stopping any further conversation and distracting her from the anguish behind what he'd said. She was all supple limbs and hot, welcoming mouth. Her tongue danced with his as they rediscovered each other with lips, teeth and hands. Nibbling his way down her neck, he found the sensitive spot made her writhe. Last time in his office, he'd been denied her beautiful breasts. He intended to make up for that.

A breathy moan broke from her lips as he swirled his tongue around her breast, making her back arch. She dug her fingers into his shoulders. Knowing exactly what she liked, he moistened her hard nipple and released a puff of air across the sensitive nub. Once again he was rewarded as her hips lifted. Her every moan, gasp and cry caressed his senses, the familiarity erasing their almost two-year estrangement.

Where once she'd been flawless, her body had now gained character. Motherhood had brought changes that he found vastly intriguing. He appreciated how her stretch marks testified to her maturity. And the extra weight she carried on her hips and butt lent her figure a lushness that enhanced her sensuality.

She protested when his fingers trailed across a stretch mark on her belly. "Motherhood isn't kind to a woman's body."

He resisted when she tried bringing his hand back to her breast. "You are more beautiful than ever."

"Next you'll be telling me it's okay that I packed on the pounds."

"You've hardly done that. And I love every inch of you. I always have."

He slid his shoulders between her thighs and filled his palms with her round backside. Her whole body trembled as he grazed his lips along the hollow beside her hipbone, and a ragged laugh escaped her.

It had been too long. Far too long. He licked her then. Her hips bucked in reaction, so he put his palm flat on her belly to keep her still. Her trembling increased as he tasted her excitement and found her ready for him. He flicked his tongue the way she liked and she moaned. At the sound he smiled. Then, he hummed against her, knowing it made her crazy.

"Yes!"

He needed her to remember how it was between them. To be the only man she thought of. Pulling out every trick in the book, he made love to her with his mouth, hands and voice.

"I want to hear that noise again," he said, looking up to watch her expression.

"What noise?" She was almost too breathless to be understood.

"The one you make when I do this." He repeated his action and wrenched a soft yelp from her throat. "Yes," he purred, "just like that."

In the past, he'd utilized his expertise to bring her to the edge of orgasm and keep her there. Once, he'd even drawn this out for an hour. But tonight she came the instant he slid one finger inside her. With her lips parted on a strangled cry, her body bowed. The length and intensity of her climax caught him by surprise.

"Words cannot describe how amazing you are at that." A single tear slipped down the side of her face, and she brushed it away with the back of her hand before extending her arms to him. "Come up here and kiss me."

He obliged, but kept the contact light and sweet despite

the temptation of her parted lips and the fingers she'd tunneled through his hair.

"I'm going to return the favor, I promise," she said, grasping his bicep with surprising force. "As soon as I've recovered."

"Later."

Trent reached to the nightstand and after two futile attempts managed to grab a condom with his shaking fingers. He caught the wrapper between his teeth and carefully tore it open. Hollowed out by the longing to be inside her, he sheathed himself in the protection and suckled her breasts as he settled between her thighs.

If the tantalizing movement of her hands down his body was intended to drive him mad, it worked. And based on the look she cast from beneath her lashes, she knew just how well. He didn't care. His level of arousal was almost painful as she wrapped her long fingers around him. A groan tore from his throat.

Fighting the urge to drive into her heat, he unclenched his teeth long enough to gasp, "I promised we'd take our time." He pulled her hand away from his erection. "I'm too close for much of that."

"Not close enough." Her pout made him smile.

Their lips came together again. The kisses were slow and sweet, a blending of tongue and breath. The mood shifted from frantic hunger to wrenching emotion. It was easy to forget the distance and hurt that had separated them.

Savannah slid the sole of her foot over Trent's muscled calf and let her hands roam over his chiseled torso. Each rise and dip of his glorious body was imprinted on her memory, but the real thing was so much better.

With her body building slowly toward another mind-blowing orgasm, Savannah stormed Trent's mouth with her tongue and nipped at his lower lip. She rocked against him until he flexed his fingers on her hip and shuddered. His erection lay trapped against her belly, hot and eager for her. Her hands dived between them and stroked him.

"I can't wait another second. I need you inside me."

"I need that, too." His voice rasped against her neck. "It's been too long."

When he shifted over her, she spread her legs and lifted her hips. Her head fell back and her breath caught as he positioned himself and thrust.

Stars exploded behind her eyes. "Magic," she murmured, closing her eyes to glory in how her body stretched and adapted to accommodate him. The fit was always perfect. He was her match in this.

"How I've missed this." Trent seized her mouth and began to move.

It wasn't like the night in his office when they'd both been hungry and frantic. This time Trent stared into her eyes and laced his fingers with hers. The emotion shading his expression was so raw it threatened to rip her heart out. Savannah wanted to turn aside and not get sucked into the whirlpool of longing for things that could never be.

Trent would never want more than this. She'd learned to accept that, but at moments like these when he gave her everything he was, her foolish heart hoped that maybe this time it would be different. Shutting the door on such thoughts, she closed her eyes and let her other senses take over.

His ragged breath fanned her hot skin as he kissed her shoulder. They were both close. She recognized the tension in his muscles and the rising intensity of his low murmurings. He wanted her to come and wouldn't let himself go until she did. Her climax waited, just out of sight. She was holding back, unwilling to reach for her pleasure, wanting to prolong the intimacy of the moment just a little while longer.

But her body wasn't about to be controlled. The first sharp bite of her orgasm stopped her breath. Her eyes snapped open. She caught Trent's satisfied smile as he watched her. The sight of him was enough to send her over the edge. Pleasure reared up and slapped her hard. Savannah exploded.

Trent's muted exclamation came a second later. Savannah had a moment to appreciate that he'd kept his voice down in consideration of Dylan sleeping in the room next door before a second wave of pleasure rolled through her.

She was sunk. The pressure in her chest told her that what had happened tonight had opened a rift in her defenses she'd be helpless to patch. It would take time and space to heal, and she wasn't sure she had the willpower to let either do its work.

In the aftermath of their lovemaking, Trent rolled over so that she was lying on top of him. He sent his fingertips skating along her spine in long, soothing caresses. She loved this part. The moments when Trent's guard was still down and she could talk to him about anything. But tonight she had trouble thinking of a subject that wouldn't lead to trouble.

Trent was the first to speak. "I'm sorry I was so angry with you for marrying Rafe."

"We'd been broken up for months. And it had ended so badly. But I shouldn't have started seeing Rafe."

"I couldn't believe how fast you got over me."

She was surprised by his admission. "I didn't get over you." She frowned. "You were the one who didn't want me."

"That's not true."

Trent shifted them until they lay on their sides facing each other, legs tangled to maintain their connection. Savannah put her head on the pillow while he caressed her cheek. Her heart thumped erratically as she took in his somber expression.

"You told me you had no interest in getting married and having children," she reminded him.

"That didn't mean I didn't want you. I just didn't want the same things you did." He kissed her forehead. "You were the one who decided to end our relationship. Not me."

Savannah remembered how she'd ached the day she'd told him they were done. "I guess in the end, it doesn't matter which of us called it quits. The fact is, we wanted different things and neither of us would be happy long term."

"I don't believe that's true. I would've been happy with you." The simple words sounded as if they came straight from his heart.

"But you didn't want…" *Children. Marriage.*

"I felt backed into a corner by your expectations."

"By my…?" She was horrified. If she could have put her dreams aside and been satisfied to just love Trent, would they have stayed together? She grew lightheaded at the thought of all the heartache she could've avoided. "How is that possible? I never put pressure on you."

"No, you didn't. At least not intentionally. But you had such an idealistic view of how you wanted your life to be." His fingers toyed with a strand of her hair, tickling her shoulder. "Were you happy with my brother?"

"Our marriage was more about an understanding than passion." She read no tension or hostility in his body as his hands played over her skin with lazy contentment. "He didn't love me."

"Did you love him?"

"Not the way a wife should. As I said, we both went in with our cards on the table. He wanted Dylan to carry on your father's dynasty." She shifted her head and kissed Trent's bare shoulder.

"And you were okay with that?"

"I was scared and alone and pregnant. I didn't know what I was going to do." Remembering that time, Savannah winced. That woman had been forlorn and in desperate need of saving. "I auditioned for anything that came along, but no one wanted to hire a woman who was three months pregnant. And I was sick. All the time. They talk about morning sickness. I had all-day sickness."

"I'm sorry it was such a hard time for you. And I'm glad my brother was there to help."

Rescuing her had always been Trent's thing. She could hear the regret in his voice and lifted her head to gaze into his eyes.

"He would have loved to hear you say that."

Trent scowled and gave her hair a fond tug. "You always see the best in people." He sounded like a weary big brother. "That's what gets you into trouble."

"I know you and Rafe never got along because of how your father favored him, but he wasn't a villain." Savannah wasn't sure why she needed Trent to recognize an alternate view of his brother. "He was as hurt and frustrated as you were. Siggy dumped the entire burden of his expectations and the weight of West Coast Records' legacy on Rafe. I'm not sure you realize how lucky you were to escape."

From his closed expression, she could tell he didn't believe her.

"Rafe wanted the business and he got it."

One thing marrying Rafe had done was give her a front-row seat to the dysfunction of the Caldwell household. During the short months she'd been Rafe's wife, she'd learned how much he'd been bothered by the rivalry Siggy had created.

"You're right, but he didn't want to be in it alone. He recognized that he needed your ability to scout new talent and Melody's talents as a songwriter and producer. Siggy ruined his dream as much as he destroyed yours."

"If you're trying to convince me to like my brother, you're wasting your time."

"It's not about you liking Rafe." Savannah laid her cheek against his chest once more. "It's about how the bitterness you carry for him keeps you stuck in the past."

If Trent understood that Rafe had been Siggy's tool, he might one day release some of the resentment that made him keep people at a distance. Maybe he'd stop running from love.

From her.

From being a family with her and Dylan.

Hopelessness swept over her. But could Trent ever see her son as anything other than his brother's child? And what would happen if he learned the truth? Would he hate her or could he understand why she'd chosen not to tell him?

Savannah kissed Trent, letting her love for him ignite her passion once more. His ardent response pushed her anxiety to the far reaches of her mind. She had time to sort everything out. Now all she wanted to concentrate on was this moment and this man.

Eight

"It's so good to see you," Savannah said, hugging her sister-in-law.

Because of Melody's touring schedule, Savannah hadn't seen her since Rafe's funeral. For the past year she'd been traveling around the country opening for Nate Tucker and his band. Melody had lost weight but gained a little rock 'n' roll flair. Dressed all in black, she wore a flared leather skirt and lacy T-shirt with ankle boots. Formerly happy to write songs and stay in the background, she'd resisted when Nate set out to convince her to open for his band. But the singer/songwriter/producer was nothing if not persistent when he recognized talent—in addition to being part owner of Club T's, Nate had started his own record label and had a recording studio downtown.

"I'm excited to be in Las Vegas and can't wait to get into the studio to put the finishing touches on my first album."

"When do I get to hear some of it?"

"Soon," Melody promised, her gaze darting to one side.

"I wrote a couple more songs that I want to get into the studio and record. After that I'll go through what I have and see what might work for the album."

"I'm sure they're going to be fantastic. All of them."

"Where's my nephew?" Melody asked. "I thought after what my father did you'd have a hard time letting him out of your sight."

"Trent has him in the pool." Savannah kept her expression as neutral as possible beneath Melody's wide-eyed regard. "He's teaching him how to swim, if you can believe it."

"I can't believe you're here," Melody said. "At Rafe's funeral, you and Trent were on opposite sides of the room from each other the entire day. What changed?"

"Your brother and I have sort of come to an understanding. I can thank your father for that. I wouldn't be here if there wasn't trouble with West Coast Records. And if Siggy hadn't threatened me with taking Dylan away."

"It seems like there's more going on here than just a simple understanding." Melody put special emphasis on the last word and gave Savannah a knowing look. "I mean, you're living with him."

"In the guesthouse," Savannah explained. "And you're right—there's more going on. Rafe's and my finances were really bad. I'm almost a million dollars in debt. And until I'm working again, I have no income to live on."

"What are you going to do?"

"My plan is to go to LA tomorrow with Scarlett Fontaine. Thanks to her, I've set up three interviews with agents."

"Who's watching Dylan while you're interviewing?"

"I'm leaving him with Trent's housekeeper. She's been terrific."

"Oh, good. Since you're leaving him here, then I can pitch in. I need a little practice taking care of a baby."

Savannah stared at Melody in confused silence, unsure if she should voice the first thing that popped into her mind. "I'd love for you to spend some time with Dylan. But why do you need practice?"

"I'm pregnant." Melody offered up a tremulous smile. "Yikes."

"That's great. I'm so happy for you and Kyle."

"Well, you can be happy for me."

From the tenor of Melody's response, Savannah sensed not all was well. "Kyle isn't happy? How is that possible? He adores you."

"I haven't told him yet."

Savannah closed her eyes briefly, recalling the confusing muddle of uncertainty and joy when she realized she was pregnant.

"You know he's going to be great about this."

"I don't know that. We haven't been together that long and haven't talked about marriage. I don't know where he stands on the whole kid thing."

"How far along are you?"

"Barely six weeks. I took a long weekend off from the tour and flew to LA for his birthday. It was a fantastic three days." Her eyes glowed with heartbreaking fondness for several seconds before dimming. "And then Nate called to say that they'd added an extra two weeks to the tour and Kyle got so mad. He complained about how much time we'd been apart and told me to quit. We had a huge fight." She trailed off, looking miserable.

"But he was all for it. He's been one hundred percent behind your career from the very beginning."

Melody gave a little shrug. "I don't think either one of us realized how hard it was going to be to be apart." She sat down and put her hands in her lap. "He's been so distant these last few months. I don't know what's gotten into him. I'm worried he doesn't love me anymore."

"That's impossible. I've seen you two together. He adores you."

Melody pressed her lips together, shifted on the couch and heaved a huge sigh. "A month ago, he practically accused me of cheating on him with Hunter Graves."

Savannah understood why Kyle might be worried. "Because of that photo of the two of you holding hands as you left that New York club?" She'd wondered what was up after seeing the image, even though she knew without a doubt that Melody would never risk her relationship with Kyle. "Okay, I'm sorry, but I could see where he might have gotten the impression that you and Hunter were together."

"But we're just friends. Nothing more. It was a madhouse as we left. Hunter grabbed my hand so we wouldn't be separated on the way to the car."

"You dated him on and off for a year and a half before you and Kyle got together."

In fact, at one point Melody had tried to use Kyle to make Hunter jealous. The plan had backfired, but in the best way possible. The ruse had awakened Kyle's true feelings for Melody and made her realize the man she was meant to be with had been right under her nose.

"And I was miserable," Melody said. "Why would Kyle think I would go back to that?"

"Maybe you should talk to Kyle about all this. Tell him how you feel."

Given her own situation, Savannah wasn't the best person to be offering relationship advice, but she felt compelled to say something that might ease her friend's mind.

"I don't know, but we haven't spoken more than a half-dozen times in the last three months."

And Savannah knew that wasn't like them. "You need to talk to him about this."

"I will. I promise. But I really need to get the album finished first."

"How long do you think that's going to take?"

Melody had been living with Kyle three months before going on tour with Nate. They'd been dating for six months before she moved in with him. And before that, they'd known each other and been friends since high school. Kyle had been Trent's best friend since they'd met freshman year, and Savannah had known Kyle from all the times he'd hung out with Trent. She hadn't been surprised when Melody and Kyle finally got together.

Melody looked uncomfortable. "I don't know."

"The longer you wait, the worse it's going to be." Since Rafe's death, at least once a day Savannah regretted not telling Trent the truth about Dylan when she first learned she was pregnant. She'd kept quiet because she'd been afraid to get hurt again. Which had been silly, because she'd lost Trent anyway.

"You're right. But if I go to LA and tell him, I'll know how he reacts. If I stay here and finish the album, I can pretend for a while that when he finds out he's going to be thrilled."

Melody was operating with the same faulty logic Savannah had used. It had backfired for her; she could only hope that the same didn't happen to her good friend.

"He is going to be thrilled," Savannah assured her, trusting that truth. "He loves you."

"Sometimes love isn't enough." Melody stared at her hands.

Savannah's voice rang with conviction. "And sometimes it's all you need."

Their conversation was interrupted by the appearance of Trent and Dylan, with Murphy trotting along beside them. As always when Savannah saw father and son together, her heart gave a big bump.

"How'd his swimming lesson go?" she asked, holding her arms out for Dylan's towel-wrapped body.

Trent showed no inclination to give up Dylan. "He's already learned how to hold his breath when he goes underwater." He leaned forward to kiss Melody on the cheek. "It's good to see you."

"It's good to see you, too." She looked a little startled by her brother's sunny demeanor and shot a sidelong glance in Savannah's direction. "I hope it's okay if I crash here for a couple weeks while I finish my album. Unless it's too crowded?"

"I have plenty of room. When is Kyle coming? I'll make a couple tee times to get him out of your hair."

"He's not going to come this trip." Melody made a stab at looking undisturbed, but couldn't quite pull it off.

Her brother frowned. "Why not?"

Savannah decided it might be easier for Melody to have this conversation with her brother if they were alone. "I'm going to change Dylan."

With Trent focused on his sister, Savannah had an easy time making her escape. She dressed her son in dry clothes and wondered what Trent would make of his sister's situation. He had demonstrated the same sort of protectiveness with Savannah as he had with Melody. Especially when it came to her relationship with his best friend.

While he and Kyle had always been the best of friends, Trent hadn't been wild about Melody dating him. But since she was a strong-minded woman in her twenties, with a successful career and clear idea of whom she was getting involved with, Trent's warnings had been unwelcome.

To distract herself from what was going on in the main house, Savannah took stock of her limited wardrobe and began planning for the upcoming interviews in LA. She was still operating with the same suitcase of clothes she'd brought to Las Vegas the first time. While preparing to sell the house, she'd packed up the bulk of her wardrobe and put it in storage with the idea that she would sort through it as soon as she'd gotten settled.

Dylan's swim had taken the edge off his energy, and he was content to sit on the floor in her closet and play with his musical bear. By pushing on the bear's right paw, he was able to scroll through the playlist until he found his favorite song. Then he waved his hands and sang along in his cute baby way while Murphy barked and growled at the noisy toy.

"Why am I not surprised that he's musical." Trent's voice came from the doorway. "I hope you don't mind that I let myself in."

"I don't mind. This is your house. And that's why I've been thinking that maybe Dylan and I should move out."

"Move out? Why?"

"Melody needs the peace and quiet of the guesthouse in order to finish her album."

"Where are you thinking about going?"

"I thought something nearby." She paused. "Or LA."

Trent's eyebrows crashed together. "Have you forgotten the reason you moved in here in the first place?"

"I haven't forgotten."

Trent thought she'd come to Las Vegas to keep Dylan safe, but that wasn't the only reason. She'd foolishly hoped that once Trent spent time with her and Dylan that he'd miraculously decide that being a family with them was all he wanted.

"But things are different now," she continued. "And depending on how my auditions go in the next couple days, I might need to be closer to make the most of the opportunities."

"That's not the tune you were singing two days ago, and don't give me the excuse about Melody. You knew she was coming. Why the sudden change of heart?"

Savannah couldn't explain the real reason to him: the

awkwardness of living in his guesthouse and wanting to be more than just a convenient fling. Falling in love with him all over again wasn't good for either of them. For a second, Savannah's chest became tight and her lungs refused to work. She searched for calm.

It was good for Dylan that she and Trent were getting along, but keeping things friendly and uncomplicated would be best. In addition, she needed to stop relying on Trent to save her and stand on her own two feet.

"I guess it comes down to not having a plan and not having much in the way of options because of my financial situation. What Siggy did spooked me. I reacted before thinking everything through."

"There's no reason to believe he won't try something again."

"That's why I'm leaving Dylan here while I meet with agents. I know he'll be safe with you."

"I don't understand why you're so determined to get back to work. You're more than welcome to stay here as long as you want."

"That's generous of you, but I really need to move forward with my life." And if it wasn't going to be with Trent, then she needed to put some distance between them as soon as possible. "And speaking of Melody, have you spoken with her about what's going on between her and Kyle?"

"She said they're having a little trouble." He ran his hand through his hair and his mouth tensed. "She warned me to leave things alone and mind my business."

"She's right. Melody's a big girl. She doesn't need her brother messing in her love life."

"So what am I supposed to do? Sit by and let her be miserable?"

"Why don't you focus on what we're going to do about West Coast Records and let Melody sort out her own problems? If she wants you to step in, she'll say so."

"Fine. I found a guy who can take over running the company. I'll text you his number so you can meet with him while you're in LA. I think you'll like him."

"That's wonderful. I'll look forward to talking with him. And if I want to hire him, do you have a plan for how to get him past Siggy and Gerry?"

"If things go the way I think they will, you won't have to."

Savannah shook her head. "Will it do me any good to ask you what you have planned?"

"Grab dinner with him at Cuts Beverly Hills."

"So your father will get wind of the meeting?"

"Exactly. The restaurant's practically in his backyard, and he's sure to hear if you show up."

"And then what? We sit around and wait?"

"If I know my father, we won't have to wait for long."

Pushing a stroller that contained his sleepy nephew, Trent sauntered into the recording studio of Nate Tucker's indie label, Ugly Trout Records. Since Savannah had left for LA this morning, Trent had been feeling edgy and out of sorts. While he knew it was important to her that she get back to work, he couldn't help but feel as if it was a huge mistake for her to think about returning to LA. After what had happened the week before, he'd assumed she would hide out in Las Vegas with him at least until they figured out how to handle Siggy. Trent's intention was to untangle Savannah from his father's company. Today, he was going to present to Nate an idea for how to go about that.

The receptionist directed Trent to studio B, where Melody and Nate were doing some recording for her album. When Trent entered the studio's production booth, Nate's gaze flicked over his two visitors before returning to Melody.

Trent leaned against the wall and listened to his sister.

Accompanied by a guy in a knit cap playing the guitar, she sat at an electric piano, her strong, pure voice pouring out a song of heartbreaking angst. The uncomplicated arrangement allowed her songwriting to shine. Trent felt the hairs rise on the back of his neck at the emotion resonating through the lyrics. What was going on with his baby sister?

As she finished the song, Nate blew out a breath and rocked back in his chair. "She sounds amazing. This album is going to be a knockout."

A little dazed, Trent nodded. "It sure sounds like it."

Although Trent had seen his sister perform in several large venues, he continued to be amazed at her talent. Unlike Trent, who'd dabbled a bit here and there, Melody had embraced her musical side. As soon as she could pick up a violin, she'd started taking lessons. At eight, she'd taught herself how to play the piano and had begun composing silly little songs that her friends sang all the time, driving her two older brothers mad.

All this had ended one day when she was ten. Melody had written her first serious piece, and Trent had suggested that she record it. What was the point of having access to your very own recording studio and not using it? Trent had set up a one-hour session as a surprise for her, suspecting that if he told her in advance she'd never go through with it.

As it was, encouraged by Trent's confidence in her, she'd reluctantly agreed to record her song. She'd been struggling with the start of it when their father walked in. Or perhaps *stormed in* was a better description. Siggy had been furious at what Trent had done. He didn't want the expensive studio time wasted on his daughter. Melody had been so upset she never finished recording the song and stopped singing altogether.

From that point forward, she concentrated solely on her

violin and piano, in her own way trying to please her father, just as Rafe did. Trent had gone the complete opposite direction, aggravating his father at every turn.

"Nate," Melody said from the booth, "can you play the song back so I can hear it?"

"Sure." Nate cued the song before turning to Trent. "She's such a perfectionist. I think she's recorded fifty songs."

"And I'm sure each one is better than the last. She just doesn't think she's any good. We have our father to thank for that."

Dylan was awake, his eyes bright as he listened to Melody's song. Trent unbuckled him from the stroller and lifted him so he could see his aunt. She grinned and waved. Dylan blew her a kiss and wiggled in Trent's arms.

"I've told her she has a month to whittle her album down to fourteen songs. I'm just afraid that in that time she's going to record a dozen more."

"A month? Is she planning on sticking around that long?"

"I don't know." But Nate looked troubled. "Originally I gave her two weeks, but she asked for more time."

"Is there something going on between her and Kyle?"

The way Nate's expression shut down told Trent everything he needed to know. "It's none of my business. And it's none of yours."

"She's my sister. He's my best friend."

"Stay out of it."

"Fine." He ground out the word, taking his frustration out on the wrong person.

In truth, Trent didn't want to meddle in his sister's love life, but focusing on her distracted him from fixating on Savannah. His initial intention to keep his distance had been shattered in his office the night she'd come to Club T's. Since then, he'd involved himself in her struggles with his father and had tumbled back into her bed and under her spell.

"Melody and I agree that the album could use a duet," Nate said, unaffected by Trent's bad mood. "What would you think about recording 'She's the One' with her?"

"Me? Sing?" He preferred to make music with a guitar.

"Melody said you're pretty good."

Trent felt his face grow warm. Singing was something he enjoyed doing in the privacy of his car or shower. "I'm not professionally trained."

"You think I am? I'm just a poor kid from North Dakota who happens to like playing in a band."

Nate might be from North Dakota and he might have grown up without money, but his talent and ambition as a singer, songwriter and producer made his statement laughable.

"I'll sing," Trent said, surprising himself. "As long as you promise not to put it on the album."

"Let's record it and see how it goes."

"She'd be much better off doing a duet with you. She needs someone established to kick-start the album so she can make a pile of dough."

"You know she'd really love to put the album up for free, right?"

Trent wasn't surprised. Melody had always been about the art, not the money. "But you talked her out of that, I hope."

"Not exactly. She's pretty adamant, and she's making enough money from touring and her songwriting royalties not to worry about a paycheck."

"But to give it away?" As a businessman, the idea pained him.

"I'll see how she feels once the whole album is done. In the meantime…" Nate leaned forward and pushed the button that would let him be heard in the recording booth.

"Trent is here and he's agreed to record 'She's the One' with you."

Trent groaned as his sister's face lit up with a broad smile. "After I do this, we have some business to discuss," he said to Nate.

"Is something going on with the club?"

"Club T's is doing great. This matter is as much personal as it is business."

Nate gave him a curious look. "Does it have something to do with your sister-in-law living with you?"

Trent wasn't surprised that Nate knew about Savannah. Melody had likely mentioned that she was spending time with Dylan. "It has to do with my nephew's ownership of West Coast Records."

The two men had been friends as well as business partners for several years. Nate knew all about the family business and the difficult Siggy Caldwell.

"The shares he inherited from Rafe?"

"The company isn't doing well, and Savannah needs a large influx of cash to pay off the debt my brother stuck her with."

Nate gave a solemn nod. "Sounds like the lady needs our help. Why don't you get in there and do a little singing, and then we'll talk."

"Is Dylan okay in here with you?"

Nate took the boy and set him on his lap. "I've been dealing with temperamental artists for the last ten years. I think I can handle a one-year-old."

Grinning, Trent headed into the recording booth. The guitarist had left his instrument behind, and Trent picked it up. "Think he'd mind if I borrow this?"

"Jay's pretty cool about that sort of thing," Melody said, a half smile on her face as she watched Trent settle onto the stool and test the strings. "Are you really going to do this?"

Trent might not have been interested in a music career, but that didn't mean he couldn't have had one if he'd wanted it. Back in high school, he and a few of his buddies had formed a band and even played a few gigs. It had enhanced his bad boy mystique and got him as much action as the school's jocks. Plus, he hadn't been all banged up from playing sports.

"Nate has promised me it will never make the album," Trent said, "so I don't see what harm there is."

"We'll see." Melody gave him a sly smile. "Do you remember how it goes?"

"I think I can manage." And he started to play.

Nine

Savannah hummed as she descended in the hotel elevator, eager to head to LAX for the flight back to Las Vegas. She'd spent an eventful three days in LA and couldn't wait to get home to Dylan.

The dinner the night before at Cuts with Fred Hammer had given her a sense of what Trent was trying to provoke his father to do. It was obvious that the man knew the music business and would be a fantastic CEO for West Coast Records. The fact that he'd stolen several of the label's best artists over the last five years was a testament to his business acumen. It wasn't hard to imagine just how much it would upset Siggy to have this guy in charge of the company.

Morning sunlight poured through the lobby windows as Savannah crossed the marble floor in the direction of the exit. She was so preoccupied with thoughts of her son, she was completely caught off guard by the woman who stepped into her path.

"Savannah Caldwell."

"Yes?" She didn't recognize the brunette in snug jeans and a white T-shirt and at first thought she might have been an assistant to one of the agents she'd spoken with the day before.

The woman held out an envelope. "This is for you."

Reflexively, Savannah took it. "What is this?"

"You've been served." Without another word, the woman headed for the hotel's front entrance with the confidence of someone who had done this a thousand times before.

With her mind blank with astonishment, Savannah opened the envelope and pulled out a legal document. It didn't take her long to get the gist: contesting Rafe's bequeathing the company stock to Dylan, citing the fact that he wasn't Rafe's biological son. Every bit of optimism Savannah had gained over the last seventy-two hours vanished. Instead of leaving the hotel, she made her way to the nearest chair and dropped into it.

How was she going to explain to Trent what his father was up to? Savannah had stopped worrying about the stock and the money since she'd decided to return to acting. She would figure out a way to restructure the debt and be able to pay it off eventually. But if Trent discovered Dylan wasn't Rafe's child, he would despise her for lying to him. She needed to talk to Siggy. At least one good thing had come of this—she didn't need to fear losing her son to her father-in-law.

Savannah got in her car and headed to Siggy's house. Half of her thought she'd be denied entrance, but Siggy obviously expected her, because she was ushered right in. He was sitting behind his large desk in his office and didn't get to his feet as she entered the room.

"You're suing me?"

"I'll not have you pass off your bastard as my grandson."

Savannah resisted the urge to tell the old man that Dylan was *still* his grandson. "Dylan is Rafe's son."

"Not his biological son."

Savannah went cold. She stared Siggy down, utilizing every bit of Courtney Day she possessed to keep her panic from showing. Did he know something? Or was he guessing? She had no way of knowing without tipping her hand.

"You have no idea what you're talking about."

"I know exactly what I'm talking about. You tricked my son into marrying you and into making that boy his heir."

"That's not at all what happened." Even as she said the words, Savannah knew she was wasting her breath. "And you have no way of proving that it did."

"But I can prove that Dylan isn't Rafe's biological son. The last time he was here, I took a sample of his DNA and had it tested."

What after all this time could have prompted Siggy to do something like that? Was it because she and Trent had joined forces and were threatening his business? Her relationship with Trent while she lived in New York had never been a secret, but Siggy rarely paid attention to his son's activities. Would he have been aware that they were romantically linked? Or because he'd never viewed Savannah as being good enough to be Rafe's wife, had Siggy merely been grasping at straws?

"It doesn't matter what you can or can't prove. Rafe wanted a son and he got one."

As she spoke, Savannah began to calm down. Siggy would have a hard time contesting the will. Rafe never specified that he was leaving the stock to his biological son, and Rafe's name was on Dylan's birth certificate as his father.

"But I can drag this issue through the courts for a very long time. And when the DNA tests come back, you'll get to explain to Trent why you've been lying to him all this time." Siggy looked pleased with himself, leaving Savannah to wonder what he knew or what he thought he knew. "Meanwhile, I'll be taking back control of my company."

Now Savannah understood what Siggy was driving at. She'd helped Trent provoke his father and this was the result. And she knew Siggy was right about Trent. He'd be furious that she'd lied about Rafe being Dylan's father all this time. The only thing Savannah could do to salvage the situation was to figure out how to negotiate so Dylan's paternity never became public knowledge.

"You want your company back? I want to be out from under the debt your son created."

Siggy's eyes narrowed. "What are you offering?"

"I'll sign the stock back over to you if you'll give me the million I owe. It's Rafe's debt, not mine, and you and I both know the stock is worth way more than that." At least until the company went under.

"If we go to court, I'll get my stock and I won't have to pay you a cent."

"Are you sure? Because if you take me to court, I'll make sure everyone knows how badly the company is doing. Including the royalties not being paid to your artists and how close you are to bankruptcy. In the meantime, I've hired Fred Hammer to take over as CEO, and his first act will be to fire Gerry and have him arrested for embezzlement. Think about it."

Leaving behind an uncharacteristically speechless Siggy, Savannah made her way out of the house. Head held high, but knees wobbling with each step, she made it to the driver's seat of her car before deflating with an enormous exhale. Determined not to break down while in sight of the house, she started the car and headed down the street. Savannah turned into the first parking lot she reached, found a vacant spot and shut off the engine.

Her forehead was halfway to the steering wheel when her phone rang, startling her. Convinced Siggy was calling to level more threats at her, Savannah was tempted not to answer. But she was a mother before anything and knew she at least had to check to see who was trying to get hold of her.

To her surprise, it was Corrine Scott, the agent she'd signed with late the previous afternoon. Corrine's offer of representation was the second one she'd received, and after spending half an hour with her, Savannah knew Corrine understood her priorities as a single mom as well as her preferences for roles.

"Hi, Corrine." With the way her day was going, Savannah braced herself for bad news. "I didn't expect to hear from you so soon."

"I didn't expect to be calling you so soon either, but when we spoke yesterday you said you were interested in looking at some movie projects. I had dinner with a producer last night and pitched you to him. He just sent over a script for a part that sounds perfect for you."

"Wow," Savannah said with a startled laugh. "You work fast." Her head was spinning from the rapid seesawing of her fortune over the last hour.

"Sometimes the perfect match between client and project takes a while—other times the stars align. I know you're flying back to Vegas, but do you have time to swing by and pick up the script to start reading?"

Savannah hadn't built in enough time for all the detours she'd encountered this morning. She closed her eyes and let her head fall back.

"I'll be by in half an hour. Would you possibly have a little time to talk about something of a personal nature? I could use an impartial point of view."

If Corrine was surprised that her new client was reaching out for some personal help, she didn't show it. "Sure. I'm happy to help any way I can."

Next, Savannah called the airline and changed her flight to later in the day, and then contacted Melody to give her the new schedule. As much as Savannah wanted to hug her baby boy, she had a legal issue and needed professional help.

Her phone rang again as she drove to Corrine's office. This time it was Trent.

"Melody said you were delayed in LA because of a project."

"I'm heading to my agent's office right now."

"Sounds like things are moving for you already."

"I'm surprised that they are. I never imagined she'd be able to find me something so fast. Of course, it's only an audition." Nevertheless, Savannah was consumed by optimism.

"What time is your flight? I'll pick you up at the airport."

"You don't need to do that."

"I have a surprise for you that won't keep."

"That sounds like trouble."

Savannah couldn't imagine what he could be up to and caught herself smiling as she ended the call. However, her delight didn't last long once her gaze fell upon the envelope containing the summons that she'd tossed onto the dashboard.

She had a tricky legal problem to deal with and if Trent learned the truth, he'd never forgive her for keeping such a huge secret from him. Which brought her thoughts back to the scene at Siggy's house. Had she really told him she'd hired Fred? And threatened to turn Gerry over to the police?

Trent was going to be unhappy with her for stomping

all over his clever plan, whatever it was. He'd been cagey when she'd quizzed him about his plot to save the label. Well, if he'd wanted her to stay on script, he should have given her more information.

It was too late to worry about that now. She had a lawsuit to fight and her future to secure. On the way back to Las Vegas she would figure out what sort of explanation she should give to Trent.

Airline passengers streamed past Trent as he scanned the arrivals display to find out which carousel would contain the baggage from Savannah's flight. His timing was perfect. Her plane had touched down five minutes before. He positioned Dylan's stroller where it wouldn't be missed when Savannah came to claim their luggage.

Savannah had only been gone three days, but it felt like a lot longer. They'd spoken frequently, their exchanges revolving around Dylan and her agent while Trent's mind formed the words that would convey how much he missed her. He hadn't said any of them. His reaction to her absence disturbed him. When she'd married his brother, he'd resolved to be done with her. And for the last sixteen months, he'd believed that was the case. What a shock to discover he had been lying to himself the whole time.

The way his heart leaped when he spotted her demonstrated that he was in deeper than ever. All too aware his emotions were on display, he crouched beside the stroller and focused on unbuckling his nephew.

"Dylan, there's your mommy. Let's get you out of here so you can give her a big hug."

"Oh, I've missed you," Savannah cried, snatching Dylan into her arms and plastering noisy kisses on his cheeks. "Goodness, you've grown."

"You've only been gone three days," Trent pointed out. His arms ached to enfold her in a passionate embrace, but he shoved his hands into his pockets and welcomed her with a smile instead. "I'm sure it's impossible for him to have gotten measurably bigger in such a short period of time."

"I know." Savannah began walking in the direction of the baggage carousels. "It's just my guilt tricking me because I left him."

"He did just fine." Trent meant the words to be reassuring, but when Savannah winced, he realized he was in a no-win situation. "Even though he missed you. But Melody and I did our best to keep him entertained."

"There's no one I'd rather he spend time with than you two."

Trent decided to switch to a less emotionally charged topic. "So your trip to LA was successful. Not only did you get an agent, but also an audition for a movie role. That's great."

"It was an eventful trip. I never expected things to go so well."

"Tell me about the movie."

"It's a bigger part than I expected it to be. I skimmed through the script on the flight here. It's a romantic comedy. If I get it, I'll be the lead's best friend."

"Where is it shooting?"

The carousel began to move and the first bags appeared moments later.

"It sounds like they'll be shooting in LA." Savannah split her attention between her son and the luggage circling past them and missed Trent's frown. "I'm going back next Wednesday for the audition."

"And if you get it? Does that mean you're going back to LA?" What he wanted to know was if she was moving back permanently. Before this trip, he'd gotten the impression she wanted to make Las Vegas her home base.

"While I'm filming." She pointed to a red Tumi suitcase. "That one's mine."

Trent lifted it off the carousel while Savannah put Dylan back in his stroller. The three of them left the terminal and headed for short-term parking.

"Feels like the heat broke," Savannah commented as Trent loaded her suitcase and Dylan's stroller into the trunk of his car.

For the flight, she'd donned a sleeveless cream fit-and-flare dress with chunky gold jewelry and black-and-cream-striped pumps. The look was elegant and professional, but as she settled into the passenger seat she kicked off her high heels, unfastened her sleek updo and peeled off her jewelry. With her wavy blond hair cascading over her shoulders in luxurious disarray and her clear blue eyes sparkling as she peered at her son in the backseat, she was once again the sensual, tantalizing woman who'd haunted his dreams these last few days.

"So, I promised you a surprise," Trent said, cursing the husky rasp in his voice. He started the car's engine and turned on the stereo. The CD was ready to go—all he had to do was hit Play. "I took Dylan to the studio while Melody was recording."

Savannah's smile turned eager. "Am I finally going to hear a bit of her album?"

"It's Melody's music," he said as he backed the car out of the parking spot and headed for the exit. "But I don't think this is going to be part of her new album."

"I've been dying of curiosity for the past six hours. Are you going to play me the song or what?"

"Here goes."

He keyed the CD and waited for her reaction. Her eyes rounded with delight and she clapped her hands over her mouth. Trent found himself unable to stop grinning as the song played.

"Is that Dylan singing?"

Singing was not quite what the infant was doing, but there was no question that he was babbling all the correct notes as Melody accompanied him on the piano and sang the verses. It was one of the tunes she'd written when she was a kid, and obviously it still appealed to the under-ten-year-old set.

"Apparently they've been working on this duet since she arrived."

"It's fantastic. What a wonderful surprise. Thank you."

The song ended and Trent was about to hit the rewind button to play it again when a new song began. Nate had burned the CD for Trent. Apparently he'd decided to add a second track.

Savannah cocked her head and listened to the first strains of the new song. "I know this, don't I?"

Trent knew it all too well—it was the intro to "She's the One." He'd sung it yesterday. He had only seconds to act before it got to the part he'd recorded. "Why don't we listen to Dylan's song again."

"Wait." Savannah placed her hand over his. "That's 'She's the One.' Is Melody going to put that on her new album?"

The tension in her tone caught his attention. Glancing over, Trent noticed that Savannah's expression had grown bleak. As his sister sang the first verse, Trent wondered what about the song had caused Savannah's shift into melancholy. He was equally curious how she would react when she heard him jump in at the chorus.

"I sure hope not," he said just as his voice filled the speakers.

Hearing himself made him wince. It wasn't as if he sounded off-key or out of practice, but singing for himself and singing in the studio with his sister were meant to be private performances. Now he felt exposed. He'd been thinking about Savannah while they recorded the song, and to his sensitive ears it sounded like it.

"I had no idea." Savannah brushed back her hair with a trembling hand. She didn't finish her thought. "You guys sound great together. Melody should put it on her album."

"She needs to do a duet with someone well-known."

"You don't think anyone would remember the lead singer of Chrome Pulse?"

Trent laughed. "I sure hope not."

After a couple seconds Savannah joined him in laughing. "I can't believe Melody talked you into singing with her."

"I can't believe Nate put the song onto this CD." Trent would definitely have some choice words for his business partner. "It wasn't meant for public consumption."

"I'm glad he did. And thank you for Dylan's song. It was really a fantastic surprise."

For a while they rode in silence, each occupied by their own thoughts. Trent wrestled with the urge to reach out and take her hand in his. Every shift in her body and subtle change in her expression caught his attention. He yearned to demonstrate how much he'd missed her. But her posture warned him that something was bothering her.

"You haven't told me much about your meeting with Fred. How did it go?"

"He's really great. I think he'd do a fantastic job running the company." She quit speaking before she ran out of air and seemed to hold the remaining breath in her lungs. It gave her statement an unfinished feel, as if she wanted to say more but decided against it.

"But?" he prompted as the silence stretched.

"I had a run-in with your father." From the way she was gripping her purse, it hadn't gone well. "I think your attempt to provoke him worked better than you thought it would."

"If he did anything to upset you…"

She blew out a shaky breath. "I might've tipped our hand about Gerry."

So that's what was bothering her.

"Why don't you start at the beginning and tell me what happened."

She took a few moments to collect her thoughts and Trent grew concerned at her reluctance.

"As I was leaving the hotel this morning, I was served with papers. Siggy is suing me for Dylan's shares in the company."

"On what grounds?"

Another long pause. "He's claiming Dylan isn't Rafe's son."

Trent tamped down irritation at his father's ridiculous tactics. "Obviously we have my father on the run, and I am glad to see that, but I'm sorry that you're the one on the receiving end of his despicable tactics. We'll get a lawyer and fight it."

"I already spoke to one today. I thought I'd better get ahead of this thing."

"Is this why you told my father that Fred would be taking over the company?"

"When I got the papers, I wasn't thinking very clearly. I stormed over to his house to confront him. I let my temper get the better of me."

Trent found this last bit rather funny. "Since when do you have a temper?"

All the times he'd stepped in and rescued her, she'd never shown any signs of being willing to fight for herself. Now that she had someone of her own to protect, she'd become more lion than mouse.

"Apparently I've grown a spine since giving birth to Dylan." The corners of her mouth lifted in a sad, ironic smile.

"You always had a spine," Trent told her, thinking about how many times she'd braved his temper after his father had gone off on him. Her only motivation had been to see if he was okay. And more often than not, he'd directed his misplaced anger at her. It had taken him years before he understood and appreciated her kindness and bravery. "You just didn't let anyone see it."

"Anyway," she said, her shoulders lifting and falling in a dismissive little shrug, "I told Siggy that I had hired Fred and intended to turn Gerry over to the police for embezzlement."

"You hired Fred?"

"I didn't. Or I hadn't at that point, anyway. But I called him later and explained the situation. He's willing to go into hostile territory and do what needs to be done. I told him it might be an interim position. Until the lawsuit is settled, everything is up in the air."

Trent blew out a breath. "You were busy."

Given all she'd accomplished, he didn't know if she needed him anymore. That bothered him more than it should. Their former dynamic gave him a mission he was comfortable with. She got into trouble. He helped her out. What role did he play in her life going forward?

"I just hope I didn't create a bigger mess."

"Whatever happens, we'll tackle it together."

Ten

Savannah considered Trent's statement in silence. When she'd explained how Siggy's lawsuit claimed Dylan wasn't Rafe's son, she'd expected Trent to grill her for answers. Instead, he perceived the legal action as a simple matter of his father playing dirty. Not for a moment had he doubted her. Savannah felt sick. Lying to Trent was eating at her. But telling him Dylan was his son would be so much worse. He'd never forgive her for deceiving him.

"I'm beginning to wonder if you shouldn't let me finish this up alone."

Trent's eyebrows went up. "You want me out just as things are getting interesting?"

"Who knows what crazy thing your father will come up with next? I don't want you hurt because of me."

"My father lost the ability to hurt me a long time ago."

Although that might be true, it didn't mean the damage had ever healed. Trent remained wary of becoming emotionally invested. And Savannah couldn't love him enough to fix what he refused to be made whole.

"That doesn't mean he won't try, and you know how he likes to play dirty."

"Trust me, when it comes to my father, I'm bullet-proof."

Savannah nodded. "I should also tell you that before I spoke to a lawyer, I offered to settle with Siggy. I offered him the shares back for the million in debt I owe." When Trent shook his head, she rushed on. "I know it was foolish, but I'm sick to death of the whole thing and just want to be done."

"What did he say?"

"He told me he's going to take back the shares and not pay me a cent."

Trent nodded. "He's a pretty good poker player, and he knows you pretty well. He probably expected a bluff like that would scare you. Was this before or after you told him about Fred and Gerry?"

"Before." She didn't want to admit that she'd been scared. "His arrogance made me so mad. And after what he pulled the day I closed on my house, I don't see him as an all-powerful threat anymore."

She didn't care about the shares and she didn't care about the money. Once she was working again, she could pay off the debt she owed. The only danger she faced was if the lawsuit made public the truth about Dylan's biological father.

"Don't get between a mama and her baby."

"Darn right."

Trent laughed. The sound made Savannah smile. She was enjoying being on the same team. Being estranged from him this last year and a half had plunged her into a bleak, gray world. They might not ever be together as a family the way she wanted, but being able to laugh with him and watch him with Dylan was pretty great, too.

When the trio entered the house, Melody was in the kitchen fixing dinner while Murphy sat at her feet, his huge brown eyes luminous as he begged for handouts. Trent had given Rhoda the night off. After having her offer of help rejected, Savannah took her suitcase to the guesthouse and unpacked while Dylan sat on the bed and checked out the new puzzle she'd bought him.

Half an hour later, the four of them sat on the terrace and ate hamburgers loaded with jalapeño, guacamole and fresh tomatoes. It was a familiar family gathering. While Melody and Savannah had lived in New York City, they'd made an effort to eat together at least twice a month—more often when Trent visited.

"I really liked the duet you and Trent sang," Savannah said as talk turned to Melody's new album.

"He played that for you?" Melody shot a surprised look at her brother.

"I don't think he meant to. It was on the same CD with the song you and Dylan sang. Which was amazing, by the way." Savannah saw Trent drop a bit of hamburger to the waiting Murphy and frowned at him.

"Wasn't he great?" Melody said. "I think if the album doesn't work out I might do one for kids."

"Your album's going to be great," Trent said. "But you might think about recording your other songs, as well. I can hear kids singing about noses, roses and toeses all around the world."

"I second that," Savannah said. "So when do I get to hear more of the album?"

"She's not including the duet on her album," Trent insisted. "As a matter of fact, I'm going to get Nate to destroy the master."

"So I'll have the only copy?" Savannah rather liked the idea.

She recalled the first time she'd heard the song. Melody had written it during their days in New York. It had been a collaboration of sorts: Savannah's life put to Melody's music. Trent had never caught on that the song was about him. Originally the song had been titled "He's the One," but that had hit a little too close to home. Once Melody had changed the gender, Savannah could pretend that the lyrics were about anyone.

"Can we talk about something besides my album?" Melody said.

"Sure," Trent said, sliding a look his sister's way. "Kyle's coming into town next week. He, Nate and I are going to talk about a new business venture."

Noticing that Melody hadn't commented on Kyle's imminent arrival and was instead fussing with her nephew, Savannah picked up the conversation. "Another club?"

"Kyle wants to open one in LA. Something he can manage on a day-to-day basis." From Trent's manner, he was trying to engage his sister. Obviously Melody hadn't divulged any details about what was going on between her and Kyle. "He's been scouting properties and has narrowed it down to three."

"I'm not surprised you're looking to expand, given how well Club T's is doing."

"Of course, LA is a different market. But one that Kyle knows pretty well. He said he's been out a lot lately. I suppose it's because he's been missing you while you're on tour." This last was directed at his sister.

"It has nothing to do with me," Melody said. "Kyle's never been one to sit around for long. He likes being busy. I'm surprised it's taken this long for him to take this step. I know whenever you need him to fill in for you at Club T's he really enjoys it."

"I know he does. That's why I've asked him to stick around for the next month. I have some business in LA that's going to require me to be gone from the club quite a bit."

"He's going to stay here?" Melody didn't sound happy. "Can he do that? Take time off from his other investments, I mean."

A line formed between Trent's brows. "I thought you'd be happy to have him around while you're working on your album."

"I'll be too busy to spend time with him."

"I'm sure you can make time to be together." Trent cocked his head. "Is there something going on?"

Melody pushed back abruptly from the table, her wrought-iron chair screeching against the patio tile. "Everything is fine," she snapped, picking up her plate and heading for the kitchen.

"What the hell is going on with her?" Trent looked to Savannah for explanation. "Are she and Kyle having problems?"

"I think the tour was hard on their relationship." Savannah didn't feel bad about sharing that bit of information. It only made sense that not everyone could handle a long-distance romance. "I think it will be good for them to spend some time together here." On neutral territory.

"And it will give you and me a chance to spend some time together in LA."

"You and I? Together?" Savannah's breath caught. What was he suggesting?

"I've been thinking about it since you left. I don't feel comfortable with you and Dylan in LA by yourselves."

"If you're worried about Siggy trying to take Dylan away from me, I think his attitude on that score has changed."

"I'm not worried about my father." Trent reached over and took her hand. "I missed you these last couple days."

Savannah's throat tightened. She lowered her gaze so he wouldn't see the tears that brightened her eyes. He'd never said anything to her like that before, and the joy she felt left her paralyzed.

"I missed you, too," she whispered, the strain on her vocal cords almost painful. "It would be nice to have you with us in LA."

"Then it's settled. Let's get this cleaned up and then I want to hear all about the movie you're going to audition for."

When they carried the dinner dishes into the kitchen, Melody chased them out before they could offer to help. "The kitchen isn't big enough for all of us."

Which wasn't at all true, but Savannah could tell Melody needed time to herself. She and Trent took Dylan to the comfortable couches in the outdoor movie theater. With the screen retracted, they enjoyed watching the sunset decorate the mountains in shades of orange and gold.

"It's beautiful here." Savannah let her head drop onto Trent's shoulder as they watched Dylan running around the open gas fireplace, currently unlit.

"Staring at that view, it's hard to believe that less than five miles away there are millions of lights and people."

"Do you ever get tired of just how crazy it is on the Strip and in the hotels? That was what drove me crazy about New York. It was always people, people and more people. I think that's why Tennessee appealed to me. Wide-open spaces where days could go by without seeing anyone."

"That's why I bought this place. To get away from it all."

"You do have your own little vacation spot here."

"Do you really want to go back to LA? The traffic? Everyone on top of one another?"

"If I want to get jobs, I'm pretty sure that's where I need to be."

"Scarlett makes it work, going back and forth."

"She has two careers and a husband who lives here." Savannah hadn't meant to imply anything by this last remark. Nevertheless, she felt Trent stiffen. Containing a weary sigh, Savannah patted him on his knee and got to her feet. "It's past Dylan's bedtime."

She expected Trent to be happy to escape after the direction the conversation had gone, but he surprised her by dogging her steps to the guesthouse. When she gave him a questioning look, he shrugged.

"I've been reading Dylan a bedtime story. I know it's something you do for him every night, so I thought he'd expect it."

Once again Trent had taken her by surprise. "That's nice, but I've got this."

"Sounds like you're trying to get rid of me."

"Not at all." But suddenly she understood a bit of what Melody was feeling. Keeping disappointment or upset hidden wasn't easy. But the last thing she wanted to do was talk about how she was feeling and have it end in an argument. "I just thought maybe you'd be tired of babysitting."

Savannah entered Dylan's room and began pulling out what she needed to get him ready for bed. Trent demonstrated just how much time he'd been spending with Dylan as he made himself useful, gathering diapers and baby wipes.

"We still haven't talked about the movie," he said, spreading a changing pad on the bed.

Savannah laid Dylan down and began stripping off his clothes. "We can talk about it tomorrow."

"You are trying to get rid of me."

She didn't answer right away but kept her hands busy and her attention focused on her son. But their nighttime routine of tickling and giggling couldn't distract her from the tall man standing beside her, observing their antics. At last all the snaps on his pajamas were closed and her son was ready for bed.

"Who's ready for bed?" she crooned, making her son smile. His upper teeth were starting to come in, and she was struck by how fast he was growing up. Overcome by a rush of sentimentality, she lifted him into her arms and snuggled him against her chest, but to her shock, he reached out to Trent.

"I think he wants me to read him a story."

Flabbergasted, Savannah turned her son over to Trent. He settled with Dylan in the chair and pulled out a board book. While Savannah watched her two favorite men, Trent read one book after another until he had gone through Dylan's library.

"That's enough reading for one night," Savannah said, her tone firm.

She picked up her sleepy son and settled him in his crib with his favorite toy. She turned on the lamp that threw dancing shadows on the ceiling and then headed to the door. With one last glance at the crib, she turned off the overhead light.

"Are you okay?" Trent asked as they made their way into the living room.

"Fine. Why wouldn't I be?"

"You and Dylan have been alone for a long time. With so many of us taking care of him now, I thought you might miss having him all to yourself."

He'd captured a little of what she was feeling. "Not at all. I'm thrilled that he has so many people in his life who love him."

What bothered her was how attached Trent had become to Dylan. It made her all the more conflicted about not telling him that Dylan was his son. While she'd watched Trent reading the silly stories Dylan loved so much, she'd been consumed by guilt. All the time she'd kept the two of them apart, never imagining Trent had any interest in children.

Trent took her hand and guided it to his cheek. Her other hand he pulled around his waist. Held close, she inhaled the comforting masculine scent of him and her pulse danced. She could get used to coming home to Trent. When he'd visited her in New York, she'd rushed back to her apartment and fallen into his arms after a long day of shooting.

But those moments, wonderful though they were, had been short-lived. Trent might enjoy a week or two of domestic bliss, but he grew restless soon after. Having her and Dylan stay with him was a novelty. Soon enough they'd be in his way. She wanted to be gone before that happened.

"On the way back from LA, I did some thinking."

"Tell me later."

Before she could protest, his mouth found hers and she was lost in the sweeping power of his kiss. What good was it to fight the magic between them? In the future, she would have months and years to ache for him. Today, she intended to take whatever he would give her.

Trent didn't know why this particular Friday night at the club was driving him crazy. It wasn't as if more things than usual were going wrong. At the moment he was staring at his most experienced waitress. She'd messed up the tab for one of their biggest VIPs. Trent had to decide whether to eat the twenty-thousand-dollar mistake and keep the client happy or risk pissing off someone who had been known to drop upward of three hundred grand in the club when he was in town.

"Give this to Jason and tell him not to bother Khalid." Trent signed off on the report she brought to him about the discrepancy and handed it over.

"I'm really sorry, Trent."

"Figure out what happened and get it fixed."

Gina nodded and raced away. Trent watched her go with more than a trace of impatience. Normally he wouldn't be this short with his staff even over a mistake of this size, but Savannah had been in LA for four days and this time she'd taken Dylan with her. Dammit, he missed her. He missed both of them.

"So this is where you're hiding." Kyle Tailor entered Trent's office, his long legs carrying him across the room in four strides. "I've been looking all over the club for you. The place is packed."

"When did you get in?"

"Half an hour ago. I came here straight from the airport."

Trent was wondering why his best friend had chosen to visit Club T's over reuniting with the woman he loved first. "Are you meeting Melody here?"

"No, it's late. I'll see her tomorrow."

"I'm sure she'd like to see you tonight."

"I really don't want to bother her."

"Bother her?" Trent stared at his friend in dismay. "I was right. There is trouble between you two. Is it because she was on tour for so long?"

"What has she said?"

"Nothing. And that's what's weird. Normally she talks about you all the time. It's kind of annoying."

"Well, maybe that's because she's not in love with me anymore."

"Has she said that?"

"Not in so many words."

"Then what are you basing it on?" Trent waited for his friend's reply. When Kyle kept his lips pressed together, a belligerent scowl pulling down his brows, Trent said, "I know my sister. If she wasn't in love with you, she'd let you know." Still, Kyle said nothing. "Did you do something?"

"What makes you think it's my fault?"

Disgusted, Trent shook his head. "Because she's down in the dumps and you sound defensive."

"Can we not talk about your sister? I'm here to have some fun. Let's grab some drinks and find some women who want to have a good time."

Trent couldn't believe what his best friend was saying. They'd just been talking about the problems he and Melody were having and Kyle wanted to chase women? But when he took a harder look at Kyle, Trent recognized the desperate edge in his friend's expression. As if he intended to have fun even if he didn't feel like it. Deciding Kyle wasn't as indifferent to his problems with Melody as he was trying to appear, Trent swallowed the harsh lecture he'd been about to deliver.

"I can't right now," Trent said. "It's been a crazy night, with one thing after another going wrong." Almost as if on cue, Trent's phone buzzed, delivering another text message. Now they were running out of a particular vodka that one of their VIPs preferred. He exhaled and got to his feet. "To top it off, our DJ got sick at the last minute, so I've got Nate up on stage."

"I saw. The crowd seems to be enjoying him a lot."

"You know, for an introvert, he's a pretty decent showman."

They both laughed. Few people would characterize the front man for Free Fall as an introvert, but in truth, as much as he enjoyed making music, Nate needed a lot of downtime during his tours.

"Come on," Trent said, heading for the door. "Why don't you come with me while I put out a couple fires, and then I'll show you some of the upgrades we've done to the outside since you were last here."

Kyle grumbled about coming to Vegas to play, not work, but he accompanied Trent on his rounds. To Trent's surprise, his friend stuck with him the whole night, even though he had several offers to hang out with some very beautiful women. They parted ways at three. Kyle was heading off to try his luck at the tables and Trent still had work to do.

At five he debated the feasibility of heading home for a couple hours. He had a meeting with a new liquor distributor at eight. If he stayed on his couch, he could catch an extra hour of sleep. But as he lay staring at the shadowy ceiling, his overactive mind kept him awake.

He was back to thinking about Kyle and Melody. Although Trent had been opposed to their relationship when he'd originally learned of it, he'd come around after seeing how happy his sister was with Kyle. Now, however, he was worried that Melody was going to get hurt, and he knew she would be furious with him if he interfered.

A few hours later, the meeting with his potential distributor went well. Trent had managed to catch enough sleep to give the guy a fair hearing. The addition of some unique, high-end product would enhance the appeal of Club T's in an already cutthroat market. The club's closest competitor might be seven million a year behind them in sales, but that could change if Club T's had a couple bad months.

Eager to catch a few more hours of sleep, Trent headed home. The smell of coffee hit him as he entered his open-concept living space from the garage. He sucked in a big breath and felt revitalized. All thoughts of heading off to bed vanished as he spied Savannah and Dylan out on the terrace. She was sitting on the concrete while Dylan put a ball through a miniature basketball hoop.

Leaving his tie and suit coat draped over the banister, Trent poured himself a cup of coffee and headed out to enjoy the cool morning.

Savannah glanced his way as he approached. "Are you just getting home?"

"It was a late night and I had a meeting at eight this morning." He sat in the chair nearest the pair and sipped from his mug. Murphy came over to greet him, and Trent lifted the Frenchie onto his lap and gave him a thorough scratching. The dog snorted with pleasure. "I grabbed a couple hours' sleep on the couch in the office."

She acknowledged his statement with a nod and arced the ball through the hoop. Given the size of the target and her distance of five feet, it was an impressive toss.

"Score," she called, raising her arms, and Dylan mimicked her.

Despite her obvious pleasure in watching her son, Savannah seemed quieter than normal. Trent noticed that although her lips curved in a smile, her eyes never lit up. Given her friendship with Melody and the fact that Kyle's car wasn't parked in the driveway, Trent suspected she was worried about his sister.

"Is something wrong?" Trent asked, not wanting to come straight out with his own concerns until he knew which way the wind blew.

"My lawyer called a little bit ago and told me your father's backing down on the lawsuit." Savannah's gaze tracked Dylan as he chased his ball along the terrace. "Not only that, but he's offering to pay me one point five million for Dylan's shares."

Given her somber mood, this wasn't at all what he'd been expecting. "That's not even close to what those shares are worth."

"I know, but it's enough to pay off Rafe's debts and give me a nest egg."

"You should counter."

Savannah looked horrified at his suggestion. "I'm just relieved to have it all done."

So why didn't she look as if things were going her way?

More than anything Trent wanted her to be happy. His father had caused her enough harm. And should have to pay.

"Do you have any idea what caused him to change his mind?" Trent asked.

"No, and my lawyer also questioned his abrupt turnaround, as well. He did a little investigating and discovered someone wants to buy West Coast Records."

"So there's a chance for you to make even more money."

"And a chance for Siggy to ruin the whole thing."

"So you've made up your mind." He set the dog back on the ground and watched him run over to Dylan.

"I've already given the go-ahead to sell the shares back to Siggy."

"Then why aren't you celebrating?"

"I should be. It's stupid that I'm not."

Trent was starting to understand. "You wish you'd been able to fight him to get what the shares were worth."

"No, I'm happy with our deal the way it stands. I didn't marry Rafe for his money. I married him to give Dylan a traditional family. Now that Rafe is dead, I have accepted that Dylan and I will be fine on our own."

It wasn't the first time Trent was filled with admiration for her. The girl he'd grown up with, the woman he'd known in New York, hadn't been confident and strong. Savannah might still need help from time to time, but she didn't need rescuing. She'd stood up to his father and participated in Trent's scheme to provoke his father into acting. She might not have anticipated what Siggy would do, but she'd taken charge when he threatened her with a lawsuit.

"So what is really going on?"

Her big blue eyes turned sorrowful. "There's something I should've let you know a long time ago."

Anxiety twisted his gut at the pained expression on her face. "Like what?"

"It has to do with your father's lawsuit. He claimed Dylan isn't Rafe's son." She clenched her fists and leaned forward. "It's true."

Trent's thoughts froze. Once again his perception of her changed. "So that's why you chose not to fight him? Because you knew you'd lose?"

"No. I meant what I said about the money. I only wanted what's fair."

"Did Rafe know Dylan wasn't his son?" For the first time since he'd found out that Rafe and Savannah were getting married, Trent felt sorry for his brother. "Or did you lie to him, too?"

Hurt flickered in her eyes, but she didn't let her chin droop. "Rafe knew before he proposed to me. At the time I didn't understand why he would want to raise a son who wasn't biologically his. I didn't realize it at the time, but the cancer treatments had made him sterile. Your father had drilled the concept of dynasty into Rafe's head for so long that even as he was dying, he was determined to make Siggy happy."

"So you both lied to my father."

"Yes. At the time I was in a vulnerable place—pregnant and terrified of raising Dylan alone." She didn't need to add that Rafe had been there to pick up the pieces after she and Trent had broken up.

"That first night in my office, when you told me Dylan was Rafe's son." Trent wasn't sure he recognized the woman standing before him. "You were lying."

She shook her head. "As far as Rafe was concerned, Dylan was his son. But he wasn't his biological child."

Never before had he perceived Savannah as being duplicitous. But she'd lied to him and to his family. Could she also be lying about Rafe knowing that Dylan wasn't his?

"Is lack of money for a long, drawn-out legal case the

reason you're no longer fighting Siggy for Dylan's right to the stock? Or are you suffering a guilty conscience?"

"Will you condemn me if I tell you it's a little of both?"

Trent held perfectly still and stared at her. A question was burning a hole in his heart. Who was Dylan's father? He thought he knew Savannah inside and out. Had she had a fling or a one-night stand? The thought disturbed him.

"I never in a million years thought you'd do something like this." His voice sounded flat and wooden.

"Like what?"

"Pass a stranger's child off as Rafe's."

"I didn't. Don't you understand?" Savannah released a long-suffering sigh at his head shake. "He has your smile."

"Who does?" Trent had no idea what she was getting at.

"Dylan."

What was she trying to say? Trent stared at her, his mind blank.

Savannah looked miserable. She'd obviously been expecting a different reaction. "Trent, Dylan is your son."

Eleven

Funny how easily the confession slipped free. She'd been dreading this moment since the pregnancy test had come back positive. But in the end it wasn't as traumatic as she thought it was going to be. She'd already lost her self-respect and her uncomplicated future to the lie. Trent's confession that he'd not wanted their relationship to end had cut deep. What if instead of being afraid to be rejected she'd gone to him when she first found out she was pregnant? Her life might have turned out very differently.

"That's impossible," Trent said. "We were always very careful."

"This is going to sound crazy." Savannah braced to defend herself, suspecting Trent would be skeptical of her convoluted explanation. "When I came to visit you in Vegas that last time, I did so on Rafe's recommendation."

"Rafe told you to come see me?"

"As I was getting settled in LA, he and I began to spend time together. He said he'd been in love with me a long time and wanted us to be together. I liked Rafe, but he knew I loved you."

"If he wanted you, wouldn't it make more sense for him to keep you away from me?"

"Yes, if he'd actually loved me. But as I found out after we got married, he was merely using me." She studied Trent's face and saw only confusion and doubt. "And using you."

"Using us how?"

"He needed an heir. He wanted one who looked like a Caldwell." She raised her eyebrows and stared at him, waiting for him to understand what she was saying.

"But we were careful," he repeated.

"That last time we were together…the condoms we used… Rafe gave me those condoms and told me to get you out of my system."

"Seriously?" Trent looked completely shell-shocked. And angry. "You didn't think that was strange?"

"Maybe." She thought back to how desperate and miserable she'd been at the time. "I thought he was trying to be helpful. I never imagined he'd do something as crazy as sabotage the condoms."

"He *wanted* you to get pregnant? To what end?"

"So that there'd be a Caldwell to eventually take over at West Coast Records."

"Do you hear how insane that sounds?"

"I've been living with this for the last year and a half." Savannah's strength was draining. She crumpled into a nearby chair and put her hands in her lap. "I was the one he duped. How do you think I feel?"

"You don't think we're both victims in this?"

Trent paced away toward the terrace and stood with his back to her. He remained as still as a statue for a long time until he finally asked, "Were you ever planning on informing me Dylan is my son?"

She should have been better prepared for this question. As it was, she'd spent all her time worrying about what the fallout for her and Dylan would be if—when—Trent learned the truth.

"To what end?" Her response might have been harsh, but Trent had made his opinion clear. "You never wanted to be part of a family. Rafe did."

"You had no right making that decision for me." Trent turned to face her. His expression was bleak.

Remembering how that final conversation with him had gone, Savannah hardened her heart. "That last morning we were together, you told me you had no time or energy for anything but the club."

"And at that particular moment I didn't. We'd been open barely six months and every day there was something new going wrong. We'd made a huge investment and in order to make it pay off, I had to give it a hundred and ten percent."

"I heard that loud and clear. You didn't have time for me. Why would I think you would have time for me and our child?"

"You should have told me," he insisted.

Savannah refused to regret the decision she'd made. Loving Trent had led to heartache. Marrying Rafe had seemed a safe and sensible alternative.

"You know now," she said, her strength returning as she settled on a course of action. Savannah got to her feet and headed toward him. "You have a son, Trent. What do you intend to do about it?"

She'd never challenged him directly before. Her question was born of frustration and longing. More than anything she needed him to step up and demand to be in Dylan's life. To be part of her life.

"Honestly, I don't know." He raked his hand through his hair. "I need some time to think."

She barely registered the disappointment that washed

through her. His answer didn't surprise her at all. "You know, nothing about your life needs to change the least bit," she told him. "Something's going to break for me in LA. In fact, I just found out I have to head back there tomorrow."

"Already?"

"My agent is excited about my acting prospects. She was able to line up another audition. It looks like my future is there."

Maybe she'd look for a rental. It hurt to give up her plans for buying a house in Las Vegas and living near Trent, but he didn't appear as if he was going to step up and be Dylan's father.

"Your future?" he echoed. "You're not going to stay in Las Vegas?"

The question gave her the opening she needed to ask what was burning in her heart. "Do you want us to stay? Dylan needs a father. I…" She sucked in a breath for strength before putting it all out there. "I need you. I always have."

Trent's features turned to stone. "You can't expect—"

"No." Between one heartbeat and the next, Savannah embraced Courtney Day. The character gave her the dignity to speak mildly and conceal her anguish. "I don't expect. And that's why I'm leaving. Moving to LA is practical. I'll be closer for auditions and meetings." When Trent didn't say anything, Savannah rushed on. "I need to pack. I'll be by later to say goodbye."

And before she was overwhelmed by the sobs tearing at her throat, she left him.

Outrage consumed Trent as he watched Savannah pick Dylan up and walk away with her head held at a defiant angle. He couldn't get past how many times she had looked him in the eye and let him believe Dylan was Rafe's son.

And then today she'd acted as if by keeping the truth hidden she'd done him some sort of favor.

Realizing his hands were clenched into fists, Trent shook his arms to release the tension. But nothing could unravel the knot in his chest. He headed for his room and grabbed a quick shower. There was no way he was going to be able to sleep, so he headed back to the club.

In the months following his breakup with Savannah, Trent had thrown himself into making Club T's into the go-to spot on the Strip. Besides having a killer lineup of DJs, he was constantly looking at ways to improve service and ambience. He had a list of things he wanted to upgrade, including the lighting and sound.

When he got to his office, he was surprised to find Kyle there.

"Where have you been?" Trent asked. If he asked a little more forcefully than he needed to, it was due to his concern for Melody. "I expected to see you at the house. Tell me you didn't hook up with somebody."

"Nothing like that." Kyle didn't overreact to Trent's aggressive tone or nosiness. "I took a suite here at the hotel."

"Why aren't you staying at the house? Have you called Melody? What the hell is going on with you two?" Trent knew he wasn't giving his friend a chance to answer, but his own troublesome morning had put him on edge.

"Look, I didn't say anything last night, but we've had a rough patch."

"How rough?"

Kyle's expression darkened. "I'm here, aren't I? In Vegas, I mean. And at Cobalt. I don't know what's going on at the moment."

He looked utterly miserable, so Trent decided to cut him some slack.

"So what brings you here this morning?"

"You got your start in the LA club scene. I know they

make a tenth of what we bring in at Club T's. Do you think it makes sense for us to open something in LA?"

"I'm looking at some other business opportunities in LA," Trent said, thinking about Savannah and the rebirth of her acting career. Of course, when he'd started considering ventures that would take him to LA and into her orbit, he hadn't known she'd been keeping his son from him for a year. "I thought I would explore expanding into LA."

"Great. I talked with Nate for a while last night and he's on board, as well." Kyle crossed the office to the window that overlooked the club. "He told me that you have Savannah staying with you. Are you sure that's a good idea?"

"I'm just helping her out for old times' sake. She and Siggy have been at odds over the label and he's been playing dirty."

Kyle gave a rough laugh. "Just like old times, then."

"Just like."

"I found out something just now." Trent had no idea he was going to share Savannah's revelation until the words came out of his mouth. "Savannah told me Dylan is my son."

"She cheated on Rafe with you?"

Trent had no idea why Kyle had leaped to that conclusion. "No, she married him after finding out she was pregnant with Dylan."

"She never told you she was pregnant?" Kyle looked appalled. "That's messed up."

Hearing his own opinion echoed by his best friend, Trent began to feel a little vindicated. "She should've come to me."

"Absolutely. Your poor brother."

"Rafe knew. Apparently his cancer had made him infertile. He was glad to be a father and have a son to pass the business along to."

Trent felt at that moment that he understood what his

brother had been up against. Maybe setting up Savannah to get pregnant had been a crazy act, but with the cancer eating away at his mind, no doubt he hadn't been thinking rationally.

"What would you have done if she'd told you before marrying Rafe?"

This was a question Trent should have asked himself already, but he'd been so consumed with anger at being lied to. "I don't know. Obviously I would have taken care of her and the baby." Taken care of her financially was what he meant to say.

"But would you have married her? I know how you feel about getting tied down, but you've been crazy about Savannah for a long time."

"Maybe." *Probably not.* "We'll never know." Funny how twenty-four hours earlier he'd been thinking how great things were between them and how much he was enjoying having Dylan around.

"So that's it then? You guys are done?"

Were they done? Of course they were. A bone-deep chill struck Trent.

"She's planning on restarting her acting career." He sounded calm and detached. Numb. "That means she's going to be spending time in LA."

"How much time?"

He had to think about their last conversation. "Probably full time."

And just like that it hit him. Savannah wasn't going to be back and forth between Las Vegas and LA like she'd first talked about doing.

She was leaving and taking Dylan. His son. Trent was still reeling from the knowledge that he was a father. Now it occurred to him that he and Dylan were going to be very far apart.

"How are you going to see Dylan if they're living there?

I mean, if it was my kid, I'd never want to be away from him."

Kyle had made a good point. Did Savannah expect that Trent would just give up his son? "I haven't really thought the whole thing through."

"You should talk to her about sharing custody."

"I don't know if she'd be open to that."

"You could demand it."

Trent recoiled from Kyle's suggestion. He was sick of being at odds with Savannah. Until recently he hadn't been able to admit how his world had been disrupted when he'd lost her.

"I'll think about it."

"I don't envy you," Kyle said. "When the kids come into the picture, it messes everything up."

With that said, Trent changed the subject. The two men talked business for a couple hours before grabbing lunch. Then they went to Nate's studio and brought him up to speed. By the time Trent returned to his house at three, he was fighting the drag of exhaustion from his sleepless nights.

Unfortunately any hope of a catnap before he headed back to the club was shattered when he opened up the door between the garage and the house and discovered his houseguests in high spirits. Their excited voices reached his ears and raked across his raw nerves before he stepped across the threshold. On the edge since he left the house earlier that day, Trent felt a snarl form on his lips.

"What's going on?" he demanded, eyeing the open bottle of sparkling grape juice on his breakfast bar and the almost-empty flutes.

"We're celebrating," Melody said. "Savannah just found out she got the movie."

Trent should've been happy for her, but he hadn't gotten over what he'd learned that morning. "You must be thrilled."

If she noticed that he was less than enthusiastic, she didn't react. "I'm more nervous than anything else."

"You don't have to be," he said, mood softening as he noticed her uncertainty. "You're going to be great." He remembered watching her on the set of *Loving New York*. She'd been confident and professional. Before that, he'd been accustomed to thinking of her as a naive girl. The transformation to accomplished actress had forced him to reevaluate who she was. "When do you start filming?"

"Next month, but they want me next week for wardrobe." She looked dazed by all the sudden changes.

He understood how she was feeling. He was off balance, as well.

"How long is shooting supposed to take?" Melody asked.

"I was told to expect ten to twelve weeks."

"You're going to need a place to stay," Melody said. "I have a friend who might be able to help you with that."

"Actually, I've already found a small house to rent for the next six months."

"Sounds like everything's working out." Trent tasted bitter disappointment at how fast everything had been arranged. He wasn't prepared for her to leave him and take Dylan away. His gut twisted and sweat beaded on his skin.

The conversation with Kyle rose in his thoughts. Should he demand partial custody? But was that really what he wanted? For his son to be shuttled back and forth between Las Vegas and LA?

Savannah didn't look at him as she said, "Dylan and I have imposed on you long enough. We'll be out of your hair tomorrow."

"That's not how I feel about having you here." But the words lacked sincerity.

She'd lied to him, and he couldn't get past that. Even so, her expectant expression tore at him. She was waiting for him to say something heartfelt and romantic. Maybe that he wanted them to stay. That he couldn't live without her or their son.

But so much was wrong between them and anger was a familiar, uncomplicated emotion. He held on to it even as concern over losing her and Dylan gnawed at him.

"Nevertheless, it's time we start the next chapter of our life." Savannah glanced at her son as he yawned. "Looks like someone's ready for his nap. I'd better go put him down."

Savannah had barely stepped out onto the terrace when Melody rounded on Trent.

"You're not really going to let her move to LA, are you?"

"She has a part in a movie that's filming there. I don't know why you think I'd stop her."

"I'm probably the last person to be giving romantic advice, but you two belong together. I've known it since those days in New York. I know it upset you when she married Rafe." Melody held up her hand to forestall the denial that leaped to his lips. "Don't even try to deny it. I saw you at the wedding."

"Sometimes it doesn't work between people."

"Sometimes people are unwilling to work at it."

"Are we talking about Savannah and me? Or you and Kyle?"

"All four of us, I think."

"So what are you going to do about it?"

"This isn't about me. This is about you. You are about to let go of the only woman you've ever loved. And why?"

"She lied to me. She's been lying to all of us. Dylan is my son."

"Yikes." Melody grimaced but didn't look surprised. "She finally told you."

"You knew?"

"Since the day before she married Rafe. She was having serious doubts about going through with the wedding. I told her to follow her heart. I thought that meant she would tell you about the baby."

"But she didn't." Trent remembered how he'd expected her to call off the wedding right up until the moment she actually said, "I do." He'd left right after the ceremony and never congratulated her or his brother. "Obviously she found what she needed in Rafe."

"In some ways, I think she did. You should've seen her that morning. She was a wreck. Pacing. Hyperventilating. I thought for sure she was going to call it off. And then Rafe came in." Melody's eyes took on a faraway look. "He sat her down and knelt before her. He took her hand in his and very calmly convinced her that he would make sure everything was going to be all right." Melody blinked back tears. "None of us knew that he wouldn't be around to fulfill that promise."

A complicated mix of emotions churned in Trent's gut. He'd loved his brother and resented him in equal measure. He'd learned that Rafe had betrayed him, but he also had to acknowledge that by marrying Savannah, Rafe had tried to take care of her the way Trent had refused to.

He didn't want to think about Rafe being a good guy. It was easier to dwell on all the things he'd done wrong. And yet without Rafe, there would be no Dylan and Trent might never have had a second chance with Savannah.

A second chance that had ended as badly as the first one.

"I wonder," Melody continued, "after all this time, Savannah changed her mind about telling you the truth."

"Siggy was suing her for the shares in the company Rafe left Dylan. He was claiming Dylan wasn't Rafe's son. I think she expected the truth to come out. So she let me know."

"Are you sure that's why? Maybe she hoped once you knew Dylan was your son that you might ask her to stay. She still loves you. I just know it."

"That's not the way it seems to me."

Savannah had given up her dream of a blissful, traditional family with him. She'd decided being Dylan's mom was enough. And for some strange reason that angered Trent more than all the rest put together.

"Is this really what you want?" Melody demanded, irritation snapping in her voice.

For the last twelve hours, Trent had been too preoccupied by how he'd been wronged by the people who should have his back to give much thought to what he wanted.

"What do you mean?"

"Do you really want to live here alone while your son and the woman you love live in a different state?"

"The woman I love?" He gave a bitter laugh, wishing he'd kept his distance from Savannah the way he had for the last year and a half. "What I want is to take back the last two weeks."

"You don't mean that."

"I do. I wish Savannah had never come to Vegas to ask me for help. Because if she hadn't, I'd never have learned the truth."

On the terrace edge, out of sight of the living room's occupants, Savannah heard Trent's declaration and felt neither shock nor hurt. In fact, she was a little relieved. Now she didn't have to wonder if returning to LA was the right decision. Trent didn't want her or Dylan in his life. She could stop looking back and move forward.

Savannah entered the guesthouse and closed the sliding glass doors to the patio. With her bags packed and her flight several hours away, she kept herself busy cleaning the bathroom and little-used kitchen until Dylan woke.

Feeling restless and needing to get away from the house, Savannah took Dylan to the nearby mall and window shopped for a couple hours. She kept melancholy at bay by thinking about what homey touches would warm up the cute mission-style house she'd rented. By the time she returned to Trent's house, it was close to six and she knew he would have left for the club.

Melody's car was gone as well and Savannah was able to relax knowing she wouldn't run into either of them. She set about heating up the leftover chicken she'd fixed for dinner the night before. Dylan was a good eater. He scarfed down the chunks of carrots and potato as well as the bits of thigh meat Savannah arranged on the high-chair tray.

Later, Savannah sat with Dylan on the couch and read to him, losing herself in the rhythm of the words and her son's delight. When she ran out of books, she turned to her phone and the playlist that contained all his favorite songs. He laughed and clapped his hands while she sang. For a while longer she was able to escape her sadness. And then she heard the first few notes of the song Dylan and Melody had recorded. Days earlier, she'd uploaded the song, and now she played it for him often. His ability to mimic the tune amazed her. Before she could hit the repeat button, the other song from the CD began to play.

Savannah's finger hovered over the stop button. Dwelling on her foolish dreams wasn't conducive to moving forward. But the magic of Melody's lyrics being sung in Trent's deep voice was hard to resist. She didn't realize she was crying until she noticed that Dylan was watching her with solemn eyes. He put his palms on her wet cheeks. With a shaky laugh, she kissed his damp fingers and dashed the remaining moisture from her skin.

"Mommy's being silly, isn't she?" The last strains of

"She's the One" faded and the room grew silent. Needing a distraction, Savannah got to her feet. With Halloween a week away, she'd bought Dylan a costume but hadn't yet tried it on him. "You're going to be the cutest dragon LA has ever seen," she promised as she slipped his chubby thighs into the blue-and-green suit with orange wings and spikes down the tail.

Once she had the zipper up and the hood lifted into place, she started working on his roar. He was slowly learning his animal sounds and mastered the dragon's growl after a few minutes. Laughing at the cuteness overload, she spun with Dylan in her arms and he shrieked with delight.

Why had she once worried so much about being a part of a traditional family with Trent when what she should have wished for was a perfect family? Because somehow that's the exact sort of family she'd become with Dylan. Perfect.

Twelve

Club T's throbbed with ear-blasting electronic music and pulsed with a dazzling light display. Trent sat in his favorite spot and watched the crowd drink and dance, laugh and flirt. A stunning blonde sat to his right. He'd forgotten her name as soon as they'd been introduced. She was a friend of the redhead Kyle had plucked out of the crowd waiting behind the velvet ropes.

Trent's cell phone buzzed with an incoming text from Nate.

You don't look like you're having fun.

He glared over to where Nate sat on the far end of the curved couch, his lips twisted in a sardonic smile. The club was too noisy for conversation to carry over that distance, so Trent texted back.

I'm working.

Nate checked the incoming message and responded without looking up.

Kyle and I have this. Maybe you should get out of town for a few days.

Where the hell was he supposed to go? He rejected the first idea that popped into his head. Going to LA to check out the potential club properties Kyle had scouted would put him too near Savannah and Dylan. He wasn't ready to deal with that situation yet. His emotions were too raw.

Amid the loud music in the club, Trent reflected on the playful growls and unrestrained laughter that had drifted across his quiet backyard the other night. He'd been standing on his terrace, overlooking his pool when the sounds had first caught his attention. Drawn by the joyful noise, he'd crossed half the distance to the guesthouse before reality had caught up with him. Unfortunately, although he'd stopped himself from joining them, it had taken him ten minutes to turn away. The memory of how he'd ached standing there alone in the dark compressed his lungs.

He would head to New York City and put the entire country between him and Savannah. Visiting his mother would take his mind off his troubles. She was directing her first off-Broadway musical and had been pestering him for months to fly out and see it. He texted Nate back.

Sounds good.

Figuring he might as well get started immediately, Trent left the couch, shaking off the blonde woman who'd clutched at his jacket sleeve. He hadn't consumed more than a single scotch, but as he made his way out of the club, he felt disconnected from his environment, as if he'd overindulged.

Six hours later he checked into his hotel in Times Square and ordered breakfast from room service. By the time he ate and showered, it was late enough that he could call his mother without waking her.

"You're in New York City?" At eight in the morning, she sounded wide-awake and delighted to hear he was in town.

"I came in a few hours ago. Kyle and Nate are both in Las Vegas, so I thought I'd take some time off and come visit you."

"I'm so glad. I have to be at the theater at ten. We're making some minor changes to one of the scenes." The play had opened a week before to mixed but mostly positive reviews. His mother was a perfectionist, always taking her craft up a notch. "You can take me to lunch and tell me all of what's going on in your life."

"I'll be there."

Trent hung up and headed for the lobby. His favorite thing to do when he came to New York was to walk the streets and absorb the energy. The city's pace was just as hectic as Las Vegas's, but here people moved with purpose, the vibe oriented toward both business and artistic pursuits.

At five minutes before ten, he met his mother on the sidewalk in front of the theater. She wore a long gray sweater belted over black leggings and a slouchy black trench coat. Bright red lipstick emphasized her broad smile. These days she was always happy. It hadn't been that way when he was young. Sometimes when Siggy hadn't been home she would sing with Trent and Melody, but even then her eyes had carried shadows.

"How wonderful to see you." His mother trapped his face between her hands and brought his head down so she could kiss his cheek. Then she peered at him. "You look tired."

"I flew the red-eye and didn't sleep."

"With all the crazy hours you work at that club of yours, I would think you'd be used to it." She linked her arm through his and drew him into the theater. "I hear Melody's back in the studio. Is she ever going to finish her album?"

"Nate has given her a deadline and threatened to pick the songs himself if she doesn't start making some decisions."

"Is she happy?"

Trent gave his mother's question serious consideration. It wouldn't do to fire off a hasty answer. "Yes and no."

"Why, yes?"

"I think she's glad to be done with the tour. The traveling and performing are not her cup of tea. And she's having fun playing in the studio. It's what she loves. It wouldn't surprise me if one day she stopped singing and went into production full-time."

"It's too bad Siggy can't appreciate musical genius. She would've been a great asset to West Coast Records." His mother slipped off her coat and draped it over her arm. "So would you."

Trent shrugged. He'd given up on pleasing his father before he'd become a teenager. "Siggy didn't want me within a mile of his company, and he only sees Melody as a little girl."

Naomi shook her head. "So why is my daughter unhappy?"

"I don't know for sure, because neither of them is confiding in me, but I think Melody and Kyle are having problems. Right now they are both in Las Vegas, but from what I can tell they haven't seen each other yet."

"That's the feeling I get, as well," his mother said, her sigh speaking volumes. "She stopped talking about him three months ago. I think something happened when she broke from the tour to visit him in LA."

"They'll figure it out."

His mother regarded Trent with surprise. "That's very optimistic of you."

"You don't think I'm right?"

"No, I think you're right." Her eyes narrowed and she seemed to be searching for something in his expression. "I'm just surprised that your opinion is so upbeat."

"I don't understand what you mean."

"You aren't exactly a believer when it comes to romance and relationships. Do you remember saying that your brother's marriage wouldn't last a year?"

And it hadn't. Just not for the reason Trent had thought.

"I didn't think Rafe and Savannah were meant for each other."

"Because she was your girlfriend first?"

Two years ago he'd never imagined he would lose her. By the time he figured out that he didn't want to live without her, she'd been engaged to his brother.

"I had my chance."

And he'd blown it. But he couldn't say the words out loud. His regrets were private.

"I understand she's been staying with you in Las Vegas."

"Siggy threatened her, saying he was going to fight for custody of Dylan. I offered her my guesthouse until things could be sorted out."

"Why would Siggy try to take away Dylan?"

"He lost Rafe and saw Dylan as his replacement."

"And he wanted control over the shares of the company that Rafe left his son."

"And he didn't want to pay for them. Rafe left Savannah a lot of debt, and she was trying to sell the label's shares back to Siggy so she could get out from under it."

His mother rolled her eyes. "Tell me you haven't left her to deal with Siggy alone."

"Everything has been sorted out. Another record company offered to buy West Coast Records, so Siggy bought Rafe's shares back and Savannah should be able to pay off her debts. She's moved back to LA and has taken a part in a movie."

Trent decided this was the perfect opportunity to tell his mother about Dylan being his son, but as he opened his mouth, they were approached by an obviously frazzled man. After his mother introduced her assistant director, they headed off. Trent chose a seat in the dim theater and watched his mother work, enjoying the competent way she directed the actors. It was obvious she had a vision in her head regarding the changes, but it took her an hour and twenty minutes to achieve the results. At long last she clapped her hands and sent everyone on their way.

Collecting her coat and purse, Naomi came up the center aisle toward Trent. "Shall we go to La Masseria for lunch?"

Located in the theater district, the Italian restaurant was one of her favorites. During one of his many trips to visit Savannah, they'd met his mother and her current husband there before a Broadway show. The entire evening had been a great success. His mother had talked about Savannah for months afterward, prodding him about his future plans. Trent had given her noncommittal replies, and as time went on she'd stopped asking questions.

After they were seated, Trent gave the menu a quick glance. He wasn't really hungry. Being in this restaurant brought up happy memories of his time with Savannah, of his mother's hopes for his future and the satisfaction she'd found with a man who supported and loved her.

"Earlier I mentioned that Siggy threatened to seek custody of Dylan, but what I didn't say is that he gave up after discovering that he isn't Rafe's son."

"It sounds just like Siggy." His mother waved to someone, apparently unconcerned at the bombshell regarding her grandson's legitimacy. "He's obsessed with his legacy."

"Doesn't it bother you about Dylan?"

Naomi met her son's gaze. "Why should it? I love Dylan. Whether or not he's Rafe's biological child doesn't change the fact that he's my grandson." She studied Trent for a long moment. "Does it bother you?"

"It bothers me that Savannah lied."

Why had he thought his mother would be outraged that Savannah had lied, too? Melody hadn't been bothered. Rafe had created the situation in the first place. At this point, the only other member of his family who seemed at all upset was Siggy.

"I don't see why. As you said earlier, you had your chance with her and things didn't work out. It seems as if this is her business and Rafe's. He married her, after all." His mother turned her attention to the waiter who'd approached the table, leaving Trent to stew over her matter-of-fact assessment.

As soon as they'd placed a drink order, Trent spoke again. "It bothers me because Dylan is my son."

"I see." His mother had been perusing a menu she no doubt knew by heart. Now she set it down and gave him her full attention. "Can I assume since you haven't mentioned this before that you just found out?"

"Savannah told me a few days ago."

Naomi laced her fingers together and set her clasped hands on the table. "Does this change things between you?"

"By change things, do you mean am I going to marry her?" Trent heard his aggrieved tone and saw his mother's eyebrows lift.

"You love her, don't you?"

For some reason the question threw salt on his already raw wounds. "She and I were together a long time. I didn't want to end things, but I couldn't give her the normal family life she craved."

"So marriage is off the table. Do you intend to have a relationship with your son? Or are you going to be like your father?"

If she had stood up and shrieked at him, he would've been less shocked. That she would place him in the same category as his father in anything cut deep. Trent slammed the door on his emotions. Ice filled his veins.

"I haven't decided what I'm going to do."

"Oh, don't be like that." His mother picked up her menu and once more began to peruse the entrées. "Your father used to shut down the exact same way."

"Stop comparing me to him."

"I will when you stop behaving like him. Siggy has no heart and very little soul. He is bullheaded and unforgiving."

"But you married him and had three children. Why do that if he's so terrible?"

"I was young, idealistic and ambitious. He told me I was talented, and I thought with him backing me I would have an amazing career as a singer." Trent's mother sighed. "And in the beginning he charmed the pants right off me."

"What changed?"

"He thought I had an affair."

The waiter brought their drinks, giving Trent a moment to assimilate what his mother had said.

"Did you?"

Naomi didn't look surprised or annoyed by his question. "I didn't sleep with Marco, but I did fall in love with him. He was an incredibly talented musician I met shortly after he signed with West Coast Records."

"Marco? I don't recall anyone by that name at the label."

"That's because your father destroyed his career. He never made an album and eventually gave up music." Naomi got a faraway look in her eye. "It was a year after Rafe was born. Siggy promised that I could record my second album. I'd been working on songs while pregnant with Rafe. One of those was a duet. Marco and I recorded it together. He had the most amazing voice. If he'd signed with any other record company, he probably would've been huge."

Trent couldn't figure out why she was telling him all of this. "Does Siggy think this Marco is my father?" It would explain why he could do no right in his father's eyes. Trent hadn't realize how much he'd needed his father's favoritism to have a basis in logic.

"No. He ran a paternity test on all three of you." Her smile had an acid bite. "That was the moment I stopped trying to make my marriage work. The day I discovered he would never trust me."

"Then why does he hate me?" It was the cry of a small child who didn't understand what he'd done wrong. And it was a question he'd never asked his mother before.

"Because you were my beautiful, musical boy and I doted on you. Rafe didn't inherit my talent or my joie de vivre. He was a serious baby with the most solemn eyes. It was almost as if from birth he was weighed down by his father's expectations." Trent's mother gave her head a sad shake. "You, on the other hand, and your sister after you, were exuberant and artistic. For all his early success with West Coast Records, Siggy was a businessman, not a visionary. He related better to Rafe."

Trent pondered what he'd learned and realized he'd never stopped being angry with his father. In fact, he'd gone a step farther and used his contentious relationship with his father as an excuse to keep people at bay.

"I don't want to be like my father."

"You're not like him at all."

"So you think I have a heart and a soul?"

His mother smiled. "I never doubted it for a second."

* * *

Savannah poured candy into a large bowl and set it on the small table just inside her front door. It was five o'clock on Halloween, but she didn't expect trick-or-treaters to show up for another hour. She and Dylan had been living in LA for a week. The mission-style house she'd rented was about the same size as Trent's guesthouse and beautifully furnished, but Savannah was having a hard time settling in.

She'd had several meetings with the director, her fellow actors and the wardrobe department, and was anxious to start filming. As she'd done after starting the soap opera, she'd hired an acting coach to help her prepare for her new role. But her down time offered abundant opportunity to worry, and lately she'd been revisiting the multitude of ways she could have handled things better since leaving New York two years earlier.

Her doorbell rang. Trick-or-treaters already? Savannah glanced to where her son sat in the middle of the living room, wearing his adorable dragon costume. Seeing that he was occupied with Murphy, also dressed like a dragon, she picked up the bowl of candy and opened her front door.

Instead of an adorable child dressed as a princess or a superhero, a tall, leafy plant with legs stood before her.

"Hello?"

The day before, she'd received a lovely fruit basket from the movie's executive producers, welcoming her on board. She couldn't imagine whom the plant was from.

To her utter shock, the face that emerged from behind the foliage was Trent's.

"I hope it's okay that I dropped by."

Savannah made no move to invite him in. "What are you doing here?"

"I went to New York to visit my mother. She wanted to send you something congratulating you on your new role. I offered to deliver it myself."

"Why would you bother?"

He ignored her blunt question. "Can I come in?"

Reluctantly she stepped back and made a sweeping gesture with her arm. Once Trent and his enormous plant were inside, she put the bowl back on the entry table and closed her front door. Trent looked around the snug living room for a place to set down his burden.

"You don't have a lot of room."

Stunned by his criticism, she crossed her arms over her chest. "It's only Dylan and me. We don't need a lot of space." That said, she stared at him.

"How about if I put it here for now." He set it on the breakfast bar, well out of reach of Dylan's grasp. "I like his dragon costume."

"He's dressed up for Halloween."

"Are you taking him trick-or-treating?"

"We went to the mall yesterday for a Halloween event. Tonight I thought we'd stay home and hand out candy."

"Sounds like fun. Do you want some company?"

She couldn't believe he was standing in her living room, acting as if he didn't wish she'd come back into his life. Should she confront him on what she had overheard? Her grandmother had often said that those who eavesdrop shouldn't expect to hear good things said about themselves.

"While I appreciate whatever this is you're attempting to do," she began in a severe tone, her broken heart jabbing at her ribs with each breath, "I can't have you popping into and out of our lives anytime you want. I grew up being shuffled between my father and grandmother, and that's not what I want for Dylan. He deserves stability and consistency."

"Is that your way of saying that you don't want me to be part of his life?"

His audacity left her dumbfounded. "Last week you wished you'd never learned the truth."

"I never told you that."

"I overheard you talking to Melody." Savannah's voice broke. "You don't want to be a father. I get it. Why do you think I didn't tell you in the first place?"

"I was upset. I should never have said that."

"But it's what you felt." And as much as the truth had hurt, she preferred it to the lies Rafe had told her.

"Only for a brief moment. You caught me off guard. All I could think was that you'd kept a huge secret from me, and I couldn't accept that you had your reasons for doing so."

"I'm sorry I didn't tell you right away. I never should have listened to Rafe."

"He told you to keep the truth about Dylan from me?"

"He explained to me about that girl in college." When Trent stared at her blankly, Savannah continued, "The one who got pregnant. You helped her take care of it?"

At last comprehension dawned. "Lisa Wheeler. What does that have to do with our situation?"

"You didn't want to be a father then any more than you do now."

"Wait." Trent raised his hands in a stop gesture. "I didn't get Lisa pregnant. I just helped her. She was a friend. She helped me get a B in a poetry class. We never even dated. She'd been raped and was severely traumatized. I tried to get her to go to the police, but she was from a conservative family and didn't want them to know."

"But why would Rafe…" Savannah's stomach turned over. "He lied to me." And why not. Rafe had deceived her several times before that.

"I had no idea your opinion of me was so low." Trent's lips twitched into a sardonic line.

Perhaps in this instance she'd judged him a little too

harshly. "To be fair, you were pretty vocal about your view regarding the whole marriage and kids thing. You didn't want anything to tie you down."

"You were right to listen to Rafe. I gave you no reason to think otherwise. At some point I let my father's negative opinions define me. I figured if I was going to be labeled selfish and no good, I might as well act that way."

"So, what did you hope to gain by coming here?" She didn't understand what he wanted from her. "If you're interested in being part of Dylan's life, I welcome that. I would never keep him from you."

Her son recognized his name and got to his feet. He toddled over to Trent and lifted his arms, asking to be picked up. Savannah's throat tightened as Trent scooped up Dylan and checked out the costume.

"This is really cute. I especially like his horns." Trent's crooked smile had a detrimental effect on Savannah's equilibrium.

She cautioned herself not to read too much into his visit. Just because he'd made an effort to stop by didn't mean his opinions had changed.

Her son was an excellent diversion from her tumultuous emotions. "Dylan, what does the dragon say?"

To her delight Dylan growled, first at her and then his father. Trent laughed.

"I heard you two doing this the night before you left. You were having so much fun. I didn't know how to handle how I was feeling." He lifted Dylan into the air, making him giggle. Trent stared at his son for a long moment, his smile fading. At last he returned his attention to Savannah. "Since then I've had time to think. I want to be part of your life."

"I think that would be great for Dylan." And she meant it.

"What about for you?"

What about her? Having him around all the time would be bittersweet. In her life, but never truly hers.

"I've really missed you." She thought that was safe to admit. But to keep him from getting the wrong idea, she continued, "We were friends for a long time before anything happened between us in New York. It'll be great to be on good terms once again."

"Do you want to go back to being just friends?"

She opened her mouth to say no, but the word couldn't make it past the lump in her throat. The last thing Savannah wanted was to be just friends with Trent, but she couldn't go down that road to heartache again.

He began before speaking again without waiting for her answer. "At one point you thought you'd be okay living in Vegas. Do you still think that's a possibility?"

"We could talk about it. Now that I'm working, my financial situation isn't so dire and I can afford more house there than here."

"And you're okay about traveling back and forth?"

Now that his father was no longer entertaining him, Dylan decided he wanted to be put down and squirmed until Trent set the boy on the floor once more.

"Scarlett has made it work. I don't see why I can't, as well." Savannah watched Dylan head to the bin where she kept his musical train. Plastic clattered as he pulled the pieces out. "My son's happiness is important to me. If living in Las Vegas means you and Dylan get to spend as much time together as possible, then that's what I'll do."

"What about your happiness?"

Since leaving Trent behind and moving to LA she'd discovered peace, but not joy. "I've learned I can be content anywhere as long as I have my family."

"I've learned something, too." He took her hands in his. "The only time I'm happy is when I'm with you."

Savannah stared at Trent while blood pounded in her

ears. Had she heard him right? Or was she imagining the words she longed to hear?

"But you said…"

"Forget what I said. I was an idiot. I've been an idiot for a long time. Nothing else explains why I ever let you go." Trent tugged her up against him. "I love you."

A stunned Savannah was marveling at her abrupt turn of fortune even as Trent's lips closed over hers. His kiss reflected all the hunger and longing that filled her. She held on for dear life as her future shifted onto a new track. When at long last he broke the kiss, she was breathless and gloriously happy.

"I love you." His deep voice gave weight to the phrase. "I made the mistake of letting you go once. I can't let that happen again."

Savannah's chest ached at the pain and loss she glimpsed in his gaze. "I'm not going anywhere." She glanced at Dylan, who could not have been less interested in what was going on between his parents. "We are not going anywhere."

"Promise?"

"I promise."

Trent pushed her to arm's length and narrowed his eyes. "I think I need something more concrete than your verbal acceptance."

She laughed. "Do you want it in writing?"

"Absolutely. I demand a legally binding agreement." He reached into his pocket and pulled out a box. He popped the lid and showed her a gorgeous diamond ring. "Will you marry me?"

The engagement ring blurred as tears filled Savannah's eyes. Unable to shake her uncertainty, she whispered, "Are you sure about this?" Her breath stopped as he plucked the ring free of the box and slid it onto her finger.

"I've never been more sure of anything in my life."

"Then, yes." Giddy beyond anything she could imagine, Savannah threw her arms around his neck and hugged him tight. Crushed in his return embrace, she couldn't stop smiling. "I love you so much."

"You and Dylan are my everything. I never want us to be apart ever again."

That brought up a logistical problem. "It's going to be a while until that happens, with me here doing the movie and you in Las Vegas running Club T's."

"I've already got that covered. Both Kyle and Nate are in Vegas for the foreseeable future. Nate plans to get back in the studio, and Kyle has his relationship with my sister to save." He put his arm around her. "I'm going to stay in LA and take care of Dylan while you're working."

That he'd obviously thought this through and was delighted with the prospect lightened her heart. Yet, she remained cautious.

"That's all well and good," Savannah said, appreciating Trent's willingness to throw himself into being Dylan's father, but unsure whether the new role would be enough to satisfy him. "But won't you be bored without some business venture to challenge you?"

"No, because in addition to looking for space for a location for a new club here in LA, I have recently become part owner of a record label in desperate need of help."

"You have?" Something about his self-satisfied expression stirred her suspicions. "You don't mean…"

"Siggy sold the label to Ugly Trout Records. Nate and I now own West Coast Records." Trent's smug grin was difficult to resist, and Savannah found her lips curving in response.

"How?"

"Nate made Siggy an offer he couldn't refuse."

"But you and Nate are business partners in the club. Didn't Siggy realize that?"

"We're also partners in Ugly Trout Records. I helped him with the start-up five years ago."

"Aren't you worried he'll find out you're behind this?"

"Siggy is a bastard. He was so determined to keep me away from West Coast Records that he was willing to dump the company to keep it out of my hands." Trent gave a dismissive shrug. "And anyway, it's too late for him to pull out. The papers are signed."

Savannah smiled as she imagined what her father-in-law's reaction would be when he found out. "He's going to have a fit."

"Too bad. He should have done his research."

"And now you own the company that should have been yours all along." Savannah lifted on tiptoe and brought Trent's lips back to hers for a passionate kiss that left them both breathing hard. "You are clever, talented, and I love you."

Trent's, his smile faded. "I never thought you'd look at me like that ever again."

"Like what?"

"Like I was someone you believed in." He grazed his fingertips across her cheeks and cupped her face. "Ever since I can remember, my father has told me I'm selfish and flawed. He said I would ruin people's lives the way I had ruined his. While I couldn't figure out what I'd done wrong, I accepted that he was right. In the end it became my excuse for the way I'd let you down." He pressed his lips to her forehead. "Every time I saw how I'd disappointed you, I ached for the pain I caused."

"I've always believed in you." Savannah had long known that Siggy was to blame for Trent's commitment issues. "It was believing in us where I lost faith."

An intense glow lit his eyes, transfixing her. "I promise to do everything in my power to make sure that never happens again."

And as he sealed his vow with a slow, reverent kiss, Savannah knew wherever she lived in the future, as long as she was with Dylan and Trent, she would be home.

* * * * *

If you liked this story of a billionaire tamed by the love of the right woman—and her baby—pick up these other novels from Cat Schield

AT ODDS WITH THE HEIRESS
A MERGER BY MARRIAGE
A TASTE OF TEMPTATION
THE NANNY TRAP
ROYAL HEIRS REQUIRED
A ROYAL BABY SURPRISE
SECRET CHILD, ROYAL SCANDAL

Available now from Mills & Boon Desire!

***

And don't miss the next
BILLIONAIRES AND BABIES *story*

ONE HEIR...OR TWO?

by bestselling author Yvonne Lindsay
Available November 2016!

MILLS & BOON®

Desire™

PASSIONATE AND DRAMATIC LOVE STORIES

A sneak peek at next month's titles...

In stores from 20th October 2016:

- **Hold Me, Cowboy** – Maisey Yates *and*
  One Heir...or Two? – Yvonne Lindsay

- **His Secretary's Little Secret** – Catherine Mann *an*
  Back in the Enemy's Bed – Michelle Celmer

- **Holiday Baby Scandal** – Jules Bennett *and*
  His Pregnant Christmas Bride – Olivia Gates

Just can't wait?
Buy our books online a month before they hit the shops
www.millsandboon.co.uk

Also available as eBooks.

ve a 12 month subscription
to a friend today!

Call Customer Services
0844 844 1358*

or visit
lsandboon.co.uk/subscriptions

***** This call will cost you 7 pence per minute plus your
phone company's price per minute access charge.

MILLS & BOON®

Why shop at millsandboon.co.uk?

Each year, thousands of romance readers find their perfect read at millsandboon.co.uk. That's because we're passionate about bringing you the very best romantic fiction. Here are some of the advantages of shopping at www.millsandboon.co.uk:

* **Get new books first**—you'll be able to buy your favourite books one month before they hit the shops

* **Get exclusive discounts**—you'll also be able to bu our specially created monthly collections, with up to 50% off the RRP

* **Find your favourite authors**—latest news, interviews and new releases for all your favourite authors and series on our website, plus ideas for what to try next

* **Join in**—once you've bought your favourite books, don't forget to register with us to rate, review and join in the discussions

Visit **www.millsandboon.co.uk**
for all this and more today!

JW